Finding Him

J. L. Perry

FINDING HIM
Copyright © 2023 J. L. Perry
All rights reserved.

Paperback ISBN: 978-0-6486828-2-0
Hardback ISBN: 978-0-6486828-5-1

No part of this publication may be reproduced, distributed, or transmitted in any form or by any means, including photocopying, recording, or other electronic or mechanical methods without the prior written permission of the publisher.
This is a work of fiction. Names, characters, places and incidents are the produce of the author's imagination, or used factitiously. Any resemblance to actual events, locales, or persons, living or dead, is entirely coincidental.
Cover Design by The Book Cover Boutique
Edited by Jess Fitzpatrick

Books By J. L. Perry

Finding Love Series

Finding Him

Finding Forever

Finding Us

Finding Forgiveness

Finding Love

Finding Her

Bastard Series

Bastard

Luckiest Bastard

Jax

Cocky Hero World

Bossy Bastard

Sexy Bastard

Standalones

The Boss

Saviour

Nineteen Letters

This book is dedicated to my beautiful Grandmother, Evelyn...

You always inspired me to be a better person. The unconditional love and support you gave me over the years never wavered. The wisdom you shared, and the kindness and compassion you showed—not only to me, but to everyone— was truly incredible. You had such a beautiful soul. I was blessed to have been born into your family, and my world is much emptier now that you've gone.

1924 - 2015

There's never a wrong time for the right person.

Not everything in life is supposed to be beautiful or long-lasting. I truly believe that we don't meet people by accident—they come into our lives for a reason.

Although things were definitely changing for the worst in my marriage, I still thought Jake was the person I was going to grow old with. I had no idea he was only there to play a small part in the greater picture, because my *destiny* lay elsewhere.

Through my husband's betrayal, life would lead me on the path to *him*—Logan Cavanagh. A gorgeous, captivating, successful Lawyer, and also the unlikely hero in my story ... a man who would touch my heart so deeply, I knew I'd never be the same again.

From the moment I laid eyes on Brooke, I wanted her, but there was one problem ... she was married to someone else, and I'd *never* come between a man and his wife.

When her life started to unravel, I was there to help pick up the pieces. I knew going in she was never mine to keep, so when she walked away, there was nothing I could do to stop her. I honestly thought it was the end ... that I'd never see her again.

But months later, fate had us crossing paths again and her situation had now changed, so the gloves were coming off. *I was all in*, and there was no way I was letting her go a second time.

Chapter 1

Brooke

"Hi, this is Jake ... I can't take your call at the moment. Leave your name and number after the tone and I'll get back to you as soon as I can."

I press *end* before the tone beeps. There's no point in leaving a voice message. He didn't reply to the one I left him at six o'clock saying that dinner was almost ready, or the one I left him an hour and a half later after the food had gone stone cold, as I sat and watched the wax drip down the sides of the candles I'd placed in the centre of the table.

Moving to Melbourne six months ago was supposed to be the beginning of a new life for us. My husband had been offered the job of a lifetime as a junior partner at Cavanagh and Associates, one of the largest law firms in the country.

It's the kind of position he'd been striving for ever since he joined the bar—his dream job, you could say. But only weeks after arriving here, the cracks in our relationship started to appear, and in the months that followed, things have only managed to get worse.

Tonight's dinner was supposed to symbolise a new

beginning for us—a fresh start in our new life, a chance to put the last few months behind us. He promised he'd be here.

The constant fighting and uncertainty is getting me down. I'm lonely and feeling isolated since our move, which hasn't helped our plight. I gave up everything to come here: my career, my friends, *my life*.

When we lived in Sydney things were different. I was content, if I'd known what lay ahead for us, I never would've agreed to this. I'm not sure if it's the stress of his new job, or the crazy long hours he's been putting in, but Jake's become somewhat of a stranger to me.

After I graduated from university four years ago, I started working as a dance teacher and head choreographer. Dancing has always been my passion. I've been doing it since I was a little girl. It's my escape when times get tough. For me, it's easy to forget all my troubles when I'm lost in the music. *It's how I cope*. Maybe that's why I'm struggling so much now.

I also miss my students, but my husband no longer wants me to work. He says we don't need the money since his new job also came with a huge salary increase. Becoming a full-time homemaker wasn't something we'd ever discussed prior to coming here, and I'm not sure I would've agreed to uproot my entire life if it had been.

Sure, I could've ignored his demands, but the constant bickering every time I bring the subject up is wearing me down. I don't deal well with conflict; I never have.

The sole purpose of coming here was so Jake could follow his dreams, but *my* dreams no longer seemed important to him.

Starting a family could give this new life of mine some purpose, but those plans—like my career—have been put on hold. *"Children will only complicate things,"* he says. He used to want kids as much as I did, but somewhere along the way, he's decided that being a father no longer fits into his life's plan. Not in his immediate future anyway.

After cleaning the kitchen, I head upstairs to our bedroom and run myself a warm bath. I'm hoping it will help relax me.

But an hour later, as I pad across the carpet towards our bed, I feel no calmer ... my mind is still racing. I place my phone down on the bedside table, plugging it into the charger. The clock reads 10.36 pm, and my husband's still not home.

I exhale a large breath as I lay down and pull the covers up around my chin. *I hate this!*

My eyelids become heavy as I stare at the digital clock, watching the minutes slowly tick by. My stomach churns and my mind is laden down with worry. All my uncertainties from the past creep back to the surface. Everything has changed, and I'm no longer sure what my future holds. I feel incredibly alone, which is something I hoped I'd never feel again.

As I drift into a restless sleep, I'm blissfully unaware that in less than twenty-four-hours, *destiny* will step in—my unexpected hero—and it will change the course of my life forever.

Chapter 2

Brooke

It's just after six when I open my eyes. Rolling over, I find my husband fast asleep beside me. I'm not sure what time he finally got in, but it breaks my heart to see what's become of us. I desperately want things to be the way they used to be, but I'm at a loss as to how I can make that happen. With each passing day, the void between us is widening. I feel powerless.

Scooting closer, I push down the anger and disappointment from last night and snuggle into the warmth of his body, causing him to stir.

"Good morning." I place a soft kiss on the side of his neck as I speak.

"Morning," he mumbles, sliding his arm around my waist and resting his lips against my forehead. His gesture provides immediate comfort. This is the sweet, caring, attentive husband I've missed. These small glimpses give me hope.

"What time did you get in last night? I tried to call you a few times."

"I don't remember ... late."

"Did you forget about the special dinner we planned? You promised me you'd be home for it."

"Jesus, Brooke." Jake sighs as he rolls onto his back and scrubs his hand over his face. "I just opened my eyes and you're already starting." He throws back the covers and rises. I'm not used to these mood swings from him. One minute he's fine, and with a flick of a switch, he changes. "I'm under enough pressure at work without getting shit from you too."

Letting out an exasperated breath, I flop onto my back and stare up at the ceiling. "I'm not starting anything. I only asked you a simple question. I spent all of yesterday in the kitchen, making all your favourite foods."

His expression softens slightly as he stares down at me from beside the bed. "I'm sorry, okay? And I'm sorry about dinner last night. My life's just ..." He throws his hands in the air as he speaks. "Things are really complicated at the moment."

"Do you think you've taken on too much with the new job?"

"What? No!"

Sitting up, I reach for his hand. "Can't you see what this job is doing to you, babe? You were never this stressed or overworked at McCabe and Brunswick."

"Just drop it, Brooke." He tugs his hand from mine and turns and stalks across the room.

The relief I felt moments ago is quickly replaced by hopelessness. But even as my head drops back down onto my pillow, my eyes follow him as he disappears into the en suite bathroom. We'll never be able to resolve anything if he keeps running from me. I'm not sure how much more of this I can take.

I lie there for a short time, stewing over what just happened, but as much as I'd like to stay in bed all day and have my own little pity party, I have things that need doing.

I feel lightheaded when I sit up and move to the side of the bed. Placing my head between my legs, I wait for the woozy feeling to pass before I stand.

After grabbing my running gear out of the drawer, I get changed. My mornings always start with a run. It helps to clear my head, and boy do I need that distraction today.

I head into the bathroom to run a brush through my long brown hair. "What do you want for breakfast?" I ask Jake.

"Nothing. I'm heading into the office early," he replies, tilting his head back to wash the shampoo from his hair. *Of course, he is.* I roll my eyes in the mirror. He may as well move into that damn office. He spends more time there than he does here at home.

After reaching for my toothbrush, I line it with paste. I can't remember the last time we sat and ate breakfast together. Trying to swallow my resentment, I remind myself that he's doing this for us, for our future.

Once I pull my hair up into a high ponytail, I wash my face. "Oh, I forgot to mention," Jake says, stepping out of the shower and reaching for a towel, "tonight is the office Christmas party."

"It's tonight?"

"You're coming right?"

"Do you want me to come?"

"Of course," he says. "You're my wife. How will it look if I'm the only one who turns up without a partner?"

"Right," I say, forcing out a smile. Is that the only reason he wants me there? "What time is the party?"

"Seven, I believe, but I'll confirm all the details for you when I get to work." As I turn to leave the bathroom,

Jake reaches for me, wrapping his fingers around my upper arm. "It will be fun; it's been ages since we've had a night out on the town."

"Yeah, it has." Maybe a night out together away from all the stresses of life is exactly what we need. "It'll be fun."

As I go through my schedule for the day, I put the coffee pot on. I wonder if my hairdresser Pierre will be able to squeeze me in for a shampoo and blow-dry? I make a mental note to call him first thing after my run.

Jake's dressed in a suit when he finally enters the kitchen, and for the first time this morning, I find myself smiling. He looks handsome, and the blue shirt he's wearing underneath his navy suit jacket makes his eyes pop. His light brown hair is neatly combed to the side, and his baby face makes him look much younger than his actual age of twenty-nine.

"You look nice," I say, handing him his lunch.

"Thanks." He brushes his lips against mine, as he reaches behind me for the travel mug I placed on the breakfast bar.

I wish he'd eat something before he goes. He's clearly lost weight in the past few months. His fast-paced life seems to be taking its toll on us both.

"I'm worried about you," I say, straightening his tie.

He gives me one of his crooked smiles, it's a feature of his I've always loved. "There's no need to worry about me."

"I can't help it. You're my life—the only family I have left. It's only natural that I'd worry."

"I know things have been rough for you," he says, sliding his arm around my waist, drawing me in closer. "Things will settle down soon, I promise."

"I hope so." Getting up on the tips of my toes, I place my lips against his. "I miss you." I'm lucky if I get to see him for a few minutes a day. "What time do I need to be ready tonight?"

"I probably won't make it home in time. I have a late meeting. I'm going to take my tuxedo with me to work, just in case."

"You're wearing a tuxedo tonight?"

"Yes. It's black tie."

"I don't have anything remotely suitable to wear. I thought it would be just a small party at the office or dinner at a restaurant."

"This is a multi-million-dollar company we're talking about here, Brooke." He pulls his wallet from his back pocket. "Use the credit card to buy yourself a nice dress. I want you to be the standout of the night."

"It will take more than a nice dress to do that."

Leaning down, he places a kiss on top of my head. "You'll be the most beautiful woman in the room, I'm sure."

A nervous excitement bubbles up inside me. This will be my first time meeting his boss and the rest of his colleagues, so I want to look my best. Despite everything I'm feeling at this moment, I know how much this job means to him.

"I hope you can make it home in time."

"I doubt I will."

"I'm not comfortable going on my own, I don't know anyone."

"You know me. I'll be there waiting for you when you arrive."

I lift one shoulder. "Okay."

"I've got to run. I'll text the information to you."

Grabbing hold of his tie, I pull him in for one more kiss. "Please do."

It frustrates me that I can no longer guarantee a call, it's getting to the point where I can't rely on him for anything.

Chapter 3

Brooke

I strap my iPod to my arm and slide the house key into the small pocket sewn into my running shorts. Placing the plugs into my ears, I press play as I jog down the path and out into the street.

When Jake and I moved here, we bought a beautiful, art deco two-storey house, just ten minutes out of the city. It was built in the 1920s.

The house had undergone extensive renovations before we purchased it, but it still had all of its original old charm with its curved walls, ornate leadlight windows and gloriously high ceilings, which we instantly fell in love with.

We took out a hefty mortgage, but Jake's salary more than covers the repayments. After the small apartment we'd had in Sydney, it took a while to adjust to living in such a vast house.

Ten minutes into my run, a sharp pain shoots across my lower abdomen. It's so intense it stops me in my tracks. Placing my hand on my side, I inhale a few deep breaths and try to walk it out.

I attribute it to a cramp and start moving again as it

slowly subsides. But when the pain returns with a vengeance minutes later, I decide to turn around and head back home. Maybe I need to schedule an appointment with the doctor, but that will have to wait until tomorrow. My day is already jam-packed.

After showering and changing into my favourite green sundress, I call Pierre. Jake always said he loved me in this dress, and that the colour suited me. Hopefully, I can find something in this colour for tonight.

"Hi, this is Brooke Johnston," I say when the receptionist answers the phone. "I was wondering if I could have a quick word with Pierre." I'll have a better chance of getting in to see him today if I speak with him directly.

"One moment, please. I'll see if he's free." I hold my breath as I wait. He's usually booked out for weeks in advance.

"*Chérie,*" he says in his sexy French accent.

"Pierre, I have an emergency on my hands."

"An emergency?"

"Yes. It's Jake's office Christmas party tonight, and I've only just found out about it. It's black tie. Please, please, please, can you fit me in sometime today?"

"For you, *Chérie,* I'll try my best. Hold on one moment." I chew on my fingernail as I wait for him to come back to the phone. "How about one-thirty? I can squeeze you in between clients."

"One-thirty sounds perfect," I say, beaming. "Thank you so much for this. I owe you big time."

"I need to keep my lawyer's beautiful wife happy."

His comment makes me laugh. Jake represented him when we first arrived in Melbourne. He'd recently split with his partner of two years, after finding out he'd been unfaithful. To make matters worse, his ex then set his sights on Pierre's fortune, which meant his salon was in jeopardy—a business he'd put twenty years of his life into.

Jake was able to use the infidelity, as well as the fact that his partner had walked into the relationship without a penny to his name, to negotiate a smaller settlement which would ultimately save Pierre from losing everything he'd worked so hard for.

I eat breakfast in between my chores, before heading to the bus stop. I pray I find a dress. I want to look perfect for my husband.

We need this.

Desperation sets in as I exit the fifth store, after having had no luck. I've tried on over a dozen dresses and none of them were quite what I was looking for. Looking down at my watch, I see I only have forty minutes to spare. I can't be late for my hair appointment.

As I'm crossing the street, I notice a gorgeous floor-length, red gown hanging in the storefront of a tiny boutique. While it may not be Jake's favourite colour on me, my hopes start to rise.

I can see the huge smile that's illuminating my face in the reflection of the glass, as I place my flattened palms against the window.

The dress is even more exquisite up close. It's slimline, with an off-the-shoulder design and tapered waistline that gathers to one side. Simple yet stylish. Could this be the one?

I head inside to find out. "Hi," the sales assistant greets me as I manoeuvre between the racks of clothes, heading towards the counter at the back of the store.

"Hi," I reply with a smile. "I'd like to try on the red dress in the window please."

Her face lights up at my request. "It's beautiful, isn't it?"

"It's exquisite"

"It's a new arrival. It only came in yesterday." Stepping around the counter, she eyes me up and down. "I think it would look magnificent on you."

"Oh, I hope so." I want to knock my husband's socks off.

"Size eight?"

"No, a ten if you have it."

My body is lean from all the dancing and running I do, but I'm well-endowed in the chest area. Jake says I have curves in all the right places.

My heartbeat quickens as I strip down to my underwear and slide the dress off the hanger. After unfastening the zip, I step into it, silently praying this is the one.

"Wow!" the sales assistant says when I emerge from behind the curtain. "You look *amazing* ... absolutely stunning!"

I inhale a sharp breath as I turn and stare into the mirror before me. This dress is everything I hoped it would be and so much more; like it was made especially for me. The tight fit accentuates my hourglass figure, and the smooth red silk glistens under the bright shop lights.

I feel my smile grow as I turn to gaze at the back of the dress in the mirror. If I'm going for the wow factor, this is most definitely the one to do it.

"It's perfect," I whisper.

I still have the silver strappy heels and matching clutch at home that I wore on my wedding day. They'll pair perfectly with this dress.

I'm still grinning to myself as I drape the garment bag

over my arm and look down at my watch. The hair salon is two blocks away, but I'll definitely make my appointment in time.

I can't wait to see my husband's face tonight.

A long relaxing soak in the tub seems to do wonders for me and I step out feeling rejuvenated. I didn't want to shower and risk messing up the gorgeous up-style Pierre has so meticulously created.

As always, he didn't let me down. My long dark locks are pulled back from my face, and the curls he placed in my hair have been strategically pinned to form a large bun at the nape of my neck. The style will suit my gown perfectly.

After slipping into my black lace underwear and matching strapless bra, I take a seat at my dresser so I can apply my makeup. Mascara and lip gloss are usually my limit, but I decide to go all out for tonight.

I'm not stupid enough to think that looking my best for Jake is enough to fix this growing rift between us, but it might help to reignite some of the passion we used to share.

Once I've finished, I gaze in the mirror and hardly recognise myself. Thanks to a makeup tutorial I watched on YouTube on my bus ride home, the smoky dark eyeshadow I applied really makes my big brown eyes pop, and the shimmering powder I applied over my foundation gives my skin a healthy and youthful glow. My ruby-red lips complete the ensemble.

I almost feel jittery as I slip into my dress. I'm hoping tonight Jake relaxes and enjoys himself. I want him to remember the fun, closeness, and deep love we once shared. He's my life and I don't want to lose him.

My mother has passed, and I don't have a relationship with my sperm donor, so Jake's the only family I have. I resent how unimportant and insignificant I've become to him since he started this job. I want back that healthy balance of work and play, which I don't think is too much to ask.

Sitting down on the side of the bed, I gather my dress up around my knees and I slip into my silver heels. When I lean forward to fasten the ankle strap a sharp pain, like the one I got while running, radiates across my abdomen.

"Ouch," I softly cry out as I stand. I inhale a large breath as my hand gently rubs over the offending area.

With only one shoe on, I hobble back into the bathroom to grab some paracetamol. By the time I've swallowed both tablets, the shooting pain has subsided to a dull throb. I don't want anything to spoil tonight for us.

Once my other shoe is on, I slide the diamond earrings Jake gave me the previous Christmas into my lobes. These and my wedding ring, are the only jewellery I wear. My ring is a simple, thin gold band.

I was in my last year of university when Jake proposed, and he hadn't been working long, so we didn't have a lot of money to splurge on a ring. It didn't bother me in the slightest. I came from humble beginnings, and I've never been materialistic. His love and companionship are all I've ever wanted.

Reaching for my favourite perfume—it's my mother's scent, the one she always wore—I spray a small amount on my wrists and behind both ears, just like she used to do. The familiar smell gives me comfort and I feel like she's with me when I wear it.

I take one last look in the full-length mirror before heading downstairs ... I hardly recognise myself.

After ordering a taxi, I shove my lipstick, mobile phone and some money into my silver clutch. I'm nervous about arriving at the function on my own, but hopefully Jake will be there waiting for me when I arrive like he promised.

As I slide the key into the front door, I suddenly feel light-headed. It has me swaying on my feet. "Whoa," I say, gripping the doorknob and resting my forehead against the wood as I wait for it to subside. *Please not now.* Deep down I know something is not right, but tonight is way too important to miss.

I stand by the kerb as I watch my ride slowly pull up. With Christmas only a few short weeks away, it's warm out tonight.

"Where are we heading, love?" the middle-aged driver asks, eyeing me through the rear-view mirror once I'm seated in the backseat.

Sliding my phone out of my clutch, I pull up the message Jake sent me earlier. "The Dome. Three-hundred-and-thirty-three Collins Street, please."

Apart from an address and starting time, that's all his text read. It hurt that he made no mention of seeing me tonight ... he didn't even ask if I'd found a dress.

As we approach the city, I send him a quick text before placing the phone back into my clutch.

Brooke: I'm on my way.

I'm not really expecting a reply, but I hope he at least takes the time to read it.

Chapter 4

Logan

"Has a court date been set?" I ask my colleague as he updates me on his latest case.

A group of us are standing around talking shop, waiting for the night's festivities to get underway. To be honest, I hate these events, but it's a way to thank all my staff for the hard work they've put in throughout the year and to celebrate all our successes.

As principal of Cavanagh and Associates, it's only fitting that I attend. Even my stuffy old man used to come to these before I took over the company. Both our Sydney and Melbourne branches wouldn't be what they are without a combined effort, and I really do have a great, passionate bunch of people working for me.

"February ..." he replies, but it's the only word I hear. I do a double take as my attention is drawn back to the entrance of the ballroom. Shoving my hands into the pockets of my tuxedo trousers, all the air leaves my body.

I watch intently as possibly the most beautiful woman I've ever laid eyes on engages with the hotel staff situated by the door. She continues to get my undivided attention as she crosses the room. Her eyes are everywhere, and despite her obvious grace and beauty, she seems unsure of herself, which I find somewhat endearing.

Who is this woman?

I make it a priority to meet all my employees, even the cleaning staff. If I'd met this stunning woman in the past, surely, I would remember her. She has a look that is unequivocally unforgettable.

The red dress she's wearing accentuates her long and lean, yet alluring figure. She looks like she belongs on a runway. Her body in that dress ... *fuck*. And the hypnotic sway of her hips as she moves across the room, has me entranced. I've dated a lot of models in my time, but never in my life has anyone had such an instant effect on me after just one glance.

Without taking my eyes off the woman in red, I place my hand on Jim's shoulder. "We'll have to continue this conversation later," I say. "There's someone I need to meet."

I don't even wait for his reply before I make a beeline in her direction.

This evening is suddenly looking up.

Usually, I'd play it much cooler, but it's like I'm drawn to her. I'm a man who knows what he wants, so I have no qualms about making this happen ... I feel absolutely no shame in approaching her. Besides, she looks like she's out of place, so it would be rude of me not to rectify that. This is my party after all.

"Excuse me," I say, once I'm standing close enough for her to hear me.

She stops walking and glances sideways, in my direction. The moment our eyes connect, I intake a sharp breath. She had me mesmerised from a distance, but fuck me if she isn't even more breathtaking up close.

She turns to face me, just as the small clutch she's holding drops from her hand, landing by my feet. I'd like to think I influenced her reaction in some way because if I'm being honest my heart is beating out of my damn chest. That in itself is a first for me.

When she makes no attempt to retrieve it off the floor, I squat down, scooping it into my hand. My eyes take her in as I stand. From her painted red toenails and silver heals, to her tight, lean body, in that sexy-as-hell dress. What I wouldn't give for a chance to unwrap her, and discover the hidden treasures that lie beneath.

Once I'm standing to full height, I hold out her clutch, and she takes a few seconds to regain her composure before taking it out of my hand. When her cheeks flush pink, I feel my lips curve into a smile.

"I don't believe we've had the pleasure of meeting, Miss ...?"

The colour on her face intensifies, and I notice her hand tremble slightly as she holds it out to me. "I'm Brooke. Brooke Johnston, my husband, Jake, works for this company."

She's married.

Damn.

Despite the instant disappointment I'm now feeling, I wrap my hand around her delicate fingers. I've never had a problem getting women, but I draw the line at the married ones. I may be a lot of things, but I'm not a homewrecker or a cheat for that matter.

"And you are?" she asks.

"Logan ... Logan Cavanagh."

"Oh, you're Jake's boss?" Her face lights up as she speaks, and my stupid heart rate continues to climb. *Pull your shit together, Cavanagh.*

I'm so lost in her beauty, I realise I still haven't

released her hand. But she seems in no hurry to break our connection. Or maybe she's just being polite.

"Yes, I am. I'm the principal of Cavanagh and Associates. I inherited the title when my father retired."

"You followed in your father's footsteps, how nice. He must be very proud of you."

"I guess." I shrug because I can't honestly answer that.

Proud is a word my father never uttered. A small part of me wants to confess that, or how he practically forced me into becoming a lawyer so I could take over his legacy, but I don't.

Brooke turns her head, as she briefly scans the room, looking for her husband no doubt. Her sudden movement sends the fragrance she's wearing wafting into the air. I inhale a sharp breath through my nose. Christ, she smells so good.

"How are you coping with the move?" I ask. Her husband had a great reputation at his last firm, hence why I hired him. He originally pushed for a position in my Sydney firm when I interviewed him, but he was needed down here. "Have you settled into Melbourne okay?"

A sweet smile crosses her face. "Yes, we've settled in fine, thank you." She has exquisite eyes; large and brown, almost doe-like. I see an innocence in them, and I love the way they twinkle when she speaks.

Neither of us notices Jake approaching until he grabs her from behind and draws her body back into his. I let go of her hand as she turns her head to glance at him over her shoulder.

"Sweetheart, you made it," he says, turning her in his arms.

"Jake."

"Sorry I'm late, I was hoping to be here before you arrived."

"It's okay. Your boss was keeping me company."

"How are you, Jake?" I say, extending my hand to him.

"Good," he replies as his eyes move between me and his wife. When he pulls her possessively into his side, a stab of guilt washes over me. Am I that transparent? "I see you've already met *my* wife."

The way he emphasises his possession of her with his words and actions, make me think he's an arsehole. It's a side of him I've never seen before. He's always been very personable in the interactions I've had with him in the past.

"I have. You're a lucky man," I reply, forcing out a smile.

"How did your meeting go?" Brooke asks him.

The adoring look on her face as she gazes up at him makes me more envious than I care to admit.

Just because I'm single doesn't mean I wouldn't like to settle down one day with the right person. It's been years since I've been in a serious relationship because I'm still bearing the scars from the last one. I date, but never long-term.

I'm looking for someone I can have a genuine connection with. But most of the women in my life are only interested in my money or taming the unattainable bachelor.

"My meeting went fine," Jake answers.

"You've been working way too hard." Her gaze flickers in my direction as she speaks. "All those long hours and late nights you've been putting in."

Was that statement for my benefit? Is she having a dig at me for overworking him? I don't know where he's been going at the end of his working day, but I'm always the last person to leave the building and can assure you he's nowhere in sight when I do. But I keep that to myself.

Jake continues to stare me down like I'm encroaching on their personal space—has he forgotten I'm the guy who pays his wage? If he's so overprotective of his wife, maybe he should've been here to greet her when she arrived.

"Well, if you'll excuse me," I say. "I need to go mingle."

Turning, I head towards the table I'm assigned to. It's probably best I keep my distance. There's no point vying for a woman I can never have.

I greet a few people as I head towards the front of the room. My personal assistant, Claire, makes the seating arrangements and changes them up each year, so I'm seated with a variety of different people at every event, ranging from the top of the chain, right down to the bottom.

The firm's success is a team effort, and I don't discriminate. I'd hate for anyone to think that what they do for my company isn't important. We each have a part to play.

My father and I butt heads on this because although he was brilliant at what he did and built the company from nothing, he's never been a people person and would have no trouble sleeping at night if he knew he made somebody feel beneath him.

Thankfully, my personality is more like my mother's. My father often tells me I'm soft, but I'd rather think of it as being a decent human being.

I've always prided myself on being a good person as well as a good boss. It took years to work off the stigma my father created within the company while he was in charge. Although he never mistreated his staff, he ruled with an iron fist, and everyone was scared of him both personally and professionally.

"Shit," I mumble to myself as my eyes scan over the place cards. Brooke and Jake are seated right beside me. Sitting next to her all night is a bad idea.

With a quick glance over my shoulder, I pick up both their place cards to do a quick table shuffle. It's too late to move them to the other side of the room, but I can at least seat them away from me.

Maybe I should've brought a date with me tonight. I don't usually bring women to business functions because my private life is just that: private. But I'm second-guessing my choices tonight.

"Mr. Cavanagh," a voice says from behind me, temporarily foiling my plan. Swinging around, I find Brooke standing there. *Damn* "We must be seated at the same table." She steps around me, looking for her name on the place card, which unfortunately is still clutched in my hand. "I'm positive the doorman said we were seated at table one."

Trying my best to look inconspicuous, I drop the cards to the floor. "Maybe they made a mistake. Give me a few minutes and I'll try and clear it up for you."

Turning, I go to make a hasty retreat.

"Wait. They're here ... on the floor," she says.

Acting surprised, I face her. She bends to pick them up, and I get a look straight down the front of her dress at the hint of black lace that covers the swell of her breasts. *Christ.* I quickly avert my eyes.

"The wait-staff must've knocked them over when they were setting the table," I lie, tugging on my black bowtie, which suddenly feels like it's cutting off my air supply.

She places both cards down on the table before reaching for the back of her chair.

"Allow me." I may not be entirely pleased to be seated

beside her given the circumstances, but at the very least I'm a gentleman.

Chapter 5

Brooke

"Thank you," I say when Jake's boss pushes in my chair.

Apart from the fact he's been working my husband to the bone, he seems nice enough. I was surprised when he said who he was, I wasn't expecting him to be so young or handsome, for that matter.

My eyes take him in as he scans his surroundings before eventually seating himself. It's hard for me not to stare, he has a rare kind of beauty. I may be a married woman, but I'm not blind.

My husband has disappeared to catch up with some colleagues, I don't understand why he has no desire to introduce me to them. He hasn't even commented on my gown.

"Where's Jake?"

"I'm not sure," I reply, shrugging.

I force a smile as I fiddle with the cloth napkin in front of me. I'm embarrassed by the way Jake acted earlier; he's never been the possessive or jealous kind.

"So, are you working here in Melbourne?"

"No, not at the moment. I worked as a dance teacher

and choreographer back in Sydney." I let out a sigh before continuing. "I loved that job so much."

"You can't get a job doing that here? Surely there are plenty of dance studios in Melbourne. I have clients in that industry. I could make some calls for you."

"That's really nice of you, Mr. Cavanagh, but Jake doesn't want me working."

My gaze drops down to my lap the second those words are out of my mouth. I didn't mean to confess that. My husband made a terrible impression on his boss earlier when he carried on like a caveman, and now I feel like I'm jumping on the bandwagon.

"Please call me Logan. *Mr. Cavanagh* is my father's name; it makes me feel old when you say it."

"Okay," I say, smiling.

"You have a beautiful smile."

"Thank you."

"So, how do you feel about that?"

"My smile?" I ask, confused.

"No," he replies with a chuckle. "How do you feel about your husband not wanting you to work anymore?"

"Truthfully, I miss everything about it."

I can tell by the way his jaw ticks that he's not impressed with my answer. Which only makes my embarrassment escalate to humiliation. He may see compliance as a weakness, but to me, it's more about keeping harmony within my marriage.

Maybe I'm going about it all wrong, but I grew up around single women, and Jake is my only serious relationship. I have no prior experience to draw from.

Our conversation ceases, but that's probably for the best. My husband's job might be in jeopardy if I keep adding fuel to the fire.

We sit in awkward silence, but Logan continues to

acknowledge everyone who passes the table with a small wave or a nod. I can tell by people's reactions that they genuinely like him.

I'm trying not to stare, but my eyes automatically keep gravitating in his direction. His dark hair, perfectly chiselled features, straight nose, and long inky lashes that frame his piercing, emerald green eyes only add to his overall appeal. Does this man have any faults? I'm sure there's something, but I've yet to see it.

When my eyes move down to his big strong hands, the first thing I notice is the absence of a wedding ring.

I turn in my seat, looking towards the back of the room. I need a distraction. Relief floods through me when I see Jake approaching us. I'm glad Logan and I are no longer conversing; that would only irritate my husband further and I have to wonder why.

I place my hand on Jake's leg once he's seated. "Everything okay?" I whisper.

"Everything's peachy."

Out of the corner of my eye, I see Logan raise his hand to flag down the waiter. "Can I get a double scotch on the rocks, please?" *A double?* He must be planning a big night.

"Make that two," Jake chimes in, and I side-eye him because he's never been much of a drinker.

"Can I get you anything, Brooke?" Logan asks.

"She'll have a white wine."

"Actually, I'm not feeling the best, so I think I'll stick with water."

"Suit yourself," Jake says, rolling his eyes.

His lack of concern stings. My eyes dart to Logan, and my husband seems to be oblivious to the death stare he's getting from his boss.

The moment Logan's gaze moves to me, his face

softens immediately. He gives me a sympathetic smile, and I feel compelled to reassure him that my husband isn't always like this, that he's just under a lot of pressure right now, but as his employer, he'd already know that.

The mood around the table mellows by the time the other employees join us and the first course arrives. But within minutes of finishing his meal, Jake gets a message on his phone and excuses himself from the table.

"Where are you going?" I ask as he stands.

"I've gotta see someone quickly. I won't be long."

"Can I come too?" I feel stupid sitting here with his work colleagues on my own.

"No, stay here, I'll be back soon."

I stare after him as he walks away, and I can feel the eyes of the entire table on me as I do.

Chapter 6

Logan

"Are you enjoying your night?" I ask when I hear Brooke softly sigh beside me as she watches her husband leave. I can already tell she isn't, but I can guarantee she's too polite to admit it.

I'm shocked he's left her alone again. The Jake I met at his interview is vastly different to the man I see tonight. I'm usually a good judge of character, but now I'm not so sure. I'll definitely be keeping a closer eye on him at the office going forward.

"I am, thank you." Her forced smile tugs at my heartstrings.

Her husband is an idiot. She's hands down the most beautiful woman in the room, yet he's paying her absolutely no attention. We've had conversations about cases and even sat in many meetings together, but I haven't had the chance to get to know him on a personal level. After his behaviour tonight, I don't think I want to.

Brooke turns her body in her seat, and my eyes follow her line of sight to the dance floor. At first, I think maybe that's where Jake might be, but I don't see him so my attention moves back to her. If I'm not mistaken, there's a longing in her eyes. Maybe she wants to dance, and I have an overwhelming compulsion to ask her, but quickly squash the thought. For one, I don't dance, and two, dancing with her is only asking for trouble.

Her attention eventually moves back to me, but just as she goes to speak, I see her screw up her face as her complexion turns a ghostly shade of white. She places her hand over her stomach, and I hear a moan of pain fall from her lips.

"Shit. Are you okay?" I ask.

"I don't know," she replies as perspiration appears on her forehead. She doesn't look well at all. "Would you please excuse me? I need to find Jake."

Standing, I pull out her chair and help her to her feet. "Are you sure you're okay? Are you able to walk?"

"I'm fine. Thank you," she replies before turning and heading towards the exit.

My eyes don't leave her as she crosses the room. When I see her stop and double over, I decide to follow her. God only knows where that prick is.

My eyes are everywhere when I reach the foyer, but she's nowhere in sight. Without hesitating, I make my way outside.

I only just make it through the doors when I spot her. She's standing at the base of the stairs on the footpath. One hand rests on her stomach, and the other covers her mouth. Her head is turned to the left, as she stares down the street with tears cascading down her pretty face.

I follow her line of sight and can't believe what I'm seeing.

If my concern for her wasn't so great, I'd go over there and rip his damn head off. He's so busy dry fucking another woman up against the wall that he hasn't even noticed he has an audience.

My gaze moves back to Brooke and the sadness etched all over her face is like a sucker-punch to my gut. I know exactly how she's feeling at this moment; I've been there.

When she abruptly turns and heads in the opposite direction. I immediately follow.

"Brooke," I call out as she breaks into a jog. I can hear her sobs as I close the distance between us, and my heart breaks for her.

Just as I get close enough to grab her, she stumbles, falling forward. My arms instinctively reach out, sliding around her waist as I pull her back into my front.

"I'm so sorry you had to witness that," I say, but when her body goes limp, my heart drops into the pit of my stomach.

Hooking my hand behind her knees, I waste no time lifting her into my arms. Her head falls back and I immediately see she's unconscious.

What the hell?

"Brooke." I shake her slightly, but when I get no response, I rush towards the wooden bench nearby and gently lay her down. Quickly shrugging out of my tuxedo jacket, I ball it up and gently slide it under her head. "Brooke, can you hear me?"

Placing my two fingers on the side of her neck, I check her pulse. I can see she's breathing by the rise and fall of her chest, but I'm perplexed as to what just happened.

"Is she okay?" a passer-by stops to enquire.

"I'm not sure," I reply, reaching into my pocket for my phone.

My first instinct is to call triple zero, but St. Vincent's Hospital is only a few minutes from here. Chris, my driver, is always instructed to stay close by in case I ever need to make a hasty retreat.

"Is there something I can do to help?" the stranger asks.

"No, but thank you. I've got this."

"Are you ready to leave already?" I can hear humour in Chris's voice, and usually, I'd have the perfect comeback for him, but this is no time for banter.

"I need you out the front of the building now."

"Is everything all right, Mr. Cavanagh?"

"Just hurry," I say before ending the call.

Relief floods through me when I see Brooke's head roll to the side, quickly followed by a soft moan.

Crouching down, I glide my fingers across her forehead, and then down the side of her face. "It's okay," I whisper in a calm and soothing voice, although what I'm feeling inside is anything but. "Help is on the way."

Brooke's eyes flutter open, and her face is contorted with pain. Her back arches slightly off the bench as a more aggressive sound escapes her. I don't know why seeing her like this affects me so much, but it does.

"Jake, help me," she mumbles.

Quickly glancing over my shoulder and down the street, I see her poor excuse for a husband is still all over that woman and totally oblivious to this dire situation unfolding with his wife.

"I've got you," I say, gently lifting her into my arms. "Everything is going to be okay."

When I see my driver approaching, I make my way to the kerb. "Shit," he says, quickly exiting the car and running around the back of the vehicle.

"Open the door."

"Is she okay?"

"Does it look like it?" I snap. I'm not usually so abrupt with him, but in my defence, I'm a bit of a mess. I've never been in a situation like this before.

Leaning into the back of the limousine, I lay her across the seat before climbing in.

"Has she had too much to drink?"

"No! Stop making assumptions and just get us to the hospital."

"Of course, Mr. Cavanagh."

Gently lifting her torso, I take a seat before laying her head on my lap. She keeps falling in and out of consciousness.

"We're getting you help," I say as I lay my tuxedo jacket over the top of her to keep her warm. I'm trying my best to keep my composure, but I'm struggling. When she draws her knees up towards her body before crying out in pain once more, I internally freak out. "Chris, hurry."

"We'll be there in a few minutes," he says, eyeing me through the rear-view mirror. "Thankfully the traffic isn't too bad this time of night."

I turn my attention back to Brooke. She's ghostly pale and clammy. "We're almost at the hospital," I tell her. "I won't let anything happen to you; I promise."

I have no right to make promises I'm not even sure I can keep, but right now, I mean every word.

Chris comes to an abrupt halt outside the emergency entrance to the hospital. I don't even wait for him to open my door.

Gently lifting her head from my lap, I slide out of the car. I see Chris jogging towards the building as I reach into the back seat for Brooke. I'm grateful that he's proactive; the quicker we can get her seen too, the better.

I'd be lost without this man. Although he's my

employee, I'd like to think that we've become friends over the years.

Brooke is semi-conscious, but her head is now flailing from side to side, as she moans in agony. I'm not sure what is going on with her, but my gut tells me it's not good.

"We're at the hospital," I say, as I lift her into my arms. The interior light is on in the car, and I momentarily freeze when I see a small pool of blood on the cream leather seat where she was just lying.

"Shit!" The sight of it has me internally freaking out.

"Jake," she cries.

"I've got you. Everything is going to be okay." I'm not even sure I believe my own words, but I feel compelled to say them. "Just hang in there."

Chris is already speaking with the triage nurse when I rush through the automatic glass doors.

"I need a doctor," I call out, panicked as I head in their direction. "I think she's haemorrhaging." I can feel the dampness from the blood on her dress, and also on my hand as it trickles between my fingers.

The nurse gets up and opens the door that leads directly through to the back of emergency. "This way," is all she says, turning and briskly walking down the hall, and I follow. She abruptly draws back the curtain surrounding one of the cubicles. "Lay her down there. I'll get the doctor in here immediately."

Stretching her arm, she presses the red button behind the bed, and within seconds the hospital staff come running from every direction.

"Can you tell me what happened?"

"I don't know. She was in pain and holding her lower abdomen before collapsing. She's been in and out of consciousness ever since. When I lifted her out of the car just now, there was blood on the seat."

"I'm going to have to ask you to step outside."

"But—"

"She's in safe hands now. I'll get the doctor to come and talk with you as soon as he's had a chance to look her over." I open my mouth to speak again, but the nurse flicks her hands, shooing me out. "Please. We can't give her the care she needs with you in the way."

Nodding, I turn and leave. Everything in me wants to stay by Brooke's side to comfort her, but the nurse is right —I'll only be in the way.

"Please look after her," I request, but it comes out more like a plea. I'm beyond concerned, and although we barely know each other, I don't want anything to happen to her.

"We will," she says, giving me a sympathetic smile before closing the curtain and shutting me out.

I stand there in shock. I should feel relieved that Brooke's getting the medical care she needs, but I don't. Her cries are going to haunt me.

I probably should make my way back out to the waiting room, but I can't. I want to stay close. Looking down at my hand, I see it's soaked in her blood, and the cuff of my white dress shirt is as well. The red stain only increases my grave fears for her well-being.

There's a sink by the wall, so I head in that direction. I remove both of my cufflinks and shove them into my pocket before rolling my sleeves up a few times.

Bile rises in my throat as the water in the basin turns pink. As I wipe my hands with a paper towel I stare blankly into the distance.

Pacing back and forth, I hear voices coming from the other side of the curtain, but nothing seems to register.

A few minutes later, I'm startled when the curtain

flies back and they wheel Brooke, bed and all, straight past me. I grab hold of the nurse's arm as they pass.

"What's going on?"

"We're taking your wife for some scans. The doctor needs to know exactly where the bleeding is coming from."

"Is she going to be okay?" I ask, ignoring their error in thinking she's my wife.

"She's in good hands," she says, placing her hand on my arm. "I'm sorry. That's all I can tell you at this stage, but I'll need her full name?"

"Brooke ... Brooke Johnston."

"Thank you, Mr. Johnston. I'm going to have to ask you to head back into the waiting room and someone will call you when we have more answers."

I feel a lump form in the back of my throat. I'm taken aback by how much this situation is affecting me. I've never felt so helpless in my life.

My shoulders slump and my feet drag as I head down the corridor and press the green button on the wall, allowing me to exit. Looking around the packed room, I search for Chris. He has to be here somewhere; he wouldn't leave without telling me. Finding no sign of him, I walk towards the automatic doors, and out into the night.

I find him leaning against one of the concrete pylons just outside the exit. "How is she?" he asks, standing up straight.

"I'm not sure." I scrub my hands over my face as I speak. "They've taken her to have scans to see where the bleeding is coming from."

"I hope she's going to be okay."

"That makes two of us."

"I wiped most of the blood off the backseat, and I'll take the car in to be cleaned in the morning."

"That's the least of my worries," I say, with a flick of my hand.

"Who is she? The woman I mean."

"One of my employees' wives."

"Where's her husband?"

"Still at The Dome, I presume."

"Okay."

I see the confusion on his face. I'm sure he's wondering why I'm here with her, instead of him. "I probably should try to contact him."

"You most definitely should."

I bet he wouldn't be so insistent if he knew the whole story. That fucker doesn't deserve her. She's better off without him.

Sliding my phone out of my pocket, I search for my assistant's number. Claire will still be at the function and may be able to get a hold of him for me.

"Claire."

"Mr. Cavanagh."

"I need a favour."

"Sure. Are you still here?" I can hear the confusion in her voice.

"No. I'm at the hospital."

"Hospital?" she shrieks, and it's loud enough that I have to pull the phone away from my ear. "Is everything all right?"

"I'm fine. I'm here with someone else."

"Who?"

"Long story. I can fill you in later. What I need you to do is find Jake Johnston. Do you know who he is?" It's a stupid question; Claire knows everyone who works for me.

"Yes, of course."

"He was seated at my table."

"I can't see him. Hold on, I'll walk around the room." I impatiently tap my foot as I wait. "I can't see him." Of course, she can't. I bet that bastard is still outside.

"Go out to the front of the building and see if you can see him there." I feel my anger spike, knowing he's more than likely still out there with that woman. I eye Chris as I wait.

"Okay." A short time passes before she speaks again. "Nope, I don't see him."

"Look to your left, follow the outer wall of the building." When I hear her gasp, I know my suspicions are correct.

"Oh my god, is that Jenny, his secretary? Shit, I think it is. Wasn't he here with his wife tonight?"

"His secretary?"

"Yes. Jesus, is he giving her a tonsillectomy with his tongue? Get a room you two," she mumbles to herself. Although there's nothing funny about this situation, her observation makes me chuckle. One of the things I love about her is her wit and lack of a filter, although it's gotten her into trouble on more than one occasion. "I'm sure when I did the seating plan, he was seated at your table with his wife."

"He was. That's who I'm at the hospital with."

The rage I feel is indescribable. I have a strict *'No fraternising with staff policy.'* It not only applies to me, but to all of my employees. It's one of the clauses in their employment agreement, but I know my anger runs far deeper than that. This situation brings back all those ill feelings from my past. Emotions I buried many years ago.

"What a snake. His poor wife." My sentiments exactly. "What happened to her?"

"I'm not sure."

"Do you want me to go over there and tell him she's in the hospital? Although under the circumstances, I'm not sure he's going to care."

"No, don't worry about it. I'll stay here until I know she's going to be okay."

"Keep me updated."

"I will, Claire. Thanks."

"Oh, and Mr. Cavanagh."

"Yes?"

"I'll cover for you here."

"Thank you."

I was tossing up whether to stay or leave, but that phone call just confirmed I'm not going anywhere, for the interim anyway. I couldn't possibly leave her here to face this all on her own.

"I'm going to hang around for a bit," I tell Chris. "You may as well head home."

"I'm happy to stay if you want the company."

"I appreciate it, but it could be hours before I know anything. I'll get a cab home."

"Okay. I'll head out, but I'll keep my phone close by. If you need me, or a lift, just call."

"Thank you."

I'm not sure how long I've been waiting to hear news on Brooke's condition, but it's been a while—a few hours, at the very least.

I've nodded off occasionally, despite my concerns. *It's been a long fucking day.*

"Mr. Johnston," someone says, nudging my leg.

Sitting up straight in my seat, I rub my eyes with the heel of my palms. I don't bother correcting him when he calls me by the wrong name. If they think I'm her husband, I might get some information on her condition. "I'm sorry it's taken so long for me to come and see you. I'm Dr. Goldstein. I'm the one taking care of your wife."

I clear my throat before I speak. "How is she, doc?"

"She's doing well, considering." I feel instant relief when he says that. "Come, we can have a chat in one of the private rooms if you like."

"That would be great."

Standing, I look down at my watch and see it's just after midnight. Shoving my hands into the pockets of my trousers, I follow him back through the doors to the emergency rooms, and halfway down the corridor. He stops at a doorway and gestures for me to enter. The room seems sterile and sparse of furniture with only a small sofa and coffee table inside.

"Sit." I do as he asks. He takes a seat on the edge of the table opposite me before speaking again. He's still dressed in scrubs. "First and foremost, I want to assure you that your wife is doing okay. It was touch and go for a while, but I'm confident she'll make a full recovery."

"Did you find out what was causing the bleeding?"

"Yes. Your wife had an ectopic pregnancy."

"Ectopic?" I ask, perplexed. That word is unfamiliar to me.

"Do you know what a fallopian tube is?"

"Not really," I say, feeling foolish.

Sure, I've heard of it, and recall it has something to do with the female reproductive system, but I have no clue what it actually is or does. I like to think I'm an expert on the exterior of a woman's body, but my mastery stops there, unfortunately.

"Would you like me to explain?"

"Please." I feel stupid for even saying that but I'm not married, and having children of my own isn't something I've thought about at this stage in my life.

"Without getting too technical, women are born with two fallopian tubes. Basically, they're the carriageway by which the fertilised egg travels from the ovary to the uterus. In a normal pregnancy, the fertilised egg implants itself into the lining of the womb where the foetus will develop and continue to grow over the coming months. But in some instances—around one in every hundred pregnancies—the egg doesn't make it to the uterus. In your wife's case, the egg implanted itself outside the womb, in one of her fallopian tubes, which resulted in what we refer to as an ectopic pregnancy."

"I see," I say.

"Her fallopian tube ruptured, causing extensive bleeding. We had no choice but to operate."

"To stop the bleeding?" I ask.

"Yes. We also had to remove one of her tubes. The damage caused by the rupture was extensive. It was unrepairable, so removing it was the only way we could stem the bleeding. She's very lucky you got her to the hospital as quick as you did." I nod but say nothing. "I'm sorry for your loss," he says, reaching out to place his hand on my shoulder. "Her other fallopian tube is still healthy so I have no reason to believe you can't try for a family again in the future."

I'm now feeling like an arse for impersonating her husband. The person who should be on the receiving end of the doctor's sympathy is Brooke, but I'm grateful to hear she can still become a mother one day if that's what she wants.

I exhale a large breath. "Can I see her?"

I'm not sure if she'd even want to see me under the circumstances—we're practically strangers—but it feels imperative that I do. At the very least, I'd like to let her know I'm here for her if she needs me.

"She's still in recovery, but she should be moved to a room in about an hour or so. We'll be keeping her in for a few days for observation, but I can have one of the nurses take you there, where you can wait for her."

"I'd appreciate that, thank you."

"No problem at all."

He stands, and I do the same, extending my hand to him. "I appreciate everything you did for ... umm ... her." She's not my wife, and I already feel guilty for misleading him.

"You're welcome. If you'd like to wait here you can. I'll have one of the nurses come and get you once your wife's been allocated a room."

"Thank you."

Chapter 7

Brooke

I feel numb as the orderly wheels me down the long corridor towards the room I'll be staying in, but it's not from the drugs they've given me.

I want to go home—I hate hospitals since I practically lived at one during my mother's illness—but I'm not even sure where home is anymore. It's definitely not with Jake.

When I close my eyes, the despair takes over and I fight back tears ... tears not only for my baby, but also for the end of my marriage. Jake can make all the excuses in the world, but there's no way I can forgive him. I saw his betrayal with my own eyes, and to say it gutted me would be an understatement. All those late nights he's been putting in now make sense. Trust is everything in a marriage, and without that, what is there?

The doctor informed me he'd spoken with my husband, and that he is waiting to see me. I don't want him here. I'm going to ask him to leave; I'm dealing with enough. I can't believe he had the gall to come.

I wasn't aware I was pregnant, that's what devastates me the most. At least if I'd known, even for the shortest time, I could've loved and been thankful for the tiny life growing inside me.

Given my current situation with my husband, people may say losing the baby is a godsend, but my mother raised me on her own. Like her, I would've managed. I have so much love inside me, and there's no one left to share it with.

My eyes remain closed when I arrive in my room. I know I need to face Jake, but I just need a moment to gather my composure. I hear the orderly close the curtains around my bed, followed by the scuffing sound of his shoes against the linoleum floor as he leaves.

I wait for Jake to approach the bed, but minutes pass and all I get is silence. Slowly opening my eyes, I look around. Has he left already? Maybe he ran back to *that* woman to seek comfort. Just the thought breaks my heart a little further.

When my eyes land on the man fast asleep in the far corner of the room, I gasp.

What is Jake's boss doing here?

He's slumped back in the chair with his arms crossed over his chest and his legs spread wide. He looks extremely uncomfortable. I stare at him for the longest time. The sleeves of his dress shirt are rolled up around his elbows. His dark hair is slightly dishevelled, and his bow tie is now draped loosely around his neck.

Minutes pass before he stirs in his seat. Quickly turning my head, I close my eyes like a coward. When I hear the curtain draw back, I clench them a little tighter. Is that Jake? Is he back?

Someone fusses around the bed before grabbing hold of my wrist. My eyes fly open to find a middle-aged nurse standing beside me.

"Oh, you're awake," she says in a quiet voice. "How are you feeling?"

Empty. "A little tired, and sore," I reply.

"I'm just going to check your vitals, then I'll grab you something for the pain."

"Thank you."

"You have a good man there," she says, flicking her head in Logan's direction. I force a smile instead of replying. Unfortunately, he's not mine. "He's been waiting for hours, and anxious for your return."

In my peripheral vision, I see him sit up higher in his chair, so I keep my attention focused on the nurse as she goes about her duties.

I'm grateful he's here since my husband didn't think I was important enough, but this situation is still awkward, I barely know this man.

"I'll be back in a few minutes with your pain medication."

"Thank you." My eyes follow her as she leaves the room. I can't bring myself to look in Logan's direction.

"Hey," he says, standing a moving towards the bed.

"Oh, hi. I didn't notice you sitting over there."

A small smile tugs at his lips, does he know I'm lying?

"I just wanted to hang around and make sure you were okay. How are you feeling?" The tenderness in his voice has my emotions flooding back to the surface.

I turn my head away, as I struggle to fight back the tears.

"I'm sorry for everything you went through last night, Brooke," he says, placing his hand on top of mine. Those words only make the tears fall faster. My bottom lip quivers as I struggle not to break down in front of him. Letting go of my hand, he walks back towards the chair, and I feel rude for snubbing him. But instead of taking a seat, he picks it up and moves it closer to the bed. "You don't have to say anything. Just know that I'm here ... I don't want you to go through this alone."

A strangled sob escapes me as his fingers wrap around mine, holding my hand tight. I have no words. My heart may be shattered, but I'm touched by his kindness, and so grateful he's here.

The room is flooded with light when I open my eyes. I must've fallen asleep. Do you ever wake and for that first split second, as the bliss of slumber still lingers, and life seems wonderful ... then reality hits? And that brief moment of serenity vanishes, as your world comes crashing down around you?

That's me in this instant. I inhale a sharp breath as memories of Jake and my lost baby hit me full-force.

I feel the warmth from the hand wrapped around mine as the grip tightens. Turning my head, I see Logan still sitting beside my bed. I can't believe he's still here.

Dark circles have formed underneath his striking green eyes, and a five o'clock shadow darkens his ridiculously handsome face. I have the urge to reach out and run my fingers across his stubble.

"Morning," he says.

"Good morning."

"How are you feeling?" he asks, as I try to sit up by myself. He immediately lets go of my hand and stands to help.

"A little tender," I answer in a raspy voice, as he raises the head of the bed. "My mouth is so dry."

"It's probably from sleeping with it wide open. I'm pretty sure you caught a few flies."

"What?" I screech as he tries in vain to suppress his grin.

"All that snoring probably didn't help."

"I do not snore."

"I'm kidding." He chuckles, and I find myself smiling at his playfulness. "It's nice to see you smiling," he says, fluffing my pillow.

"Thank you for doing that, even though it was at my expense."

"I'm sorry for making fun of you."

"It's okay."

"You actually slept soundly." His gaze moves down to the floor, as he runs his fingers through his thick hair. "Not that I sat here and watched you sleep." The insecure look he gives me has my lips curving up once more. "I just meant the nurse came in a few times throughout the night to check your vitals, and you didn't stir once."

"I'm sure that's what you meant," I tease.

"It is." When I let out a small laugh, he shakes his head and smiles. "Touché." I swallow a few times trying to get some moisture back in my mouth. "Would you like me to ask the nurse if you can have something to drink?"

"Please."

I lean back into my pillow and sigh as I stare up at the ceiling. I'm anxious about everything I'm going to have to face once I leave here. It will be tough, I know that, but in time things will work out. Life's funny like that.

"Nil by mouth until you see the doctor, I'm afraid," Logan says when he re-enters the room. "But the nurse said you can suck on some ice chips."

A triumphant smile breaks out on his face as he holds up the paper cup in his hand.

"Thank you."

Leaning forward, he whispers, "Don't worry, I didn't tell the nurse about the flies you've eaten. I'll keep that between us. I'd hate to see you get in trouble."

"Very funny," I say, laughing. As he stands to full height, he stares down at me with an endearing look on his face. It's sweet and a little unnerving. "I hope they'll let me leave today. I hate hospitals."

"The nurse said the doctor will be doing his rounds soon, but when I spoke with him last night, he said they'll be keeping you in for a few days."

His words deflate me, even though I'm not looking forward to going home to face Jake, I want to get out of here.

I watch as he places his hands on his lower back and stretches. "This seat doesn't make the most comfortable bed." He rolls his shoulders and cracks his neck from side to side.

"Why don't you head home?"

"I don't want to leave you here alone."

"I'm fine, honestly," I say. "I'm no stranger to being on my own."

"I wouldn't mind having a shower and changing into some clean clothes. Is there someone I can call to come and sit with you? Your parent's? A friend?"

"No parents, my mother has passed." I shrug, and he gives me a sympathetic smile. I refuse to even give my sperm donor a mention.

"No siblings?" He raises an eyebrow in hope.

"Nope, I'm an only child and all my friends live in Sydney."

"Well, that settles it, I'm staying. Unless of course, you'd like me to get in contact with Jake."

Just the mere mention of his name hurts. "He's the last person I want to see."

There's a brief silence before he speaks again. "Did you know?"

"Know what?"

"About the affair with his secretary?"

I feel my eyes widen with his confession. "His secretary?"

"Yes."

"No, no I didn't," I say, bowing my head. "I feel like such a fool."

"I'm sorry."

I don't know why he's apologising; he has nothing to be sorry for. "Go home and shower. If you want to call back later, you can. If not, that's okay too."

"Are you sure?"

"Positive. You've already done so much." I pause for a moment, as my emotions resurface. "I'm extremely grateful for your kindness."

He reaches into his back pocket and pulls out his leather wallet. "If you need anything—and I mean anything—just call."

"Thank you," I say when he hands me his business card.

By mid-afternoon, I'm feeling somewhat human again. The nurse came in earlier to help me shower, and she was nice enough to remove the abundance of bobby pins from my hair, so I could wash it. I even managed to get a few more hours of sleep.

Understandably, I'm still feeling down, but I'm trying

not to let my situation overcome me. Instead, I'm throwing all my energy into getting well enough to leave this godforsaken place.

Earlier, when the doctor did his rounds, he strongly advised me to stay in the hospital for at least one more day. When I begged and pleaded for him to release me, he promised to call by towards the end of his shift to re-examine me.

If bed rest is all I need to recuperate, I can get that at home. Although what awaits me there won't be pleasant, it's got to be better than spending another night here. We have other rooms at the house that I can sleep in, at least until I make new arrangements.

I'm flicking through the channels on the television when someone pops their head through the curtain.

"Are you up for a visitor?"

My heart skips a beat the moment our eyes lock. "You didn't have to come back."

"I wanted to. I hated the thought of you being here all alone."

He draws back the curtain slightly, before entering. The first thing I see is the roses in his hand. *Yellow roses.* I know he has no idea how significant that type of flower is, but they're enough not only to bring tears to my eyes, but also a huge smile to my face.

Is it an omen? I'd like to think so. Although my mother is no longer walking this earth, I feel her presence often. And to me, this is another sign. Yellow roses always remind me of her.

At least I have the comfort of knowing my baby is with her in heaven.

"These are for you."

My gaze moves from the flowers to him. He's clean-shaven and dressed casually in a pair of jeans and a t-shirt, but he looks no less debonair than he did last night in his tux.

"Thank you," I say as he holds them out to me. Taking them from him, I bring them to my nose and inhale their sweet scent. "They're beautiful."

"I also got you these." He places a large, brown paper shopping bag on the bed beside me. "You'll need something to wear home when you leave. Your dress ..." His words drift off, but I already know what he isn't saying. I vaguely remember being cut out of my clothes before they rushed me into theatre. "Everything should fit, I used what you were wearing last night as a guide. Your clutch purse is in there as well. You left it on the table at The Dome. Claire, my assistant, collected it for you."

Pulling open the bag, I peek inside. There sits my clutch on top of some clothes, underwear, and even a pair of shoes. I place my hand on my chest, feeling overwhelmed.

"I have no words," I say.

He flicks his hand like it's nothing.

I'll never forget all he's done, not only staying with me throughout the night, but the doctor told me earlier that my husband saved my life by getting me to the hospital as quickly as he did.

"Was it you who brought me to the hospital? I remember bits and pieces, but most of it's a blur."

"Yes. I followed you outside last night." He holds both his hands up in a defensive position. "I wasn't stalking you or anything. I was concerned. When you ran off after ..."

I nod because he doesn't need to repeat that part; I think it will be permanently ingrained in my memory. Such a huge betrayal, committed by the person I loved and trusted most, is not easily forgotten.

Chapter 8

Logan

I'm sitting beside Brooke's bed, making small talk when the doctor enters. I've been here all afternoon.

I know she said there was no need for me to return, but I felt compelled to. She's all I thought about when I left here earlier.

Jake is all she has, and look how poorly he's treated her. I'll take every ounce of pleasure in dealing with him, and his secretary, first thing Monday morning. Any retribution I can get for this poor woman, I will.

"Would you like me to step out?" I ask, standing and moving to the side.

"No, stay," Brooke answers.

"Mr. Johnston," Dr. Goldstein says, extending his hand to me. My eyes dart to Brooke, and I can see she's fighting back a smile. Could this situation get any more awkward?

"Doc," I say, shaking his hand.

"How are you feeling?" he asks, turning his attention back to his patient.

"A lot better. I haven't needed any pain medication this afternoon. I've eaten and kept it down," she says like it's a huge triumph, and it brings a smile to my face. She really is the sweetest. Her eyes dart to me briefly. "And I ... umm ... managed to use the bathroom."

Her last sentence comes out more like a whisper, and my smile grows when I see her cheeks flush the prettiest shade of pink.

"Well, that is good news. Good news, indeed."

"Does that mean I can go home?" she asks with a hopeful look on her face.

My eyes drink her in. She looks completely different to the beauty I first met, in her stunning red dress, formal hairstyle, and heavily made-up face.

The woman before me now is dressed in a simple hospital gown, her long brown hair is down, and there's not a stitch of makeup on her face, yet she's equally beautiful, if not more so.

"You know my thoughts on this," the doctor says. "I'd prefer it if you stayed at least until tomorrow morning."

"But I can get bed rest at home ... in my own bed."

The doctor's attention moves to me. "What are your thoughts on this?"

I shrug. I'm kind of agreeing with him. My gaze moves to Brooke and the pleading look she gives me says so much. She's hell-bent on getting out of here.

"As her husband," I say, clearing my throat, "I give you my solemn word that she'll be well cared for." When I place my hand on my chest for added effect, Brooke bites her lip to fight her smile. "If there are any issues, I'll bring her straight back."

The doctor sighs. "Okay. If you promise to get complete bed rest—that includes no heavy lifting or stretching—and see your GP within the next few days, I guess I can let you go home."

"Thank you," she says, beaming.

"I'll get a letter drawn up for your GP, along with your discharge papers."

"Thanks for everything, doc," I say, shaking his hand once more.

Brooke slumps back into her pillow and starts laughing the moment the doctor leaves, and I find myself doing the same.

"I'm so lucky to have such a considerate and caring fake husband."

I puff out my chest. "You better believe it ... I'm the best!"

I'm actually disappointed she's leaving because it means the end of my time with her. I'll probably never see her again after today, and that thought saddens me more than I care to admit.

"You got everything?" I ask, picking up the brown paper bag that's sitting on the bed. She already changed into the clothes I bought her. The leggings and fitted tee only accentuate her amazing figure. How Jake would want to stray outside his marriage is beyond me. If she was my wife, I'd treasure her.

"I think so," she says, looking around the room.

"My card." I point to my business card sitting on the table beside the bed. "Please take it. If there's anything you need, just call me."

"Okay." I see gratitude in her smile as she picks it up and slides it into her silver clutch purse.

"I mean it, Brooke. Anything."

"I appreciate everything you've done for me. I really do."

"It's been my pleasure."

A comfortable silence settles between us as we walk down the corridor towards the lifts. When we reach the lobby, we both stop walking and face each other.

"Well, I guess this is goodbye," she says.

"I guess it is."

"Again, I can't thank you enough—"

I hold up my hand, cutting her off. "There's no need to thank me. As I said, it was my pleasure."

"You're a good man, Mr. Cavanagh."

I shrug. "I'm far from perfect."

"I don't believe that for a second," she says playfully poking my side.

"I was trying to play it down," I admit. "You're right, I'm pretty incredible." When she pokes me again, I chuckle. "On a more serious note, what are your plans from here?"

She lifts one shoulder. "I'll go home, face the music, and take it from there."

"You deserve better than him," I say. It's none of my business, but it needs to be said.

"Thank you." Her gaze drops down to her feet. "I should be going."

"Can I at least give you a lift? My car's parked outside."

"I appreciate the offer, but I think it's best if I take a cab."

I want to insist, but I don't. I wish I could take her back to my place and care for her like I promised the doctor I would, but she's not mine to keep.

"Bye," she says, taking a step forward and encircling her arms around my waist. It's a move I wasn't expecting, but I'm certainly not complaining. I wrap my arms around her also, holding her tight for the briefest moment. "I'll never forget you, or the kindness you've shown me."

I won't forget her either, but I don't voice that out loud.

Letting me go, she gives me one last smile before turning and walking away. Shoving my hands into the pockets of my jeans, I stand there and watch her go.

My gaze shifts to the ground and I blow out a long breath as she climbs into the back of the taxi and drives out of my life.

I can't even put into words the depth of sadness that sweeps through my entire body. Call me crazy, but I can't help feeling like I just lost something monumental.

Chapter 9

Brooke

Butterflies churn in my stomach as the cab pulls up outside my house. Our car is parked in the driveway so I know Jake's home. I have no idea what I'm going to say to him when I get inside, but one thing is for sure, our marriage is over.

After paying the driver, I exit the vehicle. I only make it halfway across the lawn when Jake comes barrelling out of the house.

"Thank God," he says. "I've been going out of my mind."

His arms are outstretched as he approaches. "Don't," I say, holding my hand out in front of me.

"Don't what?" he asks as his arms drop down by his side.

"Don't touch me."

His facial expression turns from confused to angry as I sidestep him and continue towards the house.

"Hey," he snaps, following me into the front foyer. "What's your problem?"

"My problem? That's rich, coming from you," I huff, heading towards the staircase.

"You're angry at me?" He grabs hold of my arm and swings me around before getting up in my face. "You're the one who left last night, and then disappeared for twenty-four hours. So, tell me, Brooke, where the fuck have you been?"

"I saw you last night, Jake. I saw you with that woman." Angry tears sting my eyes, but I refuse to give him the satisfaction of seeing me cry.

"What woman?" Although he's playing dumb, the fact that his face pales tells me he knows exactly what woman I'm referring to.

"The blonde in the blue dress."

"What?"

"The one you were kissing." His unwillingness to even acknowledge what he's done only infuriates me more. "Let go of me," I say, pushing on his chest. "You disgust me."

"Brooke, baby," he pleads. "I don't know what you're talking about."

"Really?"

"Yes, really."

"You're a piece of work. You don't remember having her pushed up against the wall last night?"

"It wasn't like that, I swear."

"It wasn't just a peck, Jake. You were all over each other." Never in my life have I been so mad. We've had a few arguments over the years, but it's never been this volatile.

"You're reading too much into this."

I shake my head in a combination of disbelief and repulsion. Does he think I'm stupid? "I have eyes, Jake. I know exactly what I saw. All those late nights and weekends you claimed to be working, you were with her, weren't you?" His silence speaks volumes. "Well, you know what," I say, as tears fill my eyes, "she can have you."

"Brooke." He reaches for my arm again, but I manage to turn away before he grabs hold.

"I want a divorce."

I only make it up the first step before he grabs hold of me and pins me against the wall. "You don't mean that."

"I do. You disgust me, Jake. I'm done with you. I should've known better than to get involved with a lawyer; you're all the same."

"I'm nothing like your father," he screams.

"You're right, you're worse!"

His fingers splay across my collarbone, as his hand rests at the base of my neck, but I stare him down. I'm not afraid of him.

"You don't mean that, baby."

"I mean every single word." And I do. I never thought I could despise a man as much as the one who helped create me, but Jake has somehow managed to top the list.

His facial expressions change, as something inside him snaps. His beautiful blue eyes, the ones I have always loved, suddenly look black. His hand moves up a fraction, and the grip on my throat tightens.

"You bitch!"

His murderous glare penetrates me as he shoves my head roughly into the wall. He's never been violent towards me before, but the pressure of his hold tells me he's trying to do me harm.

"Jake," I cry, but my plea goes unheard.

"You're not going anywhere—you hear me?"

I struggle to get air into my lungs, but it's fruitless. His hold is so tight, it's cutting off my airway. Panic sets in as my lungs start to burn and my vision becomes blurred.

Dropping the bag in my hand, I grab hold of his arms

and desperately try to pry his hands off me, but he's too strong. When that doesn't work, I try to claw at his face, but Jake draws his head back out of reach.

"You're my wife, you belong here with me!" Raising my leg, I use every ounce of strength I have left, kneeing him in the balls. "Ah shit," he groans, letting me go and crumbling to the floor with a thud.

I cough and splutter as I breathe in as much air as I can, barely holding on to consciousness. Jake is withering in pain on the floor by my feet, blocking my exit to the front door as he clutches his balls in his hands.

After picking up the bag I brought home from the hospital, which also contains my phone, I race up the stairs and into our bedroom, quickly locking the door behind me.

I can no longer hold my tears at bay as I slide down the wall and into a crumpled mess on the floor. My body starts to tremble from the shock of what just happened. Not only has Jake never raised a hand to me, but I've never seen him show violence towards anyone else either. I have known this man for years, but in the last twenty-four hours, I've seen a completely different side of him.

Moments later, I hear the door handle rattle, followed by a knock. "Brooke, let me in. I'm so sorry, I don't know what came over me."

His voice is soft and calm, but he's delusional if he thinks for one moment that I'm going to let him in.

"Leave me alone," I say, my voice sounding raspy. I flinch when he punches the door.

Managing to get onto my hands and knees, I crawl across the room towards the en suite. I can't trust that he's not going to lose his shit again and try to break down the door.

Once I've locked myself inside, I use the vanity to

pull myself up into a standing position. When I look at my reflection in the mirror, I see that some of the blood vessels have burst in one of my eyes, making the white part of my eye bright red. Tilting my head back, I can see his handprints visibly around my throat. The sight makes me sick to my stomach.

My hands tremble as I turn on the tap and splash water onto my face. One thing is for certain, I need to get the hell out of this house and as far away from that man as possible. But first, I need to clear my head and think this through. I'm not opening that door until I have a solid plan. There's no telling what he'll do to me if I try to walk out of the house now.

Tentatively walking back into the bedroom, I sit on the side of the bed. Maybe I should've listened to the doctor and stayed in the hospital a while longer.

From downstairs, I can hear my husband screaming and things smashing. The psychotic Jake has returned with a vengeance.

Opening my eyes, I feel dazed and confused. Sitting up, I see I've been lying on top of the covers, and my legs are still hanging over the side of the bed. I look over at the clock on the bedside table. It reads 1.08 am.

Swallowing, my throat still feels tender. I stand, and the moonlight shining through the window slightly illuminates the room. I tiptoe towards the en suite, since I presume I'm still alone, but I can't be sure.

I turn on the bathroom light before gazing around the bedroom. Jake is nowhere in sight. Placing one hand on my chest, I breathe a sigh of relief and walk towards the door to see if it's still locked. It is. I feel lethargic and emotionally drained, but I have to get out of here.

Opening the wardrobe, I pull out a small suitcase. I can't take much—only the essentials.

After placing it on the bed, I unzip it and then grab as many clothes and underwear as I can squash in. In the bathroom, I get my face cream, makeup bag, toothbrush, and hairbrush. I can buy whatever else I need.

Glancing in the mirror, I'm not surprised to see that I look like shit. The bruises have started to form on my neck. My fingers glide over the offending area. *I still can't believe he did this to me.* You think you know someone, only to find out you don't really know them at all.

After splashing some water on my face, I grab an elastic out of the top drawer and pull my hair back into a ponytail.

Rushing back into the bedroom, I strip out of the clothes I'm wearing, slipping into a pair of jeans and a red top. After sliding into a pair of red ballet flats, I rummage around in the wicker basket at the base of the wardrobe, looking for my red silk scarf to tie around my neck to cover the bruises.

I grab my mobile phone charger off the bedside table and take my phone out of my silver clutch purse. I see Logan's business card and for a split second I contemplate calling him, but I've already disrupted his life enough. Placing the card back inside, I drop the purse on the bed. He doesn't need to be involved in any more of my drama.

Reaching inside the brown paper shopping bag, I grab the prescription and letter from Dr. Goldstein and shove them in my back pocket.

Dashing back around to the wardrobe, I reach up to the top shelf and feel around for my album. It's one of my most treasured possessions. In it are photos of me growing up and, more importantly, photos of my mother. The stretching sends a shooting pain across my abdomen, but there's no way I'm leaving without it. Most material things are replaceable, but this is not.

Once it's safely packed in between a few layers of clothes, I go to my jewellery box and retrieve the gold heart-shaped locket my mother gave me for my eighteenth birthday. It was one of the last gifts I ever received from her. Inside is a small picture of us together.

Taking off my wedding band, I place it down on the dressing table. I no longer want it. That part of my life is over.

My hands are shaking, and the adrenaline is coursing through my body as I close the suitcase and zip it up.

"It's now or never," I say to myself, picking up the suitcase and heading towards the door. I place my ear against the wood and listen carefully before unbolting the lock. I hear nothing, only silence.

Please don't let him be out there, I silently pray as I grip the door handle. My heart is thumping furiously against my ribcage as I creep out into the hallway. My eyes are everywhere. I'm just waiting for him to pounce.

When there's no sign of him, I tiptoe towards the stairs and descend. I pause in the foyer where the damage Jake caused in his fit of rage becomes apparent. The TV is on in the main room, but he's turned the volume right down. There's just enough light for me to see the holes in the walls, and furniture upturned. How can you live with someone for five years, and never know about the monster that lived within?

Gazing down, I see Jake passed out on the floor, an empty bottle of scotch lying next to him. Even that surprises me. In the eight years we've been together I rarely saw him drunk, let alone intoxicated. Alcohol has never agreed with him.

My handbag and sunglasses are lying on the floor, beside the now overturned hall table, so I grab them before ever so quietly opening the front door. Slowly moving down the front steps, I wait until I'm a metre or so away from the house, before breaking into a slow jog. My stomach hurts, and I'm unable to sprint due to the operation—even at this pace, I'm suffering—but my need to get away far outweighs the pain. I won't stop until I'm a few blocks away.

I'm grateful that it's dark out, but I still stand behind a tree out of view from the road before pulling out my phone to call a cab.

Minutes pass, but it feels like hours before I hear a car approaching. Peeking out from behind the tree I see the headlights as it comes over the hill, followed by the illuminated light on the roof. Only then do I step out from my hiding place and flag it down.

"The airport, please," I say once I'm seated in the backseat.

When we arrive at the departure terminal a short time later, I pay the driver and exit the vehicle. I'm constantly looking over my shoulder as I head inside. I'm still on edge and don't doubt that Jake will come looking for me the moment he notices I'm gone.

Keeping my head down, I walk briskly towards the check-in counter. "Can you tell me when the first available flight to Sydney is?" I ask the attendant manning the desk.

"The next flight out isn't until six o'clock," she says.

"Six o'clock?" It's only just after two in the morning, so that's four hours away. "Nothing sooner?"

"I'm sorry, no."

Four hours gives Jake ample time to track me down. He probably knows I'll head back to Sydney—I have nowhere else to go. I sigh. Although I'm still completely shattered by the events of the past few days, my first priority at the moment is my safety. I'll have plenty of time to grieve my losses in the coming days.

"Can I get a one-way ticket please?" There's no way I'm coming back. Sydney is my home, and since Jake is no longer in my life, it's where I belong.

"Can I see some ID?" she asks.

"Sure." I pull out my driver's licence and hand it to her, all the while scanning my surroundings. I feel like I'm out in the open here. I'll need to find a safe place to wait until it's time to board my flight.

"Do you have any check-in luggage?"

"Just this one bag," I say, pointing to the small suitcase by my feet.

I face another dilemma when it comes time to pay for my ticket. I don't have enough cash on me to cover it, and using my card is going to leave a paper trail, making it easier for Jake to track me. The only thing in my favour is that it's Sunday and the banks are closed. Thankfully, Jake doesn't trust internet banking, so he won't be able to look online.

"Can you tell me where I need to go?" I ask her as she hands me my boarding pass.

"Just head towards the gates," she says, pointing to the large departure sign on the back wall. "You'll need your boarding pass when you go through security. From there, you'll head to gate fifty-two. That's where your plane will be leaving from. Boarding should commence around five-thirty."

"Thank you." Butterflies churn in my stomach as I head in that direction.

Once I'm through security, I move towards the ladies' room. I hate public toilets but I'll be safe in there. Entering one of the cubicles, I pull down the lid and take a seat. Not the most ideal hiding spot, but it'll do.

Rummaging through my handbag, I retrieve my phone. I'm relieved to see there are no recent missed calls or texts from him. Hopefully, he's still passed out on the floor. Turning my phone off, I place it back in my bag. These next few hours are going to drag, but as things stand right now, it appears I'm going to escape Melbourne with my life.

Chapter 10

Logan

It's just after four in the morning when I throw back the covers and rise from my bed. I've been tossing and turning for the past few hours. I can't sleep because my mind is laden with thoughts of Brooke.

Crossing the room, I slide open the glass doors that lead out to the balcony. I'm dressed in only my silk pyjama bottoms, and the cool air is refreshing as it dances over my skin. Resting my hands on the balcony railing and staring out into the night, I inhale a large breath. Melbourne looks spectacular all lit up, and the views seem to go on forever from the top floor of my penthouse apartment, but my mind is far too preoccupied to enjoy it. I wish I'd been more insistent about dropping her home yesterday. She's all I've thought about since then.

So many unanswered questions swim around in my mind. Is she okay? How did things go with Jake when she arrived home? Did she end up forgiving him? *Jesus, I hope not.* She deserves so much better than that arsehole.

Maybe I'll get a hint of what went on between them from Jake when I organise an emergency meeting with him and his secretary first thing this morning. They're both in breach of their contracts, which gives me the right to terminate their employment if I see fit. I'll make that decision once I've had a chance to speak with them both. I have to remain professional and not let my personal feelings influence my decision, but I'll make sure they don't get away without consequences. There's no place for that shit in the workplace. I pride myself on the reputation of my company, and the last thing I want is for one of my employees to incite a sexual harassment claim.

Heading back into my bedroom, I change into my gym gear. It's too early to go into the office, so maybe a good workout will clear my mind and give me back my appetite. I've barely eaten in the past two days.

Jill, my housekeeper, should be here at five to make me breakfast before I leave for the office. She spends her days cleaning and running errands for me, but always has my dinner prepared before she leaves in the evenings. I'd be lost without her. Along with Chris, my driver, she travels with me between Sydney and Melbourne. I trust them both implicitly. Neither of them is married or has children of their own, so they're both free to travel with me wherever I go.

My hands are shoved into the pockets of my suit pants, as I stand in my office in front of my floor-to-ceiling window, staring out across the Melbourne skyline. I'm still stuck in some kind of weird limbo. I had a conference with Claire earlier this morning and filled her in on everything. She's going to schedule a meeting for me with Jake and his secretary once they arrive. I've instructed Jim

Maloney, one of my senior lawyers, to sit in on it. He handles things around here while I'm in Sydney.

From the reception area, I hear Rose. "You can't go in there. Mr. Cavanagh has asked not to be disturbed. Mr. Johnston!" The mere mention of his name gets my blood pumping.

I turn and take a few steps towards the door before it flies open. "Where the fuck is my wife, Cavanagh?" he screams, throwing the small white piece of cardboard he's holding in my direction. My eyes briefly gaze down at the floor where it lands—it's my business card. It must be the one I gave Brooke at the hospital.

There's a look of contempt on my face as my eyes move back to him. "Excuse me?"

"You heard me. Where is she?" His face is bright red and he's practically frothing at the mouth as he takes a step towards me. He looks like a hot mess. Nothing like the well put together man I'm used to seeing.

My fists are balled at my side. I'm not intimidated by him in the slightest. "I have no idea where your wife is, but I can only hope she had enough sense to leave your sorry arse."

"You're hiding her, I know it. Tell me where she is, or so help me ..."

I take a step towards him, getting up in his face. Being able to keep my composure in highly volatile situations is something I've always prided myself on, but this guy presses all my buttons. "And what are you going to do?" I ask through gritted teeth. "You and your idle threats don't scare me in the slightest."

Through my peripheral vision, I see Marco, one of the security guards, rush into my office, just as Jake lunges at me. I manage to sidestep him before Marco tackles him to the floor. He's six foot four and built like a brick wall, so

Jake doesn't stand a chance. For a split second, I actually feel sorry for him as he tries to thrash his body around under Marco's heavy weight.

Marco gets to his feet, effortlessly bringing Jake with him. "What do you want me to do with him, boss?"

"Escort him out of the building." When he nods, my eyes lock with Jake. "You're fired. If you step one foot inside this building, I'll have you arrested." He doesn't say a word as he's dragged from my office. I walk around my desk, buzzing my receptionist, Rose. "Have his office cleaned out immediately."

"Of course. Are you okay?"

"I'm fine, thanks."

"I tried to stop him, Mr. Cavanagh …" I can hear by the tone of her voice that she's on the verge of tears.

"I know you did. It's not your fault. Take some time to regroup if needed."

"I'm all right," she says. "Just a little shaken."

Pulling out my phone, I dial Claire's number. She walked down to the courthouse to file some urgent papers for me.

"What's up?" she asks.

"Change of plans: I just fired Jake. He stormed into my office demanding I tell him where I've hidden his wife."

"No way!" she says. "Damn, I missed all the fun." Her response makes me chuckle.

"When you get back here, have his secretary come to my office. I'm going to let her go also."

"I think that's wise, considering what's gone on. I should be back in about twenty minutes. Do you want me to send Jim in as well?"

"Please."

Hanging up, I drop the phone onto my desk, exhaling

a long, drawn-out breath as I run my fingers through my hair. That's not how I anticipated the morning would go down.

My thoughts again turn to Brooke as I start to pace back and forth. I hope she's okay. I'm pleased she left him, and pray she had the sense to get as far away from that unstable bastard as possible. If only there was a way I could contact her, just to check, or at the very least see if there is anything I could do to help.

I'm deep in conversation with Jim when there's a knock on my office door. "It's me."

"Yes, Claire."

She opens the door and pokes her head inside. "I have Jenny Morris, here to see you," she says.

"Send her in."

"You wanted to see me, Mr. Cavanagh," Jenny asks, her hands fidgeting by her side.

"Please, take a seat," I say, gesturing towards one of the two leather seats opposite me. "You know Mr. Maloney?"

"I do," she utters in a quiet voice before greeting him with a nod.

"Miss Morris," Jim says in an authoritative tone. When it comes to business, Jim can be extremely tough when needed, but ultimately is very fair. In real life though, he's a sweet man. He's worked at this company for many years, and my father has the greatest respect for him, which speaks volumes. My old man hates everybody.

Jenny places her hands under her legs once she's seated and leans forward slightly in her chair. She looks anxious and has every reason to be. I take a few moments to observe her. She's not what I'd call ugly, but she's certainly not beautiful either. She doesn't hold a candle to Brooke, and I'm puzzled as to why Johnston would even consider risking what he had with his wife for this woman.

"Do you know why I've asked you here?" I place my flattened palms on the desk as I speak. I've calmed down considerably, but I'm still pissed. I shouldn't even be dealing with this shit.

"No. No, I don't," she answers.

"Are you familiar with the company's policies, Miss Morris?"

"I'm not sure what you mean."

Her answer annoys me. "The policies regarding your employment."

"Umm ... policies? What policies?"

I look over at Jim, and he seems just as unimpressed as I do. "Okay, let me spell it out for you. Do you remember the '*No fraternising with staff*' clause in your contract?" I rummage through her employment file in front of me, removing the contract she signed before starting. I flick through the pages until I find what I'm looking for. "Clause eight," I say, passing it to her.

"Oh." All the colour drains from her face as she reads it. "I don't remember reading that in my contract of employment."

She's lying. I can spot a liar from a mile away. I insist that all employees read it thoroughly before signing it. She passes it back to me, and I skip to the last page.

"Is this your signature on the bottom of the page?" I hold it out in front of her.

"Yes, but I still don't understand what this is about."

"Really?" I sit up straighter in my chair. "You don't

remember being intimate with Mr. Johnston at the Christmas function on Friday evening?"

"No," she screeches as her eyes widen. "Whoever said that is lying."

I bang my hand down on the desk. I'm through playing games. "I saw it with my own eyes, Miss Morris, along with a few other people."

She swallows hard before answering. "Well, it was outside of work, so technically it doesn't count." The arrogance in her voice only irritates me further.

I take a deep breath and count to five in my head. "Do I need to remind you that it was at a *work* function? Would you like me to read the clause out to you?"

"I'm sorry," she says, reining in her attitude.

"You do realise Mr. Johnston is married?"

"So?" She shrugs. "Obviously not happily."

Again, I feel my anger rising. Getting involved in an employee's personal life has never interested me, but I feel compelled to ask her if that's something Jake mentioned. I can't seem to wrap my head around any of this. I've also been in the exact situation Brooke is now facing, so in some ways, this feels personal to me.

"Regardless, the fact that you knew but didn't reconsider appals me."

"I've learnt my lesson, Mr. Cavanagh. It won't happen again." The tone of her voice, combined with her flippant attitude tells me she's learnt nothing from this. I've met women like her before. They'll stop at nothing to get what they want, and will stoop to any level to get it.

"I will make sure it doesn't. Please collect your belongings from your desk. Security will escort you out of the building."

"You're firing me?"

"You breached your contract of employment; I have every right to do so."

Standing abruptly, she straightens her skirt. "And what about Jake? I suppose you'll just sweep his part in this under the carpet?"

"I fired him earlier this morning."

Her eyes widen slightly before narrowing into slits. "You're an arsehole."

"That may be true," I say, feeling somewhat amused by her insult. I've been called a lot worse in my time.

Turning, she storms from my office. I have to suppress my smile when she flips me the bird over her shoulder.

Leaning back in my chair, I run my hand through my hair. Before I get a chance to speak, Rose buzzes me from her desk. "Can I speak with you for a moment, Mr. Cavanagh?"

"Can it wait, Rose?" I've had enough excitement for one day.

"It's in regard to something I found in Mr. Johnston's desk."

"Okay, I'm all ears."

A few seconds later she knocks on my door. "Come in."

"Do you want me to leave?" Jim asks.

"No, stay." He's in charge when I'm not here, so he needs to stay in the loop.

I gesture for her to take a seat when she enters. Before doing so, she places two items on my desk—a small clear satchel filled with white powder, and what looks like part of a plastic straw.

"These were pushed to the back of one of his drawers," she says. "I'm no expert, but it looks like drugs to me."

"Interesting," I reply, reaching out to pick them up. I

can see remnants of the white powder on the inside of the straw. He must've been using this to snort whatever is inside the satchel. My guess is cocaine. Like Rose, I'm no expert, but I'm also not stupid. "Call the police, and send them in when they arrive."

"Of course."

"Are you feeling okay after the ruckus earlier?" I ask.

"Yes, thank you," she replies with a smile.

"Do me a favour, Rose. Get me Mr. Johnston's personal details. The police are going to want them."

"I'll do that now."

Once she leaves, I stand and walk towards the window.

"The plot thickens," Jim says to my retreating back.

"It sure does," I reply without turning around. I find myself wondering if Brooke knew about this. I highly doubt it, but it does explain his erratic behaviour earlier.

Chapter 11

Brooke

Eight months have passed since I fled Jake and moved back to Sydney. The first few days were tough, and I shed a bucketload of tears. But after receiving a barrage of nasty and threatening messages from him that week, I decided enough was enough. I changed my number and haven't looked back.

It's sad considering he was my life for so long, but given how things ended, moving forward was the only way to go. As my mum always said, *'Being strong doesn't mean you'll never get hurt; it means even when you do, you'll never let it defeat you.'* Those words were something she lived by.

Within days of arriving here, I secured a small Victorian terrace house. It's not far from the city, but far enough away from where I once lived with Jake. The easiest way to prevent him from finding me was to completely start over, which is what I've done. That meant no contact with my old friends, and not going back to the dance school where I used to work. It was incredibly hard, but necessary.

When I first returned, I lived off the savings I'd put

away to start my own dance school, but it didn't take me long to get a job—well, two actually, or three, if you count the occasional piano lessons I'm now teaching from home. Apart from my plane ticket, I didn't touch the money in our joint account. I don't want or need anything from him. It's way more satisfying knowing I'm doing this all on my own.

I work part-time at a dance studio during the day, and waitress in the evenings at a small restaurant down the street from where I live. I squeeze the piano lessons in during my free time. Keeping busy helps to curb the loneliness. I've even managed to save a little money each week, which is helping to rebuild my dance school dream fund. It's going to take me longer than I'd like to reach that goal, but every day is a step closer to achieving my dream, and that's what I try to hold on to.

The place where I'm now living is old but has had some renovations done over the years, so it's pleasant enough. The kitchen is less than five years old, and I love to cook, so that's a bonus. The bathroom renovations are a little older, but it's still in good condition.

The bright colours on some of the interior walls weren't to my liking, so I repainted every wall white. It gave the space a fresh new look. My landlord was even nice enough to take the cost of the paint off my rent.

My lovely red sofa, bedroom suite, television, fridge, and washing machine were all purchased new, but the rest of the furniture although bought second-hand, is in great condition. I even managed to pick up some old black and white prints of the area in a yard sale, which I reframed. They look great hanging against the stark colour of the walls and coordinate well with my furniture.

I'm so proud of my humble little abode; it's not much, but it's home. It makes me appreciate what my mum went through so much more. There's something really satisfying about accomplishing all this on my own. Who needs a husband? *Certainly not me.*

"I'll just run the mop over the floor before I go," I tell Andy as he finishes up balancing the night's takings. He and his partner Mark own the restaurant where I work.

"I like closing with you," he says. "I never have to ask you to do anything. You just do it."

When I'm finished, I rinse the mop and empty the bucket. After placing them in the storeroom, I grab my bag. "I'm going to head off," I say.

"I'm almost done. Wait and I'll drop you home."

"It's only down the street."

"I know," he says. "But I don't feel comfortable with you walking home in the dark."

We've had this conversation many times. I've rarely accepted his offer in the past, for no other reason than I don't want to put him out. However, today I did three back-to-back classes at the dance studio, and we were run off our feet at the restaurant tonight, so I'm exhausted.

"That would be great, thank you." My answer makes him smile.

I give Andy a wave when I reach my front porch, but the car remains idling out front until I'm safely inside. He's very sweet, and I'm grateful to have someone watching out for me. He's expressed concern about me being on my own, though I've never discussed Jake or the fact that technically I'm still married. He even tried to set me up with his brother once, but as lonely as I am at times, I'm not interested in another relationship right now. I'm not sure if I'll ever be. The two main men in my life, my father and my husband, both turned out to be the biggest disappointments.

Dumping my bag in my room, I grab my pyjamas out

of the drawer and head into the bathroom to shower. This place gets too quiet at times. I've considered getting a pet for company, but I'm away from the house so much, it wouldn't be fair.

I double check all the windows and doors are locked before turning off the lights and climbing into bed. I'm so tired I know sleep will come easy tonight.

A loud bang awakens me, which is followed by what sounds like glass shattering. Bolting upright, I glance at the clock on the bedside table. It's just after one in the morning. Sitting perfectly still, I listen intently, but all I hear is silence. Throwing back the covers, I slide my feet into my slippers and get up to investigate. It's usually such a quiet neighbourhood, and I'm not aware of any problems since moving here.

I'm still half asleep and a little disoriented as I pad down the hallway in the dark. Entering the front room, I walk towards the window. A street light on the other side of the road illuminates the dark night enough for me to see if anyone is outside.

"Shit," I say when I hear something crunching beneath my feet. Switching on the lamp sitting on the side table, my eyes scan the floor. The first thing I see is a brick sitting in the middle of the room and shards of glass everywhere. My heart starts to race as my gaze moves to the now smashed window. My hands tremble slightly as I reach down and pick up the brick. I gasp the moment I see the word 'BITCH' written on the face of it.

Dropping it to the floor, I take a step back. *Who would do such a thing?* I've made no enemies since moving here.

Not to my knowledge, anyway. My mum brought me up to be polite and courteous to everyone. *'Treat others how you want to be treated,'* was something she said often.

I wrap my arms around myself as I stare out into the night. Panic sets in when I think I see a shadow move across the front porch. I bolt to my room and lock the door, then rummage in my bag for my phone. My hands are shaking as I sit down on the edge of the bed and call triple zero.

I'm startled when I hear a loud knock. "Police." Leaping off the side of my bed, I unlock the door and poke my head into the hallway to scan the surroundings before stepping out.

"Coming," I call out, rushing down the hallway to open it.

After explaining the situation, I let one of the officers in while the other searches outside the property. I feel intense relief now that they're here.

"Do you have any idea who may have done this?" the officer asks as he surveys the damage.

"No, not really. I've made no enemies I'm aware of since moving back to Sydney. Although ..." I pause briefly, contemplating whether I should mention Jake.

"Although?" The officer turns to face me. "If you know something, this is the time to tell us."

"My initial thought was my estranged husband. I haven't seen him in over eight months, and as far as I'm aware, he has no idea where I'm living."

"Hmm," he says, eyeing me. "Is this normal behaviour for him?"

"No, but things didn't end well for us."

I never reported the assault; I'm not sure why. Maybe I was worried it would affect his career. His job means everything to him, and the way he behaved that day was out of character. It was much easier for me to just walk away.

"Are you in the middle of a custody battle or property dispute? Or something that may have recently upset him?"

"No, nothing like that." I haven't asked Jake for anything, and I don't intend to. "We've had no contact since I left."

"I think we can rule out your ex then. It may have been kids having fun."

"Throwing bricks through people's windows is not what I'd call fun," I say abruptly as I take a seat on my sofa. I slide my hands under my legs in an attempt to stop the tremors. I'm still incredibly shaken by what's happened.

"I'm sorry. I didn't mean to sound insensitive, Mrs. Johnston." I give him a tight smile but don't reply. In my day, the idea of fun was playing knock-and-run on your neighbour's door, not throwing bricks through people's windows.

My eyes move towards the small archway when the other officer appears. "Whoever it was is long gone," he says.

I don't know if that should make me feel relieved or more terrified. What if they come back?

I feel like death warmed up as I climb out of bed, but

also a little safer now that the sun has risen. It was close to four by the time I laid back down. After the police took my statement and left, I cleaned up the mess and waited for the twenty-four-hour emergency glass company to come and fix the broken window.

I wasn't able to fall asleep again with my mind going a hundred miles an hour as I tried to make sense of it all. Every noise I heard as I lay there in silence made my heart beat faster. The police said it was possibly a case of mistaken identity, or maybe connected to the previous tenants, which did nothing to ease my mind. I'm now rethinking living here, which sucks. I've put so much time and effort into making this my home.

After busying myself with housework, I finally change into my running gear. I'm not even sure if I feel safe enough to leave the house, but a long run should help clear my mind and give me some clarity.

Paranoia sets in as I step outside and lock the front door. I didn't bring my iPod today. I can't afford to get lost in the music; I need to remain aware. If that brick was aimed at me, I'll have to watch my back from now on.

"Morning," I say to one of my elderly neighbours who's out early watering her garden.

"Good morning." I always greet my neighbours when I see them out and about, but maybe I need to make more of an effort to get to know them on a personal level. Especially after last night.

Breaking into a jog, I head up the hill towards the restaurant where I work. Andy's partner, Mark, is standing on the sidewalk talking to a police officer as I approach. An uneasy feeling settles in my stomach.

"Everything okay?" I ask Mark when I'm close enough for him to hear me.

Shaking his head, I can see he's visibly distressed as

he points over his shoulder towards the restaurant. My heart drops into the pit of my stomach when I see the word 'WHORE' spray-painted in red across the front of the building.

Surely this isn't a coincidence. Somebody obviously went on a rampage last night, but the question still remains: is any or all of this directed at me?

Chapter 12

Logan

I'm showered and dressed early, ready for work. "Morning, Jill," I say to my housekeeper as I enter the kitchen. I've been back in Sydney for a few months now, and it feels good to be home.

"Morning, Mr. Cavanagh," she practically sings with an ever-so-cheery smile, as she hands me a freshly brewed cup of coffee. "Your breakfast is almost ready. I've put this morning's paper on the table for you."

"Thank you."

In all the years Jill has been working for me, I've yet to see her be anything but happy. Even Chris, my driver, has his off days, but Jill is a constant ray of sunshine.

Once I'm seated at the table, I take a sip of my coffee before pulling out my phone and texting Chris.

> Logan: I'll be ready to leave in about twenty.

I get a quick reply.

> Chris: Heading your way now, Boss.

Chris is leaning against the car by the kerb when I exit the lift and cross the foyer of my building. I smile and nod at the doorman as he holds the door open for me.

"Morning," I say as I approach the vehicle.

"Good morning, Mr. Cavanagh," Chris replies, opening the back door of the limousine.

Laying my leather briefcase on the seat beside me, I open it and retrieve my laptop as we manoeuvre into traffic. I usually use the commute to the office to get a head start on my day. It's only a ten-minute drive from my penthouse apartment in Circular Quay to the Cavanagh building in Darlinghurst, but city traffic is always horrendous this time of the morning.

We're stopped at a set of traffic lights alongside Hyde Park when I look up from my laptop and glance out the side window. A horde of people are bunched together on the sidewalk, waiting for the signal to turn green so they can safely cross the road. A leggy brunette in a pair of short shorts catches my eye as she jogs on the spot at the rear. Blondes were always more my thing, but my tastes have changed of late. A certain beauty I met in Melbourne is the reason for that. But sadly, none of the women I've gone out with since meeting her, have been able to spark the same interest in me that Brooke did.

I'd be lying if I said I've never thought about her. It always leaves me wondering where she ended up, and if she's okay. I hope she found happiness after leaving her husband. If nothing else, she deserves that.

Sitting forward in my seat my eyes follow the jogger as she passes in front of the car, and my heart skips a beat the moment she comes fully into view. I'd recognise that face anywhere. Before it even registers in my mind, I'm opening the back door and exiting the vehicle.

"What the hell are you doing?" Chris asks, winding down his window.

I flick my hand at him as I move around the front of the vehicle. "Drive around the corner and park, I won't be long."

The pedestrian light has already turned red as I jog across the road, earning myself a few beeps from the cars. "Brooke." She doesn't stop, and for a moment, I think I've made a mistake. "Brooke," I call out once more. My heart starts to thump against my chest the moment she stops running and looks over her shoulder. *It's her.*

"Mr. Cavanagh."

"Hey," I say, sliding my hands into my pockets and trying to act casual. On the inside, I'm feeling anything but. "Fancy running into you here."

"I know, right? Small world."

"How have you been?"

"Great, and you? Are you in Sydney on business?" she asks.

For a moment I'm lost for words as I drink her in. *Fuck, it's good to see her.* The face that's been haunting my dreams is so much more breathtaking in the flesh, even if she's a little red-faced and sweaty from her run.

"No, I live here."

"In Sydney?"

"Yes, I fly between here and Melbourne often, but Sydney is my home. You look amazing, by the way."

She lets out a nervous laugh as the colour on her face intensifies. "I'm a hot and sweaty mess," she says, tucking a piece of stray hair behind her ear.

Is it wrong I like her hot and sweaty?

"What are you doing in Sydney?"

"I moved back here eight months ago."

"After you left Jake?" I'm presuming they're still not together.

"You heard about that?" she asks, her gaze moving down to the sidewalk.

"He accused me of hiding you."

Her head snaps back to me, as her pretty brown eyes widen. "What?"

"The morning after you left the hospital. I guess he found the business card I gave you, he thought you were with me."

"I'm so sorry he did that," she says.

I shrug. "I'm presuming you two aren't together anymore?"

"No way." She shakes her head as she speaks, emphasising her words.

"I'm glad ... I mean ..." I run my hand through my hair. "Nobody deserves to be treated the way you were treated." A huge smile breaks out across her face, and it's enough to steal all the air from my lungs. Moments pass as we stand here in silence with our eyes locked. "It's good seeing you again," I finally say.

"It's nice seeing you too, Mr. Cavanagh."

"Logan," I remind her.

"Logan. Well, I'm sure you have somewhere you need to be, and I really must finish my run. I have to work later."

"You're working again?" That knowledge makes me happy.

"Yes, I'm back doing what I love."

"Teaching dance?"

"Yes." She looks surprised that I remember.

She takes a step backwards, ready to make her retreat, and a panicked feeling overwhelms me. Running into her this morning was a freak encounter, the chances of it happening again are slim at best. I don't want this to be the end of us. I need to see her again. There's something here, I can feel it. I only hope she feels it too.

"Have dinner with me, Brooke."

"Oh, umm ... I don't know about that."

"It's just dinner. I'm not asking you to marry me."

My reply makes her laugh. "Well, you did save my life."

"That's right, I did. Technically you owe me." I don't mean that, but if it will help convince her, then I'm running with it.

"You drive a hard bargain."

"You better believe it."

She's fighting a smile before speaking again. "I'll have dinner with you on one condition."

"Anything." My reply is instant, and I don't care if it makes me look pitiful.

"Let me cook for you."

"Deal. You can cook, right?"

"I'm okay," she says, shrugging. But the humour I hear in her voice tells me she can.

Reaching into my pocket, I pull out my wallet. "Here's my card. Call me and we'll make plans." My hand pauses mid-air. "Can I trust you'll actually use it this time?"

"Cross my heart." She even mimics her words as she moves her finger over her chest as she speaks. I try not to notice how incredible her cleavage looks in that tight top, but it's kind of impossible. That thought is only amplified when she takes hold of the business card and slides it into her bra. I bite my lip to suppress the groan. I'm suddenly envious of that tiny piece of cardboard. "I'll call you," she says with a shy smile.

"I look forward to it," I reply as the corners of my mouth curve up.

With that, she turns and jogs away. I remain fixed to the spot until she rounds the corner and disappears, but unlike the time she left me at the hospital, I'm not overcome with sadness—I'm filled with hope.

Chapter 13

Brooke

I'm in two minds as I jog away. I barely know the man, and yet I just invited him to my place for dinner. But he did save my life, and I'd hoped to get a chance to repay him for his kindness one day. He's given me no reason to believe he'll be anything but a gentleman.

The last thing I'm looking for is a relationship. I'm enjoying finding myself again, and although it's lonely at times, I'm happy with my new life.

There's no denying Logan is gorgeous—it should be a crime to be that good-looking—and from what I know of him, he's kind and considerate, but I can't dismiss his occupation. I've had more than my fill of the lawyers in my life behaving badly—both my father and Jake—and from the moment I walked away from my husband, I swore he'd be my last.

I could always throw away his business card and avoid running in this area, but that would be rude. He could've ignored what was going on with me that night back in Melbourne, and if he had, chances are I would've bled out on the sidewalk. What can one dinner hurt? I'll just feed him, then send him on his way.

Once I arrive back home, I shower and change into my dance gear before quickly eating some breakfast. I have two classes to teach this morning.

I pull out my phone as I take a seat at the bus stop and search for locksmiths in the area. I'll feel safer if I upgrade the locks on the windows and doors.

I pace back and forth in my front room after my last piano student leaves. Logan's business card is clutched in my hand, and butterflies are fluttering in my stomach as I psych myself up to call him.

My hands shake as I type his number into my contacts, and a smile tugs at my lips when I cheekily save it under Hot Stuff.

Pausing, I take a deep breath and instead of pressing call, I open the messenger app. *This is ridiculous.* Why does this man have me tied up in knots?

> Brooke: Hi, it's Brooke. I have to work tonight, but I am free tomorrow night if you would like to come over for dinner. Say about 7? If this doesn't suit you, let me know.

I feel instant relief once I press send. Staring down at the screen, I berate myself. *That wasn't so hard.* But when my phone starts ringing in my hand, I jump.

"Hello."

"Brooke, it's Logan." *Oh god.*

"Hey." Not the greatest reply, but it's the best I've got.

"How are you?"

"Good." I draw the corner of my lip into my mouth and bite down on it.

"I'm happy to hear that." There's an awkward silence, and this is what I was afraid of. This is why I went with the text message; it was easier. "So, seven sounds good," he finally says.

"Okay, great. Well, I ... umm ... guess I'll see you then."

"I guess you will."

The line goes quiet again, and now I'm regretting agreeing to this dinner thing. "Umm ... bye."

"Wait, Brooke," he says. "Before you hang up, I need your address. That's why I called. You didn't include it in your text."

"Oh." I slap my palm against my forehead. Of course, he doesn't know where I live.

"Well, are you going to give it to me, or would you prefer I guess."

"Right," I say, with a nervous laugh. "I feel silly for not including it in my message."

"I'm not complaining. It gave me the perfect excuse to call you." His words have my stomach doing a flip-flop. Is he flirting with me?

"Fifteen Lilyfield Parade, Waterloo."

"That's a fair distance from where I saw you today. Do you always run that far?"

"Yes, usually around five kilometres, but some days I can do up to ten. It just depends on how I'm feeling."

"Wow. That's impressive."

"I guess. I've been doing it for a long time so I'm used to it."

"Well, I'm in awe."

"Thank you." I'm grateful he can't see my face

because I'm pretty sure I'm blushing. "I better let you go ... I need to get ready for work anyway."

"Sure. I'll see you tomorrow," he says.

"Okay. Bye."

I hang up before he gets a chance to say anything else. But a few seconds later my phone chimes with a message.

> Hot Stuff: You hung up before I had a chance to ask you if I need to bring anything.

He must think I'm rude. I exhale a drawn-out breath before replying.

> Brooke: No, just yourself.

I put a smiley emoji at the end of my message, and I no sooner send it when his reply comes through.

> Hot Stuff: I'd be lying if I said I wasn't looking forward to seeing you again.

He ends his message with a wink emoji, and a huge smile breaks out on my face. It's been a long time since anyone has made me feel so ... giddy.

I don't bother replying. There's a part of me that's looking forward to seeing him as well, but I'm also feeling a little apprehensive.

I'm rushing around trying to get everything perfect before my dinner guest arrives. I've already changed outfits five times. For someone who's not interested in dating, I certainly seem to be going out of my way to impress him.

This morning, I skipped my run and headed to the market early to buy all the food I needed for tonight. Since it's a *'Thank you for saving my life dinner,'* I'm going all out and making him a three-course meal. I hope he's hungry. It's been a while since I've had to cook for someone other than myself.

I barely slept at all last night, I'm anxious about having Logan here, but I was also petrified that the person who threw the brick through my window may return. It's been a long day and I'm dead on my feet. I'm running purely on adrenaline, and pray I have enough energy left to get through dinner.

Opening the oven door, I check the savoury tarts I made for the starter. They're just about done. I didn't even think to ask him if he has food allergies or dislikes. This night could very well turn out to be a disaster.

My heart starts to race when the doorbell chimes. *Shit, he's here.* Glancing at the clock on the microwave, I see he's right on time. I do a quick scan of the kitchen to make sure nothing is burning or boiling over. I probably should've planned a much simpler menu.

Rushing into the hallway, I stop and glance in the mirror. *Crap, my apron.* Slipping it over my head, I stuff it in the drawer of the hall table before smoothing out my hair. I've worn it down tonight, which is something I haven't done in a long time. It's usually pulled back in a ponytail or a bun.

After my numerous outfit changes, I decided on a pair of skinny jeans and a fitted white lace top, which shows off just a hint of cleavage.

When the doorbell chimes again, I stop procrastinating and open the door.

"Hey," I say, the second my eyes land on him. He looks so handsome in his white linen button-up shirt and designer jeans. A smile tugs at my lips when I realise we kind of match.

I watch as his eyes travel the length of my body before finally meeting mine. By the time they do, he's beaming. "Hey."

"You found the place all right?"

"My driver dropped me off," he answers. *Of course, he has a driver.*

He probably lives in a thirty-bedroom historic mansion on an expansive estate by the water. I bet his butlers name is Jeeves, and has a posh British accent. I'm suddenly regretting inviting him here. His servants probably live better than I do.

"Come in," I say, sounding a little more deflated than I did when I first greeted him.

"These are for you." He hands me a long white box, and through the clear window of the lid, I can see long stem yellow roses inside. Again, with the yellow roses. I feel a lump form in the back of my throat. *Is this another omen?*

"They're beautiful. Thank you."

"They don't hold a candle to you."

I smile at his compliment as I take a step back, allowing him to enter.

"I brought a bottle of champagne as well."

"How nice." I've never had champagne before, but I don't tell him that. He only has to look around to see that our lives are worlds apart.

He follows me through the main room towards the dining table. I was so proud of how nice the table was set before the realisation that he's mega-rich set in. I have to suppress my smile when I imagine him sitting down to dinner at a table fit for royalty with the finest China and twenty-four-carat gold cutlery. Tonight, he'll be dining at a tiny, second-hand table and eating off dishes I purchased from Kmart. I hope he's not allergic to stainless steel cutlery because that's all I have.

"Your home is lovely," he says as I gesture for him to take a seat. "Have you been living here long?"

"About eight months."

He nods, and although I was expecting to see judgment in his eyes, I don't. He looks completely at home. "Do you have any glasses?" he asks, lifting the champagne bottle.

"I'll grab some, and put these in water." I hold up my beautiful flowers before disappearing into the kitchen.

Placing the box on the countertop, I take a few deep breaths to calm my nerves. I turn the oven down to low so I don't burn the tarts as I search under the sink for a vase. I know I have one here somewhere.

Once the flowers are sorted, I admire them briefly before grabbing two wine glasses.

I hold the glasses up to the light to make sure they're clean before dashing back out to where he's waiting.

"Perfect," he says when I place them on the table.

I admire Logan's masculine hands as he effortlessly pops the cork and pours us both a drink. There's no ring on his finger or a mark from one. I have no intentions of taking tonight beyond dinner, but I find myself praying he bears no resemblance to my ex, or my poor excuse of a father, by being married. He may get the wrong idea if I ask him though, so I keep those thoughts to myself.

I'm sure if there was a Mrs. Cavanagh, she'd be less than thrilled about him being here tonight. She'd have every right to feel that way. I get a pang in my heart thinking back to how I felt the night I saw Jake with his mistress. I'd never want to be the cause of making someone feel so worthless.

I take a seat opposite him and notice his Gold Rolex watch as he passes me a glass of champagne. I'm again reminded of how different our worlds are. Pushing that thought out of my mind, I take a huge gulp of my drink, followed closely by another, almost emptying the contents of the wineglass.

"Thirsty?" he asks with humour in his voice.

"Just nervous," I admit.

"Makes two of us." That surprises me. He exudes confidence. "It's just dinner, Brooke. Two old friends sharing a meal."

His words put me at ease. "Speaking of food, are you ready to eat?"

"Yes. I'm starved."

"Give me a few minutes and I'll get the first course ready."

"We're doing courses?" His eyebrows rise as he speaks. "You didn't have to go to so much trouble."

"I wanted to." I look down at the table before speaking again. "I appreciate everything you did for me that day ..." My words drift off. I've tried to push those memories from my mind; it's just easier that way.

My eyes move back to him when he places his hand on top of mine. "I've thought of you often since then and wondered how you were. I can't tell you how happy it makes me to see you're doing well."

A smile tugs at my lips. "I am doing okay."

"I'm glad."

With that, I stand and head into the kitchen.

After pulling the tarts out of the oven, I place them on a plate. I grab the salad and the sirloin steaks that I prepared earlier from the fridge. The meat is for the main course, and I've pre-stuffed them with wild mushrooms. I quickly sear them in a pan before placing them in the oven.

After another glass of champagne and the first two courses, I feel much more relaxed. Logan complimented me throughout the entire meal and ate everything I put in front of him, which pleased me.

"Let me help with that," he says as I stand to clear the table.

"You don't have to."

"I want to."

"Thanks," I say, smiling. I was quick to judge him tonight, which was unfair. Maybe he doesn't have a Jeeves.

As he passes them to me, I rinse the plates and stack them in the dishwasher. It's been nice having company, and if I'm honest, I'm not ready for him to go yet.

"Do you mind if we hold off on dessert for a bit? I'm stuffed," I say, placing my hand on my stomach.

"Wow, dessert too? You've really gone all out."

"A bit, but I've missed cooking for others," I say, wiping my hands on a tea towel.

"There's been no one else since Jake?"

"No." I see a small smile tug at his lips when I say that, though I don't know why he finds that pleasing. "What happened with him has put me off relationships for now." My words come out a little sterner than anticipated, but it's the truth. Having my heart broken by someone who meant the world to me, isn't something I can get over easily.

"That's understandable. I went through something similar years ago, so I can relate."

His reply surprises me. "Your wife cheated on you?"

"No, I've never been married." He chuckles as he leans up against the kitchen counter, crossing his arms over his chest. "I'd been dating this woman for a while—well, two years, actually. We met at uni, and I thought one day we'd get married." That's where Jake and I met, but I don't tell him that. "My father had me working ridiculously long hours. He was getting ready to retire and thought it was imperative I learn the ins and outs of the company before taking over." He uncrosses his arms and his fingers grip the edge of the countertop. "Anyway, to cut a long story short, I felt bad for not being around as much as I would've liked, so I surprised her with tickets to see her favourite band, but then something came up last minute at the office, and I couldn't make it. I asked my best mate to take her, which turned out to be one of the biggest mistakes of my life."

I gasp when I realise where he's going with this. "Something happened between them?"

"Let's just say they're now married with two kids."

Reaching out, I place my hand on his arm. "I'm sorry that happened to you ... and with your best friend of all people."

"In hindsight, he was a player, so I should've known better. We'd been friends for fifteen years though, so I thought I could trust him."

"That's awful. I can't believe either of them did that to you."

He shrugs before pushing off the bench. "Would you like another drink?"

"Sure."

I follow him back into the main room. Talking about it

obviously still bothers him. I guess I can understand that. Reliving my situation with Jake is something I avoid at all costs, and I don't know if I'll ever get past the betrayal.

He pours champagne into both glasses before picking up his and downing it in one gulp. Reaching for my own drink, I take a seat at the table.

"So," he says, joining me, "where did you learn to cook?" He's changing the subject, and I'm okay with that. Sometimes the past is better left just there.

I run the tip of my finger around the top of my glass as I speak. "My mum worked in a lot of restaurants when I was growing up and taught me all the basics, but Miss Jones, the old lady who cared for me while my Mum worked her many jobs, taught me how to bake. She was old school and did everything from scratch."

I smile when I think of her. She became like a surrogate grandmother to me over the years. She was also the one who taught me how to play the piano. She was so patient and kind, and I miss her so much. She died when I was fourteen. Even though we were close, her death did nothing to prepare me for losing my mother years later. That's a grief I don't think I'll ever recover from.

"She was obviously a good teacher," he says. "Your cooking skills are very impressive."

"Thank you."

His eyes meet mine across the table, so I lift my glass towards my mouth. There's something about the way he looks at me that's unnerving—it's not creepy, but it's a look that says I need to be wary around this man. My heart will be in danger if I'm not cautious.

"You know a way to a man's heart is through his stomach, right?" Placing the glass against my lips I take a drink to avoid replying. "If you keep cooking for me like this, I'm going to have no choice but to marry you."

His words have me inhaling too much air, causing me to choke on the liquid in my mouth, which has the champagne projecting out and spraying all over him. My hand flies up to my face. "Shit," is all I manage to squeeze out between my coughing.

He throws back his head and bursts out laughing.

Picking up a handful of the paper serviettes from the table, I quickly stand. I'm still trying to regain my composure as I desperately wipe the champagne from his face. "I'm so sorry." He's still laughing, but I'm mortified. "Please forgive me."

"Stop apologising."

"Things were going so well ..." I feel tears sting the back of my eyes as I speak, so I retreat a step and bow my head.

"Hey," he says, standing and closing the distance between us. Logan places his finger under my chin to raise my face to meet his. "Things are still going well. It will take a lot more than a champagne shower to ruin it. This is the best evening I've had in a very long time."

I see the sincerity in his beautiful green eyes as he speaks. "Your life must be pretty boring then." When he smiles, I do the same.

"I don't get out much," he says, with a shrug. "All work and no play, so they say."

"I can relate to that."

I take in a sharp breath as his thumb tenderly glides across my cheek. "I'm so glad I ran into you again."

"Me too," I reply, but it comes out more like a whisper.

We stand there for the longest time, and a part of me wishes he'd kiss me, but I can't let that happen. Breaking the moment, I pull back, making sure to put some distance between us.

"My bathroom is at the end of the hall if you want to clean up. I'll go and get dessert ready."

"Right," he says.

I see disappointment flash through his eyes before I turn and head into the kitchen. The moment I'm alone, I blow out a puff of air. As much as I've enjoyed his company tonight, I'm going to need to keep my distance from this one ... he makes me feel things I shouldn't.

Chapter 14

Logan

After washing my face in the basin, I place my hands on either side of the porcelain sink and stare into the mirror. It's been years since I've opened up about my ex, but I wanted her to know that I understood what she went through. To be honest, what happened with Amanda turned me off relationships, that is until Brooke came into my life.

I knew before coming here tonight that I'm attracted to this woman, but the sheer volume of just how much scares me. Never in my life has someone had me so captivated. I wanted to kiss her so badly just now, and for a moment I thought she wanted that too.

"Damn it," I mumble, tightening my grip on the sink. I let her walk out of my life once; I won't make that mistake again. I need to play it cool, to give her time. Rushing in is only going to scare her away.

For months I've thought about her. After a while, I tried to convince myself that it was only pity I was feeling, sympathy for all she went through that night. But now that we've reconnected, I can no longer lie to myself. I want her in my life. She may not see it, but there's something special here. I've been with enough women in my time to know that. She's not only beautiful, but incredibly sweet, and so easy to be around. And I'm in awe of her strength and the new life she's forging for herself, despite the odds.

Picking up the hand towel, I wipe my face. *Do not blow this, Cavanagh.* Shoving my hands into the pockets of my jeans, I head back into the main room. The champagne bottle is empty, and I'm wishing I brought a second one because I need another drink.

Pulling out the chair, I go to sit, but as I do, something crashes in the kitchen. Without hesitating, I dash in that direction. I come to a grinding halt in the doorway when I see the look on her face. She's as white as a sheet. My eyes follow her line of sight and a smile tugs on my lips when I see the plate she must've been carrying shattered on the floor. Looks like dessert is ruined.

"Let me help you with that." Her eyes dart to me as I step into the room and crouch down in front of the mess. "As amazing as this looks, I'm still full from the other two courses," I say, trying to put her at ease. When Brooke doesn't speak, I look up at her, and I'm surprised to see tears welling in her eyes. "Hey, it's nothing to get upset about." I see the other dessert still sitting on the counter. "We can share the other one if it means so much to you."

"I'm not upset about the dessert."

I stand to my full height, extending my hand to help her up. "But you look like you're about to cry."

"It's nothing. Don't worry about it," she says, turning away from me.

Is it me? Maybe our little moment earlier has spooked her. "If I've done something to upset you, then, of course, I'm going to worry about it." Her back remains to me, so I lightly grip her upper arm and turn her around. "Hey."

When I see the tears cascading down her pretty face, I pull her into my arms.

"Who's doing this?" she whispers.

I draw back to meet her eyes. "Doing what?"

She turns her head and points to the floor. I see her phone lying near the cupboard. Letting her go, I walk towards it and pick it up. The screen is cracked, but I can still read what the message says.

> Unknown: I'm watching you, YOU FUCKING BITCH!

I swing around to face her again. "Did someone just send you this?" She replies with a nod as she wipes the tears from her face with the back of her hand. "Who?"

"I don't know. Probably the same person who threw a brick through my window two nights ago."

"Someone threw a brick through your window?" I ask, my eyes widening.

"Yes. The word 'bitch' was written on it. The police said it could've been a case of mistaken identity, but after this ..." She shrugs and points to the phone in my hand, and I see red.

"Go pack some stuff. You're not staying here."

"What? No."

"Brooke, I'm not leaving you here while some lunatic is throwing bricks through your window, and sending you messages like this." I hold up the phone to prove my point.

"I can't just leave."

"You can and you will. Now go and pack some clothes, or I'll pack some for you." She crosses her arms over her chest, but I'm not intimidated one bit. I raise an eyebrow when she opens her mouth to speak again. "I'm dead serious," I threaten.

When she turns in a huff and storms from the room,

her sass has me rolling my lips together to hide my amusement. Pulling out my phone, I text Chris.

> Logan: I'm ready.

He replies straight away.

> Chris: Be there in ten.

Shoving my phone into my pocket, I go in search of Brooke.

After bundling her into the backseat of the limousine —under duress—I search the perimeter of her house. Either the perpetrator has already fled, or wasn't even here to begin with. Either way, I'm not comfortable leaving her here.

When I climb in beside her, I can feel her body trembling next to mine. Sliding my arm around her, I pull her towards me.

"It's going to be okay," I say, placing a kiss on her hair. "We'll get to the bottom of it."

"I hope so," she whispers.

"To the penthouse, Mr. Cavanagh?" Chris asks, starting the ignition.

"No, to the police station."

I can't let this slide. It could be someone trying to frighten or intimidate her, but there's a chance it's something more sinister, like Jake, so I won't rest until this person is caught.

I turn my attention back to Brooke. "Do you have any idea who would do this? Do you think it's Jake?"

She pulls back from me as her eyes meet mine. "He did cross my mind, but I haven't had any contact with him in eight months. And this doesn't seem like something he'd do. Wouldn't he just knock on my door or approach me in the street?"

"I don't know him as well as you do, but if he's still taking drugs, who knows what his frame of mind is."

"Jake doesn't take drugs," she scoffs. "He's always been against them."

"Well, maybe you didn't know him as well as you thought you did. When I had his office cleaned out after I fired him, cocaine was found in his drawer."

She pauses and looks down at her lap. "I had no idea," she eventually says. "But if it's true, it explains so much."

"I'm not making it up."

"Wait, you fired him?"

"I did." She sighs as she turns to look out the window. "Brooke, I had no choice."

"I know," she says, looking back at me. "I just feel bad, his career meant everything to him."

Her comment pisses me off. "Obviously, the drugs meant more to him than his career, and his secretary meant more to him than his wife." I remove my arm from around her when she gasps, and scrub my hands over my face. "I'm sorry. That comment was uncalled for."

"You're probably right," is all she says, as she wraps her arms around herself before gazing back out the window.

Tilting my head back and resting it on the seat, I rub the palms of my hands down the front of my jeans. I feel like an arsehole now.

No words are spoken on the drive to the police station. It's a short commute, but it feels like an eternity. Her comment caught me off guard because I can't fathom why she'd have any empathy for him, especially after what he did to her. I exhale a long breath. I guess I need to understand that Jake was once her husband and probably meant the world to her. Either way, he doesn't deserve her compassion, but she's probably not as cynical as me. My job has hardened me over the years. I've dealt with enough scum in my time and stopped giving a fuck a long time ago.

"You okay?" I ask as I extend my hand, helping her from the vehicle. She just shrugs. "You don't have to deal with this alone."

She squeezes my hand before mumbling, "Thank you."

We have to wait for a while to be seen, and Brooke's on edge. When I ask, she assures me that she's okay, but the consistent biting of her thumb nail tells me otherwise.

Eventually, someone comes to greet us, and I learn he's one of the officers who attended her home the other night. I'm glad it's someone who's already familiar with the case.

"Take a seat," he says, leading us into one of the interview rooms. "I believe you received a threatening text message?"

"Yes," Brooke answers, taking a seat. I take the chair beside her as she proceeds to pull out her phone and pass it to him.

"A restaurant was vandalised down the street from your place the same night as the brick went through your window, so we presumed it was just some punk being a dickhead. Now I'm not so sure."

"I actually work at that restaurant," she says, bowing her head.

"I see," he replies, leaning back in his chair. My jaw ticks as I listen.

"I know we spoke about this the other night, but do you have any idea who could be doing this?" She shakes her head. "Have you ever received messages like this in the past?"

She pauses briefly before answering. "Yes, but that was months ago."

The officer picks up his pen and jots something down. "Do you know who sent the other messages?"

"Yes. My estranged husband."

"Were they threatening in any way?"

"Mostly, yes. But then I changed my number and they stopped. As I told you the other night, I've had no contact with him in eight months."

"Has he ever been violent towards you in the past?"

Her eyes dart to me before falling to her lap. "Once—the day I left him. He tried to strangle me."

Keeping my composure and trying not to react to everything I'm hearing is imperative, but in this instance, I'm struggling. Pushing my chair back, I stand and start to pace as I analyse her words. The day she left him was the same day I let her go home to face that animal on her own. *Fuck.*

Chapter 15

Brooke

My head is spinning as we leave the police station. Logan barely spoke a word the entire time, which concerns me. Is he upset with me? I know he said I wasn't in this alone, but I'm okay if he's changed his mind. After all, this is my problem, not his.

The moment we step into the night air, he stops and turns towards me. I can see the anguish marring his features as his eyes scan my face. Is this where he sends me on my way? I wouldn't hold it against him if he did.

I open my mouth to speak, but before the words are even out, I'm bundled in his arms. "I'm so sorry I wasn't more insistent about taking you home from the hospital that day."

"What?" I say, looking up at him confused. "Is that why you were pacing back and forth like a caged animal in the interview room?"

"As soon as you mentioned what he'd done to you that day, I felt like I was going to burst an artery."

"Why?" I ask. "None of that was your fault."

His hands move to my shoulders as he draws back to

make eye contact with me. "Don't you see? I could've stopped it from happening."

"How? If I'd pulled up outside with you, knowing what I know now, I think it would've made the situation worse."

He wraps me in his arms again, holding me tight. "I'm an arsehole. I feel like I let you down."

"You are the furthest thing from an arsehole. You saved my life, remember?"

He doesn't let go for the longest time. I'm not going to lie—it feels good in his arms. It's been so long since I've been held like this. I inhale through my nose; I could drown in his manly scent.

"Did you just sniff me?" he asks.

"What? No!"

"I think you did."

"You're delusional if you think that."

When I hear a chuckle from beside us, my eyes move to his chauffeur. He's looking up at the stars as he patiently holds the door open for us, but there's no mistaking the grin on his face.

Pulling back, Logan reluctantly lets me go. I smile at him as he steps aside, allowing me to climb into the car first.

"Thank you," I say to his driver as I climb into the backseat of the limousine.

"You're welcome," he replies with a nod.

"Not a word," I hear Logan grumble as he passes him and takes a seat beside me.

"Sure thing, Boss. The penthouse?"

"Please."

"Maybe it's best if I go home," I say. I'm not entirely comfortable going to his place, and this may give him the out he needs. I don't want to be a burden.

"Not a chance in hell. I'm not letting you go back there until we have some answers."

"Maybe I should stay at a hotel for the night, then."

"Nope, you'll be safer with me."

"What if I don't want to stay with you?" I ask, a tad annoyed at his insistence.

"I'm not going to bite you, Brooke."

"Maybe I'm into biting," I retort. I'm not impressed with his forcefulness, despite his good intentions.

"Well, if that's the case, I could possibly accommodate."

My eyes widen, as my head snaps in his direction. "I was joking."

"I know," Logan says, chuckling. "Relax. I have a spare room; besides I've heard how loud you snore, remember?"

I gasp. "I do not snore."

He looks over at me with a huge smile on his face. "Right."

"I don't," I say, playfully elbowing him in the side.

"I'm kidding. Just humour me, okay. I won't sleep well tonight unless I know you're safe."

"Fine." Crossing my arms, I settle back into my seat as my gaze moves to the window. *One-night,* Hot Stuff, that's all you get. *Tomorrow, I'm going back home.*

Chapter 16

Logan

Exhaustion must have taken over as I feel the weight of Brooke's lithe body get heavier and heavier during the drive back to my penthouse. I smile openly hearing her soft snores even out. Lifting her into my arms, I breathe in her sweet scent. I don't know why I have this overwhelming desire to protect her, but I do. When she rests her head on my shoulder, snuggling into me, my smile grows.

"Can you grab her bag?" I whisper to Chris.

Grinning smugly, he does as he's asked. He's probably amused because he hasn't seen this side of me before.

I look down at her as I walk towards the lift. Yet again, I'm overcome by her beauty. The fact that she's asleep and totally oblivious to me admiring her is even better. I was constantly reminding myself not to stare at her during dinner. She has the kind of look that I could observe endlessly and never tire. How anyone would want to hurt her is beyond me.

My eyes dart to Chris when he presses the button to bring the lift down. He's still smirking, the prick.

"Not a word," I mouth.

When the doors open, he places Brooke's bag inside and pulls out his key that allows the lift to take me up to the penthouse. "Have a good night," he says, raising his eyebrows.

"Fuck off," I say to his retreating back.

I hear him chuckling as the doors close. If he gives me shit tomorrow, I might have to sack him. I already know that's not going to happen, but the thought amuses me nevertheless.

Brooke stirs the moment the lift starts to move. A look of horror clouds her face when she realises I'm carrying her. "Umm ... can you please put me down?" she asks, squirming in my arms.

"Sorry," I say, removing my hand from behind her knees. When her feet are firmly on the ground, I completely let go and retreat a few steps. "You fell asleep in the car, and I didn't want to wake you."

"Oh, okay." She tucks her hair behind her ear, and things suddenly feel awkward between us.

Leaning back against the wall, I watch the numbers climb, hoping to reach my floor sooner rather than later.

When the doors finally open, I scoop up her bag and extend my hand for her to exit first. Her eyes are everywhere as we walk through the foyer and into the great room. The lights are dimmed and the blinds are drawn, showcasing the magnificent view you get from up here. The floor-to-ceiling windows span the entire wall, and I've got to say, even after all these years, I've yet to tire of the city skyline, especially at night when it's all lit up.

"Wow, you live here?" she asks, glancing at me over her shoulder.

"I do."

"This room alone is bigger than my entire terrace house." I stand back as she walks towards the windows.

"Look at the view from up here. Oh my god, you can see the Harbour Bridge."

"The Opera House is just to your right."

"Wow." She takes another step forward until she's almost pressing up against the glass. "I've never seen the city from up this high before. It's breathtaking."

"It sure is." But I'm not looking at the skyline or the harbour—my eyes are trained on her. I bought this place because I fell in love with the view the moment I saw it, but now that she's here in my space, there's no comparison. She's far more stunning.

Brooke stares out into the night for the longest time, and I find myself smiling as I watch her. "I can't believe you live here," she eventually says. "Well, I can believe it, but you know what I mean. I'd probably never leave this spot if it was my home. I'd place my bed right here."

I chuckle at her words. "I have the same view from my bedroom." I don't offer to show her, though. I know she's already here under duress, and the last thing I want to do is scare her off. My intentions for bringing her here were purely honourable. "Unfortunately, you can't see the bridge from the spare room, but there's still glimpses of the harbour and a great view of the botanic gardens. You won't be able to see it until morning."

"I look forward to morning, then."

"Can I get you anything? A drink, or something to eat?"

"No, thank you. I'm still full from dinner," she says, glancing at me once more.

"Me too. It's a shame I missed dessert though. I'll have to get a rain-check on that course."

She laughs at my comment but makes no offer for a redo. I'll work on that one, though. "Come, let me show you to your room."

I walk over to where I placed her bag and pick it up. She takes another glimpse of the view before following me. She only makes it a few metres before she stops in her tracks. "You have a grand piano?" she asks. "Can you play?"

"Hardly," I scoff. "I bought it for my niece when she started piano lessons."

"How old is she?"

"She's seven."

"How sweet."

I see her fingers glide over the black gloss finish as we pass. It has me wondering what her fingers would feel like against my skin. I can't let my mind go there. *Your best behaviour, Cavanagh,* I silently remind myself.

I'm acutely aware of her closeness as we climb the staircase that leads to the bedrooms. We walk down the long hallway, passing the other rooms as we go. I'm going to put her in the room closest to mine because I don't want her too far away. I know my building is safe, but this whole situation doesn't sit well with me. Is Jake really behind all of this? She may not even be in danger, but that's a chance I'm not prepared to take.

Opening the door, I switch on the light. "This will be your room for the night."

Placing her bag down, I stand just inside the doorway. Again, her eyes are everywhere. "This room is exquisite," she says, smiling. I love how she appreciates the littlest things. Some of the spoilt brats I've dated over the years would have expected nothing less. I chuckle when she sits on the side of the king-size bed and bounces, testing its comfort. She has no idea how adorable she is.

"You'll find everything you need in the en suite." I point to the far door.

"Even your spare rooms have their own bathroom?"

I shrug. "It's a penthouse." I grew up with money, so I'm used to the grandeur. "If there's anything else you need, I can have my housekeeper pick them up for you in the morning."

"Your housekeeper?"

"Yes. Jill."

She smirks like she finds that amusing. "Not Jeeves?"

"Jeeves?"

"Never mind, I'm being silly." She walks over and picks up her bag before lying it on top of the bed. "Thank you for letting me stay here tonight; I really appreciate it."

"It's no problem. I'm happy to have you here."

"I mean it," she says. "I know it may not have seemed like it earlier, but I really am grateful." Her gaze moves down to the carpet. "I probably wouldn't have gotten much sleep at my place."

When her eyes meet mine again, the vulnerability I see hits me straight in the chest. I take a few steps towards her, holding out my hand. As soon as her fingers grasp mine, I tug her closer and wrap her in my arms.

"Everything is going to work out. I promise you that. I won't let any harm come to you."

She doesn't reply, but I feel her arms tighten around my waist. I hold her for a short while, before reluctantly letting go.

A smile forms on her face as her eyes lock with mine. "Are you always this wonderful, Mr. Cavanagh?"

"Absolutely," I answer, dazzling her with my charming smile.

"Of course, you are," she says, laughing.

I take a step back before I do something stupid, like kiss her. "I hope you're comfortable in here tonight."

"Are you kidding me? It's going to be like staying in a luxury hotel."

Her response makes me chuckle. She's like a breath of fresh air. "Goodnight, Brooke," I say, turning and walking towards the door.

"Goodnight, Logan."

Grasping the door handle, I glance at her over my shoulder. "My room is just next door if you need anything during the night."

When her eyes slightly widen, I quickly close the door behind me without waiting for a reply. A few seconds later, I hear the lock latch on her door.

That sounded more suggestive than intended.

Chapter 17

Brooke

When I open my eyes, the room is bathed in darkness. Looking over at the bedside clock, I see it's nine forty-five. Shit! I hadn't meant to sleep so late. I'll blame it on the mattress. It was like sleeping on a fluffy cloud.

Throwing back the covers, I jump out of bed. When I draw the thick curtains, I'm blinded by the light and it takes a few seconds for my eyes to focus. When they do, the air hitches in my throat. He wasn't joking about the view. Pushing up onto my toes, I lean forward to take it all in.

I'd love nothing more than to jog around those gardens, but under the circumstances, I don't think that's a good idea.

After a quick shower, I head downstairs to find Logan. It's mid-morning, and I'm probably holding him up. I'm sure he has places to go, and I need to get home.

My eyes are glued to the view as I cross the main room. It looks different, but just as spectacular during the day.

I jump when a figure steps out of the shadows. I'm

expecting to see Logan standing there, but instead, I find an attractive older lady. "Good morning, dear. I'm sorry if I frightened you. You must be Brooke. I'm Jill, Mr. Cavanagh's housekeeper."

"It's nice to meet you, Jill," I say, holding out my hand to her. "I was just looking for ... umm ... Logan, I mean, Mr. Cavanagh."

She smiles. "I'm afraid you've missed him by about three hours. He had to go into the office this morning."

"Oh," I say. I was hoping to at least say goodbye before I leave.

"Come." She reaches out and grabs hold of my arm. "I'll make you some breakfast. There's a package for you on the counter. Mr. Cavanagh's assistant dropped it off about an hour ago.

"A package? For me?"

"Yes, dear." I smile when she calls me dear for the second time. My mother used to call me that often.

As I take a seat at the breakfast bar, she slides a small package towards me. The box is wrapped in white paper and tied with a red bow. I open the card pinned to it.

Brooke,
I'm sorry I missed you this morning. I hope you don't mind, but I've taken the liberty of buying you a new phone. It has a new number. I've transferred all the contacts from your old phone to this one.
See you this afternoon.
Logan.
P.S. I was touched to find you had my number saved under Hot Stuff.

I gasp when I read the last line.

"Is something wrong?" Jill asks.

"Umm ... no," I reply as I feel my cheeks heat.

"Can I get you a coffee?"

"Please."

"Milk and sugar?"

"Yes, please. One sugar."

Unwrapping the box, I find a new iPhone inside. The one I had was almost five years old, but I'm not sure how I feel about him buying me this. My first thought is how he got a hold of my old phone, and then I remember the officer handing it to him at the police station last night after Logan gave him his business card. Buying a new phone wasn't an option for me. It's money I don't have, and it will take me one step further away from my dream.

Removing the lid, I take it out and turn it on. I open the messenger app and search through my contacts. I die a little inside when I see his number is still under Hot Stuff. I'm mortified that he now knows my secret name for him.

"Here you go, dear," Jill says, sliding the mug of coffee towards me.

"Thank you."

Raising the cup to my mouth, I take a sip before typing my message.

> Brooke: Morning, Thank you for the phone. It was very thoughtful of you. Please let me know what it cost so I can reimburse you.

I was tempted to write Hot Stuff, but I don't want him getting the wrong idea. A friendship is all we'll ever have.

Placing the phone down on the counter, I reach for my coffee once more.

"What would you like for breakfast?" Jill asks.

"You don't need to wait on me."

"It's my job. Besides, Mr. Cavanagh left me with strict instructions to look after you. It's not often he has house guests. Apart from family, you're the first."

That surprises me. I assumed women would be beating down his door. "Just a piece of toast will be fine," I say.

My eyes move around the room. The kitchen is just as magnificent as the rest of the place. And though he appears to live an opulent life, it's nothing like I imagined.

Butterflies churn in my stomach when the phone chimes with a reply.

> Hot Stuff: Good morning, beautiful. It's a gift, so there's no need to repay me. I'm looking forward to seeing you this afternoon. We can go somewhere nice for dinner if you like.

I ponder his message for the longest time. As much as I'm flattered that he called me beautiful, I'm not comfortable with where this is heading. My heart is at risk here, and my best bet is to cut all ties.

> Brooke: I plan on heading back to my place this morning, so I won't be here when you get home. Thanks for letting me stay last night though, and please let me know what I owe you for the phone. I insist!

I read over my reply numerous times before finally pressing send. It feels abrupt, and for that, I feel bad. He's been nothing but nice to me, and if it wasn't for his occupation, I might even entertain the idea of something more, but my track record with lawyers is less than stellar.

Only seconds pass before the phone starts ringing. Looking down at the screen I see *Hot Stuff*. I blow out a long breath before answering.

"Hey."

There's a brief pause before he replies. "Please don't go."

"I can't stay here, Logan."

"But it's not safe for you to return to your place."

"I can stay at a hotel, but I need to go home and get some things. I have to work."

I hear him sigh through the phone. "I have a few meetings this morning that I can't get out of. I don't want you going back there on your own. Promise me you'll wait for me. If I shuffle a few things around, I should be able to get home around three."

"Okay, I'll wait," I say, although it's against my better judgment. But after everything he's done for me, I at least owe him a proper goodbye.

Chapter 18

Logan

My head hasn't been in the game all day, probably because my thoughts have been consumed by Brooke. I've called Jill twice just to check she hasn't left, which is pathetic. I'm not usually so needy, but this one has got under my skin. I know my reasons run much deeper than my attraction though. I feel for her in so many ways. Brooke told me down in Melbourne she had no family, which means she has nobody to turn to. *I hate that.* I desperately want to be that person for her, but I can't be if she won't allow it.

"It's unusual to see you this time of day, Mr. Cavanagh," the doorman says as he holds the door open for me. He's right, I've never left the office this early before, but what's going on upstairs in my apartment is far more important. Who knows what's awaiting her back at her place. There's no way I'd let her face that alone, especially after another text came through on her old phone this morning. This one included a threat. I contacted the police, but I've yet to tell Brooke. I'm not sure I want to.

The first thing I notice when the lift doors open, is her bag sitting on the floor in the foyer. The sight of it makes me anxious. As much as I don't want her to go, I can't force her to stay. If I've learnt anything in my short time with her, it's that she's fiercely independent. It's a trait I admire.

Stepping out of the lift, I hear music. *The piano.* My first thought is Lara, but she can't play that well yet. She can't play much at all, to be honest. I regretted buying that thing for her almost immediately. I'm pretty sure my ears were bleeding by the time she left that first day. But it made her happy, so it was worth the sacrifice.

Placing my briefcase down and pausing at the opening to the main room, I see Brooke's eyes are closed and there's a smile on her face as she gets lost in the melody. I'm mesmerised by her passion and blown away by her talent. She plays beautifully, and I can only hope one day my niece will be half as good.

A contented sigh falls from her lips when she strikes the last note, and I have the urge to applaud, but I don't. "That was beautiful," I say, stepping further into the room.

Her eyes spring open the moment I speak. "Logan. I'm sorry." She quickly stands. "I hope you don't mind."

"Not at all."

"I've never played anything so grand before."

"You're very talented," I say. "How long have you been playing?"

"Since I was a little girl, the lady who looked after me while my mother worked taught me."

"Miss Jones?"

Brooke gives me an inquisitive look; does she think I've been researching her? "Yes, how did you know that?"

"You told me about her. She was the one who taught you how to cook."

"Oh." Her face lights up as she speaks. "I'm

impressed you remembered that." Doesn't she realise I hang on her every word? I want to know everything about her.

"And I'm impressed with your playing skills."

"Thank you."

"I should hire you to give my niece lessons." She smiles, but it doesn't quite reach her eyes. She may think I'm joking, but I'm dead serious. Not only does Lara need the lessons, but it may also be a way of keeping Brooke in my life. I get the impression she's pushing me away, and that's the last thing I want. "How was your day?"

She shrugs. "I didn't do much." Of course, she was stuck here.

"Yours?"

"Busy. I would've come earlier if I could've."

"That's okay," she says. "You're here now. I cancelled my classes at the dance school, and my shift at the restaurant tonight, but I have to work tomorrow. I need the money."

"I admire you for working two jobs?" I don't like that she has to, but I respect her for it nevertheless.

"I have three, actually. I teach piano lessons in my spare time."

"Wow. I bet that keeps you busy."

"It keeps my head above water."

"Let me help you."

Her face drops, and it's only then I realise what I've said. "I'm not looking for a handout, Mr. Cavanagh. I manage just fine on my own."

"It's Logan, and I'm sorry," I say, running my hand through my hair. "That came out wrong." It's commendable that she wants to do this on her own. A lot of the women I've dated in the past were always looking for handouts or a free ride. *Brooke is nothing like them.*

"Look." Her face softens as she speaks. "I'm grateful for everything you've done for me, truly I am, and as much as I've enjoyed spending time in your spectacular apartment with that killer view, I have a place of my own, and commitments. I need to get back to my life."

"I understand that," I say. "But I'm concerned about you going back there."

"And I appreciate that more than you know, but I'm not your problem."

I want her to be my problem, but I don't voice that out loud. She steps forward and grabs a hold of my hand. "You are one of the kindest people I've ever met, and I'm glad I stuck around long enough to say a proper goodbye, but I need to get back to *my* life now."

"So, are you saying you don't want to see me anymore?"

Her grip tightens on my hand. "It's more like I can't."

"Is the thought of being around me so terrible?" I ask. My words come out more abruptly than expected, but what she just said hurts.

She lets go of my hand as her eyes move down to the floor. "No."

I place my finger on the base of her chin, moving her gaze back to mine. "Then what?"

"It's not you, personally," she says. "It's more what you do for a living."

My eyebrows pinch into a frown. Am I hearing this right? "I can't be in your life because I'm a lawyer?"

"Pretty much."

"That's a little unfair."

She blows out a long breath. "Can we just drop it?"

"No!" I cross my arms over my chest, letting her know I intend to get to the bottom of this. There's nothing wrong with what I do for a living. I'm a lawyer, for fuck's sake, not a serial killer.

Ignoring what I said, she steps around me, heading towards the lift. I stand there in complete shock as she picks up her bag. I'm not used to being dismissed.

"Thank you again for everything."

If she thinks I'm letting her just walk away she's mistaken.

Chapter 19

Brooke

I only make it as far as the lift before Logan corners me. "Brooke, wait. I'm not letting you go back there alone."

"Fine."

I was more than willing to catch public transport, but I have no clue where the bus stops are around here. Truthfully, I'm kind of glad. The last thing I want is to leave things like this. What I've just said would sound incredibly shallow to him, but he has no idea my insecurities with men span a lot further than just Jake. Hopefully, I can smooth things out on the drive back to my place.

"Let me grab my keys." He walks towards the long hall table in the foyer, it sits below a large mirror that expands the entire wall. I can see the deep frown lines etched on his forehead through the reflection and I feel awful. How do I tell him it's me and not him, without it sounding like a copout?

He insists on carrying my bag. Instead of getting out on the ground floor, we head to the basement level, which I presume is the car park. Fishing in the pocket of his suit pants when the doors open, he pulls out his keys as we cross the polished cement floor. Extending his arm out in front of him, he presses a button.

The lights on a black sports car ahead flash. His car is almost as sexy as him. "Nice car," I say as he opens the passenger-side door for me.

"Thanks." The tension between us is clearly visible.

"What kind of car is it?" I ask once we're both seated inside.

"An Audi convertible R8 Spyder." That means absolutely nothing to me; I don't know a damn thing about cars.

"It suits you," I say, looking over at him and smiling.

"Why, because I'm a lawyer?" There's sarcasm in his tone, and although I choose to ignore his comment, it still stings.

As the automatic garage door to the car park opens—allowing the light from outdoors to flood in—Logan flicks a button on the centre console, opening the roof of the convertible as we drive up a steep driveway. Never in my life have I been in a flashy car like this. Jake and I owned a regular, everyday vehicle. It was all we could afford. And now that I'm on my own, I don't even have one. Our lifestyles couldn't be any further apart if we tried.

We travel in silence all the way to my place, and the closer we get, the more knotted up my stomach becomes. I'm not sure if it's because this is the end of the road for us, or because I'm anxious about being back here.

He pulls up outside my house, and I remove my seatbelt. "Thank you again for everything," I say, reaching for the door handle.

"Let me get that for you." Before I have a chance to protest, he exits the car. I find his gentlemanly ways very sweet, just like him. He opens my door and extends his hand to me. "Would you mind if I at least came inside and checked that everything is okay?"

"I'd like that, thank you."

There's a small smile on his face as he grabs my bag out of the boot, the last thing I want to do is hurt him. I wish I could find the words to help him understand, but my past is not something I've ever liked to talk about.

When we reach the front porch, he places my bag down as I rummage around inside my handbag for the keys. As I go to place the key in the lock, I notice the door is slightly ajar. "I remember locking this before I left," I say.

"I do too. Step aside."

"Hold on," I say, grabbing hold of his arm. "What if someone's still in there?"

"Wait out here!"

"Shouldn't we call the police first?" Ignoring my question, he opens the door and enters the house. My heart is beating out of my chest. I can't let him face this alone, so despite what he said, I follow him in. He only makes it a few steps inside before he stills. I'm not expecting it, so I crash straight into his back.

He spins around to face me. "I told you to wait outside."

Stepping around him, I gasp when I see the state of my living room. The furniture is upturned, and the picture frames that were hanging on the wall now lay broken on the floor. But what makes my blood run cold is the word 'WHORE' that's spray-painted in large red bold letters on the wall. Before I even realise what's happening, I'm being ushered towards the front door. The moment we're outside, Logan gathers me in his arms. Tears sting my eyes, and I can feel my body trembling as he holds me tight.

When he finally lets me go, he cradles my face in his hands. "Are you okay?" I just nod, because I'm unable to speak. "I'm going to call the police." He takes a few steps away from me, and although I can still hear him talking, nothing he says registers. My mind is spinning, and my gaze keeps flicking back to the front door. When he ends the call, he slides his phone back into his pocket. "They're on their way. I'm going to look around inside while we wait."

I reach for him as he takes a step towards the door. "Don't," I say, suddenly feeling terrified. "What if they're still in there?"

"I can handle myself." He grips my upper arms and kisses my forehead. "Don't move from this spot."

"But—"

"I mean it, Brooke."

"Here, drink this," Logan says, handing me a glass containing a small amount of amber liquid. "It will help calm your nerves."

"Thank you." He sits beside me at the breakfast bar in the kitchen of his penthouse.

After the police took photos and fingerprints from the scene, Logan brought me back here. This time I didn't even mention a hotel. It's one thing having a rock thrown through your window, or a threatening text sent, but knowing someone invaded my personal space, my sanctuary, is on a whole new level.

It was obvious I could no longer stay there, so the police allowed me to gather a few things from my bedroom, but even that wasn't spared. The contents of my drawers and wardrobe were strewn everywhere, but the most troubling part was seeing my now-unmade bed and the dent that sat in the middle of the pillow from where a head had clearly been. It wasn't mine. Whoever was in my house was also in my bed. It both spooked and disgusted me.

I'm so grateful Logan insisted on driving me home, I would've hated to face all that on my own.

"Are you hungry?" he asks, placing his hand on my leg. He's been so kind and gentle with me. "Jill left some food in the fridge for us, I can heat it up if you'd like."

"Okay." The last thing I want is food, but I know he won't eat unless I do.

He doesn't say much during dinner, but I can feel his eyes on me as I push the food around on the plate. "Try and eat something," he pleads. "You need to keep up your strength." For his sake, I force a small amount down, but when I eventually slide my plate away, he doesn't protest. "I'll clean up if you want to go and have a shower or lie down."

"I'll help." He eyes me as I pick up the plates and walk into the kitchen. Can he sense my unwillingness to leave his side?

"I have a bit of work to do in the office," he says once the plates are rinsed and packed in the dishwasher.

"You're leaving?" My question comes out more panicked than planned.

"Hey." He pulls me into his arms. "I'm not leaving you," he says. "I have a home office on the other side of that door." He points across the room. I wondered what was behind that door earlier today when I was here on my own. "Do you want me to walk you upstairs to your bedroom?"

"Please." I squeeze my eyes shut, trying to fight back

the tears as I bury my face in his chest. I'm trying my best to keep it together. I don't want him to see me cry; he'll think I'm weak.

He picks up my bag before reaching for my hand. "Come." Once there, he places my things on the bed. "Are you going to be okay?"

I shrug. "Eventually. I'm just a little spooked at the moment."

"That's totally understandable, but you know you're safe here, right?"

I wrap my arms around my torso. "I don't feel safe anywhere right now."

He gives me a sympathetic look. "How about I work on my laptop in my bedroom, that way I'm just next door."

"You wouldn't mind?"

"Of course not."

"Thank you."

"I'll run downstairs and grab my briefcase."

"Okay." I lock the bedroom door when he leaves, and sit on the side of the mattress until I hear him return. Once I know he's nearby, I gather what I need for my shower. I lock the bathroom door also. I hate how rattled this has gotten me.

The warm shower doesn't have the relaxing effect I was hoping for. My mind is racing as I struggle to understand the reasons behind what's happening. My heart tells me the Jake I fell in love with isn't the one behind this, but my gut is conflicted. Who else would harbour such hatred towards me? The detective we spoke to earlier said they're still trying to track Jake down. Apparently, the house we bought together has been repossessed by the bank, and there is no record of a forwarding address.

Walking over to the bedroom door, I make sure it's still locked before climbing into bed. I leave the light on because I don't feel safe in the dark right now. Even though Logan lives on the top floor in a secure building, I'm still feeling uneasy. Pulling the covers up around my chin, I stare up at the ceiling. Sleep won't come easy tonight.

I lie there for the longest time—possibly hours—listening and internally freaking out with each sound. I jump when I hear a soft knock on the bedroom door. "Brooke, it's me. Is everything okay?"

Throwing back the covers, I leap out of bed and rush towards the door. "Hey," I say the moment I open it. He's changed out of his suit into a t-shirt and sweats. Even casually dressed, he looks good enough to eat.

"I thought you might still be awake. I saw the light under the door."

His eyes move down my body, and even though I'm dressed in the least flattering thing I own—an oversized pink t-shirt—I'm suddenly feeling exposed. My skin prickles under the weight of his stare. The way he's eyeing me is almost predatory, so when I reach for the hem of my top and tug it down, his gaze immediately snaps back to my face.

I move my focus to the floor. "I can't sleep," I admit.

"Do you want to come and sit with me for a while? I'm still working, but I have a TV in my room.

I don't hesitate with my answer. "Please."

"I was just heading downstairs to grab a bottle of water; would you like one?"

"Sure."

"Great. Make yourself comfortable," he says, gesturing towards his bedroom. "I'll be right back."

"I'll come downstairs with you," I blurt out, and he's

either oblivious to my eagerness or sympathetic to my plight because he doesn't bat an eyelid.

"Wow," is the only word out of my mouth when I enter his bedroom.

My eyes are everywhere because I don't know where to look first. On the far-right wall, the rich mahogany door to the large walk-in robe is partly open, and I catch a glimpse of his suits meticulously hung in a neat row along the back wall.

My gaze moves over the thick wooden posts of his king-sized bed. The chunky bedside tables and huge dresser match perfectly. Unlike the bright and airy room I've been staying in, this one is darker—moodier, even—and way more masculine. Like everything he owns, it reeks of money and it suits him.

My eyes are drawn to the floor-to-ceiling windows to the left. There appears to be a balcony set off the glass sliding doors, the idyllic place for morning coffees. He wasn't lying, the view from here is just as spectacular as the one in his main room.

He picks up a remote next to the bed and presses a button. I watch in awe as a large flat-screen television rises out of the foot of the bed. "You can watch TV, or come sit with me over there." He points to the long, chocolate brown, leather-winged back sofa.

As much as I feel the need to be as close to him as possible, I'm happy just to be in the same room. "I don't want to disturb you any more than I have. I'll watch TV."

"Watch whatever you like," he says, handing me the remote.

I'm so thankful for him at this moment.

Chapter 20

Logan

Standing beside my bed, I stare down at Brooke. She looks so fragile and vulnerable, lost amongst the sea of pillows. It's just after midnight, and she's finally fallen asleep. A number of times throughout the evening I caught her watching me. She'd quickly turn away and focus on the television every time I noticed. It had me constantly fighting back a smile.

I'm in two minds about whether to carry her back to her room or leave her here. She looks so comfortable and at peace. Deciding against moving her, I walk around to the other side of the bed, remove my t-shirt and clamber in beside her. I don't usually sleep in my sweats, but tonight it's warranted. She's the first woman I've ever had in this bed—in this apartment, actually.

The business side of my life is so public, with both me and my company frequently ending up in the headlines due to the high-profile cases we take on, that I like to keep my personal life private. I date often enough when my busy schedule allows it, but I never bring any of those women back here. Some of them I want to see again, others I don't, so them not knowing where I live is a bonus.

Rolling onto my side, I watch her sleep. I keep my distance though. The last thing I want is for her to think I'm taking advantage of her vulnerable state. My intentions are purely honourable—I just want her to feel safe. As much as she tried to hide her unrest earlier, I saw straight through her false bravado.

Reaching out, I gently brush back a piece of hair that's fallen across her face. The TV is still on, so it illuminates her delicate features. I'm mesmerised by her flawless skin, the long dark eyelashes that fan over her cheeks, and her plump lips that I'm aching to kiss.

My heart races whenever I'm around her. It scares me to think how quickly I've become attached. I never believed it when people said, *'when the right girl comes along, you'll know,'* and yet, my heart is telling me it's her. In Melbourne, I felt the attraction immediately, but she was married, so I would've never taken it further. The only thing standing in my way now is the giant walls she's erected. In time, I hope I can bring them down.

My eyes fly open when I feel a heavy weight on my chest. Raising my head off the pillow, all I see is a mountain of brown hair. It brings an instant smile to my face. My movement has her stirring, and I wait to see her reaction. While I kept my promise and stayed on my side of the bed, at some stage during the night it appears she's cuddled up to me.

Lifting her head, her eyes squint as she tries to focus. The moment she realises she's been using my body as a pillow, she jumps, scrambling back to her side of the bed. "I'm so sorry," she says, horror lining her voice.

Throwing back the covers, she goes to rise, but I reach out and clasp her arm. "It's okay."

"I'm so embarrassed," she says, covering her face with her hands.

Sitting up, I pry her hands away. "Don't be."

I see a smile tug at her lips. "Why do you always have to be so nice?"

"It comes naturally," I say, making her laugh. I flop down onto my back and look over at the clock. "I don't have to get up for another hour." I tap the space beside me. "Lie with me for a while?"

She looks a little unsure of herself as she lays back down, far enough away from me that our bodies are no longer touching. Everything in me wants to reach out and pull her closer, but I know that's not a wise move.

"How are you feeling this morning?" I ask.

"Surprisingly better."

"I'm glad. Hopefully, the investigators will get a match with the fingerprints."

"I hope so too," she says, turning her head to look at me. "I'm so glad you were with me yesterday. I'm not sure how I would've coped with all that on my own."

Rolling on my side to face her, I gently rub my hand down the length of her arm. "I'm glad I was there too."

"I don't know where to go from here."

"What do you mean?"

"I can't go back there. I'll have to find somewhere else to live."

"You're welcome to stay here as long as you want," I offer, and I genuinely mean it.

"That's really sweet, but it's not an option."

"Why, because I'm a lawyer?" Under the circumstances, it's not something I wanted to bring up today, but it's been eating away at me ever since she said it.

"You make me sound so judgemental."

"Well, isn't that what you're doing? Judging me because of what I do for a living. That's unfair, Brooke." Rolling onto my back, I blow out a frustrated breath. "I'm nothing like Jake."

"My father was a lawyer too," she says, her voice so quiet I can only just make out her words.

My head snaps in her direction. I remember her mentioning that she didn't have a relationship with her father. *Now we're getting somewhere.*

"And?" There has to be more to it.

"My mother was only nineteen-years-old when she met him. She interned at the law firm he worked for whilst putting herself through university." She pauses briefly, taking a deep breath before continuing. "Her future looked promising until she fell in love with that snake."

"I see."

"This is hard for me. It's something I don't talk about. *Ever.*"

Rolling back onto my side, I reach for her hand. "And I appreciate you opening up to me." When she doesn't continue, I pry a little further. "So, she found out she was pregnant after their relationship ended?"

"No, before," she says, averting her eyes away from me. "That's when he informed her about his wife ... the one she had no idea about."

"Oh." I tighten my grip on her hand.

"He demanded she have an abortion."

Shit, this is worse than I thought. "I'm so sorry he treated your mother so poorly."

Her eyes move back to me. "She was the sweetest and

most loving person. She didn't deserve that." When I see her bottom lip quiver, I shimmy my body closer to hers.

"No, she didn't."

"She walked out of his office that day and never heard from him again."

"I'm glad she didn't listen to him."

"Me too," she says, as a smile tugs at her lips. "Her life was never the same. With a child on the way, she had to leave university and get a job. I think she always intended on going back to finish her law degree, but she never got the chance. She worked two, sometimes three, jobs at a time just to keep both of us clothed, fed, and housed."

"It sounds like you inherited her strength."

"Hardly," she scoffs.

"I disagree."

"I still feel guilty when I think of what she gave up for me, but she never once complained."

"It's what mothers do—they put their children first. Well, most mothers anyway."

"What's your mother like?" she asks.

"Amazing. I'm fortunate to have her."

"That's how I always felt about my mum. She was the best."

The smile on her face says so much. I feel bad for her; I'd be lost without mine. "What happened to your mother?" I ask.

"She got sick. She was tired all the time and put it down to the long hours she worked. I don't think she realised she had cancer until it was too late. She was already stage four by then."

"How sad."

"I'd always planned on looking after her when I left university. I was going to start up my own dance studio, and in my mind, it was going to be an instant success."

She lets out a small laugh before continuing. "I desperately wanted to repay her for everything she'd done for me growing up. I knew how tough things had been. She deserved a better life, a chance to live again. But unfortunately, I never got to do that for her."

"I'm so sorry." When I see tears well in her eyes, I slide my arm around her waist, pulling her to me.

"I miss her so much." A lump forms in my throat as she softly cries into my chest.

Life has been hard for her, and she has no one left to turn to. I make a silent pledge to myself as I hold her tight: Going forward, I'll be that one person she can always count on, if she'll let me, of course.

Chapter 21

Brooke

Finally pulling myself together, I draw back. I didn't mean to cry in front of Logan. It's been a long time since I've mourned my mother. I remember Jake getting angry with me the last time he found me lying across our bed sobbing. It was the anniversary of the day she'd passed, and I'd just gotten back from the cemetery. *'She's been dead for years, get the fuck over it,'* he'd said. Her death is something I don't think I'll ever get over.

There's so much compassion on Logan's face as his eyes meet mine. "My heart hurts for you," he whispers.

Reaching up, he glides the pad of his thumb gently across my cheek, wiping my tears away. I'm touched by his tenderness. It's nice having somebody in my life who cares.

When he places his lips against my forehead, something inside me cracks. I'm not sure if I'm just lost in the moment or craving his attention, but when he draws back and stares down at me, I inch my face forward and place my lips against his.

For a moment neither of us move, but our mouths stay connected. "Brooke," he murmurs, as his fingers slide into my hair. I'm probably going to regret this, but right now I need his comfort more than I need air.

I part my lips, giving him the clarity he needs. At first, his movements are slow and precise—god, this man knows how to kiss. It's been over eight months since I've had any kind of affection, and it's not until now that I realise how much I've missed it.

He rolls me onto my back, and part of his body covers mine. I can feel his erection pressed up against my leg, as his hand glides over my outer thigh before cupping my arse.

"Logan," I croon when he palms my flesh and groans into my mouth.

He draws back, making eye contact with me once again. So many questions are etched on his face, and I can tell he's searching for permission to take this further. Walking away now would be the most sensible thing to do, but I want this—I *need* it. Not just the closeness; but the escape.

A primal growl rumbles in the back of Logan's throat as I wrap one leg around his waist and draw his body closer, before pulling his lips back to mine. He deepens the kiss as he shifts between my thighs. I curl my other leg around his, entangling them at our ankles.

Rocking his body forward, he grinds against my core. "Fuck, Brooke." We may only be dry humping, but I already feel like I'm on the edge of coming undone. Is there anything this man isn't good at?

When my body starts trembling, he must sense that I'm close because he picks up the pace, and the added friction is just what I need. His free hand slides under my t-shirt, palming my breast before pinching my nipple between his forefinger and thumb, and I'm gone.

"Oh god," I moan, pushing my head back into the

pillow as my orgasm rocks through me. Logan doesn't stop moving until he's drained every ounce of pleasure from my body.

Pulling back, he observes me. The corner of his bottom lip is held captive between his teeth as he stares down at me with so much heat in his gaze.

"Do you have any idea how hot that was?" he states, as his mouth moves down to pepper kisses along my jawline. "You drive me wild."

Placing my hand on his shoulder, I push him over onto his back, so I can straddle his lap. I've had a taste of what this man can do, and now I want more. I'm aching to have his hands and mouth all over me. It's been too long.

A sexy smirk lights up his face as I reach for the hem of my pink t-shirt, pulling it over my head and tossing it across the room.

The way his eyes drink me in makes my skin prickle. I tilt my head back and whimper as his fingertips glide up my sides until he's cupping my breasts, giving them a firm squeeze. "You're perfect."

Lifting his head off the pillow, he swirls his tongue around my nipple before sucking it into his mouth. My fingers weave into his thick, dark hair holding him in place, as I throw my head back.

"Yes," I cry out, encouraging him to keep going.

Logan manoeuvres one of his hands between our bodies. When his fingertips slip down the front of my underwear, and over my sensitive flesh, I rock my hips forward.

He slides one of his thick fingers deep inside me and I whimper. "Fuck, Brooke, you're so wet for me."

That statement should embarrass me, but I can't ever remember feeling this turned on. "I need you," I whisper. Because I *need* him so much.

Flipping me onto my back, he removes his finger and reaches over to his bedside drawer to grab a condom. Once he has one in his hand, he pauses briefly as his eyes scan over my face. "Are you sure?"

"I want this."

Smiling, he clambers off the bed, tossing the condom onto the sheets beside me. This is my first time seeing him without a shirt on, and I'm in no way disappointed. His body is a work of art, and I feel no shame as my eyes drink him in. From his tanned skin, defined abs, and the sexy little V that disappears into his low-riding sweats, which are tented from his arousal. This man obviously works out.

His gaze doesn't leave mine as he hooks his thumbs into the waistband of his pants and removes them in one fluid motion. He reaches for the condom, tearing the foil packet open with his teeth. He's so damn sexy. I watch him effortlessly roll it onto his impressive length, and with each movement he makes, the anticipation of what's to come only amplifies. I've never craved a man as much as I do him at this moment.

His gaze moves back to me, as I lay here wearing nothing but a tiny piece of pink lace. I should feel self-conscious by the intensity of his stare, but I don't. There's something comforting in the way he looks at me.

He wastes no time stripping me out of my underwear, growling as he slides them down my legs. "Do you have any idea how beautiful you are? I've wanted you from the moment I first saw you," he admits as he kneels between my now parted legs and crawls up my body.

When he's hovering over me, I reach for him, running my fingers through the side of his hair. His eyelids flutter shut, and he intakes a sharp breath as he settles between my thighs.

A beautiful smile curves his lips when his eyes lock with mine. "I guess we're really doing this?"

"I guess we are."

"We don't have to if you're not ready."

"Are you trying to talk me out of it?"

"I hope not," he says, chuckling. "I just want you to be sure."

"I'm sure."

Leaning down, he brushes his lips with mine. "It's going to complicate things."

"We're two grown adults, I'm sure we will figure it out."

He arches an eyebrow and smirks as he grabs hold of his cock and glides it back and forth through my slick heat. When he pushes the tip inside, we both moan in unison. He feels so good. *So damn good.*

"It's only fair to warn you, sweetheart," he whispers into my ear, as he rolls his hips forward, thrusting all the way in, "once I've had you, I'm going to want to keep you."

I get the feeling there's some truth behind his words, which should alarm me, but I'm too far gone to turn back now.

Reaching over to the bedside table, I grab my mobile phone. It chimed with a message a few minutes ago, and I've been hesitant to read it. I already know it's from Logan since he's the only one who has this number.

What happened between us this morning was like nothing I've ever experienced in my life. He ended up taking me twice, once in bed, and the second time against the wall in the shower, which in turn made him late for work, but he didn't seem to care. My time with him was insanely hot. He was so passionate and knew exactly how to command my body, wringing multiple orgasms from me without even trying.

Once Logan left, I made my way back to the spare room. I was embarrassed to go downstairs and face Jill after what we did, worried she might have heard us.

For the past few hours, I've been lying on top of the covers, staring up at the ceiling and analysing every single second of our time together.

I'm feeling like I'm at a crossroads. I like this man, I really do. Never in my life have I felt the kind of hunger Logan and I shared earlier. *It was off the charts.* Not even with Jake. It was like we couldn't get enough of each other.

He makes me feel so much it scares me. But I promised myself after leaving my husband, I'd never put myself in that position again. I'm so torn.

Holding the phone in front of my face, I read the message on the screen.

> Hot Stuff: I can't get you off my mind. x

Releasing the breath I didn't realise I was holding, my hand drops back down onto the bed. He's been on my mind all morning too, I'm so conflicted. It's times like this when I really need my mother. She always gave the best advice.

Deciding to sit on the message a while longer, I push up off the bed and head downstairs. I can't hide up here forever. Jill's probably wondering where I am.

"Good morning," she says the moment I enter the kitchen.

"Morning, Jill."

"Can I get you some breakfast, a coffee maybe?" I'm more than capable of making my own, but Logan's coffee machine looks way too complicated for me to even attempt it.

"Coffee sounds perfect. I don't have the stomach for food right now."

"That's understandable, dear," she says, placing her hand on my arm. "Logan told me what happened this morning."

"Oh my god, he told you we had sex?" I screech, as my eyes widen.

"My goodness, no," she replies, averting her gaze.

I want the ground to open up and swallow me whole when I see her cheeks turning pink.

"He told me that your place had been vandalised."

"Oh." I let out a sigh as the realisation hits home. My mind has been so preoccupied with a certain hot lawyer; I hadn't given my current situation much thought.

"Don't be upset with him. He only told me so I could keep an eye on you. Mr. Cavanagh is very fond of you, but I guess you already know that since ..." She waves her hand around in the air instead of finishing her sentence.

I know she's referring to the fact that we've had sex. To say I'm mortified she now knows about that is an understatement.

"He's a good man, but I guess you already know that too."

"Yes," I say, smiling.

What I've seen of him so far is pretty much perfect, and there lies the problem. What is the other side of him like? I had no clue about the monster inside Jake until it reared its ugly head. From what little I know about my father; my mother was oblivious to his dark side too.

"He deserves to find happiness. His life pretty much revolves around his work, I'm afraid."

"You're very fond of him, aren't you?"

"Although he already has a beautiful mother, he's like a son to me."

"That's sweet," I say, taking a seat at the breakfast bar. "He's lucky to have you both."

She slides the coffee across the counter, and I stare down into it as my finger circles the edge of the mug. "You seem preoccupied today, dear."

I shrug. "I've got a lot on my mind."

She reaches out, placing her hand on top of mine. "Well, I'm a good listener if you ever need someone to talk to."

Looking up at her, I smile. "Thank you."

I may need to take her up on that offer. I have nobody else to confide in.

Chapter 22

Logan

I check my phone for the umpteenth time since sliding into the back of the limousine. There's still no reply from Brooke, and it concerns me. My entire being wants to call her, but I need to give her space. She let some of her walls down this morning, so putting pressure on her now is the worst thing I can do.

My disappointment only deepens when I arrive home and find Brooke is not there to greet me. It's the first time I can ever remember looking forward to coming home. This place is basically where I eat and sleep, but with her here, things feel different.

"You're home already, Mr. Cavanagh," Jill says, as she walks into the kitchen. I usually work late, so she's gone by the time I get home. But today I really wanted to be here.

"Where's Brooke?" I ask, grabbing a bottle of water out of the fridge.

"In her room. She's been there most of the day."

"Oh."

"Just be patient with her. She'll come around."

"Did she say something to you?"

"She opened up a little. She's dealing with a lot of demons right now."

"I know," I say, but it still ticks me off to know I'm guilty by association. Just because we have the same career path, doesn't mean I'm anything like her father or her ex. I can only hope she gives me the chance to prove that. "I'm going to go up and see her."

Jill nods. "I'll have dinner prepared for you both before I leave."

Knocking on the spare bedroom door, I wait for an invitation to enter.

"Come in," she calls out.

Opening the door, I find her sitting in the middle of the bed with her legs crossed. There's a photo album laid out in front of her.

"I just thought I'd come up and say hi."

"Hi," she says, smiling up at me.

"Can we talk?"

"Sure." She taps the bed beside her.

Walking over, I sit on the edge of the mattress. What I really want to do is pull her into my arms and kiss her—that's all I've thought about today—but Jill's words are swimming around in my head. If I have any chance of making this work, I need to be patient.

"Are they photos of you?"

"There's some of me, but they're mainly of my mum." She lifts the album, bringing it closer so I can see the image on the page.

"Is that your mother?"

"Yes."

"Wow, you're the spitting image of her." The likeness is uncanny.

"I know. The older I get the more I see it."

She closes the album and places it down beside her. "So, what did you want to talk about?"

"I heard from the detectives today."

"Oh."

"They got a positive ID on the prints. Our suspicions were correct."

Her eyes widen to saucers. "Jake?"

"Yes."

Her whole body deflates as her gaze moves down to her lap. "I can't believe it. Why is he doing this?" Although in her heart she already knew it was him, I can see the confirmation has upset her. "Have they caught him?"

"No, they haven't." Reaching out, I wrap my hand around hers. I'm grateful when she doesn't pull away. "But they're looking. His parents reported him as a missing person over a month ago, he allegedly stole a large sum of money from them before he vanished ... he hasn't been seen since. A warrant for his arrest was issued a few months ago, for failure to appear in court."

"For the money he took from his parents?"

"No, drugs."

"Wow."

"The detective also told me they're applying for an Apprehended Violence Order on your behalf. Once it's put in place, Jake will be prohibited from coming anywhere near you." *On paper, at least, but I doubt that will stop him.*

"I see."

"I had a meeting with an old friend today. He's a private investigator and ex-detective. My company has used him many times in the past. He's one of the best in the business. He's on the case now too, and if anyone can find Jake, he can."

"But until then, what? I'm a prisoner? I need to go back to work, my students rely on me."

"We'll work something out."

"I can't afford to lose my job, Logan," she says.

"I understand that. I can have Chris take you if need be." My gut tells me not to let her out of this building until he's found, but the last thing I want is her feeling like a prisoner. "It's not safe to be out there on your own."

"I couldn't ask that of you. You've already done enough." Uncrossing her legs, she moves to the edge of the bed and stands. Her back is now to me, as she gazes out the window. "Maybe it's best if I move to a hotel."

Rising, I close the distance between us and place my hand on her shoulder, turning her until she's facing me. "If he found you at your place, he can find you in a hotel. Stay here with me. You don't have to share my bed—my offer has no strings attached ... I promise. Just let me care for you until he's found. I'd never forgive myself if any harm came to you." Tears well in her big brown eyes, and it tugs at my heartstrings. I want to see her smiling again because it tears me up seeing her like this. Pulling her into my arms, I hold her tight. "Please stay."

Picking up my phone, I dial Chris's number. "How are things there?"

He's under strict instructions not to let Brooke out of his sight. I even asked him to escort her inside the dance studio, to be safe. Who knows if this maniac is lurking in the shadows, just waiting to pounce? Chris is a veteran, so I know he can handle himself. I trust this man implicitly.

"Good. She's inside. I'm just sitting out the front, but

there doesn't appear to be any movement."

"I'm glad. Keep me updated."

"Will do," he says.

"And Chris."

"Yes, Mr. Cavanagh."

"Guard her with your life."

"You have my word."

I can't think straight. Neither the detectives nor Mike, the private investigator I hired, have yet to find a lead on Jake's location. Unlocking the top drawer of my desk, I pull out Brooke's old phone and turn it on. I haven't checked it since yesterday, so I'm curious to see if anything more has been sent.

The phone alerts me of a new message the moment it comes to life.

> Unknown: I'm going to ruin you, just like you ruined me, BITCH!

Reading it makes my blood run cold. If he harms one hair on her head, his life won't be worth living. Leaning forward, I buzz my secretary. "Rose."

"Yes, Mr. Cavanagh."

"Something's come up, and I have to go out for a few hours. You'll need to reschedule my appointments."

"Okay."

"Do you want me to move them up for later today?"

"Please." I'll work into the night if need be. By then Brooke will be home and safe, and I'll be able to relax.

"Oh, and Rose, I need you to courier something to Mike for me."

"No problem."

Standing, I grab my suit jacket from the back of my chair and slide into it. I can't just sit here. Jake found out where she lives, so I presume he's familiar with all her movements. I place Brooke's phone on Rose's desk as I pass.

"Send him this, but I need it done immediately." She nods as she pulls a large envelope out of her desk drawer.

"Do you want me to enclose a note with it?"

"No, I'll call him now and explain."

When I arrive at my destination, I hand the driver a fifty-dollar note and exit the taxi. "Keep the change."

Chris's eyes widen the moment he notices me crossing the street. "Couldn't stay away?" he remarks, smirking as I approach. Watching me lose my nuts over a woman is obviously amusing to him.

"Four eyes are better than two, fucker," I retort, passing him and entering the studio. I shake my head when I hear him chuckle. He's seeing a side of me that even I don't recognise. This woman has me tied up in knots.

All eyes are on me when I enter the reception area. "Can I help you?" the young girl behind the desk asks.

"Hi. I'm here for Brooke."

"Brooke Johnston?"

"Yes," I say, inwardly cringing at the use of her last name. She needs to divorce Jake, or at the very least change her surname.

"She's in the middle of a class, but if you'd like to take a seat, I'll let her know you're here."

"Thank you."

I turn my head towards the line of seats along the far wall. There are at least a dozen sets of eyes on me as I walk in that direction. It seems like I'm the main attraction for the assembled dance mums. Surely, I'm not the first man to ever enter these premises.

Loosening my tie, I take a seat. When loud music starts playing in one of the other rooms, I feel it vibrating through the floorboards. There's a large viewing window opposite me, and I see the dancers scramble to get into place. Brooke walks into the frame, and my heartbeat instantly accelerates. She's so goddamn beautiful. She's dressed in a black leotard and peach-coloured stockings, with a sheer, flowing skirt hanging from her waist. Her hair is pulled back into a tight bun, and she looks every bit the professional dancer that she is.

She stops in the centre of the window, facing towards me. She's looking in my direction, but her face is void of emotion. Is she upset that I'm here?

Raising my hand, I give her a small wave, and the two ladies beside me giggle. My head snaps in their direction. I'm about to ask them what's so funny when one of them speaks. "It's a two-way mirror. We can see in, but they can't see out."

"Right," I say, running my hand through my hair. I feel like a fool. Thank christ Chris is still outside and didn't see me do that. I would've never lived it down.

Clearing my throat, I settle back into the chair and cross my arms over my chest while I wait. I'm going to sit here and not move until she's done.

I find myself smiling as I watch Brooke. Her movements are so graceful; she looks like she's swept away in the music. I've noticed her face light up whenever she talks about dancing, and I can see firsthand why. There is no denying her talent.

I don't dance. I even hid away in the bathroom for close to an hour at my sister's wedding reception, just so I didn't have to participate in the bridle waltz. If someone had told me a few weeks ago that I'd be sitting in a dance studio in the middle of a workday, I would've laughed. But fuck me, I could happily sit here all day and watch her.

Chapter 23

Brooke

When the class is finished, I say goodbye to my girls and gather all my stuff. I've only missed a few days, but it feels so good to be back.

"Psst, Brooke." I turn around to see Laura, the receptionist, coming towards me. "There's a guy out there wanting to see you," she whispers, pointing her thumb over her shoulder.

"A guy?" My heart drops. Please don't tell me Jake has shown up here. "Did he give you a name?" I haven't mentioned anything about what's going on in my personal life, not even to Ellen, the owner of the studio.

"Crap, I forgot to ask."

"What does he look like?"

"He looks like my future husband," she says, placing her hand on her chest and swaying on her feet. "Talk about hot. He made all my lady parts tingle."

"Oh my god," I reply, playfully slapping her arm. There's only one man I know who could evoke that kind of reaction. "Dark hair, green eyes?"

"Ah-huh. And dressed in a suit. Is he your boyfriend? If not, can you introduce me?" She holds both of her hands up in front of her in a praying motion. My first reaction is to say no, he's mine. But the truth is, he isn't. When I don't reply, she sighs, pouting her bottom lip. "You want me to send him in?"

"Sure. Thanks." The butterflies are instant. This man makes me feel way more than I'm comfortable with.

"Hey," I say when he enters the room. Shoving his hands into his trouser pockets he stalks towards me. He looks as gorgeous as ever and I can see exactly where Laura was coming from.

"Hey."

"I'm surprised to see you here. Is everything okay?"

"I was in the neighbourhood, so I thought I'd drop in and say hi."

"That's sweet of you."

"I got to watch you dance through that," he says, flicking his head towards the mirror. "You were amazing."

"Thank you." I fight a smile as I bow my head. Jake hated being dragged along to anything related to dancing. He wasn't a fan of that part of my life. "I'll just pack up, and then I'll be ready to leave."

He extends his hand to me. "Will you dance with me first?"

"But there's no music playing."

"We don't need it." Before I get a chance to respond, he pulls my body towards his. "Please?"

I'm quickly learning I'm powerless when it comes to this man. He slides one of his arms around my waist, entwining our fingers together with his other hand. My body melts into his as he takes the lead. I hear him softly humming as he sweeps me away. It feels like we're the only two people in the world.

"Dancing isn't something I normally do, but for some reason, I wanted to do it with you." He shakes his head like he can't believe his own words. "I want to experience it all with you, Brooke."

I bury my face in his chest instead of replying. I want to experience so much with him as well, but I can't bring myself to say it. I'm still fighting these feelings I have for him.

He gently places a finger under my chin, raising my eyes back to his. "I can understand your reluctance to jump into another relationship," he says. "It's been years since I've been in one. It seems like a lifetime ago now, but there's no denying what my ex did changed me. When it comes to matters of the heart, I've become completely guarded." I give him a sympathetic smile because I understand those words completely. "But it appears I'm losing the battle this time around."

He continues to hold me close as he stills. The pull between us is just too strong. My eyes flutter shut the moment his face inches towards mine. *He's my kryptonite.*

I pick up my phone when it chimes with a message.

> Hot Stuff: Just picking up dinner, I'll be home soon. x

When Chris dropped me off after my dance class, Logan walked me in, escorting me safely to his apartment before heading back to work.

I type my reply.

> Brooke: See you soon.

I want to add a kiss too, but I don't want to give him false hope, but I'm trying to be more open-minded.

My talk with Jill yesterday was insightful. One thing she said rang true. *'You can't judge many by the actions of a few.'* It brought my behaviour towards Logan into perspective. My judgement of him has been unfair. My track record with lawyers isn't great, but that doesn't mean they'll all screw me over. I have to try and remain focused on that.

I can't seem to settle as I pace back and forth, waiting for him to return. But the moment I hear the lift ding, I quickly seat myself on his white leather sofa and try my best to look inconspicuous.

When the doors open, I see Logan juggling two large brown paper bags, as well as his briefcase. "Let me help you with those."

He stills when I jump up and rush towards him. There's a smouldering look on his face as his eyes travel the length of my body. I see a smile tug at his lips when he gets to my bare legs.

I showered and changed into a pair of cut-off denim shorts and a light blue, long-sleeved top when I got home. It's August, and the middle of winter, but Logan's ducted air conditioning and heated floors make his penthouse warm and cosy.

I take the bags out of his hands, and as soon as I turn towards the kitchen, I hear him groan behind me. When I glance over my shoulder, I find his eyes glued to my backside. The moment I place the Chinese food on the counter, he drops his suitcase to the floor and spins me around, pulling me into his arms.

"I've been dying to do this all afternoon," he says, crashing his lips into mine. "Mm, minty."

When our mouths finally part, I smile, feeling grateful I brushed my teeth earlier.

"How was the rest of your day?"

"Busy." His hands move up to gently cup my face. "I could get used to coming home to you."

I have no reply to that. Well, not one he'd like. I've enjoyed my time here with him, but things are moving way too fast. Even if a relationship does eventually blossom between us, I'm only here until Jake is found.

When he lets me go, I busy myself unpacking the food while he puts his briefcase in his office.

"Geez, how much food did you get?" I ask when he re-enters the kitchen. It looks like he ordered the entire menu.

"I didn't know what you liked, so I got a bit of everything. You do like Chinese food, right?"

"I love it."

Leaning forward, he plants a soft kiss on my nose. "Good. I'll set the table."

"Do you want me to dish these onto plates?" I ask.

"No, just leave them in the containers." He opens a few drawers. "I'm sure Jill has a table runner here somewhere." I inwardly smile. I'm surprised he even knows what a table runner is.

"Wine?" he asks once we're seated.

"Please." Things just seem so easy with him, *but they always are in the beginning.*

"My sister called me today," he says, dishing some food onto my plate.

"That's nice."

"It's my niece's eighth birthday in a few weeks. Will you come with me? I'd love for you to meet my family."

The fork in my hand pauses midway to my mouth. "You want to introduce me to your family?"

"Of course. Why wouldn't I?"

"You barely know me."

He shrugs. "I know enough."

"Do you take all your girlfriends home to meet your parents so early in a relationship?" My words have a huge smile exploding onto his face. "What?" My eyes narrow slightly as I wait for his reply.

"You just implied that you're my girlfriend."

"No, I didn't," I shriek. "I was just speaking generally."

"I'm sorry, but you did."

"I did not!"

"You can't take it back now."

"There's nothing to take back."

"For the record, I love being your boyfriend."

"Oh my god, I'm not your girlfriend," I say, laughing.

He reaches across the table and grabs my hand, as he turns serious. "I want you to be, Brooke. I want that more than I've wanted anything in my life."

Those words both scare and excite me.

Chapter 24

Logan

I'm grinning the moment I open my eyes. Brooke is still fast asleep in my arms, her back pressed against my front. It was late when we headed to bed last night. After dinner, we moved onto the sofa, where we finished off the bottle of wine and just talked about anything and everything. I've always loved the solitude of my home, but last night I realised something: it's far more pleasant when there's someone to share it with.

My grip on her tightens as I bring my face forward to plant a soft kiss on her bare shoulder. She stirs, so I lightly nip at her earlobe before sucking it into my mouth. "Morning, beautiful."

"Good morning, Hot Stuff." My smile widens. I've known that's her pet name for me since finding it in her phone, but it's the first time she's actually said it.

She turns in my arms, brushing her lips against mine. When I walked her to her room last night, I gave her what was meant to be an innocent goodnight kiss. Respecting her wishes, I'm trying my best to slow things down, but the kiss became heated and before I knew it, I had her pinned against the wall with clothes flying everywhere.

"Will you come shopping with me today?" I tuck her hair behind her ear as I speak. "I need your help to pick out a gift for my niece."

"I haven't said I'm going to the party with you yet."

"I know, but I still have a few weeks to rectify that."

Brooke laughs.

Pushing her onto her back, I move my body over hers. I rain tiny kisses along her jawline, and down her neck. We were awake until the early hours of the morning, but I've yet to have my fill. I'm not sure I ever will with this woman. She's under my skin, and the grip she has on my heart seems to be tightening with each passing day.

My mouth travels down to her cleavage.

"I'd like to go for a run this morning," she says.

Raising my face, I make eye contact with her. "You're not safe out there alone."

"You could come with me."

"Sorry," I say, "I don't do stuff like that."

"Stuff like what? Exercise?" She screws up her pretty face as she talks. "I've seen those abs, Mr. Cavanagh. You're not fooling me." I chuckle when she pokes me in the side.

I arch one of my eyebrows. "I exercise. I got plenty last night."

"Sex? That's your only form of exercise? I call bullshit." She's so adorable when she's sassy.

"I've worked out almost every day since moving in here." Her eyes widen slightly, and I know I've reeled her in. She thinks I'm referring to sex, but I'm not. "There's a private gym in the building." When she slaps my arm, I chuckle.

"I thought you were referring to something else."

"I know," I say with humour in my voice.

"You made it sound like I was one of many. Although

I don't doubt there's a long line of women waiting to bed you. I was waiting for you to get your calendar out and allocate me to Wednesdays or something." I throw my head back and laugh. I love her wit.

"Seven days a week or nothing with you." I give her a look that would melt her panties off if she was wearing any. "And even if there was a long line, there's no one else I'd rather be with than you ... *No one else!*" I emphasise those last three words. "I'm an all-or-nothing kind of guy."

I'm speaking the truth, but it's also an attempt to reassure her. She's been burnt just like I have, so I know the uncertainty lingers. It took me years to rebuild enough trust to let people in again, and Brooke's betrayal is only recent. I hope she knows I'd never do something like that to her.

"I'm an all-or-nothing kind of girl." Although her words are spoken with confidence, the vulnerability I see in her eyes tears me up inside.

"I'm glad," I say. "That's why you're the perfect girlfriend."

"I'm not your girlfriend," she laughs. She is; she just doesn't know it yet.

"You could use the treadmill in the gym for your run."

"I guess. It's not the same as being in the fresh air, though."

My heart goes out to her, I hate that she's not free to live her life how she wants. "This will all be over soon," I say, brushing my lips against hers.

"I hope so."

Jake may have the upper hand now, but he'll slip up eventually, and we'll be right there waiting.

It was mid-morning before we finally climbed out of bed. If I had my way, I would've kept her there all day. From there, we headed down to the gym, where we stayed for an hour—Brooke is a damn machine. I don't know where she gets her energy from. She was relentless on the treadmill, just watching her was exhausting.

By the time I step into the shower, I ache all over. I think it's a combination of the weights I lifted and our marathon sex session. Not to mention, I did twice my usual number of sit-ups. I was showing off, but I know I'll be paying for that later.

While Brooke is upstairs getting ready, I call Mike and ask him to organise a car to trail us today. I emphasise discreetly; if Brooke sees it, it will only frighten her more. But I'm not taking any chances where she's concerned. The extra security will give me peace of mind during our date. She thinks we're going gift shopping for my niece, which isn't a lie, but I've also booked us a table at the revolving restaurant at the top of Sydney Tower for lunch. One of my clients took me there once, and since Brooke loves the view from my penthouse, I know she'll enjoy this one.

"You look lovely," I say when she appears at my office door.

"Thanks, so do you."

"You ready to go?" I ask, closing my laptop.

"Whenever you are."

"I just have to send a quick message."

"Okay."

I pull up Mike's number.

> Logan: We're on the move.

As we get into the lift, his reply comes through.

> Mike: The car's waiting downstairs.

"Mrs. Johnston," Chris says smiling, as I usher Brooke into the limousine. I give him a look as I pass. I need to do something about changing her damn name. "Mr. Cavanagh."

"Chris," I reply with a nod. "Can you take us to Pitt Street Mall?"

"No problem," he replies.

I raise the privacy petition before settling back into my seat.

"So," I say, reaching for Brooke's hand. "I was going to bring this up last night, but when I saw you in those short shorts, all logical thoughts vanished from my mind." She bumps her shoulder against mine and laughs, but I'm dead serious. "Have you given any thought to changing your last name?"

"Not really," she shrugs. "Don't I need to be divorced first?"

"You need to be living in a separate residence from your spouse for twelve months before you can apply for a divorce."

"I didn't know that," she says.

"You can still change your name, though, but it needs to be done legally."

"Oh. That's something I could look into, I guess."

"I can get the paperwork for you."

"Okay," she says, a little unsure.

I pull her hand up to my mouth, placing a chaste kiss on her knuckles. "No pressure, of course. Just something to think about." As much as I want Brooke to lose Jake's last name, the decision is ultimately hers.

"Thank you. It's definitely something I should think about."

"Have you given any thought to what we can buy Lara for her birthday?"

"I've never met her, so I have no idea what she likes," she says.

"She's a typical eight-year-old girl."

She shrugs. "Maybe some jewellery? What female doesn't like jewellery?" I make a mental note of that statement. Although, apart from her watch and the small gold studs in her ears, I've never seen her wear any other jewellery. "When I was around her age, or maybe a little older, I remember my mum bought me a silver ring for my birthday. It had a small pink tourmaline gem in the centre, which is my birthstone. It was the first piece of jewellery I ever owned. I loved that ring so much." She sighs before continuing. "My mum wasn't well off, so I knew it wouldn't have much value, but I felt like the richest little girl in the world wearing it." A huge smile graces her face, and that sentence says so much about her. I love how unspoilt she is.

"Do you still have it?" I ask.

"No, I lost it years later. I was devastated."

"That's a shame," I say, squeezing her hand. "When is your birthday?"

"October eighteenth. I'll be turning twenty-six this year." Her birthday's only a few months away. I also make a mental note to write that down.

"And you?" she asks.

"I'll be thirty-three next January." We sit in silence for a while before I speak again. "What's your favourite colour?"

"Why?" she asks with a nervous laugh.

"I'm just trying to get to know you better."

I know her body inside and out after last night, but the important pieces that make her the person she is, are what interest me most. I know she's a good cook, loves to dance, and plays a mean piano, but that's about it.

"Yellow."

"Why yellow?"

"It's bright, cheery and makes me feel happy, I guess." Her answer makes me smile.

"So, I need to buy more yellow clothes if I'm going to convince you to become my girlfriend."

"It will take more than that, Mr. Cavanagh." I chuckle because I don't believe that for a second. "What's your favourite colour?"

"Red," I say without hesitation. I don't mention it's because she was wearing red the first time I met her.

When we arrive at the mall, I exit the car first, along with Chris. Our eyes are everywhere. Brooke is oblivious to the fact that the messages are still coming in on her old phone. I'm grateful I kept hold of it, but I want to shelter her from this as much as possible.

She smiles as I help her from the vehicle. I spy the car that was parked outside the Penthouse fifteen metres away. Pulling Brooke into my arms, I place a soft kiss on her forehead. "I want you to have a nice day today," I say before releasing her.

"It feels good to be out." She seems happy and relaxed, unlike me. I'm on edge.

"Can I get you something to drink?" the waitress asks after we're seated at the restaurant. I usually hate shopping, but today is different. I've enjoyed every second of my time with her. Well, not the part when she refused to let me pay for the clothes she bought.

"Your best bottle of champagne," I answer.

"Oh, champagne," Brooke says, rubbing her hands together. "What's the occasion?"

"We have a lot to celebrate." I reach for her hand across the table. "Like us becoming boyfriend and girlfriend, for one."

"I'm not your girlfriend," she says, laughing.

"I disagree."

The smile on her face is bright as she turns her head to gaze out the window. "It's beautiful from up here, isn't it?" she says.

Sydney Tower is the tallest structure in the city—over three hundred metres tall—and the rotating restaurant gives us a three-hundred-sixty-degree view of the entire city and beyond from up here.

I want to tell her it doesn't hold a candle to her beauty, but I don't. "It's even more spectacular at night. I'll have to bring you back here for dinner so you can experience it."

Her eyes move back to me, and this time her smile doesn't quite reach her eyes. I'm a man of my word. In time, she'll see I'm nothing like them.

"I've never eaten somewhere so fancy."

"Well, get used to it." I plan to do a lot of things with her, for as long as she'll let me.

"Do they have a bathroom around here?" she asks, avoiding what I just said.

"Yes." I point to the sign on the wall on the opposite side of the room.

I know she's worried I'll eventually hurt her, just like the other men in her life have, but she's not the only one with her heart on the line here.

"I'll be back," she says, removing the white napkin from her lap and placing it on the table.

The protective side of me wants to escort her, but she wouldn't like that. She's safe up here. "Okay." My eyes are on her until she disappears down the short corridor. Once she's out of sight, I pull out my phone, to update Mike.

> Logan: We've moved upstairs to the restaurant.

He replies instantly.

> Mike: My guy's downstairs at the entrance to the lift. He's eyeing everyone who enters. No sign of him yet, but I'll forward you the message that came through a few minutes ago.

I stare at the screen impatiently waiting.

> Mike: I'm watching you!

My head snaps up, and my eyes scan the room. When my phone chimes again, I read his next message.

> Mike: There's no evidence that he's actually watching. It could just be an intimidation tactic.

I'm not fooled so easily. He sent her a similar message the night I was having dinner at her place, and I don't doubt for a second that he was there. I go to type my reply, but another message comes through before I finish.

> Mike: Scrap that. He's just sent another message.

My adrenaline starts to pump.

> Mike: Are you enjoying your time at Sydney Tower? You might be laughing now, but not for long. He can't keep you by his side forever. When you least expect it, I will be waiting, BITCH! You can count on that.

I stand so fast that my chair topples over, but I ignore it as I rush towards the bathroom. "Brooke, are you in there?" I say in a raised voice, bashing on the door that leads to the ladies' room. When I don't get a reply, I enter. This isn't something I'd usually do, but under the circumstances, I'm left with no choice. My blood is coursing through my body at an alarming rate as I push through the second door. I freeze the moment I see her standing at the basin washing her hands.

"What the hell, Logan? You can't come in here!" Her face screws up in confusion, as I close the distance between us, pulling her to me. She squirms in my arms as I briefly crush her body to mine.

"Thank fuck," I whisper into her hair.

"Logan, what's going on?"

No time for that. "I'll explain later. We need to get out of here."

"But—"

"No buts, Brooke."

Wrapping my arm around her, I guide us towards the exit.

"Logan," she protests, trying to free herself.

"Please just trust me on this."

She stops resisting as we approach the lift. "Our bags are still at the table," she says when I press the down arrow.

"I'll send Chris back up to get them."

Chapter 25

Brooke

I pace back and forth in the main room of Logan's penthouse. A guy named Mike sits on the opposite side of the room watching my every move. I'm an equal mixture of nerves, concern, and pissed off. We were having the best time until everything went to shit.

After rushing me into some strange man's car, I was brought back here alone, where Mike was waiting to escort me up to the apartment. I watch him from the corner of my eye. Ugh!

I got a brief message from Logan on the way home.

> Hot Stuff: I'll explain everything when I get there. Mike will look after you until then. x

That was two hours ago.

When the lift doors finally open half an hour later, and a weary-looking Logan steps out, I don't know whether to cry or to punch him.

Rushing towards him, I wrap my arms around his waist, but the relief of knowing he's okay is short-lived as my anger takes over.

"What the hell?" I say, taking a step back and pushing on his chest. I see a smile tug at his lips, but I find no humour in this situation. None whatsoever.

When my eyes narrow, the smirk quickly drops from his face. "He was there."

"Who was where?"

"Jake. He was watching us."

"What? Did you see him?"

"No."

"Well, how do you know he was there then?"

He exhales a long breath. "Jake's been sending messages to your old phone."

"My old phone?" I'm confused.

"Mike has it," Logan says, flicking his head in the direction of the other man. "We were originally going to use it to track him, but he's been messaging you from a burner phone that's not fitted with a GPS tracker. All we've been able to find is the store where it was purchased."

"How many other messages are there?" I ask.

"Five or six."

"And they were all sent today?"

"No." He bows his head. "Over the last few days."

"And I'm only finding out now?"

He takes a step towards me. "I was trying to protect you."

"I have a right to know these things," I say, a little angrier than I anticipated. "This isn't your battle."

"Brooke." He reaches for my arm as I turn away, but I shrug out of his grip before fleeing to my room.

"Knock, knock," I say, standing in the open doorway of Logan's bedroom. He's sitting on the edge of his mattress, his head cradled in his hands. He lifts his gaze to me, and the look I see on his face hurts. "Can I come in?"

I've been sitting in my room for the past hour stewing on what happened earlier. Once I calmed down, I tried to see things from Logan's perspective. I'm not happy that he kept things from me, but I understand why he did.

"Please." A small, hopeful smile tugs on his lips as he taps the bed beside him.

"I'm sorry for overreacting," I say once I take a seat.

He slides his arm around my waist, pulling me closer. "You have nothing to apologise for. I honestly thought I was doing what was best for you, but I see now that wasn't the case. I—"

"It's okay," I say, cutting him off. "I understand why you did it."

"I'm still sorry I upset you, that was never my intention." He turns his face, planting a soft kiss on my hair.

"Did you find him?"

"No. We searched the mall and the surrounding areas for over an hour, but there was no sign of him."

I sigh. "So, nothing's changed?"

"Yes, and no."

"What do you mean by that?" I ask, drawing back to see his face.

"We're going to have to be extra careful from now on."

"I'm not giving up dancing. I've already quit my job at the restaurant, and my piano lessons are on hold for now, but I draw the line at teaching ... it's important to me."

"You won't have to give that up. We'll work something out," he says. He points to the pile of shopping bags sitting just inside the door. "Chris brought your bags up. I'll make some space in my wardrobe for your things."

"There's a wardrobe in the spare room."

"I want you in this room, with me," he says.

"Whoa. This is moving way too fast."

Logan shifts his body around until he's facing me and reaches for my hands. "Brooke, I know this is only temporary, and that you're planning on leaving once it's safe to do so. I'm not asking you to move in, but for the short time I do have you here, I want you close. I get this situation is less than ideal, but you seem happy enough being here with me, right?"

"I hate feeling like a prisoner, but you're definitely the silver lining in all of this." Plus, I do feel safer when I'm with him.

"I'm great boyfriend material."

"And I'm sure you'll make some lucky woman very happy one day," I say, trying to keep a straight face.

"Very funny. You're the only person I want to make happy."

Standing, he pulls me to my feet. "Come. I'll help you unpack your things later, right now I need a stiff drink."

"Come back to bed, Hot Stuff," I plead, holding up the covers. I thought long and hard about his offer last night, and he's right—I want to enjoy every second of this while it lasts. Once Jake's found, I'll look for another place to live, and who knows where that will leave us.

Logan stalks towards the bed as he effortlessly ties his necktie. "I'd give anything," he says, leaning down to brush his lips against mine. "And I mean *anything*, but the meeting I have this morning is important."

"You're no fun," I reply, pouting.

He chuckles as he nips at my bottom lip. "You're insatiable, you know that?" When I narrow my eyes slightly, he raises one of his hands. "I'm not complaining, trust me."

"I suppose I better think about getting up anyway. I have to leave for work soon."

Throwing back the covers, I rise from the bed naked. It's pointless wearing pyjamas, they never stay on long enough. I've only had one prior sexual partner, but I'm quickly learning my past experiences don't compare to what I have now. Logan is such a generous and selfless lover.

I can feel his eyes on me as I walk toward the en suite, so I add a little sway to my hips. I squeal when he reaches out and grabs hold of my arm, spinning me around to face him.

"I know exactly what you're doing," he says, slapping my bare arse.

"I have no idea what you're talking about," I reply, batting my eyelashes, and giving him a look of pure innocence.

"I'm not fooled for a second, you minx." He's grinning as his arm snakes around my waist, drawing me closer. I moan into his mouth when our lips connect. A minute later, he abruptly pulls out of the kiss, turning me around until my back is facing his front. "Put your hands on the wall," he commands. I do exactly as he asks because I crave his touch. His fingertips glide across my hip, before moving down between my legs. "Always wet for me," he whispers. His warm breath against my skin makes it pebble with goosebumps. He uses his knee to nudge my legs further apart. "Spread them."

I'm grinning to myself when I hear his belt unbuckle. His hand moves back between my legs, while the other grips my hip. I throw my head back and whimper when he enters me in one long, hard stroke.

"You drive me fucking wild," he groans into my ear, and just like that I'm lost in a sea of pleasure. I'll never tire of the way he makes my body feel.

Chapter 26

Logan

Steve, my agent, pulls up outside the real estate at the same time Chris and I do. He agreed to come in early to meet me.

"It's been a long time," he says, extending his hand. "A good two or three years."

"It has," I reply, wrapping my fingers around his.

"Let me open up, and we'll chat." He ushers me through the reception area and into a large office towards the rear of the building. "Take a seat." He opens the blinds, allowing the light to filter in, before joining me. "So, what can I do for you?"

"I'm after a large commercial space."

"Okay. We have a few on the books right now. Are you looking at expanding the business?"

"No, I have something else in mind."

"Expanding your portfolio?"

"Something like that," I chuckle.

"Do you have any idea what size it needs to be?"

"At least five to six thousand square metres. Preferably on the one level." He takes down notes as I speak.

"What about location?"

"Somewhere close by, but with easy access and plenty of parking."

"If we're talking in the city, that narrows it down considerably."

"Price isn't a factor," I say because it's not. I just need to make this happen. "If you have to go a little further out, that's fine, but not too far."

"I'm sure I'll be able to find something suitable."

"Great."

We both stand. "Give me until midday, and I'll get some options to you."

I extend my hand to him. "I'd appreciate it."

After Chris drops me at the office, he heads back to the penthouse. I've arranged extra security to get Brooke safely to and from work this morning. She'll probably be pissed off, but it's a necessity.

"Claire," I say when I find her waiting for me in my office. There's a stack of files in front of her.

"Hey." She eyes me as I walk around the desk, removing my jacket before taking a seat. "Someone got out of bed on the right side this morning."

"I don't know what you're talking about. I get out of bed on the right side every morning."

"You're always pleasant," she says. "But that permanent smile that's been planted on your face for the last few days is nice to see. I gather things are going well with Brooke."

"She makes me happy. Happier than I've ever felt."

"It shows." Claire has been nagging me for years to find a healthier balance between work and my personal life.

This company has always been my first priority since I took over, but I can already feel the shift. I was never in a hurry to get home in the evenings, sometimes working until late into the night, but now I can't wait for the end of the day to come, so I can go home—*to her*.

"While we're on the subject of Brooke, I need you to get forms from the deed poll, so she can legally change her name."

"Speaking of which, any news on Jake?"

"No. We had a close call on the weekend, but he managed to slip through our fingers."

"I hope they catch him soon," she says.

"Makes two of us."

I pick up my phone when it chimes.

> Brooke: Really? Four security guards?
> That's a little overkill, don't you think?
> Two of your goons rode in the back of the limousine with me, and the others followed in another car.

I chuckle to myself as I write my reply. I knew she wouldn't be impressed.

> Logan: It's my priority to keep you safe. x

I bark out a laugh at her next response.

> Brooke: When I got to the studio, the four of them surrounded me like a human shield. Way over the top! I felt ridiculous. Two of them are sitting in the reception area as I type this, and the other two are manning the door. I ended up having to tell Ellen, my boss, what's going on, which is something I didn't want to do.

To be honest, I hate this as much as she does, but until Jake's caught, I'm left with no choice.

> Logan: I know you didn't want them to know, babe, but it's probably for the best if they're aware of what's going on. What if he shows up there?

A few minutes pass before she replies.

> Brooke: I hope I don't lose my job over this.

I'm sure that won't happen, but I jot down *'Call Ellen'* on the notepad that's sitting on my desk. There's something I need to discuss with her anyway.

Standing, I grab my jacket from the back of the chair. "Rose," I say, as I walk past her desk. "I'm stepping out briefly. I won't be long."

"Okay, Mr. Cavanagh."

I have some making up to do.

I smell the delicious aroma the moment I step out of the lift. It's after six, so Jill should've left by now. It's rare for me to see her in the evenings, but I always have a cooked meal waiting for me when I get home, which I appreciate. Even though that's what I pay her for, she goes above and beyond her job description, and looks after me well.

Placing my briefcase down in the foyer, I set off in search of my girl. "You're home," Brooke says when I enter the kitchen.

"I wanted to come home hours ago, but I had a lot of work to get through." Closing the distance between us, I pull her into my arms. "I've been missing you all day."

"You're sweet." Getting up on the tips of her toes, she places her lips against mine. "I'm cooking dinner, I hope you don't mind," she says. "I gave Jill the rest of the day off."

"Does this mean you're no longer upset with me?"

"I never was. I appreciate the lengths you're going to, to keep me safe—I really do. I'm just not used to so much attention."

I find that hard to believe. She may be oblivious to it, but her beauty attracts attention wherever she goes. I saw the way strangers were looking at her the other day when we were shopping together. I was no different the first time I laid eyes on her.

I find myself grinning as I think back to that day. I was instantly besotted, and nothing has changed. I'm still completely captivated by her.

"I just don't want anything to happen to you," I say, brushing the hair back from her face. "I care about you."

I more than care about her, but I'm not about to tell her that. She's already having reservations about how fast things are moving between us. I understand her apprehension, but when your heart knows, it just knows. It's been a long time since I've felt anything close to this.

"I care about you too." Her confession makes me

smile, but I already knew that. I can feel it whenever we're intimate.

"What's for dinner?"

"I'm cooking a roast chicken and cashing in the raincheck on the dessert you missed out on when you came to my place."

"I was hoping to have you for dessert," I say, raising an eyebrow.

"Nice try, Hot Stuff, but I'm not on the menu."

I'm an expert when it comes to the law, and it's not a crime to have two desserts. "That reminds me," I say. "I have a gift for you."

"For me? What's the occasion?"

"I know things have been difficult lately, and I just wanted to brighten your day."

Reaching up, her hands cup my face. "What did I do to deserve you?" she says, brushing her lips against mine. I shove my hand into the pocket of my suit pants, pulling out a small black box. Her eyes widen when I hold it out in front of me. "What's this?"

"Your gift. Open it." Her hand slightly trembles as she takes it from me.

"Logan," she breathes the moment she flips the lid on the box.

"It's your birthstone." I bought her a four-carat pink tourmaline on a white gold band; the semi-precious gem is surrounded by tiny white diamonds. I learnt today that tourmalines come in a variety of colours, but I distinctly remember her telling me that the ring her mother bought her had a pink stone in it. "I know it will never replace the one you lost, but I wanted to buy it for you anyway." Her eyes move from the ring to me, and my heart drops when I see they're brimming with tears. "You don't like it?"

"I love it," she says. "But it's too much."

"You're worth so much more."

"You don't have to buy me things, Logan."

And that's one of the many things I love about her. "I know." Using the pad of my thumb, I brush away the stray tear that leaks from her eye. "I just wanted to see you smile."

The corners of her lips turn up. "Just being with you makes me smile." And that right there is my reward.

"I wasn't sure of your finger size, but the jeweller will resize it if need be."

"Thank you. This is the sweetest and most thoughtful gift. I'll treasure it."

Chapter 27

Brooke

"What are you doing?" Logan asks, entering the kitchen. "I woke up and you were gone."

He comes up behind me, sliding his arms around my waist and placing a soft kiss at the nape of my neck. "I'm making cupcakes for Lara's party." I'm both eager and nervous about meeting his family today.

"Really?" he says, sounding both surprised and happy. "She'll love them. Sometimes she comes over on the weekends to hang out, and I take her to the bakery not far from here. They have the best cupcakes and milkshakes."

Turning my head, I place my lips against his cheek. "That's sweet. You're a big softy, Mr. Cavanagh."

"There's nothing about me that's soft." I laugh when he nips at my earlobe. "Don't tell my sister I'm filling her kid up with sugar when she comes to visit. She'll kill me."

"Your secret is safe with me."

I can't put into words how magical the last two weeks have been. My feelings for this man grow deeper with each passing day. He's so thoughtful and attentive, always showering me with affection. If I'm honest with myself, it's the happiest I've felt in my life. Instead of looking forward to moving back into my own place when things settle down, I'm now finding myself dreading the thought of leaving here. I'm enjoying playing house with him.

There's been no word from Jake—nothing whatsoever. I'm hoping he was spooked by almost being caught, but Logan is leaning more toward the calm before the storm. I pray that's not the case.

When the timer goes off, I grab both trays from the oven, placing them on the counter to cool. "Can I try one?"

"No." I slap his hand when he reaches over. "You'll get to try them at the party."

"Are you serious? You're not going to let me have one?"

"Nope," I say, fighting a smile.

"Wow. Your ugly side is coming out now."

"What?" I swing around, facing him.

"Who knew I was shacking up with the cupcake Nazi?"

"That's a bit harsh," I shriek, slapping his chest.

"If the shoe fits, my love. You remind me of the *Soup Nazi* from Seinfeld. No cupcakes for you!" He even tries to mimic the guy's accent with his last sentence, making me laugh.

I lunge at him, but he's too quick and manages to sidestep me. Before I know what's happening, he captures me around the waist and throws me over his shoulder. I squeal when he brings his hand down hard on my arse.

"Someone needs to be punished," he says, heading in the direction of our bedroom.

"I made a few cupcakes for you, Chris," I say, taking the small container from Logan, and passing it over the seat.

He smiles at me through the rear-view mirror. "That was really nice of you. Thank you."

"You're welcome."

"Hey! How come he gets to try a cupcake before me?"

"You'll have plenty to eat at the party," I say. "Stop being a baby."

I hear Chris chuckle from the front seat. "Me, a baby?" he scoffs. "I wasn't the one crying out half an hour ago."

"Oh my god," I mouth as I pinch his leg, which only makes him laugh. I can't believe he just said that in front of Chris.

Leaning closer, Logan whispers in my ear. "Seeing you blush like that turns me on." So, I pinch him again.

I'm a bundle of nerves by the time we arrive at Logan's sister's house. I see the car that's been following us for the past few weeks pull up behind the limousine when I exit the vehicle. Security's still tight, and for the most part, I don't notice them. I hate that this is what's become of my life. Will things ever go back to the way they used to be?

I push those thoughts to the back of my mind. I don't want Jake spoiling today for me.

"What if your family hates me?" I ask, coming to stand beside Logan on the sidewalk.

"Not possible. They'll love you."

"How can you be so sure?"

"Trust me, you're very loveable."

"You're biased," I say, nudging him with my shoulder.

Leaning forward he places a chaste kiss on my lips.

"When it comes to you, I am. But I'm also telling the truth."

"Do I look okay?" I'm wearing a white sundress I bought on my shopping expedition with Logan.

"You look good enough to eat." He has a one-track mind, but I'm okay with that.

Logan is carrying the two large containers that hold the cupcakes, as well as Lara's present which is balancing on top. "Let me carry something?"

"I've got them."

"Always the gentleman, Mr. Cavanagh."

"You better believe it, Miss Ryan," he says, winking. He calls me that often now that I've finally gone back to my maiden name. It feels nice to be Brooke Ryan again.

Logan holds his elbow out to the side, so I link my arm through it as we walk up the long path toward the front door. My eyes take in the expansive mansion before us. His entire family must be rich.

"Grab the handle for me, babe?" he asks when we reach the door.

We only make it into the foyer before a young girl comes barrelling down the long hallway. "Uncle Logan," she squeals.

He places what he's holding on the hall table, before crouching down and opening his arms wide.

"Happy birthday, Princess," he says, capturing her as he stands to full height and swings her around. It's a beautiful sight. He places her back down before introducing me. "Lara, this is Brooke. She made you chocolate cupcakes."

"Happy birthday, Lara." I hold out my hand to her, but she wraps her small arms around my waist instead.

"Thank you for making cupcakes."

"You're very welcome." My eyes dart to Logan, and he smiles as he watches us.

Stepping back, she looks up at me. "You're pretty," she says.

"Isn't she," Logan agrees.

Her attention moves back to him. "Did you get me a present?"

"I sure did," he says, chuckling.

Seeing them together melts my heart. I not only see, but feel, the bond they share. Logan ended up getting her a gold necklace with a heart pendant and matching earrings. He also put some money in a card.

"Thank you," she says when he passes her the gift bag. Turning, she starts running down the hallway from where she came. "Mum, Uncle Logan is here, and he brought his girlfriend."

He looks at me and the smile on his face grows. "You told her to say that, didn't you?"

"Nope." He draws a cross over his heart with his finger. "That's two to one. I believe you're outvoted."

"I'm not your girlfriend," I say as he entwines his fingers through mine.

"I disagree."

We find his mother and sister in the kitchen, busily preparing food. When they look up from what they're doing, I see the same piercing green eyes as Logan, but their hair is fairer.

"My boy," his mum says, making a beeline for him. She cups his face in her hands, before kissing both his cheeks. "You haven't been around to the house in weeks, I've missed you."

"I've been busy."

"Too busy to see your mother?"

Her eyes dart to me. "This is Brooke, my girlfriend,"

Logan says, stepping aside, and bringing me into full view. His mother and sister share a brief look.

When her attention comes back to me, she throws her hands in the air. "Do you know how long I've waited for this day?" She wraps me in her arms, before drawing back to scan my face. "Look how pretty you are."

"Mum, stop it," Logan's sister chimes in. "You're going to scare her off."

"Well, she is—just look at her."

Logan's sister gently shoves their mum to the side, extending her hand to me. "I'm Michelle. It's lovely to meet you."

"It's lovely to meet you too."

"She made cupcakes," Logan says, holding up the containers.

"You cook too?" His mum clasps her hands together. "Did you hear that, Michelle? She cooks as well? She's a keeper."

"Mum," Michelle screeches, and we all laugh. "Excuse her. She's not normally like this. I think she's just a little overwhelmed."

"I'm happy, that's all," his mum says, coming to her own defence. I think she's cute. I like her already.

"Hey, sis." Logan steps forward and kisses the top of his sister's head.

"Hey, bro." I feel a twinge of envy when she wraps her arms around him. I pined for a sibling growing up.

"Can I give you a hand with anything?" I ask.

"Yes, come." Logan's mum grabs my arm, pulling me further into the kitchen. "It will give us some time to get to know each other."

I glance at Logan over my shoulder. "You okay?" he mouths, and he smiles when I nod. "I'll go out back and see if Craig needs my help."

Logan's mum hands me an apron. "Here, put this on. You don't want to spoil your lovely dress." She runs her hand affectionately down my arm, which I find really sweet. "Look how pretty her dress is, Michelle."

"Mum!"

"Okay. I'm sorry." Her eyes move back to me. "Forgive me if I seem a little forward. I'm just thrilled you're here."

"I swear to god, Mum, if you mention marriage or grandchildren to her, I'm putting you in a taxi and sending you home."

"Michelle," she gasps, placing her hand on her chest. "I'd never." I bite my lip to suppress my smile when Michelle looks at me and rolls her eyes. Pulling the apron over my head, I tie it in the back. "Can I get you a glass of wine, sweetie?"

"That would be lovely, Mrs. Cavanagh, thank you." I was worried for nothing; his family is amazing.

"Please call me Patricia ... or Mum if you like."

"That's it, I'm cutting you off," Michelle says, reaching for her mother's wine glass. I can't help but laugh.

Chapter 28

Logan

"There's my girl." I place down my beer and give Brooke my undivided attention as she makes her way towards us. I can understand my family's shock at me bringing her today; they've been pressuring me to find someone and settle down for years. "You okay, babe?" I ask, draping my arm over her shoulders.

"I'm great." She looks happy. I love having her here.

"This is my brother-in-law, Craig."

"Nice to meet you." She extends her hand to him. "Thank you for having me here today."

"Oh, beautiful *and* well-mannered," he says, winking at her and bringing her hand towards his mouth. It immediately gets my back up. I know he's goading me, and he succeeds. *Arsehole*. Jealousy is something new for me. Even when my ex cheated on me with my best friend, what I felt was more hurt, betrayal, and anger. But right now, the green-eyed monster is rearing its ugly head. Everything is different with this woman. I guess it's because she means the world to me.

"You can let her hand go now," I snap, and Craig throws back his head and laughs.

"Wow, this one's got you good."

"Fuck off," I grumble, even though his words ring true. He's still laughing as he leaves us, heading towards the house.

"Your family is really nice."

"I told you they'd love you."

"I snuck this for you," she says, producing a cupcake from behind her back. "What kind of girlfriend would I be if I continued to deny you?"

"So, you are finally admitting it?" The smile on my face speaks volumes.

"Well, only because I was outvoted." I brush my lips against hers. I couldn't be happier if I tried.

"You're the best girlfriend a guy could ask for," I say, before taking a huge bite out of my cupcake.

"Do they taste okay?"

"Almost as delicious as you." Because nothing in this world tastes as good as she does.

I eye John as he steps out onto the back patio. I'm excited for Brooke to meet him. Although he's only my uncle through marriage, I love him like a father. He's the complete opposite to my old man, who can be a ruthless bastard at times. I've turned to John for advice on many occasions throughout my life. He gets me because he's married to my father's sister. Those two are like peas in a pod. Actually, my aunt is a lot worse, which says so much. Never in my life have I met such a selfish, materialistic, nasty, cold-hearted bitch as her.

"Come. There's someone I want you to meet."

"I wouldn't believe it if I didn't see it with my own eyes," John jokes as he approaches us. I'm guessing my mum has already filled him in on my girlfriend status.

"It's good to see you," I say, pulling him in for a hug.

"You too, kiddo," he replies, patting my back. He's

called me kiddo since I was a young boy, and many times throughout my life, I wished I was his kid. Not taking anything away from my mother, of course; she's always been wonderful, but my father not so much. I don't know if it's because I'm his son, but he was always a lot harder on me than he was on my sister.

I slide my arm around Brooke's waist, pulling her into my side. "John, I'd like you to meet Brooke."

The smile on his face is huge as his eyes move to her. But before he speaks, he stumbles back a few steps as all the colour drains from his face. When he clutches his chest, my heart drops into the pit of my stomach.

I remove my arm from Brooke, reaching for him. "Jesus, are you okay?"

"I'm fine," he says, placing his hand on my shoulder to maintain his balance.

"Come, sit." I walk him back into the house.

"John," my mum says, the moment she notices me helping him through the door. "What happened?"

"I don't know," I reply. "He had a turn out back."

"Are you unwell?"

"I'm fine, stop fussing."

He's not fine. Enough is enough. The way my aunt treats him infuriates me, and the constant stress she puts him through can't be good for his health. It's time she set him free. I want him to find happiness in his life, while he's still young enough to enjoy it.

I can't stop grinning as I watch Brooke. She's totally enthralled by the magician as he performs for Lara and her little friends. "Are you having a good time?" I ask, reaching for her hand.

"The best." Her eyes move to me briefly, before focusing back on the magic show. "I never had parties growing up, so I'm living vicariously through your niece."

"You've never had a birthday party?"

"Nope. I knew my mum couldn't afford it, so I always told her I didn't want one." That both warms and breaks my heart all at once. Things will be different for her from now on, I'll make sure of it.

Leaning forward, I place a kiss on the side of Brooke's head. "I'm just going to grab another beer," I say. "Can I get you anything?"

"I'm good," she replies, her eyes never once leaving the magician. *He's not bad, but I've seen better.*

"So, you two are pretty serious," Craig says, joining me at the fridge.

"Want one?" I ask, holding up a beer.

"Sure. But you didn't answer my question."

"Yeah ... yeah, we are."

"Where did you meet her?"

"I met her in Melbourne late last year."

"You've been seeing her that long, and we're only finding out about it now? You better keep that information from your mother." His words make me chuckle.

"I've only been dating her for a month."

"You seem pretty smitten."

"I think I'm in love with her," I admit.

"Wow. Have you told her that yet?"

"No."

"Why not?"

"I don't want to scare her off."

"She feels the exact same about you."

"How do you know that?" I ask, frowning.

"I can see it. She looks at you the same way your sister looks at me."

"You think?"

"I'd put money on it," he says, slapping my back as he walks away.

"I'm not ready to go home," Brooke says, as we settle into the back of the limousine. I love that she referred to my penthouse as home. Hopefully one day it will be her home permanently. I can't even contemplate the thought of her leaving, which I know is on the horizon. I just want to hold her tight and never let go, but with each passing day, I feel her slipping through my fingers.

"There will be other parties."

"And dinner at your parents during the week," she says. Now, that I'm not looking forward to. I inwardly cringed when my mother insisted we join them for dinner Wednesday night. I know Brooke thinks the world of my mum and sister, but she's in for a rude shock when she meets my father. "How come your dad wasn't there today?"

The same reason my aunt didn't show up. "He hates children."

"What?" she says as her head snaps in my direction.

"True story. He eats them for breakfast."

"He does not," she says, slapping my chest.

"Okay, maybe that was a slight exaggeration. He loves Lara—she's his only grandchild—but he can only handle her in small doses. He was the same with Michelle and me growing up, probably worse. He's mellowed with age, but I think it's only fair to warn you, he pales in comparison to my mother. What you saw today was the best of my family. My father and my aunt are the worst."

"Is that John's wife?"

"Yes, my father's sister."

"I didn't see him before we left. I hope he's feeling better."

"I think my mum dropped him home earlier."

"So, your aunt, she didn't come today because …?"

"Probably the same reason as my dad. My sister and I were scared shitless of them both growing up, especially my aunt. Our nickname for her was the Wicked Witch of the West. My dad has his rare moments, but basically, he's just a prick."

"That's an awful thing to say about your father," she says.

"It's true. He wasn't as bad with my sister, but he was pretty mean to me growing up."

"Aww, you poor thing," she says, placing her hand on my leg. "Is he like that with your mother too?"

"No, he's great with her. He worships the ground she walks on, which I'm thankful for."

"Me too. Your mum is really nice."

"Yeah, she is."

Letting out a contented sigh, Brooke rests her head on my shoulder and closes her eyes. She's had a big day.

When I feel my phone vibrating in my pocket, I pull it out.

> Mike: This just came through … Having fun playing happy family, you fucking WHORE?! I wish I'd snapped your neck the day you left me. When I get my hands on you, I'll rectify that. You won't be able to walk away this time because you'll be DEAD!

Bile rises in the back of my throat as I place my phone face down on the seat beside me. Glancing at Brooke I see her eyes are still closed. I promised to keep her in the loop, and up until now I've done just that. But I'm not sure if I want her to see this one. I rest my head back into the seat, exhaling a long-drawn-out breath.

"Are you okay, Hot Stuff?" she asks.

"I'm fine, babe."

Chapter 29

Brooke

"It's such a beautiful day out today," I say, resting my forearms on the railing of the balcony off Logan's bedroom. "Far too glorious to be cooped up inside."

We're not long out of bed, deciding to have our coffees out here this morning. The low rising sun is reflecting off the harbour, giving it a golden hue. He is so lucky to wake up to this view every day.

Reaching forward, he grasps my hips, pulling me back onto his lap. "I wish I could take you somewhere, even for a walk along the harbour-front, but it's just too dangerous."

"There's been no activity from Jake in weeks. He's probably given up by now." Logan scrubs his hand over his face, he's been on edge all week. Is my situation getting too much for him? "Is there something you're not telling me?"

He blows out a long breath. "You really want to go somewhere?" It doesn't go unnoticed that he avoided answering my question.

"Yes, more than anything. I hate that Jake is ruling our lives."

He lifts me off his lap and stands. "Go shower. I have an idea."

An hour later we're standing on the rooftop of his building. He's holding a large cooler bag laden with goodies, compliments of Jill, but it's obvious we won't be having our picnic up here.

I hear it before I see it, and my heart starts to race. "We're going on a helicopter ride?"

"You deserve to have a day where you're not constantly looking over your shoulder. We both do," he says, pulling my body into his.

"You're too good to me." But my words are drowned out by the noise of the helicopter hovering above us, preparing to land.

Once Logan helps strap me in, he places headphones over my ears and points to the small microphone attached. "We can communicate through these." After slipping his own on, he reaches for my hand. "You're shaking," he says.

"I'm excited."

"Have you ever been in a helicopter before?"

"Never."

He gives my hand a squeeze. "I love how unspoilt you are."

My eyes move to the window as soon as we start to rise. When I fled Melbourne, I was in no state to enjoy my first time in the air. I plan on making up for that today. "The boats look so tiny," I say, as we fly over Sydney harbour, heading north.

I spend the entire flight oohing and aahing as I take in all the spectacular scenery below. I can't believe how different everything looks from up here. On the odd occasion when I glance over my shoulder, I find Logan grinning as he watches me. He seems more interested in me than the view. Given his extravagant lifestyle, he's probably flown in a helicopter countless times.

The trip takes just under an hour. When we finally land on a vast patch of land, I can't see any houses or roads anywhere.

"How was that?" Logan asks, sliding his hands under my arms and lifting me down.

"Amazing! How did you organise this in such a small amount of time?"

"I have connections," he says, shrugging. *Of course, he does.*

"If you head that way," the pilot says, pointing towards a line of trees, "you'll find a track that will lead you to your final destination."

"Thank you."

"I'll pick you up in this spot in four hours."

"Perfect," Logan says, shaking his hand.

"Smell that fresh air," I say, as he entwines his fingers through mine.

"Today I don't want to think about anything but us." He pulls our conjoined hands towards his face, placing a kiss on my knuckles.

When we reach the end of the long trail and step out from between the trees, I pause, taking in the white sand and crystal-clear water before me. This hidden gem is spectacular. "Wow!"

"Our own private beach for the day," he says, beaming. "You like?"

"I love it here ... *I love it so much.*"

Logan turns to face me and places the cooler bag on the sand before sliding his arms around my waist, tugging me to him. His expression turns serious as he brushes a strand of wayward hair from my forehead.

"I doubt you love it as much as I love you."

"You love me?" I can hear the shock in my voice as I speak. That's the last thing I expected him to say.

"With every fibre of my being ... more than I've loved anybody or anything in my life?" When I stand there stunned at his confession, he pulls my face into his chest, holding me tight. "You don't have to say it back. I just wanted you to know how much you mean to me. I know we haven't been together that long, and you may even think I'm crazy for saying it so soon, but I can't help how my heart feels."

Tilting my head back, I look up at him. "I don't think you're crazy." It's probably not the reply he was hoping for, but I don't know what else to say.

"When I'm with you, I'm the happiest I've ever felt, and when we're apart, you're all I think about." The corners of his mouth turn up into a smile as he speaks. "If I'm being honest, I think you stole a piece of my heart all those months ago back in Melbourne, but you belonged to somebody else then, so there was nothing I could do about it."

"Oh, Hot Stuff."

Reaching up, I run my hand tenderly down the side of his face. In my heart, I know I love him too, but I'm not ready to admit that just yet. Pushing up on the tips of my toes, I place my lips against his.

"If I'd known what awaited you the day you left the hospital, I never would've let you face that alone."

"Let's not talk about that today."

"You're right," he says, looking down at his watch. "We have three hours and forty-two minutes left until the helicopter comes back." He takes hold of my hand, leading me further down the beach. "What do you think of this spot?"

"It's perfect." *Just like him.*

He places the bag down and unzips it. I see there's a folded blanket sitting on top. Pulling it out, he shakes it open. "Help me spread this out."

I'm smiling as I reach for it. I hope he knows how much he means to me.

I open my mouth and take a bite of the plump red strawberry as Logan holds it out to me. Today has exceeded all my expectations.

"We should've brought our swimwear," I say. "The turquoise water looks so inviting."

"Who needs swimwear?"

Standing, he reaches behind him, grabs the neckline of his t-shirt and pulls it over his head before dropping it down on the blanket. My eyes drink him in. His shorts sit low on his hips, revealing his delicious 'V'. My gaze travels up his body and over his sculpted abs. He's so beautiful.

My eyes widen when he pops the button on his shorts, before slowly dragging down the zip. "What are you doing?" I ask.

"Going for a swim," he replies, hooking his thumbs into the waistband of his boxer briefs and sliding them down his legs.

"Logan!" My head darts around, as he stands there in all his naked glory.

"Relax. It's a private beach—just the two of us here. It's only accessible by air." He extends his hand. "Join me."

"You want me to strip naked too?"

A growl permeates in the back of his throat. "You know having you naked is one of my favourite things."

"I've never skinny-dipped before," I confess as he pulls me to my feet.

"Well, let me be the first to take you to the dark side." I laugh when he wiggles his eyebrows. "We've still got over an hour before the helicopter returns." I stand there for a moment, contemplating the idea. "Come on. You know I'd never let you get naked if there was a chance anyone else could see you. Your body, Miss Ryan, is for my eyes only."

I'm smiling as I gather my sun dress in my hands, before pulling it over my head.

"Do you have any idea how sexy you are?" He pulls my body possessively into his as he speaks, and I feel him hardening against my abdomen.

Our eyes are locked as he uses his fingers to unclasp my bra, before moving to my underwear and dragging them down my legs. As soon as I step out of them, I turn and take off towards the ocean. "Last one in the water is a rotten egg," I call out over my shoulder.

"Hey!" He's yet to see my competitive side, so when I hear him running behind me, I pick up the pace. I'm grinning like a fool as I sprint into the ocean. I feel his hand swat my arse just as I dive in.

"You tricked me," he says as my head pops out of the water.

"Is someone upset that he's the rotten egg?"

I squeal when he lunges at me, tackling me back down under. We're both laughing when we resurface. "You don't play fair."

"All's fair in love and war, Mr. Cavanagh." My bottom lip is trapped between my teeth as I wrap my legs around his waist.

"I'd rather love you than be at war with you," he replies, bringing his mouth to mine.

When we finally come up for air, I smooth my hand over his wet hair. "I've had the best day. Thank you for bringing me here."

"Your day's about to get even better," he says as his hand moves between us. "We can make water babies."

I gasp. "No babies!"

"Relax, I'm joking," he says, chuckling as he skilfully rubs my clit. "I'll pull out, I promise." I tilt my head back and moan when he moves his fingers lower, sliding two deep inside me. "I can't seem to get enough of you, Miss Ryan."

I know exactly where he's coming from. He's like my drug, and I'm slowly becoming addicted.

It doesn't take him long to drag my first orgasm from me, he knows exactly how to work my body. My fingernails dig into his flesh and I tremble with anticipation, as he removes his fingers and slowly enters me. I'm too lost in the moment to even worry about the fact we're having unprotected sex out in the open. If I'm honest, there's something thrilling about it.

Logan draws back his hips before thrusting all the way in, filling me completely. His tongue runs along the length of my neck, from the base of my throat to my chin. "One day I'm going to see my baby growing inside you," he growls.

I'm still floating from yesterday and because of that, I'm completely unperturbed as one of the security guards escorts me into the lift and back up to the penthouse after my day at the studio. These men have become a permanent fixture in my life.

Pulling out my phone, I type Logan a quick text.

> Brooke: I'm home safe and sound. x

His reply comes through within seconds.

> Hot Stuff: I'm happy to hear that. You've been on my mind all afternoon.

I smile as I read what he's written.

> Brooke: I'm looking forward to seeing you tonight.

The bond we've formed in such a short time is crazy.

> Hot Stuff: Me too, babe. x

He told me he loved me again this morning before he left for work, but I still couldn't find the courage to say it back. Hopefully, when he gets home this evening, the opportunity will arise. I know we haven't been together that long, and there's a part of me that's still terrified by the depths of my feelings for him, not to mention the pace at which they have grown. But I can't deny what Logan and I share runs far deeper than anything I felt for Jake in the five years we were together.

Things with my husband were different, I can see that now. When you're on the outside looking in, the clarity becomes clearer. Things weren't all bad, we had plenty of good times, but he was at his happiest when he was getting his own way. It's taken nine long months of soul-searching to come to the conclusion that I only stayed as long as I did because he was all I had left.

He came into my life when I needed him most, I'd just lost my mum and was all alone. But looking back now, I was the one who put the majority of the work into our relationship, constantly sacrificing my own needs to please him. Jake was selfish, and his wants always rose above others. Logan, on the other hand, goes out of his way to do things just to see me smile.

After changing out of my dance gear and showering, I put on my denim cut-off shorts, the ones Logan seems to love so much. Just thinking about him has my stomach fluttering with nervous anticipation. The feelings he evokes in me are so foreign.

I'm downstairs in the main room, flipping through the channels on the TV, awaiting his return. Jill has already left for the day, so he should be home soon.

A few minutes later the lift dings, and I scramble off the sofa. I only make it halfway across the room when John, Logan's uncle, steps out. He was the last person I was expecting to see, and I can't help the disappointment that rises within.

"Hi."

He pauses the moment he sees me. "Brooke, I wasn't expecting you to be here."

"I'm staying with Logan for a while," I say, not bothering to elaborate further.

I'm just getting to know his family, and it concerns me that my current situation may cause them to see me in a different light.

"Oh, I didn't know that." He gives me a pleasant smile that doesn't seem judgmental. I know from the outside looking in, it would seem weird because we haven't known each other long, but this arrangement is only temporary.

"Logan isn't home yet, but you're more than welcome to wait. He should be here soon."

"I'd like that, thank you. It will give me time to get to know you better."

"Logan was concerned for you at Lara's party; I hope you're feeling better."

"Yes, and no," he says, shrugging.

"Can I get you a drink?"

"Please. Something strong if you have it."

"It's been one of those days, has it?" I ask.

"You could say that."

"Sit," I say, walking towards Logan's bar. "Is scotch okay?"

"Perfect."

"Ice?"

"Please." I've noticed that's how Logan likes his scotch. "Thank you," he says when I hand it to him before taking a seat. "You're not joining me?"

"No. I'll have a wine with dinner when Logan gets home."

"Fair enough."

There's a slight shake to his hands as he brings his drink to his mouth, downing the amber liquid in one gulp. I barely know this man, so I'm not sure if that's a common occurrence. Logan did mention that his wife isn't the nicest person, which immediately makes my heart go out to him. My eyes scan over his handsome face. He looks like a kind man, and I trust Logan's judgement.

After a brief awkward silence, he finally speaks. "So, I'm curious, how did you two meet?"

"I met Logan last year when he was down in Melbourne."

"You've known him that long?"

"Our first meeting was only a brief one," I say, leaning back on the sofa. "I ran into him again weeks ago and things kind of progressed from there."

"You're originally from Melbourne?"

"No, Sydney. I moved to Melbourne for a few months, but it ended up not being for me."

"What about your family, are they still in Sydney?"

"Umm ... no."

"Oh."

Placing his empty glass on the coffee table, he crosses one leg over the other, resting his ankle on his knee. The curious look on his face as he observes me is unnerving.

"What do they do for a living, your parents, I mean?"

"I don't see the relevance."

Maybe it's my paranoia, but I feel like I'm being grilled. Or possibly it's because I'm worried my answers won't be enough for him. Will he think I'm not good enough for his nephew?

"I'm sorry," he says, leaning forward. "I hope you don't think I'm overstepping the line. I can see how much you mean to Logan, and I was just hoping to get to know you better. That boy is like a son to me."

"Can I get you another drink?" I ask, trying to steer him away from this conversation.

"Please." Standing, I collect his glass.

"Where in Sydney did you grow up?"

"Surry Hills."

"Oh, not that far from here."

"No."

"And your family, were they originally from that area?"

Again with the questions about my family. There's no denying we're from two different worlds, but just because my mother didn't have a lot of money doesn't make her—or me, for that matter—a bad person.

"No, my mother grew up in Strathfield."

"And your father?"

I hand him his drink before taking a seat. "I have no idea where my father grew up." His eyes slightly widen at my answer, and I can't help but feel like I'm being judged. It's not the first time in my life I've felt this way. Even when I was young, kids at school often teased me for not having a dad. I hated the way it made me feel back then, and nothing's changed. "I was raised by my mother, but everything she did more than made up for only having one parent. She worked hard her entire life and did the best she could with what little we had."

"I'm sorry to hear that."

His shoulders slump as his gaze moves down to the polished floor, and my temper rises a little. I shouldn't have to justify my upbringing to anyone.

When his gaze moves back to me, I can see the pity in his eyes. "I grew up in humble conditions," I say, straightening my spine. "But if you think I'm here to get my hands on your nephew's fortune, then you're mistaken. I'm not—and never will be—interested in his money."

"Please, you have me all wrong." He holds his hand up in front of him as he speaks. "I just wanted to clarify a few things before saying something that's completely off the mark. How old are you, Brooke?"

"Twenty-five. I'll be turning twenty-six next month. Why?"

He pauses for a moment. "What's your last name?"

"Ryan."

"I knew it," he whispers under his breath. "Is your mother's name Maree?"

"Yes," I say, with surprise in my voice. "How did you know that?"

"Your mother never mentioned me to you?"

"No. Why would she? Did you know her?"

He stands and digs into his back pocket to retrieve his

wallet before closing the distance between us. "You're probably going to think this is crazy, but maybe showing you this will help explain."

An uneasiness settles over me as he opens his wallet and pulls out a tattered photograph. The moment he holds it out in front of me, I clamber backwards on the sofa.

"Why do you have a picture of her in your wallet?"

"I've carried that picture around for over twenty-seven years. When I saw you on Saturday, I knew straight away who you were. You look so much like her."

"Knew what?" Although I asked the question, I immediately cover my ears because I don't want to hear his answer.

"Does the name Johnathan Sanders mean anything to you?"

He sits down beside me so I retreat a little further. Johnathan Edward Sanders is a name that has haunted me for many years. It's also listed under *Father* on my birth certificate. My head starts to spin as all the pieces suddenly fall into place. John is short for Johnathan—it can't be. *Oh god, I think I'm going to be sick.*

I leap to my feet. "You should leave."

"Brooke, please."

"Just go!"

"Let me explain."

"There's nothing to explain," I scream as the tears start to fall. "If what you're saying is true, you abandoned my mother when she needed you most. You ... you told her to abort me."

He buries his face in his hands, shaking his head from side to side, and I use that moment to make my escape. "I should've never said those things to your mother that day. I just panicked. I loved her, Brooke—I still love her. Please believe me. For years, I searched for her." Turning, I run towards the lift. I can't listen anymore. I frantically press the button. "Brooke, give me a chance to explain," are the last words I hear as the doors close behind me, separating me from that monster.

I stumble backwards until I hit the wall. Huge sobs rack my body as I slide down to the floor. *It can't be true, it just can't.*

The moment the doors open on the ground level, I scramble to my feet. "Miss Ryan," the doorman says as I pass him. "Is something wrong?" But I don't stop to answer. I need to get as far away from here as possible.

After pushing my way through the hordes of people that occupy the sidewalk, I take off at full speed. My feet are bare, but that's the least of my worries. I have no clue where I'm heading, but I already know I'll keep going until I can't go any further. This revelation changes everything.

"Are you okay?" a lady asks as I pass, but I don't stop. There's nothing anyone can do to fix this.

I turn down a side street, and I'm so lost inside my own head that I don't even notice the white van that pulls up beside me until it's too late.

Before I even realise what's happening, I'm grabbed from behind. "Got ya," I hear as a damp cloth is placed over my mouth, muffling my scream. A strong sweet smell invades my senses as I thrash around, trying to free myself. I'm dragged backwards and a hot burning feeling consumes my mouth and throat. My movements diminish as my body weakens. "Nighty night, Princess."

A feeling of dread overwhelms me when a needle pierces my skin. My legs instantly give way as everything fades to black.

Chapter 30

Logan

A nervous kind of excitement bubbles within as I step into the lift. I feel like a little kid on Christmas morning. It's insane how affected I am by this woman. I've never felt this happy or content ... nobody has the power to make me feel as exhilarated as she does. It's been about ten hours since I last saw her, but given my current state, it feels more like weeks.

I'm clutching my briefcase in one hand and the biggest bunch of yellow roses in the other. I picked them up on the way home because I love the way her face lights up whenever I give her flowers. I can't quite explain it, but it's a look I'd gladly witness over and over. It's the simple things about her that I crave most.

My whole perspective on life has changed. I no longer leave for work at the crack of dawn and come home late at night, but I need to keep reminding myself that this arrangement is only temporary. She's leaving once Jake is found, and I know when that day comes, it will more than likely crush me.

When the lift doors open to my apartment, I exit, placing my briefcase down in the foyer, freeing one of my hands. I'm itching to touch her. My eyes are everywhere as I enter the main room, but instead of seeing my girl, I find my uncle. He's sitting on the sofa with his head buried in his hands.

"John," I say.

He stands, and the devastation on his face makes me feel immediate unease. What has that bitch done to him now? "I've screwed up, kiddo. I've screwed up bad."

"What do you mean? Did something happen with Kathleen?" My eyes again move around the room. "Where's Brooke?"

"She left."

"Who, Brooke?"

"Yes."

"Left? What do you mean she left?"

He lets out a deflated breath, as his bloodshot eyes meet mine. "I came here to talk to you; I wasn't expecting her to be here. Believe me, I never meant for this to happen."

"Never meant for what to happen?" My initial worry is quickly morphing into anger.

"I told her the truth, but it didn't go so well."

"The truth, what truth?" I'm baffled. He's not making any sense.

When he doesn't answer, I instinctively reach for him, fisting his shirt in my hand. Never in my life have I shown such hostility towards this man, but my only concern is Brooke.

"What did you say to her?"

Tears fill his eyes and instead of compassion I only feel rage. "I told her I was her father." Letting him go, the flowers in my hand drop to the floor.

"What? Why would you tell her that?"

"Because it's the truth."

I'm currently in no state to wrap my head around any of this, I have tunnel vision. I need to find my girl and make sure she's okay. "Where did she go?"

"I don't know," he says. "She ran out of here in tears."

It feels like the bottom has dropped out of my world as I frantically dig into my pocket and pull out my phone. My hands are trembling as I desperately search for her number. *"Pick up, pick up,"* I chant as I wait for my call to connect.

My hopes are instantly dashed when I hear her ringtone nearby. My head darts around the room, and my heart sinks when I see her phone sitting on the coffee table. "Fuck!" Ending the call, I ring Mike. "Mike, it's Logan. Has there been any contact?"

"I'm in the middle of dinner. I can look when I'm done and call you back."

"No, I need to know now. Brooke's gone."

"What do you mean she's gone?"

"She got upset and left." My eyes narrow at my uncle. This is all his fault. "What if he has her?"

I hear Mike's chair scrape across the floor through the line. "Give me a sec, I'll go get the phone from my office." My eyes dart to my uncle, as I wait. "Are you there?"

"Yes."

"A message came through thirty minutes ago. I'm sorry I missed it."

"What does it say?" I ask.

"Bingo. All it says is Bingo."

What the fuck does that even mean? My head falls back as I pinch the bridge of my nose. "He has her, Mike; I feel it in my gut."

"Don't jump to conclusions. Have you tried contacting her?"

"Yes, but her phone's here."

"Christ. I'm on my way," he says. "Don't do anything until I get there."

Desperation sets in the moment I end the call. "If he hurts her, I'll never forgive you."

"If who hurts her?" my uncle asks.

"Her ex-husband. He wants to kill her, that's why she's been staying here."

"What? I had no idea."

I scrub my hand over my face. I can't just stand here and do nothing. "I'm going to look for her."

"Let me come with you," he says.

"No. You've done enough. If you really want to help, stay here. When Mike arrives, call me."

"Logan, I'm sorry." Ignoring him, I rush towards the hall table to get my car keys.

I dial Chris's number as I travel down to the basement. "Chris, Brooke's taken off. I'm worried Jake may have her."

"Did you two have a fight?"

"No."

"Then why would she leave?"

"Because my uncle has lost his fucking mind. I'm heading down to the basement now. I'm going to drive around and search the area."

"Do you want me to do the same?"

"Please. Try her place first and call me if you see anything."

I highly doubt she'd be there under the circumstances, but who knows. It's not like she has anywhere else to go.

The tyres screech as I hastily pull out of my car space. "Come on, come on," I scream in frustration, banging my hand down on the steering wheel as the garage door slowly rises. My mind is scrambled. As much as I pray

Jake doesn't have her, I can't rule out the possibility that he does.

Pulling out into the street, I turn right. I don't even know where to start my search, but I won't give up until she's home safe and sound.

"Where are you?" I whisper into the darkness. I feel like I'm going out of my mind as I drive around in circles. Every time I see someone with long brown hair, my hopes rise, but they're dashed the moment I realise it isn't her.

Manoeuvring the car over to the side of the road, I reach for my phone. "Anything?" I ask Chris when he answers.

He sighs. "Nothing yet, I'm afraid."

"What was she thinking? She knew he was out to get her?"

"I can't answer that," he says.

I bow my head because the truth is, I know what her feelings towards her father are, so I can only imagine how much John's words fucked her over. I bang my hand down on the steering wheel. His news would have devastated her. Why would he say something like that? It makes me furious just thinking about it.

"We just need to keep looking." My phone beeps, so I pull it away from my ear and see Mike's name on the screen. "I have an incoming call. Keep me updated."

"I will."

I press accept. "Mike."

"You need to come back here."

My heart drops the moment he says that. I'm almost

too afraid to ask why. Leaning back, my head rests against the seat. My stomach churns. Life couldn't be so cruel.

"Why?"

"We've been going over the building's security footage. We think we have something."

"What?" Holding my breath, my grip on the phone tightens as I brace myself for his answer.

"A white van. It was sitting across the street all day. The moment Brooke ran out of the building, it appeared to follow her."

"Fuck." The words from Jake's last message swim in my mind. *'You won't be able to walk away this time because you'll be DEAD!'* And then it dawns on me, I never told her about that one.

"Shit," I scream. *I should've fucking told her.*

In hindsight, I thought I was doing the right thing, but now I know better. Hindsight can go fuck itself. If I'd said something, maybe she wouldn't have fled like she did.

"We haven't been able to get a clear enough picture of the plates, but we're working on it."

"We need to call the police?"

"Not yet," he says. "I'm calling in a favour and hoping to get more footage from the CCTVs in the area."

I pinch the bridge of my nose. "I still think we should involve them."

"Logan, it's only been a few hours. She needs to be missing for twenty-four hours before they'll do anything."

"Not under these current circumstances," I snap. "The police are aware of her situation."

"Look, trust me, I know what I'm doing. If and when we need them, we'll take that route."

I let out a deflated breath. I hired him for a reason: he's the best at what he does. He's proven that to me many times over the years.

Ending the call, I look down at my home screen. It's an image of us, taken on the day we spent at the private beach. Tears cloud my eyes as my fingertip runs over her beautiful face. She looks so happy in this picture. I make her happy, that I'm sure of. She may not realise that she loves me, but in my heart, I know she does. I feel it in every kiss ... *in every touch.*

"I won't rest until I find you, my love." Because I can't fathom any other outcome.

Chapter 31

Brooke

Opening my eyes, I find the room bathed in darkness. My head is pounding and my body feels weak. My left arm is numb and tingling from laying on it. The bed's springs creak as I move, and panic sets in when I realise my hands and feet are bound.

Managing to lift myself into a sitting position, I try to remember. Where am I, and how did I get here? My memory seems clouded and I feel groggy.

My heart starts to race as everything slowly comes back. I listen for a moment, but all I hear is silence. "Help. Can anyone hear me?" I call out at the top of my voice. Am I in a house? Are people nearby? I have no clue, but I can't just sit here and do nothing. If I have any chance of getting out of here, I need to at least try.

Scooting myself to the edge of the bed, I swing my legs over the side. Just as I go to stand, the door flies open and the loud bang it makes when it hits the adjoining wall startles me. The light switches on, and I squint at the brightness. It takes a few seconds for my vision to finally adjust, and for my eyes to zero in on the tall figure that stands in the doorway.

"Well, well, well. Sleeping Beauty awakes."

"Jake."

Although this situation is less than ideal, the first thing I feel is sympathy as my eyes scan over his face. The last nine months have not been kind to him. His haggard appearance, long unkept hair, and full beard make him almost unrecognisable.

"How are you feeling?"

"How do you think I'm feeling? Did you drug me?"

I'm crippled with fear as he starts approaching. The last time I saw this man, his hands were wrapped around my throat. I scramble back.

"Don't," he says, holding his hand up to stop me, and my body freezes. I swallow hard as he sits on the edge of the bed and turns his body to face mine. I no longer know this shell of a man before me. The gleam that once shone in his beautiful blue eyes has diminished to the point they appear almost lifeless. I can hear my erratic heartbeat thumping in my ears as I await his next move. He's already kidnapped and drugged me, so I have no idea what to expect next. "I'm not going to hurt you," he whispers.

I don't believe that for one second. His eyes flicker down to my bare legs as his hand slides across the mattress, coming to rest on my upper thigh. I instantly recoil. A kaleidoscope of emotions bursts through me when my gaze meets his, and I see the sadness permeating his eyes.

"What happened to you, Jake?" I ask as a lump begins to form in my throat. Despite everything he's put me through, I can't help but feel sorrow for what has become of him.

He bows his head, and I can feel the shame radiating off him. "I fucked up. I fucked up so much—my marriage, my career, everything ..." You often hear how addiction destroys lives, but the gravity of those words hold so much more meaning to me in this situation. He raises his face back to mine. "I miss you, baby. I miss our old life together. I want things to go back to the way they used to be." I have to look away. Any feelings I had for this man died a long time ago. "Have you missed me?"

I can hear the vulnerability in his voice, but I'm not going to lie to him. At the end of the day, he's done this to himself and had no consideration for me, or my feelings when he decided to have an affair with that woman. My eyes dart back to him, and his slightly narrow as he waits for my reply.

"In the beginning, yes. You were my life once, Jake, but that's in the past. You cheated on me and tried to strangle me. I can't forgive you for that."

"I didn't mean it."

"You didn't mean to cheat on me, or strangle me?"

"Both," he says.

"How can you not mean to cheat? And please don't insult me by saying you tripped and accidently fell into your secretary's vagina."

He chuckles, but there's nothing humorous about this situation. "I forgot how funny you are ... there's so much I miss about you, Brooke."

I narrow my eyes. "Do you have any idea how much you hurt me, Jake?" And not just physically. The pain of his infidelity still stings. I gave this man everything.

"I know. I'm sorry."

"How long had it been going on when we were together?" No matter what he says, it won't change anything, but it's something I've always wondered about. Was it a one-time thing, or a full-blown relationship?

"With Jenny, or the drugs?"

"Both."

He shrugs. "Probably a few months. I can't remember exactly." I can't believe how naive I was. Looking back now, all the signs were there. His mobile phone used to lay around the house, until suddenly it was always in his possession. The late nights, his withdrawal from me, his constant snapping and the mood swings.

"You were always so against drugs."

"I was," he says, bowing his head.

"Then why?"

"I had a lunch meeting with a client one day, I was tired and stressed out and he sensed that. He slipped something into my drink and said it would take the edge off. He was right, it did. For the first time in a long time, all my worries seemed to vanish, I felt on top of the world." He sighs, shaking his head. "That's how it all started."

"If you were struggling, you should've talked to me."

"I didn't want to worry you. I wasn't coping well with my new position, and you seemed so proud of me." His eyes meet mine once more, and it hurts to see the tears in them.

"I was just being a supportive wife. I wasn't happy with the changes in you, or in our relationship. I was miserable in Melbourne."

"I didn't even know I was hooked until it was too late. That's when the affair started." He shakes his head again. "Jenny came on to me as soon as I started working there. Please believe me when I say I wasn't interested in the slightest, but she eventually found out about the drugs and used it to blackmail me."

His reasons don't justify what he did. If he'd only reached out to me, we could've handled this together. "I trusted you, Jake. I gave up everything to move to Melbourne with you."

The grip he has on my leg tightens, and memories of our last time together flash through my mind. The force he used around my neck still makes me shudder. "We can put all that behind us. We could have a fresh start—"

"It's too late for that," I say cutting him off. "I've moved on with my life, you need to do the same."

His nostrils flare at my response, and I can tell I've poked the bear. "With him?" *Shit.* I should've lied, or at the very least said nothing. "Answer me!" he screams, pounding his fist down on the mattress. His sudden movement makes me flinch.

"Does it really matter?"

"You're my fucking wife, goddamn it. Of course it matters!" He rises from the bed, fisting his hair in his hands. "I never picked you for a cheating whore."

"How dare you accuse me of cheating! I never cheated on you. We've been separated for months."

Reaching out, he wraps his hand around my upper arm, dragging me from the bed. "Get up," he sneers, pulling me to my feet. My ankles are still bound, so I stumble. Pain shoots up the side of my lower leg as I roll my ankle trying to regain my footing. My face is just inches from his, and the murderous look in his eyes terrifies me. "You were fucking him down in Melbourne."

"No, I wasn't."

"Liar," he shouts, making me cower.

"I'm not lying, I swear." I can hear the fear in my voice when I speak. "I didn't even know him then." Just talking about Logan fills me with despair. I'd give anything to be back in his apartment right now, tucked safely in his arms.

His hand fists in my top. "Do you think I'm an idiot?

You didn't come home that night, remember? I found his card in your purse."

"I didn't come home because I was in the hospital." I can see the puzzled look in his eyes as they scan my face. "It's the truth, Jake. I was pregnant with our child."

"You're lying." When he tugs on my shirt, my heartbeat accelerates.

"I'm not. I swear I'm not." When he sees the tears that are now cascading down my face, he lets go of me, retreating back a step. "That night I had bad pains; I went outside to look for you ..." I bow my head. "That's when I saw you with your secretary." Although that's all behind me now, talking about it makes all those feelings resurface. "I collapsed. I was haemorrhaging."

"And the baby?"

A loud sob rips from the back of my throat. "I lost it." I've often thought about the what-ifs, but as my mother always said, *'Things happen for a reason.'* But those words still don't lessen the grief I feel for our child.

He steps forward and gathers me in his arms. "I'm sorry. You should've told me."

"You never gave me the chance."

"Bullshit." He grabs hold of my shoulders, drawing back. "You've had plenty of opportunities to tell me. You should've said something."

"You tried to strangle me remember?"

"And you took off. You should've stayed and talked to me."

"Right, and give you the chance to finish me off?"

Letting me go, he starts to pace back and forth. I used to feel so safe with this man, but now he terrifies me. I have no clue what to expect from him from one minute to the next. My body stiffens when he stops and faces me again.

"We could try again." He steps forward, grasping my elbow. I hate the look of hope I see in his eyes. A rational Jake would know this could never happen, but he's no longer that person. "We can have another baby. Would you like that?"

"Jake, don't do this." He's more delusional than I thought.

"Do what?"

"What we had is over. Please just let me go. You need help."

"You're my wife. You belong here with me."

I don't belong here—I belong wherever Logan is. Will I ever get the chance to see him again ... to tell him how much I love him?

"Let me go," I plead. My words sound more desperate as reality sinks in. He's not going to let me just walk out of here.

"No!" he screams. "You're *my* wife."

"I'm not your wife anymore, Jake."

His breathing becomes erratic as he stares me down. When I see that change in his eyes, the same one I saw the day he tried to strangle me, I brace myself for what's about to come.

He retreats a few steps, and for a moment I think he's going to leave, but then he opens the top drawer of a rundown old dresser that sits by the wall. I gasp when he pulls out a gun.

"I should just kill you now," he says. "If I can't have you, I'm not going to let anyone else take what's mine. Especially, that cunt. He's been sniffing around you ever since he met you. You're my wife, Brooke, not his. *My fucking wife.*"

He's wrong ... I'm no longer his. He ruined everything we once had, tossing it away like it meant nothing. We may be legally married, but that's all we have left ... a worthless piece of paper.

When Jake closes the distance between us, I intake a sharp breath. Tears fill my eyes, but I don't plead for my life. I refuse to give him the satisfaction. If this is my destiny, then so be it. These last few weeks have been my happiest, and I'm so grateful for that. My only regret is not telling Logan how I truly feel. It hurts my heart that I'll never get to see him again, but I'll cherish the short time we had together.

My gaze moves down to my bare feet. "I love you, Hot Stuff," I whisper under my breath. This may be the only time I get to utter those words.

Jake raises his hand, and I instinctively close my eyes as I await what I know is coming. But instead of the bullet I'm expecting, his fist connects with the side of my face with such force, the blow knocks me off my feet. My hands are still tied behind my back, so I can't even break my own fall. The side of my head connects hard with the metal frame of the bed. My world instantly turns black.

Chapter 32

Logan

It seems like an eternity passes before we get anything helpful on Brooke's whereabouts. I look down at my watch as Mike makes a call to get whatever information he can on the plates. It's been over two and a half hours since Brooke left the apartment.

At this stage, we aren't even sure the white van is connected with her disappearance, but it's the closest thing we have to a lead. In the CCTV footage, it definitely appears to be following her.

I read over what Mike jots down, and it instantly has my blood boiling. The van's registration is under the name of a Mr. Jake Ryan. I'm livid that he's using Brooke's last name. It also confirms my worst fear—*he has her*—and that terrifies me. Now I just have to pray that we can get to her before it's too late.

The address Mike writes down is in Redfern, which is about a fifteen-minute drive from here. He's been right under our noses the whole time. "Should we call the police now?" I ask.

"No," Mike answers. "Let's check it out first."

"I'm calling them." I pull out my phone. "I'm not waiting another second."

"Wait," he says, placing his hand on my arm. "What are they going to do? Come in with sirens blazing, storm the place? Maybe get a hostage negotiator? We all know how that usually ends."

"What's your plan? We need to act fast. So much time has been wasted already."

"I'm going to go and check the place out myself. The element of surprise always works best in situations like this one."

"And what if they're not there. They could be anywhere by now."

"Then we'll notify the police."

He turns to leave. "I'm coming with you," I state.

"Me too," my uncle adds. I'm still pissed with him, but I don't protest. We may need him.

"Suit yourself. My car is parked across the street," Mike says.

"I'll follow you in mine. I'm parked out front too."

"I'll come with you, kiddo."

I give my uncle a look but say nothing when he climbs into the passenger seat. I'll hash this out with him later. Right now, my sole focus is getting my girl back.

We're only a few minutes into our drive when my uncle speaks. "I'll never forgive myself if she's been harmed."

I raise an eyebrow as my temper rises. "That makes two of us," I say.

I hear him sigh beside me. "Please know, I didn't mean for any of this to happen. I honestly thought I'd never get the chance to meet her. I wasn't even sure if her mother went ahead with the pregnancy."

"What even makes you think you're her father?"

"Her mother, Maree, used to work for your company as an intern."

"Cavanagh and Associates?"

"Yes."

"That still doesn't prove anything."

"We had an affair; it lasted for months. They were some of the happiest times of my life," he says. "Brooke looks just like her." I've seen a photo of her mother, so I know that part is true, but again, that proves nothing. "The last time I saw Maree, she told me she was pregnant, and I panicked. You know what Kathleen's like. She would've crucified us both." He turns his face away, gazing out the passenger side window. "I told her to get rid of the baby, and I'll never forgive myself for saying those words to her."

We come to a red light, and my eyes move back to him. Could he really be her father? What are the chances? But I can't deny his story matches up perfectly with Brooke's.

He covers his face with his hands, but instead of offering any comfort, I focus back on the road. "I loved that woman more than I've ever loved anyone in my life." I have so many questions, but I can't deal with them right now.

My adrenaline is pumping as we slowly drive past the property. I'm not surprised it's a rundown house, *a fucking dump.* The white van is parked out front, and that fills me with hope. My first instinct is to smash the front door down, but as Mike said, the element of surprise is the best way to go. I don't want to do anything that may put Brooke's life in jeopardy. She's still alive—I have to believe that. My mind cannot comprehend any other scenario.

I follow Mike further down the street, where we park.

"What's the plan?" I ask, as we exit the vehicle and approach him.

"I'm going to case the joint first, then decide," he answers, popping the boot of his car and pulling out a small torch and black leather pouch. He shoves the pouch into the pocket of his jeans, and I'm amazed at how calm he is.

I stand there with a mixture of shock and relief when he flips open a black case, revealing a small handgun. My uncle and I are both silent as he slides a magazine into the base, which is preloaded with bullets. He slips the gun into a leather holster strapped to his torso, which is concealed under his jacket. He comes prepared, I'll give him that, but I'd be lying if I said the thought of a possible shootout didn't make me feel uneasy. In a perfect world, we'd go inside, take Brooke, and leave without anyone getting hurt, but I'd be a fool to believe that's what's going to happen here.

Closing the boot, he faces us. "It's against my better judgment having you both here, but time is of the essence, so you'll need to listen to everything I say." His eyes move to me. "Do you understand?"

"Yes." I don't want to do anything that will put her at risk.

"If we have any chance of getting her out of there alive, we need to be smart."

"Okay," I reply.

"I mean it, Logan; this is no place for vigilantes. I know how much she means to you, but letting your heart get in the way of your head is going to get people killed—remember that."

"It's the last thing I want."

"Good. Let's do this then."

Mike turns and makes his way up the street; my uncle

and I follow close behind. When we reach the property, Mike signals us to stop by holding up his hand. We both stand at the foot of the driveway, shielded by some bushes.

Mike moves behind the vehicle, using his flashlight to briefly shine it inside. My heart thumps in my chest. Is she still in there?

Looking over his shoulder, he shakes his head at us, confirming she's not in the van. Again, I'm filled with a mixture of relief and dread. She must be in the house. My eyes focus on it. From here I can't see any lights on. What does that mean? It's been hours since she left, and anything could've happened in that time. I start to panic as the gravity of this situation hits me full force.

"You okay?" my uncle asks in a soft voice, placing his hand on my shoulder.

"No," I snap. If it wasn't for his actions, we wouldn't even be here.

"You need to pull yourself together, kiddo."

Despite wanting to tell him to shut the fuck up, I don't because I know he's right. I need to have my wits about me. I don't want to do anything that's going to hinder our chances of getting her back.

Mike places his finger against his mouth, quieting us before gesturing for us to follow. My uncle taps my back a few times for encouragement as I move forward. I feel bad for the way I've been treating him. I love this man, but I'm not sure if I'll ever be able to forgive him if this situation doesn't have the desired outcome.

We spot a light on in the back of the house, which lifts my spirits slightly. *Please be in there, and please be unharmed.*

Mike again holds up his hand, halting us when we near the back door. He quietly creeps up the three cement stairs and grasps the door handle. It's locked. Great, how the hell are we going to get inside now? Busting the door down is only going to alert Jake.

Reaching into his pocket, he pulls out the black leather pouch before passing me the torch. I press the small button on the side as I move closer, shining it in his direction. Pushing my hand down slightly, Mike points the light towards the ground. He holds the unzipped pouch below it, and I find myself smiling when I see what's inside. This man is a genius, and I'm so glad he's on our side. He pulls out two of the metal tools and gets to work picking the lock on the door. It only takes seconds before we hear the click.

"I'm going inside to have a look," he whispers. "I need you both to stay out here for now."

"But—"

He holds up his hand again, ending my protest. "Just let me see what we're dealing with first."

I know exactly what we're dealing with: a deranged fucking lunatic.

Despite my desperation, I'm not familiar with situations like this, so I need to trust him. My hands are fidgety as John and I stand there and wait. I can hear his heavy breathing beside me, while I'm holding my breath. So much is running through my mind at this moment as I try my best to remain positive. Surely the universe couldn't be so cruel as to take her away from me when we've barely scratched the surface of our relationship.

A few minutes pass before Mike reappears. He points to me, gesturing with his finger for me to come forward. He then turns his attention to my uncle and holds his palm up. He wants John to wait outside. I'm relieved by this, he's already made a mess of things. Mike points to his eyes, then his ears, and that's when I realise, he wants John to keep watch.

"Is she alive?" I whisper.

Mike puts his finger up to his mouth before turning and re-entering the house. I'm right on his heels. When we round the corner, I can see light pouring out of the room down the hallway. My heart thunders in my chest as we get closer, and I mentally try to prepare myself for what I'm about to see.

As we sneak down the hallway, I can hear soft moans in the distance. "Brooke," I whisper, pushing past Mike. Reaching out, he grabs my arm. "She sounds like she's in pain." My voice is soft, despite the panic I'm feeling on the inside. "He's hurting her."

"Remember, think with your head, not with your heart."

He's right. I can't go off half-cocked. The last thing I want is to jeopardise Brooke further.

He pushes me back behind him as we continue down the hall. The noises cease when we reach the doorway. Mike stops before carefully peering into the room.

"Stay here," he mouths, and I nod, but the grim look I see on his face makes me feel sick to the stomach.

My adrenaline is pumping as Mike swings around, filling the doorway with his large frame. "Freeze," he screams, his gun raised. "Move away from the girl."

The few seconds of silence that follow are deafening.

"Drop the gun, or I'll kill her," Jake yells, and I feel my legs buckle beneath me. Mike pauses, weighing up his options, but when I see his body deflate, my heart sinks. "Now!" The anguish on his face as he lowers his arms before dropping the gun by his feet, is profound. *Fuck!* "Kick it towards me." Again, Mike does as he's asked. His plan has now backfired, and I have no clue what to do next. "Get up against the wall." I release the breath I've been holding when he disappears into the room. I have to do something.

Turning, I head back down the hallway. Maybe my uncle can call for help. Both Brooke's and Mike's lives are now in danger. I could charge into the room all heroic, but that's liable to get us all killed. I may be able to handle myself, but even I know I'm no match for a bullet.

I only make it a few steps when I hear Jake's voice behind me. "Well, well, well. Look what the cat dragged in."

I swing around to face him. He's only a few feet away from me and pointing a gun at my face, but it's his blood-soaked hands that send chills through my body. Is that Brooke's blood? What has he done to her?

I'm in no way prepared for what I see when I'm forced to join Mike in the small bedroom. Brooke is on the floor, lying on her side, with a small pool of blood by her head. My first thought is she's dead, and my legs buckle from beneath me. I can't even put into words how that makes me feel, but when I notice the slight rise and fall of her chest as she breathes, some hope returns. Her arms and legs are bound, and there's a needle and a small vial of liquid lying on the ground beside her. Did he inject her with something?

Rage courses through my veins as my eyes meet his. If the others weren't in the room, I wouldn't hesitate to risk my own life, just so I could get my hands on him.

"What did you do to her?" I seethe through gritted teeth.

He releases a small laugh before replying. "It's called karma. How does it feel to lose the one you love?" There's a sadistic smile plastered on his face as he speaks, and I want to rip his damn head off.

"What did you do to her?" I repeat.

"I should kill you right now for what you've done."

"What I've done?"

"You seduced my wife."

"She's not your fucking wife," I scream.

I feel Mike's hand come to rest on my arm. "Don't," he whispers.

"She *is* my wife. She's fucking mine, not yours." I know better, but I keep my mouth shut. His hands are trembling as he aims the gun at my head, and I doubt he could make a clear shot, but that's a chance I'm not willing to take. "Did you sleep with her?" When I don't answer, he takes a step closer. "Did you?"

"What has gone on between Brooke and me is none of your damn business."

I may be playing with fire by antagonising him, but he doesn't scare me. Any man who raises a hand to a woman is a coward, and I bet he wouldn't feel so tough if he wasn't holding a gun.

Something changes in his expression and my gut tells me this is it, but I stand tall. I'm prepared to take a bullet for my girl. At the very least, it may give Mike an opportunity to overpower Jake and get Brooke safely out of here.

His arm lowers slightly, moving the gun away from my face and further down my body. "A bullet to the head is too good for you, Cavanagh. I'm going to enjoy watching you suffer."

I hold my breath waiting for him to fire, but before he does, I see movement out of the corner of my eye as my uncle rushes into the room. He lunges at Jake, just as the gun goes off. Mike doesn't flinch, but I instinctively stumble backwards. The sound from the shot in this confined space is ear-piercing.

All the air leaves my body, as John falls to the ground

with a thud. My eyes are fixed on Jake, and I notice all the colour drain from his face as he stares down at my uncle who's now bleeding profusely from the abdomen. I side-eye Mike, and he too is focused on Jake. Maybe together we can overpower him. He can't shoot us both at once.

My attention returns to Jake when he raises his weapon once more. His gaze has shifted back to me as he stares blankly into my eyes. I see a lone tear roll down his cheek ... the gun is pointed at his own head when he pulls the trigger.

The moment he hits the floor, Mike rushes forward, retrieving the gun that's still clutched in his hand. It's unnecessary because logic tells me Jake's not getting back up.

Chapter 33

Logan

My ears are still ringing as I fall to my knees beside Brooke. Untying her wrists and ankles, I scoop her into my arms and stand. Her body is limp as I gently lay her on the bed. Tears cloud my eyes as I stare down at her.

"Brooke," I say. "Brooke, it's me, Logan. Can you hear me, sweetheart?"

Mike is on the phone with triple zero as he tends to my uncle. Shrugging out of my suit jacket, I scrunch it into a ball and hold it against the gaping wound on the side of her head.

When there's no response from Brooke, I reach down to the vial on the floor and read the label on the front. I see the word ketamine—not something I'm familiar with—but I'll give it to the paramedics when they arrive, which will hopefully be soon. Seeing her like this brings back so many horrific memories of the first night we met.

"You're safe now," I whisper, running my free hand down the side of her face. "How's John?" I ask Mike, glancing over my shoulder.

My uncle's grey polo shirt is soaked with blood, and I

feel awful for how I've treated him tonight. He put his life on the line to save not just me, but possibly all of us.

"Not great."

I can't bring myself to look at Jake, I'm pretty sure the things I witnessed tonight are going to haunt me for a long time to come. I hate him for everything he's put Brooke through, but I can't help but feel bad for how things ended for him.

An eternity seems to pass before help arrives. I give the paramedics a brief rundown on Brooke, and Mike does the same with the ones treating my uncle. We're then ushered out of the room by a police officer, who immediately starts asking questions.

I'm grateful that Mike takes over, doing all the talking, as he fills him in on what went down here tonight. I didn't want to leave Brooke's side, but I understood I'd be in the way if I stayed. A part of me is grateful she's unconscious and doesn't have to witness the carnage that lies around her.

As soon as the police finish asking questions, I find myself pacing back and forth in the hallway. "You okay?" Mike asks, placing his hand on my shoulder. I shrug in reply. I'm too consumed with worry to even know how I'm feeling. "They're in safe hands now."

"I guess," I say. "I know things didn't work out how we planned but thank you for everything you did tonight. I doubt we would've been able to get to her as quickly as we did if it wasn't for you."

He blows out a long breath, and I know he's disappointed in himself.

They wheel my uncle out first. "Hang in there," I say, as they pass, but he no longer appears to be conscious. I clutch the sides of my head, my elbows spread wide, as they disappear down the hallway.

The paramedic pauses at the doorway to speak with one of the officers. "Can you radio ahead to the Royal Prince Alfred and let them know to be on standby. Tell them the patient has a critical gunshot wound to his abdomen?"

"I'll go with John," Mike says, lightly slapping my back. "I'll keep you updated."

"Please."

Pulling my phone out of my pocket, I search for my mother's number. I'm not even sure if my uncle would want to see my aunt, but she's his wife; she has a right to know.

"Logan, is everything okay?" my mum asks the moment she answers. The late hour is probably what alerted her.

"No. John's been shot and ..." I feel myself getting choked up.

"What? Shot? How?"

"Long story. I'll fill you in later. He's on his way to the Royal Prince Alfred. Will you let Kathleen know?"

"Oh, my goodness. John's been shot," my mother says, and I know she's relaying the news to my father. "I'm putting you on speaker."

My father's voice comes over the phone. "How bad is he?"

"He's in a bad way. I'm not sure if he's going to make it."

"What in the hell happened?"

"Look, I can't talk right now, Dad. The paramedics are getting ready to take Brooke to the hospital and I need to be with her."

"Brooke's been shot too?" my mother shrieks.

"No, but she's unconscious. She has a nasty cut on the side of her head."

"Oh, dear god." I hear my mum start to cry, and I can't deal with this shit right now.

"Mum, I've got to go."

"Are you injured, Son?"

"No, I'm fine. I'll see you at the hospital."

I end the call before she gets a chance to interrogate me further. I'm already regretting calling her, but if my uncle doesn't make it, they'd never forgive me for not telling them.

A soft moan falls from Brooke's lips on the drive to the hospital. Although I'm beyond relieved, seeing her in this state is almost unbearable. "Logan," she murmurs, and I can't tell you how pleased I am to hear her say my name. Unbuckling my seatbelt, I lean forward, reaching for her hand.

"I'm here, baby," I say, bringing her hand to my mouth and placing a soft kiss on her knuckles. A smile tugs on my lips when her eyelids flutter open and her big brown eyes meet mine.

"Jake," she says, her eyes wide with fright.

God only knows what she had to endure at the hands of that man.

"You're safe now. Everything is going to be okay."

I don't know how she's going to take the news of his death when I eventually break it to her. Despite all she's been through, I know the sweet and compassionate person she is, so I doubt she'll take it well.

"I think I'm going to throw up," she says, and the paramedic looking after her reaches for a white disposable vomit bag and places it near her mouth.

"Roll onto your side," he says, helping her. "I don't want you choking on your own vomit."

"Is she okay?" I ask, panicked.

The paramedic flicks his head, gesturing for me to sit back in the seat so he can examine her further. "It's normal," he replies. "My guess is, she has a nasty concussion from her head wound."

Leaning back into my chair, my hand scrubs over my face, as the worry I was feeling moments earlier, returns.

By the time we arrive at the hospital, Brooke's fully conscious and answering all the questions she's asked. I reach for her hand after she's wheeled from the ambulance and through the glass doors into the emergency department.

"I'm going to have to ask you to wait out there," the paramedic says, gesturing towards the waiting room. "Once the doctor has had a chance to examine her, you'll be able to come back in."

"Sure," I reply. I don't want to leave her, but I understand it's for the best. I lean forward, brushing the hair from Brooke's forehead. I try not to focus on the dried blood caked down one side of her face, or the dark bruise forming on her opposite cheek because it's messing with my head. "I'll be right outside."

"Okay," she says. As unwell as she looks, she still manages to give me a small smile.

Bending down, I brush my lips against hers. "I love you," I whisper, and as I pull back, I see her smile grow.

I stand there frozen to the spot as they wheel her further down the corridor. It's like déjà vu, only this time she's not just a beautiful woman I met at a party, *she's my world*.

Shoving my hands into my pockets, I head into the waiting room.

"Logan," my mum calls out as soon as she spots me. Leaping from her chair, she rushes towards me and engulfs me in her arms. "Thank goodness you're okay."

She draws back, looking up at me. "How's Brooke? Have you heard any news on John? We asked, but they haven't told us anything."

"Nothing yet."

She clutches my face in her hands. "Oh, sweetheart." My expression probably says it all. "What happened?" Her eyes move downwards, taking in my appearance. "Is that blood on your shirt?"

Following her line of sight, I see splatters of blood all over me. I'm not sure whose blood it is, but it's enough to turn my stomach.

"Excuse me," I say. "I need to use the bathroom."

My movements are hurried as I rush down the corridor towards the men's room. I just manage to make it into a stall before emptying the contents of my stomach.

As I splash water on my face at the basin, my eyes move up to the mirror before me. It's not just blood on my white business shirt; I also see small chunks of flesh. Images of Jake lying in a crumpled heap on the floor flash through my mind. Bile rises to my throat as I use paper towels to rid myself of any remnants of him.

When I finally make my way back to the waiting room, I see Mike leaning up against the far wall. The sullen look on his face speaks volumes. Like him, I'm also burdened with guilt. I know time wasn't on our side tonight, but I wish we'd thought things through a little better before going off half-cocked.

I head straight towards him. "Any news on John?"

"They've rushed him into surgery. I've just had a conversation with the investigating officers. We'll need to make a full statement at some point soon."

"Okay. I presumed that."

"Listen," he says, bowing his head. "I'm sorry for the way things turned out."

"Don't beat yourself up." I place my hand on his shoulder because I'm not sure what else to do. "He's going to pull through, and we got Brooke back safely. We couldn't have asked for a better outcome than that."

I'm unsure if I'm trying to convince him or myself, but my uncle has to survive—he just has to.

I'm jolted from my thoughts when I hear a raised voice in the background. "I demand you take me to see my husband this instance, do you hear me?"

Pinching the bridge of my nose, I turn in that direction and witness the poor nurse behind the desk practically cowering back into her seat. My aunt has arrived, and I know all hell is about to be let loose. That woman is insufferable.

Chapter 34

Logan

It's well after midnight, and I'm sitting in the waiting room with my mum, still with no news. The longer we wait, the more anxious I become.

I glance over at Mike who has fallen asleep on a chair in the corner. My father has taken my psychotic aunt for a walk to try and calm her down. She's been on a rampage ever since she arrived, even going as far as screaming at me as I tried to explain what had happened tonight. Although I would've gotten great pleasure from telling her about her husband's infidelities with Brooke's mother, it wasn't my place to say anything. I'd love to be a fly on the wall when the truth finally comes out, though.

"How are you coping, sweetheart?" my mother asks, placing her hand on my leg. I shrug instead of answering. I'm trying my best to keep it together. "Don't listen to anything Kathleen says. That woman is a bitch! I only tolerate her because she's your father's sister."

"I know. I can't believe John's put up with her for all these years."

"John's a sweet man, but you can't choose your family,

or so they say." Her comment makes me chuckle. "Speaking of family, have you notified Brooke's parents?"

"She has no family."

"What do you mean she has no family?"

"Her mother has passed."

"Oh, that poor girl. I didn't know that. What about her father?"

I let out a long breath as I lean forward, burying my face in my hands. "There's a part of the story I left out earlier."

"What part?" she asks.

"That John is Brooke's father. That's how this mess started."

"What?"

My eyes move to my mother, and I can see the shock on her face.

"Keep that between us for now. John hasn't told Kathleen yet. Well, as far as I know, he hasn't."

"How is that even possible?"

"He had an affair with Brooke's mother a long time ago when she was doing an internship with the company."

"Our company?"

"Yes."

"He never let on that he had a child. I know how much he wanted children; that's why he spent so much time with you and your sister when you were young."

"I don't think he knew anything about Brooke until he saw her at Lara's party."

"You mean Brooke's mother never told him about the baby."

"Yeah, she did, but let's just say John's reaction to the news that day was less than honourable. He never saw her again after that, and I guess he wasn't sure if she went through with the pregnancy."

"Well, I never," she says, placing her hand on her chest and sitting back in her seat. "How did Brooke take the news?"

"Not good. She took off," I reply. "That's how we ended up here. We knew her ex was after her, and I've been doing my best to keep her safe. That's why she's been staying with me."

"And you didn't try to stop her from leaving?"

"I wasn't there." I lean forward, resting my elbows on the knees of my spread legs as my gaze moves down to the laminate floor. "I would've stopped her if I'd been there."

"She means a lot to you, doesn't she, sweetheart?"

"She means the world to me, Mum. I love her."

When I get no reaction, I glance over my shoulder and see tears welling in my mother's eyes, but the huge smile on her face tells me that news makes her happy.

"You love her?"

"With everything I have."

"Oh, Logan," she says, affectionately rubbing my back. "Can I expect a wedding in the near future? I could help you pick out a ring? I'm going to get more grandbaby's, right?"

"Mum—"

The awkward moment is broken when I hear the nurse call my name. An uneasiness settles in the pit of my stomach as I rise from the seat and head in her direction. I'm not sure if I can take any more bad news tonight.

"I'm Logan Cavanagh," I say, coming to a stop in front of her.

"Your girlfriend is asking to see you."

"How is she?"

"Doing well under the circumstances. You're

welcome to chat with her doctor when he's free if you'd like more information."

"That would be great, thank you."

"Come, I'll take you to her."

"Is there any news on John?" my mother asks, coming to stand beside me.

"John?"

"Johnathan Sanders, they came in at the same time. He had a gunshot wound to his abdomen."

"He's in surgery I believe, but I can check and see if there's an update."

"I'd appreciate that," my mum says before turning her attention to me. "Go see my future daughter-in-law. I'll hang around until we get an update on John."

I shake my head, already regretting my confession. I'm never going to hear the end of this. "Thanks, Mum." Leaning forward, I place a kiss on her cheek.

"Send my love to Brooke."

"I will." I give her a hopeful smile before disappearing through the double doors.

The nurse draws back the curtain slightly when we reach the cubicle Brooke's in. "You have a visitor," she says, in a cheery voice. "Would you like me to adjust the bed so you can sit up?"

"Please."

I stand back as the nurse makes her comfortable. "How's that?" she asks, fluffing one of the pillows.

"Great. Thank you." Brooke smiles, but it doesn't quite reach her eyes. What she went through was traumatic, and I'm concerned for her mental health.

"If you need anything, just buzz." The nurse gives me a sympathetic smile as she leaves.

As soon as we're alone, I grab the chair sitting against the back wall and carry it towards the bed. I reach for Brooke's hand after taking a seat. "How are you feeling?"

She lifts one shoulder. "I've been better."

"What did the doctor say?" I ask, eyeing the bandage wrapped around her head.

"I'm still waiting for the results of my X-ray and CT scan, but they stitched up my wound."

I'm struggling not to get emotional as I bring Brooke's hand up to my mouth to place a kiss on her knuckles.

There's so much I want to ask, but for now, I think it's better to stick to small talk. She's been through enough and I'm just grateful to have her back.

I force out a smile as my eyes scan over her face. The bruise on her cheek has darkened, and the distinctive marks from where she was hit are now clearly visible. The guilt I was feeling earlier comes back tenfold. If that fucker wasn't already dead, I'd want to kill him for this alone.

"I'm sorry I didn't get to you sooner."

"I'm surprised you even found me." Her voice is soft as her gaze moves down to the white sheets that cover her.

"I had no plans of stopping until I did."

"Did they catch Jake?"

I blow out a long breath. I was hoping to leave this conversation for another day. "You don't have to worry about him anymore."

"Did they arrest him?"

"Can we talk about this later?"

"No, please. I want to know."

"He's dead, Brooke."

She gasps, bringing her hand to her mouth. "How?"

"After he shot John, he turned the gun on himself."

"Your uncle was shot?"

"Yes." I divert my eyes as images of Jake's lifeless

body, again flash through my mind. "He jumped into the line of fire." She probably doesn't want to hear this, but it needs to be said. "He saved my life; he probably saved all our lives."

"Is he okay?"

"He's in surgery now."

The moment I see the tears pooling in her eyes, I stand and gather her into my arms. When she begins to sob into my chest, I have to fight to keep my own tears at bay.

"Knock, knock," my mum says before entering Brooke's room. I notice a large bunch of colourful flowers clutched in her hand as she approaches the bed. "Hi, sweetheart."

"Hi, Mrs. Cavanagh."

"Patricia remember ... or *mum*, I don't mind either. Whatever you're comfortable with, honey." I clear my throat, and their eyes dart in my direction. My mother doesn't even flinch as she turns her full attention back to Brooke. Mum can be a little forward at times, but her heart is in the right place. I would've freaked out if she'd told anyone else I dated to call her that, but in this instance, I don't mind in the slightest.

A smile bursts onto Brooke's face, and it's the first genuine one I've seen from her since we've been here. "Okay."

"Good. 'Mrs. Cavanagh' seems so formal, and we're family now." She takes a seat on the side of the bed, placing her hand on top of Brooke's as she speaks. "Logan told me about your mother. I'm so sorry to hear that you lost her. That must've been really tough for you."

"Thank you, and yes it was."

"I know I could never replace her, but I'm here for you if you ever need me."

"That's really sweet of you. I appreciate it."

"I mean it."

"I know," Brooke says, smiling.

"How are you feeling today? You've been on my mind all morning."

"I'm feeling a lot better."

Brooke was moved into a ward around three o'clock this morning. The nurses tried to get me to go home, but I was so persistent they ended up letting me stay. All her scans came back clear, but the doctor wanted to keep her overnight for observation. I'm hoping I'll be able to take her home later today. She has ten stitches on the side of her head and a severe concussion but she hasn't complained once. I'm in awe of her strength. Life's constantly knocking her down, yet she just dusts herself off and keeps moving forward.

"I'm glad. Oh, here, these are for you."

My mum passes the flowers to Brooke, and she immediately brings them to her nose, inhaling their scent. "They're beautiful. Thank you."

"You're very welcome. I'm actually on my way to visit John, but I wanted to come and see you first." Brooke nods, but her face remains passive. My uncle survived his surgery and was placed in intensive care. His condition is still listed as critical, but I'm trying to remain confident that he'll pull through this. "Logan said they may be letting you go home today."

We've yet to discuss where home is, but for now, I want her with me. I know she said she'd only stay with me while Jake was a threat, but when the conversation arises, I'll try my best to change her mind. My place wouldn't be the same without her in it.

"I hope so. I'm not a fan of hospitals."

"Me neither," my mum says. She taps Brooke's hand before standing. "Well, I'll leave you two lovebirds alone. Don't forget dinner at my place as soon as you're feeling up to it."

"I'd like that," she replies.

Leaning forward, my mum places a kiss on Brooke's forehead, before turning and giving me one too. "Bye, Mum," I say.

"Bye, sweetheart."

"Give my love to John."

"I will. I'm hoping Kathleen isn't there. I could throttle that woman at times."

Her comment makes me chuckle. "She wasn't there when I went up to ICU."

I ducked out earlier while Brooke slept, but he wasn't awake. It was awful seeing him connected to so many machines, looking so pale and lifeless. They had to remove his spleen and part of his stomach to stem the internal bleeding. The next twenty-four to forty-eight hours are crucial, but if he can get through that, they're confident he'll make a full recovery. The doctors said he was extremely lucky. Apparently, the bullet missed his spinal cord by mere millimetres.

"Kathleen left the hospital when your father and I did," my mother says. "She complained the chairs in his room weren't comfortable enough, so she was going home to her bed." My mother rolls her eyes. "God forbid she put someone else's needs above her own. John's her husband for heaven's sake. I know if it was my Robert lying there, I wouldn't leave his side."

"You went to see John?" Brooke asks as soon as my mother leaves.

"Yes, while you were sleeping. I didn't stay long."

"Did he tell you he thinks he's my father?"

"Yes."

"What are your thoughts on that?"

I shrug. "To be honest, when he first mentioned it, I thought it was ludicrous, but when he explained what happened between him and your mother, his story was almost identical to yours."

"I see," she says, her gaze moving to the window.

"How do you feel about it?" I ask.

Her bottom lip starts to quiver before she answers. "He ruined my mother's life; he left her heartbroken and destitute." Her eyes move back to me, and there are tears brimming in them. "I hate him for what he did."

Sighing, I scoot my chair closer. "Don't worry about any of that right now. Just concentrate on getting better."

I'd like to think I know my uncle well; he's a good man. There's no denying the way he acted towards Brooke's mother was inexcusable, but in my heart, I know there are two sides to every story.

Chapter 35

Brooke

"Are you ready to blow this joint?" Logan asks, reaching for my hand.

"God, yes."

The doctors have given me the all-clear to leave. Apart from the stitches, a concussion, a few bruises, and the mental scars this ordeal has left me with, I feel grateful. Things could've ended far worse.

Logan gives me a sweet smile as he laces his fingers through mine. "Anyone would think you were looking forward to going home."

What home? I'm not sure where I belong anymore. Even though I no longer need to worry about Jake, I don't want to go back to my terrace house. It seems tainted now. "Would you mind if I stayed with you for a few more days, just until I find somewhere else to live?"

"You're welcome to stay with me as long as you'd like."

A lump forms in my throat as I tighten my grip on his hand. He's my knight in shining armour and prince charming all rolled into one. I'd be lost without him.

"Thank you."

"You don't need to thank me. To be honest, I was hoping you'd stay."

"Anyone would think you like having me around."

"I could think of worse people to have in my company."

"Hey," I say, bumping my shoulder with his.

He lets go of my hand and drapes his arm over my shoulder, bundling me into his side. "Being with you is no hardship, I can assure you." Leaning down, he places a kiss on the top of my head. When we reach the lifts that will take us to the ground floor, Logan pauses, his gaze moving to the large blue sign at the end of the long corridor—Intensive Care Unit. I brace myself for the question that I know is about to come. "I understand you're eager to get out of here, but would you mind if we visited my uncle quickly. I haven't had a chance to thank him for what he did, and it would give me some peace to see him."

The last person I want to see is John, but if it will give him some peace, then I'm willing to make that sacrifice.

"Okay."

Turning his body to face mine, he cups my face in his hands. "Are you sure? I'd never force you into doing something you weren't comfortable with, but I know seeing that you're okay, will lift his spirits." I force a smile as his eyes scan over my face. I agreed to go to the ICU, but I never said I'd visit him. I nod instead of answering because I don't trust myself to speak. "You're amazing, you know that?"

If Logan knew what I was thinking, I doubt he'd say that.

A weight settles in the pit of my stomach as we near his room. My feelings for this man aren't good ones, and just being in close proximity to him makes me feel like I'm betraying my mother.

Growing up my father wasn't mentioned often. When my mum did speak about him, her face would light up, but there was also an inimitable sadness in her eyes. It hurt me deeply to see how badly he'd broken her heart. She used to tell me how in love they'd been and how happy he had made her in the short time they'd been together.

Of course, that all ended the day she told him she was carrying his child. I never said this to her, because I didn't want to hurt her feelings, but the love was obviously one-sided, considering how poorly he'd treated her.

"You okay?" Logan asks, sensing my hesitation when we reach the doorway to John's room. Again, I just nod. I feel like I'm on the verge of hyperventilating. He wraps his hands around mine. "You're shaking." My eyes meet his, and I can see he's concerned. "Maybe I should come back and see him another time."

Knowing his uncle is a big part of his life, and understanding our paths will cross on occasions, I don't want this situation to come between Logan and me. I need to work on facing my demons and perhaps this is the first step in trying to heal.

"I'm okay," I lie. "I'm just nervous that's all."

"Are you sure you're up to this?"

"Yes."

He sighs. "Okay. We won't stay long." He squeezes my hand before we enter.

"Kiddo," I hear John say. He sounds weak, but it's hard to tell from where I'm standing—or hiding, rather—behind Logan. His large body is blocking my view.

"How are you feeling?" Logan asks, tugging on my hand as he approaches the bed. "You had us worried."

"I feel like shit," he replies, chuckling. "Oh god, it hurts to laugh."

"I brought you a special visitor."

Crap!

I step out from behind Logan, forcing a smile. I'm in no way prepared for the compassion I feel for him when our eyes meet. He looks different from the strong, vibrant man I saw a few days ago. There's no denying he's handsome, and I can see why my mother was so captivated by him, but all those machines he's hooked up to make him appear fragile.

I briefly study his face as the room falls silent. The only sound is the beeping noises from the machines. Is it possible he is my father? We look nothing alike. If anything, I may have inherited his height. Although I look exactly like my mother once did, I'm a lot taller than she was.

My heart thumps in my chest. Sometimes when I was a little girl, I wished he would come waltzing back into our lives—for both me, and for Mum. When I found out the cold hard truth, that's when all my dreams were crushed and my resentment for him started to brew. Right now, none of that hate seems to be present.

"Brooke!" His face lights up when he says my name, and for some reason, it makes me happy.

Logan slides his arm around my waist, pulling me into his side. Having him with me gives me the courage to speak. "Hi."

"I've been so worried about you," he says. "Pat reassured me earlier that you were doing well, but I feel much more relieved now that I can see it with my own eyes."

"She's been discharged, so we thought we'd pop in and see you before we left."

"I'm so glad you did." Although he's replying to Logan, his eyes never leave me.

It's twenty-six years too late, I remind myself. He can't just come into my life after all this time and expect to have a relationship with me. If my mother had listened to him all those years ago, I wouldn't have even been born.

"I'm surprised Kathleen isn't here," Logan says, pulling his uncle's attention away from me.

"She was here earlier," he replies, rolling his eyes. "But when she started to scream at me, the nurses told her to leave."

"You're lying in ICU with a gunshot wound and she screamed at you?" I can hear the anger in Logan's voice as he speaks.

"You know what she's like."

"I honestly don't know why you put up with her."

I stand there in silence as John and Logan talk. His wife sounds like a horrible woman, and from what Logan tells me, she is. I can't help but wonder why he chose somebody like that over my sweet mother. He couldn't have found a better woman than her.

That knowledge has the resentment I held towards this man, for the way he treated my mum, returning full force. I have so much to say to him, but now is not the time or the place. Somebody has to stand up for my poor mum—it's not like she ever had the chance to do it. She gave up everything for me: her life, her career ... *him*.

I've often wondered if she had followed his wishes, would they have stayed together? Once she found out she was the other woman, I doubt it. Despite her deep love for him, she had morals and self-respect.

My mother was a kind and selfless person. Her finding the happiness she deserved was all I ever wanted. Every year, when I blew out the candles on my birthday cake, that was my only wish. But he stole that from her. *He ruined her life.*

My breathing becomes laboured and I get a tingling sensation in both my arms as my anxiety grows. The compassion I was feeling a few moments ago is now replaced with contempt. My nostrils flare, and my heart races as I struggle to get enough oxygen into my lungs.

"I need air," I say, turning and rushing from the room. Coming to see this man was a huge mistake.

Chapter 36

Logan

"Are you sure you're okay?" I ask Brooke for the umpteenth time. I had one of the doctors look her over at the hospital, and he assured me she was just hyperventilating, but I'm still concerned.

"Yes, stop worrying," she answers as the taxi pulls away from the kerb. I know Chris would've come and got us if I called him, but I didn't want to wait. I needed to get her home.

"What happened back there?"

"Nothing," she says, turning her face away from me to gaze out the side window.

"Brooke." I reach for her hand.

"Just drop it," she snaps.

My fingers remained laced with hers as I settle back into my seat. I know it has something to do with my uncle; I'm sure of it. It was selfish of me to encourage her to go and see him. I knew it would brighten his day, but I didn't stop to think of the effect it would have on her.

"Forgive me," I say, tightening my grip.

Her focus moves wearily back to me. "For what?"

"Making you go and see your father."

"You didn't make me do anything," she replies in a clipped tone, "and that man is not my father. He's nothing more than a sperm donor. A lousy one at that." She sighs heavily as she rests her head back against the seat. "Can we not talk about this?"

"Of course, I'm sorry." I bring her hand up to my mouth, letting my lips linger against her skin. The last thing I want is for this to come between us. She's had a horrendous few days and I feel like an arsehole for adding to her trauma.

She leans her head down to rest on my shoulder. "I'm sorry I snapped at you, Hot Stuff." Her pet name for me never fails to make me smile. "I've got so much going on inside my head. I just need some time to process it all."

I can't even begin to fathom the cluster-fuck that's raging in her head right now. "Take all the time you need."

"Thank you."

"And if you need an ear, I have two."

A small laugh falls from her lips as she lifts her face to look up at me. "I'm so glad I have you, and your two ears."

Leaning forward, I brush my lips against hers. "I'm glad I have you too." The prospect of almost losing her has only cemented how much she means to me.

The rest of the drive is travelled in silence, and I'm relieved when the taxi pulls up outside my apartment building. I'm exhausted and running on no sleep. A hot shower and some rest will do us both a world of good.

I hand a fifty to the driver. "Keep the change," I say, before sliding out and reaching for Brooke's hand. "Let me help you."

When we step out of the lift, Jill comes rushing out of the kitchen. "Is that you, Mr. Cavanagh?"

"Yes, Jill."

As she rounds the corner, her face lights up the moment she sees I'm not alone. Opening her arms, she rushes straight for Brooke, pulling her into an embrace. "I've been beside myself with worry." When they part, I see tears fill Jill's eyes as they scan over Brooke's face. "My poor sweet girl."

The nasty bruise on her cheek looks worse, and the swelling has barely subsided. The doctor removed the bandage from around Brooke's head before we left, redressing her wound and covering the stitches with a waterproof patch.

"It's just a little bump. I'm okay."

Jill's gaze moves to me, and I can see the concern on her face, but when I shake my head, she takes a step backwards. I'm grateful when she doesn't pry any further. We both know Brooke's playing down her injuries. I'm not even sure why, but if that's what she needs to do to get through this, then so be it.

Jill dabs her eyes with the tea towel she's holding. "Are you hungry? I've been cooking."

When Brooke doesn't answer, I step forward. "We're a little tired right now, Jill."

"How about I plate it up and you can reheat it when you're ready?"

"Sounds great."

"I'll leave you both to it."

"Thanks, Jill."

"Yes, thank you," Brooke adds, reaching out and placing her hand affectionately on Jill's arm.

"It's good to have you home, dear."

I second that.

"It's good to be home."

I reach for Brooke's hand and lead her up to our room.

"I might have a bath before lying down if that's okay," she says.

"Of course, anything you want." I place a kiss on her forehead. "I'll run one for you."

I still can't bring myself to look at the clumps of dried blood lingering in her hair. I need to try and bury all those horrible images from that night. It's the only way I'm going to be able to cope.

Leaving her in the bedroom, I head into the en suite. She's unusually quiet, and that worries me. Hopefully, when she's ready, she'll open up.

A few minutes pass before Brooke joins me in the bathroom. She wraps her arms around herself as she comes to a stop just inside the doorway.

"The bath is almost ready," I say. "I put some bubble bath in there. I hope that's okay."

"Perfect."

"I'm going to have a quick shower." I undo the buttons on my shirt as she stands there watching me. "Would you prefer it if I used one of the other bathrooms?"

"Don't be silly," she says. "This is your bathroom."

"If you'd prefer to be alone ..."

She closes the few steps separating us and there's a vulnerability in her eyes that wasn't there before. "I'd rather you stay."

"Okay." Slipping out of my shirt, I drop it to the floor. I must remember to tell Jill to throw it out. Even if she manages to remove the blood stains, I want the shirt gone.

Brooke slides both her arms through the holes in her top. "Let me help you with that," I say, grabbing the hem and gently pulling it up and over her head.

"Thank you."

"How about you join me in the shower until the bath is ready? I can help you wash your hair."

Since she hyperventilated at the hospital, things have shifted between us. I now feel like I'm walking on eggshells. It could be my paranoia, but the last thing I want to do is overstep my mark or upset her again.

"I'd like that," she says, with a small smile.

Reaching into the shower, I turn on the water to warm it up, before fully undressing.

Brooke follows me into the stall. "Turn around." I lift the shower head out of its cradle as I speak. "Can you tilt your head back slightly?" The dressing over her cut is sitting right on her hairline.

She places her hand over the area, protecting it further, inadvertently giving me a close-up view of the mark on her wrist where she was bound. There's also a large hand shaped bruise on her upper arm. I'm riddled with guilt for not being able to protect her. No matter how hard I try, I can't seem to shake that feeling.

"The warm water feels nice," she says, but my eyes are focused on how it turns red as it runs down her back and pools around her feet. A lump forms in my throat as I hang the shower head back on the cradle and reach for the shampoo. The suds turn pink as I gently massage her scalp. "Mm, you have magic hands."

Usually, a moan from her would spark a reaction from me, but I'm too traumatised to feel anything but immense sadness and guilt.

Once the shampoo and conditioner are rinsed from her hair, I place a soft kiss on her shoulder. "There you go."

She turns to face me. "Let me wash you."

My eyes dart to the now almost full bath. "Looks like your bath is ready."

"Oh." She pauses for a moment as she studies my face before turning and exiting the shower stall.

I feel bad as my eyes follow her across the bathroom. I don't even know why I just rejected her, but that's most certainly what I did. Having her hands on me is something I usually crave. I hope she didn't notice, but my gut tells me she did. The slump in her shoulders as she walked away from me spoke volumes.

Closing my eyes, I tilt my head back and let the hot water run over my weary muscles, as I yet again unsuccessfully try to clear my head. My gaze is drawn back to Brooke the moment my eyes reopen. She's watching me over her shoulder. The look of uncertainty on her face tugs at my heart.

Quickly washing, I turn off the water and step out. I'm not sure why I feel the need to put some space between us, but I do. Her eyes follow my every move, but when I reach for my towel, her gaze drops down to her lap and I'm pretty sure I hear a sigh.

Fuck.

"Do you want some company?" I ask.

"Please," is her only reply as she scoots her body forward to make room for me. I can clearly see she's traumatised, and I'd be an arsehole if I walked away from her now. We've both been through a harrowing experience, and the best way for us to get through this is *together*. I'm determined to show her that I am here for her to lean on whenever she needs me.

My legs straddle her hips as I position myself behind her, but she immediately turns her body to face mine. "Are you okay?"

"I will be," I admit as my eyes meet hers. The marks on her face churn me up inside. "How about you?"

She shrugs. "I just have a lot going on inside here." She points to her head, and I can relate to that.

"Yeah, me too. Seeing you unconscious and bleeding on the floor, plus what happened with my uncle and Jake ... it's really fucked me up."

She reaches up and runs her fingers through my wet hair. "I'm sorry you had to see all that."

"I'd go through it all again in a heartbeat if it meant I'd get you back."

"Thank you for coming for me." Her legs slide up until they're straddling mine. "I don't know where I'd be now if you hadn't."

"Finding you was my only option." My arms encircle her waist as I pull her body against mine. "I only wish I'd gotten there sooner."

My eyes again gravitate towards her injuries, and that sickly feeling settles in my stomach once more.

"Don't beat yourself up about it. You did the best you could. I shouldn't have left the way I did." She bows her head. "I didn't even think about Jake when I fled. I just needed to ..." Her words drift off, but I know what she was going to say. She needed to get away from John.

My hands cup her face as I bring her lips down to mine. I don't want to talk about this now. There's plenty of time for that tomorrow.

She moans into my mouth when I deepen the kiss, but when my cock stirs, I draw back. "Turn around and I'll wash your back."

She looks puzzled as her eyes meet mine but eventually does as I ask. I move her hair to the side, draping it over her shoulder, before reaching for the body wash. Leaning forward, I place a soft kiss on the side of her neck as I lather the soap in my hands.

I just pushed her away for a second time. *Fuck.*

I'm sitting on the edge of the bed when Brooke exits the bathroom after drying her hair. Standing, I pull back the covers. "You need your rest," I say.

"You're not joining me?"

I'm dead tired, but I know sleep won't come easy. "I'm going to go downstairs and do some work. I really need to check my emails."

"Oh."

I wait until she climbs into bed before pulling the sheets up to cover her. When I lean down to kiss her cheek, she turns onto her side, giving me her back.

Sitting down on the side of the mattress, I run my fingers through the strands of her hair. "I won't be long." When she doesn't reply, my hand moves to her shoulder. "Hey."

"Take all the time you need," she says, but I don't miss the crack in her voice as she speaks.

"Brooke." Again, she doesn't answer. "Babe, turn around."

"Why?"

"Please." When she ignores my plea, I rise and walk around to the other side of the bed. Her eyes are closed, but when she swipes her finger underneath one of them, I know she's crying. Without hesitating, I pull back the covers and climb in beside her. A small sob escapes her as I gather her in my arms. "Don't cry," I whisper, placing my lips on her forehead. "It kills me to see you like this."

"If you'd rather me not be here, I can go."

"What? No." Drawing back, I slide my hand under her chin and raise her face to meet mine. "I want you here. Why would you think I didn't?"

Even though I asked the question, I know exactly why she's feeling that way. "You're acting weird."

"I want you here," I repeat, as my lips brush against hers. When her eyes scan mine, searching for the truth, I say it again. "I want you here."

I'm not sure what's going on inside my head, but I mean what I say. She belongs here with me.

"Make love to me," she whispers.

"The doctor said you need to rest."

"Please. All I need is you."

"I need you too, but there will be plenty of time for that when you've recovered."

She sighs, before diverting her gaze. "I need you to help me forget."

"Jesus," I say, pulling her body closer. What does she mean by that? Did Jake do something to her? Beyond what we already know.

"Please." She pushes me onto my back and straddles my lap.

"I don't think so," I say, gently rolling her back down onto the mattress. When her face drops, I know she thinks I'm rejecting her again. "If we're going to do this, I'm doing all the work."

"Huh?"

I grin when I see the confusion on her face. If this is what she needs then I'll give it to her. There's nothing I wouldn't do for this woman. "The doctor said you're not to overdo it."

"But—"

"Shh," I say, placing my finger on her mouth to halt her protest. "My way or no way." I chuckle when she sucks my finger into her mouth, before softly biting down on it. "Sit up." Pulling myself onto my knees, I slide the t-shirt she's wearing over her head before gently laying her back down. "Just lie here and relax."

My lips brush hers before I disappear under the sheets. I'm going to caress every inch of her luscious body as I make my way down south. And by the time I'm done, the only thing she'll be able to think about is me.

Chapter 37

Logan

"Oh god," she moans as she tugs on my hair. I know she's close because her trembling legs are now gripping my head like a vice. My tongue movements quicken as I slide two fingers deep inside her little piece of heaven, crocking them so I can hit her g-spot and it's enough to send her over the edge. "Hot Stuff," she cries loudly as I milk every last drop of her orgasm. I could do this all day with her and never tire.

Wiping my mouth with the back of my hand, I make my way back up her body. "Are you okay?" I ask, popping my head out of the sheet. The huge, contented smile I see on her face tells me she is.

"I'm more than okay," she pants. She grabs hold of my face, pulling it towards hers. "You're so good at that—the best I've ever had." Her words make me chuckle, but at the same time, they spark something inside me. Jealousy. The mere thought of her doing this with another man makes me borderline crazy. *She's mine.*

Settling my body between her legs, my mouth softly meets hers as I push all those thoughts out of my head.

I'm still unsure if we should be doing this, but if this is what she needs, there's no way I'd deny her. Truth is, I could use the distraction myself.

Pulling out of the kiss, I reach over to the bedside drawer. My need to be inside her is overwhelming. She watches my every move as I place the foil packet between my teeth and tear it open.

"You still want to do this?" I ask before going any further.

"Absolutely. I need you now more than ever."

"Jake didn't, you know ... touch you, did he?" I'm not sure how I'll cope if she says yes.

She shakes her head before answering. "I don't think so. But I was unconscious most of the time."

Leaning back on my haunches, I gently lift her torso off the bed, enfolding her in my arms. Once again, images of her lying bleeding and unconscious on the floor flash through my mind. "I love you," I whisper.

She tilts her head back, gazing up at me. "I love you too."

It's the first time she's said it back. In my heart, I felt she did, but there was always that small seed of doubt.

"You do?"

"With my whole heart." When her arms encircle my waist and she buries her face in my chest, I hear her sniffle.

"Babe."

"I was worried I'd never get the chance to tell you how much you mean to me."

I'm struggling to hold back my own emotions as I think about how close I came to losing her. "I'm so glad you got the chance. I don't know how I would've coped if things turned out ..."

Laying her back down, I cover Brooke with my body. Our eyes remain locked as I drape one of her legs around my waist and line myself up. This is the moment I'll savour. I'm thankful for our second chance.

My lips meet hers as I slowly sink inside her, filling her completely. Her eyelids flutter closed when I withdraw slightly before pushing all the way back in. This is my favourite place to be. I've never felt so connected to anyone, as I do her.

"My life would be meaningless without you in it, Brooke," I say, gently brushing the hair back from her forehead. She's turned my whole world on its axis.

"I feel exactly the same," she whispers, tears once again filling her eyes.

"Knock, knock," Brooke says from the doorway of my home office. Spinning my chair around, I face her. "Sorry," she mouths when she realises I'm on a call.

Smiling, I signal with a crook of my finger for her to enter. Pushing my chair away from the desk, I tap my lap. I had Claire rearrange all my appointments so I can work from home for the next few days. There was no way I could leave Brooke; she's been clingy, and I can tell she is not ready to be on her own. If I'm honest, I need her near me too.

I slide my arm around her waist when she seats herself, and place a soft kiss on her shoulder. The swelling on her cheek has gone down considerably overnight, but the bruises on her face still disturb me.

"I'm grateful they agreed to an early settlement," I say to Steve, my real estate agent. "It'll give me some extra time to do the modifications. If you could courier the contract over, I'll sign it and get it straight back to you."

"I'll get on that now," he replies.

"Talk soon, and thanks again."

I'm so happy with what he has found me. The large building at Petersham was originally a furniture storage warehouse built in 1905, so the open floor plan has ample space for me to work with. It comes with a decent-sized car park around the back, which will be perfect for what I have planned.

It's about a twenty-minute drive with traffic from the penthouse, so not as close as I would've liked, but it's in great condition for its age. That and the sheer size of the place is what sold me in the end. I have limited time to get this project completed, so anything that needed major structural changes or repairs wasn't an option.

"I'm sorry I interrupted you," Brooke says, once I end the call.

"Never," I say. "I was just talking to my real estate agent."

"Oh. Are you thinking of moving?"

"No, I'm happy here. You're happy here, right?"

"Yes, why?"

"Just curious."

"That reminds me. I need to think about sorting my place out too. If the leasing agent calls a surprise inspection on me, I'm screwed."

Neither of us has been back to her terrace house since it was vandalised.

"I can sort that out for you."

"You're sweet," she says, resting her palm on the side of my face, "but I can handle it."

I smile, humouring her, but there's no way I'm letting

her clean that place up. I'll hire someone to do it. She may not have the money for something like that, but I do.

"By the way, shouldn't you be resting?"

"I'm bored," she says. "I don't know how anyone could stand to be bedridden. It would drive me insane."

"How about I set you up in the lounge room so you can watch a movie?"

"I'd much rather go for a run."

I sigh, running my free hand through my hair. I've been waiting for her to bring that up. "The doctor said you need to rest for the next few days."

"But it's been weeks since I've been able to run outside."

"And a few more days won't hurt." I chuckle when she pouts. Bringing my face forward, I suck her bottom lip into my mouth. "I know things have been tough for you," I say, drawing back and tucking a piece of stray hair behind her ear. "But all that's behind us now. Jake's no longer a threat, and you're free to go wherever you want once you've healed."

My words were supposed to lift her spirits, but when I see sadness wash over her at the mere mention of his name, I could kick myself.

"I saw his obituary in the paper this morning." She bows her head, and I'm conflicted by how that makes me feel. I understand she'd be sad—he *was* her husband once—but I also can't get past how he's treated her. "His funeral is on Friday."

"And you want to attend?" She shrugs, as tears fill her eyes. "Babe," I say, tightening my grip around her waist. "If attending his funeral is what you need, then go. Personally, I don't know if it's a good idea."

"I don't want his family to think badly of me for not

attending. They're good people and have always been kind to me."

"He tried to kill you twice," I say, struggling to keep my annoyance at bay. "Under the circumstances, I think they'll understand."

"I know." She turns her face away from me, wiping the tears from her eyes with the tips of her fingers. "I want them to know that despite everything, I'm sorry for their loss. He was their only child, so his death would've hit them hard."

"I understand that," I say, placing my forefinger under her chin and bringing her gaze back to me. "Call them, send them a card, or write them a letter if you have to, but I don't think attending the funeral would be in your best interest, or theirs."

Who knows how his family feel about Brooke now. None of this is her fault, but grief can sometimes bring out the worst in people.

"So, you think it's best if I don't go?"

"I can only advise you. At the end of the day, it's your decision to make. Given the circumstances, I personally couldn't attend, but if you want to, I'll organise someone to go with you so you're not alone."

"Thank you, but I think you're right. I'm not sure I'm up to it."

"I agree." I place my lips against her cheek. "You know I'd support you one hundred percent if I thought you'd benefit from being there. But it's my job to look after you, and I think you've been through enough."

She slides her arms around my neck, resting her head on my shoulder. "I'm so glad I have you in my life."

"Ditto."

"It's nice to have someone who actually cares."

"And that will never change." Standing, I bring her with me.

"Where are you taking me?" she asks, as I head towards the doorway.

"I'm going to get you set up in front of the TV. The quicker I get through my workload, the sooner I can join you."

"I can walk you know."

Ignoring her, I don't put her down until we reach the sofa. Once she's seated, I grab the remote to turn on the television.

"Jill," I call out.

"Yes, Mr. Cavanagh?" she answers as she enters the main room.

"Can you get Brooke a blanket and pillow?"

"Of course."

Brooke stands. "I can get them myself."

"Sit." I point to the sofa and smile when she does what I ask. She doesn't look pleased, but I'm not bothered by that. Part of the reason I decided to stay home was to make sure she rested and didn't overdo things. "What do you want to watch?" I ask, flicking through the channels.

"I might just listen to my iPod."

When she goes to stand again, I raise an eyebrow. "Where is it?"

"In our room, on the dresser." Turning, I walk in that direction.

By the time I return, Jill is beside her, fluffing a pillow before placing it down on the sofa.

"Thanks, Jill. I'll take it from here." I like the fact that she looks after Brooke just as well as she does me, but when I'm home, I want to be the one caring for her. "Lie down," I command.

Shaking the blanket out, I place it over Brooke before

tucking it around her sides. "I only have a concussion you know."

"A severe one," I add.

Pulling the iPod out of my pocket, I pass it to her. "Thank you."

"You're welcome." She smiles, as she places the earplugs in her ears. "Can I get you something to drink?"

"No thanks, I'm good."

"I'll leave you to it, then."

I watch as she presses play before closing her eyes. I stand there staring down at her. I'm grinning as I do. Her fingers tap down on the blanket to the beat of the tune, and if I'm not mistaken, I see a calmness wash over her.

She's so engrossed in the music; she doesn't even realise I'm still here. I'm transfixed. Minutes pass before one of her eyes slowly creeps open, and she spots me.

"What?" she asks, pulling one of the plugs out and pausing the song she's listening to. "Did you say something?"

"No. I'm just watching you. You look like you're lost in the music."

"Music does that to me. It's good for my soul." My smile grows when she says that. "It's great for clearing your mind."

"I could use some of that," I say, shoving my hands into my pockets. I barely slept a wink last night. A multitude of fucked up images from that night ran rampant through my mind.

She pulls back the blanket and taps the space beside her. I have so much work to do, but that can wait. Right now, I'd rather be here with her.

Slipping out of my shoes, I lie down beside her. She covers me with the other half of the blanket before passing me one of her earbuds. Once I place it in my ear, she restarts the music.

"Close your eyes," she says as she reaches for my hand, lacing our fingers together.

Trying to clear my mind, I focus on the words of the song. It takes a little while, but for the first time in days, I feel myself starting to relax.

Chapter 38

Brooke

Tears cloud my eyes as I do a final read-through of the letter I've written to Jake's parents. It may be the coward's way out, but just contemplating calling them on the phone made me anxious. Sure, they may have loved me once, but I have no idea what they think of me now. So much has happened between me and their son.

The letter is shorter and more direct than I would've liked, but I know all too well that words will never be enough to comfort them or take away their pain. I've been there with my mother. I'm not even sure if his parents know about the affair, drugs or the reasons behind my leaving, but no good can come from bringing that up or pointing the finger. They're grieving the loss of their only son, and I don't want to add to their pain.

Despite everything, I still can't believe Jake's gone. It was his own bad choices that ultimately led to his demise, but it still breaks my heart that his life ended so horrifically.

"There you are," Logan says, startling me as he comes to a stop just inside the doorway. "I woke up and you weren't there."

Bowing my head, I quickly wipe the tears from my eyes. "I couldn't sleep, so I came down here because I didn't want to wake you. I hope you don't mind me using your office."

"Of course not. Are you okay?"

"Yes. I took your advice and decided to write Jake's parents a letter."

"At two in the morning?"

"It's been weighing heavily on my mind, and I'd like them to get it before Friday."

"Fair enough." His face is expressionless as he closes the distance between us and takes a seat on the corner of his desk.

"I know this isn't easy for you, Hot Stuff, but it's something I need to do. I hope you understand that. These people were my family once."

"You're right, it isn't easy for me, but I do understand. I admire the compassion you have for others."

Picking up the letter, I hold it out to him. "You're welcome to read what I wrote."

"Please don't take this the wrong way, but I'd rather not." He stands and holds out his hand to me. "Come back to bed."

"Okay."

"Where are you going with those?" Logan asks as I grab my running gear out of the drawer and head into the bathroom.

"I'm getting ready for my run."

"But—"

"No buts."

"Brooke," he says, throwing back the covers and leaping out of bed. "I don't think this is a good idea."

He follows me into the en suite. "I feel fine. A run will do me a world of good."

"You should wait a few more days."

"Nope," I say, sliding my sports bra over my head and tugging it down. "You said a couple of days, a few days ago."

"Babe."

"You worry too much," I say, stepping into my underwear. "You're going to give yourself an ulcer if you're not careful."

"It's my job to worry about you."

"I love that you do, but you can't wrap me up in cotton wool."

"How about we use the gym. I can keep an eye on you there."

"Or you could come for a run with me," I say, poking my arms through the holes in my crop top. "The fresh air will do you good."

"Running is for pansies," he replies, drawing me into his arms.

"Is that so?"

"Real men work out at the gym."

"I beg to differ. I've seen plenty of hotties while I'm out running."

His eyes narrow to slits as he draws his face back to meet mine. "Hotties, eh?"

"In abundance."

He throws his head back. "Ugh, please don't make me go with you." His comment makes me laugh.

"It'll be fun."

"But I hate running."

"Well, stay here then." I break out of his hold and

continue dressing. He just stands there watching my every move. When I walk over to the sink and pick up my toothbrush, he turns and leaves the bathroom. A smile tugs at my lips as I put a line of toothpaste on my brush. I'm eager to get out there; I need this to clear my head.

I pull my hair back into a ponytail before splashing water on my face.

I expect to see Logan back in bed sulking when I enter the room, but he's not there. I head towards the walk-in robe to grab my runners, and I'm surprised to find him in there changing.

"Where are you going?"

"With you," he grumbles. "I can't have you out there running alone when there's an abundance of hotties on the loose."

Closing the distance between us, I fist my hand in his t-shirt and pull his face towards mine. "I only have eyes for one hottie, and that's you, Hot Stuff."

He's grinning when I softly place my lips against his. I can't even put into words how happy I am that he's going with me. I've never had a running partner before.

"Smell that beautiful salt air," I say, extending my arms wide and drawing the fresh air into my lungs. "It's so good to be free."

Logan slides his arm around my waist, pulling me in for a chaste kiss. "Now I can take you places and not have to worry about your safety."

My stomach does a flip-flop when he says that. I just want to forget everything for now. "Come on, let's go," I say, breaking into a jog.

"Take it easy on me."

I'll show him how non-pansy runners are. He'll be eating his words by the time we're done.

He keeps up with me for the first kilometre of the three-kilometre lap around the Royal Botanic Gardens. His breathing has become rapid, and the contorted look on his face tells me that he's beginning to struggle.

"How are you feeling?" I ask as my eyes scan over his red face.

"Peachy," he replies, breathlessly. His words don't fool me. He's anything but peachy, but he's far too stubborn to admit otherwise.

"Great, we'll pick up the pace then."

"Fuck," he mumbles to himself, and I bite my lip to suppress my smile.

I speed up slightly, but not as much as I'd like. I feel bad, but I can guarantee after today he'll never say running is for pansies. "We're over the one-k mark. Only two more to go."

"What," he says, coming to an abrupt halt. "Two more what? Kilometres?"

"Yeah, have you got a problem with that?" I try my best to keep a straight face as I jog on the spot. "You're not pansying out on me already, are you?"

"Never," he snaps as his eyes slightly narrow. I laugh when he starts moving again.

My amusement grows as I not only catch up but pass him. When I hear him groan from behind, I speed up a little more. "You okay?" I ask, turning around and jogging backwards.

"I'm fine." I see a steely determination cross his face as he passes me. As fun as this is, I can't help but feel sorry for him. He is used to succeeding in all aspects of life, so admitting defeat is probably not an option for him.

"Do you want to stop?"

He holds his head higher. "Never." See, I was right. I know him better than he thinks.

"Okay. Don't say I didn't offer."

With that, I take off, running at my usual fast pace. No more Mr. Nice Guy—or woman, in my case. I can already tell he's not going to last much longer, but if he's too proud to admit defeat, then who am I to stop the inevitable.

"I'm no quitter, Miss Ryan."

"Don't I know it, Mr. Cavanagh." His eyes dart in my direction, so I give him a cheeky wink. Bless his stubborn heart.

A few hundred metres later, we approach a steep incline, and again I'm fighting my grin. The lactic acid is building in my legs, so I can only imagine how he must be feeling. I've trained myself over the years to push through the pain, but it took a long time for me to master that.

As predicted, we only make it halfway up the hill before he stops. Turning around, I continue to jog on the spot.

"Can you give me a minute to catch my breath?" he asks, holding up his hand momentarily.

As amusing as this has been, I can't keep it up. I stop jogging and walk to him. He's bent over with his hands on his knees as he struggles to get air into his lungs.

"How about we head home?"

"You mean it?" He looks up at me with a weak smile on his face. "Because I'm not going to lie, you almost fucking killed me just now."

I hold my stomach as I burst out laughing, eventually pulling myself together enough to reach for his hand. "We can walk the rest of the way. I'm tired too."

"I call bullshit on that one. You're just trying to make

me feel better." He links his fingers with mine as we take the short route back to his apartment building.

"My legs still feel like jelly," Logan says as we step into the shower.

"Aww, poor baby." Reaching for the body wash, I squirt some into my hand. "You'll build up your stamina in time."

"Not happening. That's the first and last time I ever go running with you."

"You're quitting already?"

"I have a renewed admiration for runners after this morning."

"You mean the pansies?"

"Okay, maybe I was quick to judge."

"Yes, you were."

Stepping back into the stream, he lets the hot water wash over him. The liquid glistens against his olive skin, which only seems to accentuate every one of his delicious muscles.

"This feels so good."

"Let me wash you."

"My arms are fine. It's my legs."

"I want to do this."

"You're just looking for a reason to put your hands on me."

"Am I that transparent?" I say, laughing. Placing my palms flat on his chest, I move my hands in a circular motion across his shoulders, over his pecs, and down his defined abs. "You shouldn't be so irresistible."

"Is that so?" When my fingers move a little lower and

my eyebrows rise, he quickly captures my wrists. "I have no energy left for that."

"For what?" I say, playing innocent.

"Don't play coy with me, Miss Ryan. I've seen that look before."

"Just relax, then, and let me do all the work."

"Jesus," he groans as my fingers wrap around his shaft, moving up and down in long calculated strokes. "Are you trying to finish me off?"

"Yes, but not in the way you're implying."

I fall to my knees and take him in my mouth.

"Brooke," he groans as he places his hand on the back of my head to still me. A primal growl rips from his throat as he slowly rocks his hips, pumping into my mouth.

"Mm," I moan.

"Do that again."

"Mm."

"*Yes*. That sends vibrations down my cock." Pleasing him is such a turn-on.

He suddenly withdraws and slides his hands under my arms, effortlessly lifting me to my feet. "I need to be inside you." He backs me into the wall and raises my body off the ground. "Wrap your legs around me."

"Are you sure you're up to this? A few minutes ago—"

"Shh," he says, placing his hand over my mouth. "It may in fact kill me, but what a way to go."

We wander down to the Western Boardwalk at the Sydney Opera House for brunch after our shower. "Hmm," I say, looking over the menu. "I'm not sure what I feel like."

"I could eat a damn horse," Logan replies, making me laugh.

"I don't think they have horse on the menu."

"Very funny," he says. "After the amount of calories I burnt off this morning, I need something with sustenance. I might have the big breakfast, or the pancakes ... maybe both."

"You ran a kilometre, not a marathon."

"That's huge for me."

"Not for me," I say, shrugging. "I might have some fruit and yogurt."

He shakes his head. "I don't know how you survive on that shit, especially with the amount of exercise you do."

"It's not shit; it's good for me."

He looks at me over the top of his menu and smiles. "I know babe, and I love that you look after yourself."

The waitress approaches our table. "Are you ready to order?" she asks. My gaze moves to Logan to take the lead, but when he looks up at her, his face pales. "Logan!"

"Mandy." His eyes dart to me before moving back to her. I have no idea who this woman is, but I can tell by his reaction that she's somebody to him.

"I can't believe it." She's beaming as she speaks. "How are you?"

"I'm doing great. How are you?"

"Things are okay with me, I guess," she says with a shrug. "You look amazing by the way, but you always did."

He clears his throat, as he shuffles uncomfortably in his seat. "How's Brent?"

"We're not together anymore." His eyes don't leave her as he reaches across the table to take hold of my hand. "You of all people know what he's like. He left me and the kids a few months ago. He's shacking up with some nineteen-year-old he met at the gym. Hence why I'm working here. Somebody has to pay the bills."

"I'm sorry to hear that," Logan says, but his tone sounds anything but sincere.

"Are you still working with your dad?"

"No, he retired years ago. I'm running the company now."

"Wow. Good for you." She reaches out, placing her hand on his arm, and I don't like it. "You always were a hard worker; you deserve all the success."

He tugs at the collar of his shirt. I've never seen him like this before. My eyes move to her and take her in. She's beautiful, with a tall, slender figure, large blue eyes, and long blonde hair. She's so fixated on him that I don't even think she realises I'm sitting here.

"Have you decided what you're having, Hot Stuff?" I ask, not only as an attempt to break this moment they appear to be having, but also to alert her to my presence.

Her head snaps in my direction as a fake smile graces her face. "Hot Stuff—how cute. And very fitting, I must say."

Bitch.

I force myself to smile as my attention moves back to Logan. The corners of his lips turn up slightly when our eyes meet.

"Amanda, this is my girlfriend, Brooke. Brooke, this is Amanda."

I feel somewhat relieved when he introduces me as his girlfriend, but it doesn't escape me that he greeted her as Mandy. They must be close if he has a pet name for her.

"Girlfriend, wow." I don't miss her condescending tone as she eyes me up and down before giving Logan her full attention once more. "I thought you'd be married with children by now."

He intakes a large breath and averts his gaze down to the table. I wait for him to reply to her comment, but he doesn't. Instead, he just sits there fidgeting with the napkin in front of him. It's painful seeing him like this.

"Can we get the fruit platter with a side of yoghurt and the big breakfast please," I say, picking up both menus and passing them to her. Hopefully, she can take a hint.

"Of course."

"How would you like your eggs?" Amanda asks, her eyes moving back and forth between us.

"Not fussed," Logan says, flicking his hand slightly.

"Sunny side up," she replies, writing it down on her pad. "I remember how you like your eggs, Mr. Cavanagh." She gives him a sweet smile as she taps her pen on his shoulder.

I roll my eyes. *I remember how you like your eggs, Mr. Cavanagh.* When I notice the deliberate sway in her hips as she walks away, my eyes move back to Logan. I'm almost expecting him to be fixated on her arse, but instead, he's looking at me.

"Who is that?" I ask.

"My ex."

My eyes widen. "The one who ran off with your best friend?"

"The very one."

"Wow," I say, sitting back in my chair as a sickly feeling settles in the pit of my stomach. That feeling only intensifies when Logan runs his fingers through his hair and sighs as his gaze moves back down to the table. I reach for his hand. "Are you okay?"

"Of course." But I know him well enough to know he's anything but okay.

My worries are confirmed when the food finally arrives. I watch him push his food around on his plate.

"I thought you said you could eat a horse."

He shrugs as his eyes remain cast downwards. "I've lost my appetite."

Chapter 39

Logan

"Kiddo," my uncle says when I enter his hospital room. He's recovering well and has been moved out of ICU and into a ward. "It's good to see you." His head manoeuvres to the side as he looks around me, but it's a fruitless move because I came here alone. "Brooke's not with you?"

"No, she's downstairs with the doctor having her stitches removed." It's the truth, but I don't have the heart to tell him that she didn't want to see him. Hopefully, in time she'll open up to having some kind of relationship with him.

"How's she doing?"

"She's doing great." I reach for the chair by the wall and drag it closer to the bed. "She's going back to work on Monday."

"Are you sure she's ready for that?"

"It's what she wants, and I'm not going to stand in her way. Besides, she loves her job. It makes her happy."

"What does she do?"

"She's a dance teacher and choreographer. You

should see her; she's amazing." I feel myself smiling as I talk about Brooke.

"You're really taken with her, aren't you?"

"I've never felt like this before—ever. I'm going to marry this one."

"That's exactly how I felt about her mother. She captured my heart the moment I met her. I've never loved anyone or anything as fiercely as I did Maree, and I doubt I ever will again."

"That's how I feel about Brooke."

"Her likeness to her mother is uncanny. The moment I saw her at Lara's party I knew she was my daughter."

"That sounds so foreign."

"What?"

"You calling her your daughter."

"Like it or not, it's the truth."

"So, you're adamant Brooke is yours?"

"Yes. And when I get out of here, I plan on righting the wrongs I committed all those years ago, including telling Kathleen."

"You know you're liable to end up back in here if you do that."

He grabs hold of his side as he laughs at my response. I pity him; she's not going to take this news well.

"You're probably right, but she needs to know. I should've told her years ago."

"You're a braver man than I am."

"I'm also going to ask her for a divorce."

"Are you serious?"

"Yes."

Those words make me happier than they should. "I feel like I've waited my entire life for you to say that. Despite everything, you deserve better. You know I'll help you out any way I can."

"I know you will. It's been a long time coming. Having a near-death experience has given me clarity." He sighs. "My life would've been so different if I had followed my heart from the very beginning."

"Why didn't you?"

"Come on, you know what Kathleen's like. It would've ended badly for everyone involved."

"The alternative wasn't much better. From what Brooke tells me, life was really tough for her and her mum."

"For years I searched for them—well, for Maree. I wasn't even sure if she'd gone through with the pregnancy." He bows his head, and I can feel his shame from here. "Especially after what I said to her."

"After you told her to terminate it?"

"Yes." He clears his throat. "I panicked."

"Because you weren't ready to be a father, or you were worried about what your wife would do?"

"My marriage to Kathleen was never based on love; it was more of a business relationship, but that still doesn't excuse what I did." His gaze moves back to me, and I can see the pain in his eyes. "I could've handled whatever backlash she handed me because I deserved it, but it was what she would've done to Maree that worried me most." He pauses briefly and then a smile tugs at his lips. "She was so sweet and innocent, a lot like Brooke. You know as well as I do how brutal your aunt can be. She would've crucified her." He pauses, adjusting the pillow behind his head. "I really fucked things up, and not a day goes by when I haven't regretted my actions."

I'm still struggling to wrap my head around all of this, and I can't help but worry about Brooke and how this is going to affect her.

"Do you know when they're going to let you out of here?" I ask, changing the subject.

"Soon, I hope."

"You had us all worried. What possessed you to jump into the path of a bullet?"

"I heard screaming while I was waiting outside, but when neither you, nor Mike emerged, I knew something was wrong. That's when I decided to enter the house. When I saw Brooke bleeding and unconscious on the floor and the gun trained on you, I had to do something."

"You were willing to sacrifice your life for us?"

"Absolutely. You've always been like a son to me, and Brooke, well ..." He pauses briefly before continuing. "I've let that poor girl down her entire life, so giving up mine in exchange for hers was the least I could do."

"She's really struggling with this you know."

"I know."

"She's fiercely loyal to her mother."

"Rightly so. I'm a stranger to her, but hopefully, she'll allow me in so I can at least rectify that. If I could only just explain ..."

"Give her some time. She's been through enough."

"The last thing I want to do is hurt her any more than I have."

"Thank you," I say.

"Have you met her?"

"Who?"

"Brooke's mother?"

"No. She passed when Brooke was still in college."

When John's face pales I know that news has shocked him. 'You didn't know?'.

"No. No, I didn't."

I feel like a prick for just blurting it out like that. He

turns his face away from me, and when I see him wipe his eyes with the back of his hand, I feel even shittier.

"I'm sorry." I wait for him to say something, but he remains silent. "Would you like me to leave, so you can be alone?"

"Please." I don't miss the crack in his voice as he speaks.

Standing, I shove my hands into the pockets of my jeans. "I'll call you later." I briefly place my hand on his arm. I came here in the hope of cheering him up but have failed miserably. He nods, but doesn't turn back to face me. I turn to leave, but when I reach the doorway, a strangled sob escapes him. I pause for a moment because I feel torn. "Are you sure you want me to go?" I ask, eyeing him over my shoulder. When he nods again, I begrudgingly walk away.

"Are you okay?" Brooke asks, reaching across the centre console and placing her hand on my leg.

"Yes," I lie, as my eyes briefly leave the road to focus on her. "Why?"

She shrugs. "You're just quiet. You seem off."

"I'm fine." I remove one of my hands from the steering wheel and place it on top of hers.

"Was your uncle okay when you went to visit him?"

I let out a long breath. "He's doing much better. They've moved him out of intensive care and into a ward."

"That's good."

"How about I take you somewhere nice for lunch?" I ask, trying to change the subject.

"I'd like that. Maybe we could go back to that revolving restaurant at the top of Sydney Tower. That's if you want to, of course. I'm happy to go anywhere."

"Sure." Putting the indicator on, I turn and head in that direction. "I promised to take you back there anyway."

We're both silent as we come to a stop at a set of traffic lights. My thoughts are still on my uncle. I feel awful for leaving him. I should've stayed.

As I wait for the green light, I spot a large poster taped around a pole: *World Famous Russian Ballet Company—Sydney Opera House.* My gaze moves to Brooke, but she's looking out her window at the people passing by. Hopefully I can get tickets. I bet she'd love to see that.

I drive into the underground parking garage close to Pitt Street Mall. "I've just got to send a quick text," I say once I switch off the car.

> Logan: Claire, can you see if you can get two tickets to the Russian Ballet that's performing at the Opera House?

By the time I exit the vehicle, she replies.

> Claire: Sure, any particular seats?

I quickly respond.

> Logan: The best they have. I want to surprise Brooke.

Walking around to the passenger side, I open the door and extend my hand to her. Fingers crossed they're not sold out. Although ballet isn't my thing, there's nothing I wouldn't do to see my girl smile.

"It's only eleven," I say, looking down at my watch. "How about a little retail therapy before lunch?"

"Sounds good. Is there anything, in particular, you're after?"

"I was thinking about you."

"I don't really need anything," she says. But I've seen how sparse her wardrobe is.

"I was thinking formal wear. I have some work functions coming up."

"Oh." She goes quiet.

"You don't want to come with me?"

"Of course, but money is tight right now."

"I didn't say anything about you paying."

"And I'd rather you didn't."

A smile tugs at my lips. "Come on," I encourage. "It won't hurt to look." She gives me a dubious expression, but doesn't argue.

"This is nice," I say when we walk into the first store and I eye a red dress. I love that colour on her.

"It's okay." When she screws her face up, I chuckle. "The colour's nice, but I'm not keen on the style."

"Show me what you like then."

"This," she says, taking a baby blue dress off the rack and holding it up. "It's so pretty." I love how unspoilt and unpretentious she is. She's gone without her entire life and deserves all the pretty things. "I love, love, *love* this one." She picks up an emerald green dress and eyes it. "Oh, and that black one over there."

"Can I help you with anything?" the sales assistant asks when she approaches us.

"We're just looking," Brooke replies.

"Actually, she'd like to try on a few dresses." I have to fight my smile when I see Brooke's eyes narrow. "It won't hurt to try them on."

"But—"

"Come on, humour me."

"Fine," she says with a sigh.

"What size are you?" the assistant asks.

"A ten."

She takes the emerald dress out of Brooke's hands and grabs the right size. "The fitting rooms are this way."

Brooke follows her, but I hang back. Once they're out of sight, I grab a size ten in the other two dresses she admired.

Heading towards the back of the store, I hand them to the sales assistant. "She'd like to try these on too."

I stand there and watch as she knocks on the changing room door, where Brooke is. "Your husband would like you to try these on too."

Brooke pops her head through the slightly ajar door. When she sees the dresses, her eyes dart to me. "He's not my husband," she grumbles, making me laugh.

"I'm her future husband," I state. Her eyes narrow and my amusement grows.

"Let me know if you need a hand," the assistant says to her before turning her attention to me. "You can take a seat there."

My phone chimes the moment I sit down. Pulling it out of my pocket, I see it's from Claire.

> Claire: All the good seats are sold out for the weekend shows, but I can get box seats during the week.

I'm not concerned about what day we go; I just want her to have the best experience possible.

> Logan: Box seats sound good, just make sure you keep my schedule open that day.

I can't wait to surprise her with these tickets. She can wear one of the dresses she's trying on.

> Claire: Okay, I'll purchase them now. The contractor got back to me earlier too. He can meet you at the site tomorrow afternoon at two. Do you want me to confirm that time?

Time isn't on my side, so I'll have to arrange for someone to come to the penthouse to sit with Brooke. I only have a matter of weeks to get this warehouse converted.

> Logan: Two's perfect. Thanks, Claire.

When I hear Brooke clear her throat, I look up from the phone. "Jesus," I say as my breath hitches in my throat. "Babe, you look stunning."

"It's pretty isn't it?" Her face lights up as she admires the dress in the mirror.

"We should get it." I stand and close the distance between us.

"It's four-and-a-half-thousand-dollars," she whispers so only I can hear. "I can't afford that."

"But I can."

"No, you can't."

"I earn more than that in an hour."

Her eyes slightly widen at my admission. "Irrelevant."

I sigh. "Try one of the others then."

"They're just as expensive."

"Just try them," I demand, slapping her arse.

"It's pointless."

"Would you do it for me? Please."

She blows out a puff of air before heading back into the fitting room.

Each dress looks just as beautiful as the next, but I'm pretty sure she'd look good in anything. "Which one was your favourite?" I ask once she's changed back into her own clothes.

"I'm not telling," she answers.

"Why?" I ask, chuckling.

"Because I know you too well, Mr. Cavanagh."

"What's that supposed to mean?"

"You're not fooling me. As soon as I tell you which dress is my favourite, you'll buy it."

"Actually, you're wrong," I say, taking the dresses out of her hand. She stands there watching me, as I walk towards the sales assistant.

"How did she do?" she asks.

"Great, we'll take these."

"All of them?"

"Yes."

"No," Brooke says, coming up behind me.

"Yes," I reply, turning to face her.

"Logan!"

"Brooke!"

"I can't believe you," she says, crossing her arms over her chest. Her actions only manage to push her perky tits further up, which gives me an even better view of my girls.

Averting my eyes away from her spectacular cleavage, they move back to her face. "Please let me do this for you."

"But—"

I place my finger over her lips. "You'll be coming with me to all my work functions from now on, so you'll need these. Actually, you'll probably need a few more." My eyes move around the shop.

"Oh, no you don't," she says, placing her hands on either side of my face, turning it back towards her.

"I know your size; I can just come back another time."

"Okay," she says, sighing in defeat. "The black dress—that's my favourite. You can get me that one, but that's it."

A triumphant smile breaks out on my face as I lean forward and brush my lips against hers. "Thank you."

"You're ruthless. I'd hate to go up against you in court."

She's not the first person to say that to me. I may be a nice guy, but when it comes to my job, that's a totally different story.

Pulling my wallet out of my pocket, I head towards the counter. "We'll take them all."

When I feel Brooke pinch my side, I chuckle. I don't even flinch when the sales assistant gives me the total, but I hear Brooke gasp beside me. I've paid more than that for one of my suits. Passing over my black American Express card, my eyes move in her direction. The scowl on her face tells me she's pissed off, but I think that look is adorable on her.

"You're such a scammer," she says as we leave the store. "I'm going to pay you back. It'll wipe out my savings, but if there's one thing I'm not, it's a charity case."

"Hey." I stop walking and face her. "Is that what you think this is?"

She lifts one shoulder. "I don't want your money, Hot Stuff." When I see the tears in her eyes, I feel bad for deceiving her.

"Come here," I say, folding her in my arms. "I love

that you don't want my money—truly, I do—but I want to do nice things for you. It makes me happy." I draw back and place my finger under her chin, lifting her gaze to meet mine. "Is that such a crime?"

"I'm not used to this kind of thing."

"Well, get used to it. I want to spoil you."

"I don't need material things to be happy. Don't you understand that?"

"Yes, I understand. It's just one of the many things I love about you."

A smile tugs at her lips. "So, we can return the other two dresses then?"

"Nice try," I say, draping my arm over her shoulder as we continue walking.

"You suck." When she elbows me in the side, I laugh.

"I don't suck half as well as you do, baby."

"Oh my god," she says as her cheeks turn a pretty shade of pink.

"What? It's the truth."

Chapter 40

Brooke

"How was your first day back at work?" Chris asks as I slide into the back of the limousine.

Although it is now safe for me to catch the bus, Logan insisted that Chris continue to drive me.

"It was amazing—it felt so good to be back."

"You love it there, don't you?"

"Dancing is my life." He smiles at me in the rear-view mirror, before focusing back on the road. "Chris," I say a few minutes later. "Could you drop me off at my terrace house in Waterloo?"

"Why?" I see a frown form on his forehead.

"I need to clean the place up."

"Are you thinking of moving back there?"

"No. But I'll need to get my bond money back if I'm going to be able to afford another place."

"You're not staying with Mr. Cavanagh indefinitely?"

"No. He's been gracious enough to have me this long, but I think it's time I find a place of my own."

"He's not going to like this, you know."

"What? Me going back to clean the place up, or me moving out?"

"I'm guessing both."

I lean back into the seat.

"He offered to pay someone to clean up the terrace house for me, but I don't want that. It's something I'm more than capable of doing myself."

"I admire you for that," he says, smiling at me through the mirror once more.

We travel the rest of the way in silence, and Chris's words weigh heavily on my mind. Staying with Logan permanently is not something we ever discussed. It's way too early in our relationship to think about moving in together. I've only been there as long as I have because of my exceptional circumstances.

I undo my seatbelt when we pull up outside the terrace house. It's been weeks since I've been back here, and to say I'm feeling uneasy about going inside would be an understatement.

"Thank you."

"I'm not leaving you here on your own, Miss Ryan."

"Please call me Brooke, and you don't need to stay. I'm sure you have more important things to do."

"I'm already risking my job by bringing you here."

"He'd never fire you, Chris."

"I don't know. He's changed since he met you."

"How?" I enquire as we walk up the front path.

"Let's just say, you're very important to him. Work was always his number one priority, but now that's shifted to you."

"I'm lucky to have him," I say. "He's a good man."

"He is," Chris agrees. "And I'd say he's lucky to have you also."

"That's sweet of you to say." I rest my hand on his arm briefly before fishing in my bag for the keys. I gasp when I open the front door and step inside. "I forgot what a mess this place was." I can see the horror in Chris's expression as he takes in the room. "There's a lot to do here, but you really don't have to stay."

"Actually, I do." He removes his suit jacket, placing it over the back of a chair before rolling up his sleeves. "Where do you want me to start?"

"I have some gloves in the kitchen drawer. I'll go grab them and some rubbish bags."

Within an hour, we manage to get some sort of order back into the front room. We carried all the broken and unrepairable furniture outside and swept up all the glass and debris.

"I'm going to grab some steel wool and try to scrub off this paint," I say.

"You're going to need more than that. Do you have any acetone?"

"No. I do have some leftover white paint, but probably not enough to cover all the red."

"I've had my fence at home graffitied a few times, and acetone was the only thing to get it off."

"Oh."

"Why don't you start on one of the other rooms, and I'll run to the hardware store and get some."

"I don't want to put you out."

"It's no bother. I'm happy to be of some help."

Reaching for my bag, I pull out some money and pass it to him. "Thanks, Chris. I appreciate it."

Taking the rubbish bags into my bedroom, I start sorting through my clothes. Like the rest of the house, this room is trashed too.

After gathering everything off the floor, I start placing items into piles on the bed. At least I'll be able to salvage some of them, but what's torn will need to go in the bin.

Chris takes longer than I expected, so when I'm

finished, I carry the bags to the bin outside and place the ones I'm going to keep by the front door.

"What the hell, Brooke?" a voice says, startling me. Swinging around, I come face to face with an unimpressed Logan.

"Hot Stuff." I notice Chris standing in the doorway with an apologetic look on his face.

"Let's go," he says, reaching for my hand.

"I'm not done here."

"Yes, you are!"

"No, I'm not," I snap crossing my arms over my chest.

"I told you I'd hire someone to clean this place for you."

My hands now move to my hips. "And I told you, I'd do it myself."

"Brooke!" I can tell he's angry, but I'm not budging on this.

Ignoring him, I turn to Chris. "Did you get the acetone?"

"Yes." He lifts the bottle in his hand before walking around Logan to hand it to me. "Mr. Cavanagh called to see if you'd gotten home safe," he whispers. "I'm sorry. I couldn't lie to him."

"I wouldn't expect you to." I planned on telling him where I'd been, I was just hoping it would be after the fact. Turning, I go to walk further into the room, but Logan steps around me, blocking my path. "I don't want to fight with you over this," I say, "but it's important to me that I get this done. I can't afford to lose my bond." His eyes scan my face, but he remains silent. "Are you going to let me pass, or do I have to hurt you?"

My empty threat has a smile tugging at his lips. "You're incredibly stubborn. You know that, right?"

"Well, that makes two of us," I say.

"I don't want you to do this."

"Tough. I'm not relenting, so you can either roll up your sleeves and help or move out of the way." He raises his eyebrows in defiance, but I stand strong. He may be used to paying people to do his dirty work, but that's not how my mother raised me. "I refuse to waste money paying someone to do a job I'm quite capable of doing myself."

His nostrils flare slightly, and I'm expecting him to lose his cool, but instead, he blows out a frustrated breath before removing his jacket.

"Fine."

"Thank you." Stepping forward, I slide my arms around his waist.

"This isn't the end. I plan on punishing you later," he warns, softly enough that only I can hear. I yelp when he slaps my arse.

Drawing back, my eyes meet his. "I look forward to it."

"Minx," he mumbles under his breath as I walk away.

"Are you sure you can't come with me?" Logan asks, gathering me in his arms.

He's been unexpectedly called to Melbourne on business.

"I wish I could, but I've already had enough time off work. This job is important, and I have a lot of people counting on me. Our annual concert is coming up and there's so much to do; I'm already behind."

"I hate leaving you."

"You'll be back tomorrow."

"I know," he says, sighing. "But that's a whole twenty-four hours away."

"Absence makes the heart grow fonder, Mr. Cavanagh."

"My heart couldn't get any fonder if it tried, Miss Ryan."

"I will miss you though." He reaches out, tucking my hair behind my ear.

"I don't know how I'm going to sleep tonight without you beside me," he confesses.

"I'm sure you'll manage."

He releases me when his phone chimes in his pocket. Pulling it out, he looks down at the screen. "Chris is downstairs. I need to go; otherwise, I'll miss my flight."

Raising my hand, my fingertips tenderly skim down the side of his face. "Be safe, and good luck today."

"I love you," he says, brushing my lips with his.

"I love you too."

"I'll call you when my plane touches down in Melbourne."

"Please do."

He gives me another hasty kiss before reaching for the handle of his suitcase. "Chris will be back in time to take you to work."

"Okay." I stand in the foyer as he steps into the lift. "Bye."

"Bye, babe."

He blows me a kiss as the doors close. It's only a day, but I know it's going to feel like an eternity while he is gone.

"Can I help?" I ask Jill as I enter the kitchen.

"If you like. Since it's just you tonight, I thought I'd make your favourite."

"Salmon?"

"Yes. You can get a start on the salad if you like."

"I can make my own dinner," I say, "if you'd like to get away early."

"That's fine, dear. I have nowhere else to be. I usually travel with Mr. Cavanagh, but he insisted I stay here and care for you."

"That was sweet of him. Chris stayed behind also."

"Mr. Cavanagh thinks the world of you."

"I think the world of him too," I say. "Do you have enough salmon for two?"

"Oh, are you expecting company?"

"No, I was hoping you could join me for dinner."

"I'd like that," she says, smiling.

After gathering the ingredients for the salad from the fridge, I place them on the counter.

"Tell me about your family, Jill?"

"If you mean kids, then there's nothing to tell. I have a sister who lives in Perth. I don't see her as often as I'd like, but we talk on the phone a few nights a week."

"You never married?" She falls silent. "I'm sorry if I'm prying."

"Not at all," she says. "I guess the right man never came along."

"That's a shame."

She shrugs. "I don't have many regrets—not becoming a mother, maybe—but otherwise I'm happy with the life I've lived."

Once the salad is made, I grab a bottle of wine from the fridge. "Would you like a glass?"

"I'm not sure how Mr. Cavanagh would feel about me drinking on the job."

"I think he considers you more like family than an employee, Jill. Besides, you're my dinner guest tonight and it's no fun drinking on your own."

"Okay, you twisted my arm."

We no sooner sit down to eat when I hear the ding of the lift as it arrives at our floor. My heart starts to race. Did Logan change his mind and decide to fly back tonight? He didn't mention anything when I spoke with him earlier.

Standing, I rush towards the foyer, but I'm filled with disappointment when I see an attractive older lady standing there. Her dark hair is cut into a sharp bob, and the resting bitch face she's now sporting makes her appear far less attractive.

Who is this woman? A key is required to get up to this floor, and I'm gathering after his uncle's impromptu arrival last week that Logan isn't the only person who holds one.

"Oh, hi," I say, coming to an abrupt halt. "Are you looking for Logan? I'm Brooke, his girlfriend."

"I know exactly who you are," she bites.

"And you are?" I ask, taken aback by her rudeness.

"I'm Kathleen, Logan's aunt ... Johnathan's wife."

Although she speaks poshly, I don't miss the disdain in her voice, or the disgust in her eyes as she looks me up and down.

"I see."

John must have told her about me, so I gather this isn't a friendly visit.

"I presume you've heard of me or is that a question I should be asking your whore of a mother?"

"Excuse me?" I say, taking a step towards her. "How dare you."

"How dare I?" She laughs before taking the final stride that separates us. "You listen here, you little gold digger," she sneers, getting up in my face, "I'll say this once and once only: stay away from my husband."

"For your information, it was your husband who approached me, not the other way around."

I can tell my reply catches her off guard. "From what I remember of your mother, Johnathan was one of many, so I wouldn't bank on him being your father."

My hand's fist by my sides. As far as I know, this woman never met my mother, but if she makes one more remark about my mum or her character, I don't know how I will react.

"It takes more than just sperm to make someone a parent, so it's safe to say biological or not, he's not deserving of the title of father."

"Well, I never," she gasps, placing her hand on her chest. "But then again, I wouldn't expect anything better from you. You're trash, just like I knew you would be. It won't take my nephew long to figure that out. A pretty face with no substance is his usual modus operandi. It's only a matter of time before someone else catches his attention."

"I can see why your husband looked for love outside his marriage. You're just as cold and vindictive as I was led to believe."

I don't even see her hand rise until it connects with the side of my face.

"Oh, my goodness," Jill says, hastily appearing at my side. "Are you okay, dear?" I nod instead of replying because I'm still shocked that she hit me. Jill gently moves me behind her, shielding me. "Leave," she screams at Kathleen, pointing towards the lift.

"I don't take orders from the help."

"You'll do as I say, or I'll be forced to remove you myself."

Logan's aunt squares her shoulders before turning on her heels with a huff.

Jill and I stand there in silence while Kathleen steps into the lift. Needing the last word, she turns to face us once more.

"You've been warned," she barks, pointing her finger at me. "Stay away from Johnathan or you'll be sorry."

I don't bother justifying her threat with a reply. I have no intention of having a relationship with that man anyway.

The moment the doors close, Jill gathers me in her arms. I can feel her body trembling as she holds me.

"Let me look at you," she says, drawing back.

"I'm fine, Jill," I reply as tears cloud my eyes. They're not tears of sadness though; they're tears of anger and frustration. The nerve of that woman.

"You're not fine, you poor girl. Come, let me put some ice on your cheek." She wraps her arm around my shoulder and steers me towards the kitchen. "And don't listen to a word she said. She's a nasty piece of work that one."

Chapter 41

Logan

I'm consumed with rage as I sit on the side of the mattress, watching Brooke sleep. I'm racked with guilt for leaving her again.

The television at the base of the bed is on, but it's muted. Was she afraid to sleep alone in the dark? The light is enough to illuminate her pretty face, and her long brown hair fanned out on the pillow. A smile tugs at my lips when I spy the t-shirt I was wearing this morning tucked under her chin. She must've been missing me as much as I was missing her. It's scary how close we've become in such a short time.

I'm grateful Jill called me and told me what happened. I got back here as quickly as I could. I could've caught the red eye, but instead, I chose to charter a flight. It got me back a few hours earlier. I had some loose ends that I intended to tidy up in Melbourne tomorrow, but they'll have to wait. My priority was, and always will be, Brooke.

My aunt, however, will be feeling my full wrath as a result of her actions. Not only did she put Brooke through more unnecessary drama, but she also probably managed to widen the rift between her and John.

My anger spikes again when I spy a few scrunched-up tissues on the bedside table; *Brooke's been crying*. My fingertips gently ghost down the side of her face. I should never have left her; it was far too soon.

Standing, I strip down to my boxer briefs before rounding the bed and climbing in beside her. Sliding my arm under the crook of her neck, I drape the other around her waist and draw her close.

My actions have Brooke stirring. I didn't mean to wake her. Rolling over, she faces me.

"Hey," she says in a sleepy voice. "You're home."

I force out a smile, trying to mask my true feelings. "Jill called and told me what happened, so I chartered a flight early. Are you okay?"

"I am now that you're back."

Leaning forward, I brush my lips against hers. "I'm sorry about what happened. I'll make sure she never comes near you again."

Brooke snuggles her body into mine, resting her head on my chest. "You have nothing to be sorry for."

"I feel responsible."

"Don't," she says, closing her eyes.

She is already drifting back to sleep as I lean down and place a soft kiss on her forehead. I'm too wound up to sleep. I tried to call my aunt the moment I got off the phone with Jill, but she didn't pick up. I bet she only had the balls to come here last night because she somehow knew I wasn't home. She may have been able to intimidate me when I was a child, but that shit doesn't work on me anymore.

"Open up," I yell as I pound my fist on my aunt's front door.

"Logan," she says, placing her hand on her chest like she's surprised by my visit. *Give me a break*. Did she honestly think I wouldn't show up here?

"I'm here to collect the key to my apartment."

"What?"

I hold my hand out in front of me. "You heard me ... the key."

"But—"

"I won't ask again. Give me the fucking key." Her eyes widen in shock. Although I've never liked her, I've always been respectful. It was how I was raised. But I'm done playing Mr. Nice guy. Someone should've put this woman in her place years ago. "I'm waiting."

"Fine," she says, squaring her shoulders. Turning, she storms down the hallway. "Here." She slams it into my hand when she returns, and I have to restrain myself from reacting. It wasn't her key anyway; I gave it to John.

"If you ever talk to, call, harass, or even look in Brooke's direction again, so help me god, your life won't be worth living."

I hear my aunt gasp as I turn around and make my way down the path towards the limousine. She's lucky I'm a gentleman. No man should ever raise a hand to a woman, but I'm a big believer in what goes around comes around, and I have a feeling her karma is on its way.

I don't even make it to my office before I get a call from my father.

"What the hell just happened with Kathleen?"

"I went around there to get my key back," I reply.

"She was in tears when she called. She said you attacked her." I roll my eyes.

"She's a liar, I did no such thing. I bet she left out the part about going to my apartment last night, and not only threatening Brooke but slapping her across the face."

"She did what?" he bellows down the line.

"Exactly." My aunt is a professional when it comes to playing the victim; she's done it her entire life. She has my father wrapped around her little finger. "Open your eyes, Dad. Your sister is a nasty piece of work."

"Look—"

"No, you look." I blow out a long breath, trying to compose myself before continuing. "What's going on between Kathleen and John has nothing to do with Brooke."

"Although I wholeheartedly disagree with what she did, Kathleen seems to think Brooke's the reason John has asked for a divorce. She thinks you all are conspiring against her."

"Bullshit. Do you honestly believe that? You know as well as I do that Kathleen is the sole reason John's leaving. It's been a long time coming. The way she treats him is deplorable. In my opinion, he should've done this years ago."

Although my dad can be a jerk at times, he's never been disrespectful towards my mother, so he of all people should understand. He's seen that woman at her worst. Christ, he's had a front-row seat to it for years.

"She's my sister, Son."

"That may be true, but this has nothing to do with you, me, or Brooke for that matter. It's between Kathleen and John and we need to stay out of it. She made her bed, now she can lie in it."

With that, I hang up. I'm done with this conversation.

I take a few deep breaths before dialling my sister's number. "Michelle, it's me."

"Hey, big brother, how are you? How's Brooke?"

"News travels fast."

"What news?"

"You haven't heard about what happened last night?"

"No, what? Is Brooke all right? You guys didn't split up, did you?"

"No, of course not."

"Thank god."

"Kathleen came to my apartment while I was in Melbourne and slapped Brooke across the face."

"Oh my god. Why would she do that?"

"You really need to ask? You know what she's like."

"God, I hate that woman. Poor Brooke."

"She was pretty shaken up by it. That's actually why I'm calling. She's at work most of the day, but do you think you could call over this afternoon. I'm sure she'd love to see you, and I've got a big day ahead of me. I don't want her to be alone."

"Of course. I need to get Lara from school, but we can head over after that."

"Perfect," I say. "Oh, and please don't bombard her with questions. If she wants to open up to you, she will."

"You really need to ask me that? I'm not Mum."

"Right," I say, making us both laugh. "I should be home around six. We're going to Mum and Dad's for dinner tonight. I hope the old man is in one of his rare good moods."

"I hope so too," Michelle says. "The last thing poor Brooke needs is the alternative, especially after what she endured from Kathleen."

I'm already in two minds about going, but I know my mother will be devastated if we bail.

The first thing I hear when I step out of the lift is music. Michelle spots me straight away, but Brooke and Lara are so engrossed in what they're doing, they don't even realise I'm here.

I grin as I watch them, Lara is perched on Brooke's lap as they play the piano together. It's great to see my two favourite girls getting along.

My sister stands and makes her way towards me. "Hey," she says, kissing my cheek.

"Hey, sis. How's she been?"

"Good, considering. I didn't know she played the piano though. She's amazing."

"Isn't she?" I say, my smile growing.

"She's so good with Lara too. I don't want to impose, but do you think she'd consider giving her some lessons? Lara doesn't like the teacher she has now. She thinks she's mean."

"You can ask."

"You wouldn't mind?"

"Of course not," I reply. I'd love for Brooke to become more involved with the good side of my family.

"Okay, I'll ask her when I get the chance. I was thinking of inviting her out for lunch one day this week."

"She'd like that." *I'd like that.*

"Can you text me her number later?"

"Sure."

"I should think about going," Michelle says, looking down at her watch. "I know you've got dinner at Mum's, and Craig will be home from work soon."

"You should come to Mum's with us."

"It might be better if just the two of you go. You know how Dad gets when there's too many people around."

"Right," I say, chuckling.

God, I hope he doesn't embarrass me tonight. I'm still mortified by the way my aunt treated Brooke.

"Hey, babe," I say crossing the room.

"Hot Stuff." I love how her face lights up when she sees me.

Leaning down, my lips brush hers.

"Ooh, kissy, kissy," Lara says, making me laugh.

"Sounds like someone's jealous," I retort, scooping her up off Brooke's lap and dipping her in my arms. She squirms when I blow raspberries on her neck.

"Stop, Uncle Logan!" she squeals.

"We're going to head off," Michelle says to Lara when I place her back on her feet. "Say thank you to Brooke."

"I had the best time playing the piano with you, Aunty Brooke."

Brooke's smile brightens when Lara throws her arms around her neck. "I had the best time too. We should do it again sometime."

"I'd like that," Lara says. "Can I come back again, Mum?"

"Yes."

"Tomorrow?"

"Tomorrow, you have netball practice."

"The day after tomorrow?"

"We'll see."

That day's out too ... it's the night I'm taking Brooke to the ballet, but I don't mention it because it's a surprise. I can't wait to see the look on her face.

"Your house is lovely," Brooke says when Mum greets us in the hallway.

"Thank you. I'm so happy you're finally here." She gives Brooke a big squeeze before hugging me. "Come. Your dad's in the kitchen. He's looking forward to meeting Brooke."

I roll my eyes because my father never looks forward to meeting anyone, but I hope at the very least this means he's in a good mood.

It feels like there's a lot riding on tonight, which is why I was in two minds about coming.

I'm the first to enter the room. "Son," my dad says, rising from the table and extending his hand to me.

"Dad." I wait for Brooke to join me before introducing her. "Brooke, this is my father, Robert."

"It's nice to meet you," he says, also extending his hand to her.

"It's nice to finally meet you too," she replies, stepping forward. But instead of grasping his hand, she wraps her arms around his waist.

I instinctively hold my breath as I await his reaction. My father is *not* a hugger.

At first, he looks a little shocked, but then he slowly—and very awkwardly—raises an arm and pats her on the back. When a hint of a smile curves at his lips, my eyes dart to my mother, and she's grinning as she watches them. I, on the other hand, am waiting for the storm to hit, but surprisingly, it doesn't come.

When Brooke lets him go and retreats a step, my father clears his throat. Releasing a soft chuckle, he shakes his head. Maybe he's just as stunned by his own pleasantries as I am.

That introduction couldn't have gone better if I had

scripted it myself. However, the night is still young, so my scepticism remains.

I take a step towards the table and pull out a chair for Brooke.

"Can I get either of you a drink?" my mum asks.

"I'll get them. Would you like another beer, Dad?"

"Sure."

"A wine for you?" I ask Brooke as I place my hands on her shoulders. I smile down at her when she looks up at me.

"Yes, please."

I follow my mother into the kitchen, where we both have a clear view of the dining room table. Brooke says something to my father, and this time I'm not mistaken by his grin.

"Did you slip something into dad's drink before we got here?"

"Logan," my mum says, slapping my arm. "I'd never do anything like that."

"Is he drunk?

"Of course not."

"Huh, I wasn't expecting him to be so ... nice," I say, opening the fridge.

"Your father is capable of being nice," my mother scolds, grabbing two wine glasses from the cupboard.

Seldom, I want to add, but I refrain. The man my mother sees is very different than the one I do.

I crack the top off both beers before crossing the room to hand one to my father. The home phone starts ringing, and when my mother goes to answer it, my dad holds up his hand to stop her. "Just let the machine take it, love."

The room falls silent as the recorded message clicks in. *"Hi, you have reached the Cavanagh's residence. I'm sorry we aren't able to take your call at the moment, please leave your name and number after the tone, and we'll get back to you as soon as possible."*

The beep sounds and my aunt's voice comes over the machine. Just hearing it makes me inwardly cringe. "Robert, it's me, Kathleen. The hospital just called to say Johnathan is being released tomorrow." I roll my eyes when I hear her sniffle. "He's not welcome here after the way he's treated me. When I expressed that to the discharge nurse, she said if a family member can't take him in, he'll be transferred to a nursing home until he's fully recovered and able to care for himself. Under no circumstances is he welcome to stay with you, do you hear me?"

"That bitch," my mother mumbles under her breath. "How could she."

"Did you really expect anything less from her? You know what she's like," I say, seething. "He can't go to a nursing home, he'll hate that."

"I agree," my father replies. "But I can't go against my sister's wishes, she's going through a really tough time right now."

As usual, my father is wearing his rose-coloured glasses. Why can't he see that his sister is a bully and an emotional blackmailer? Personally, I'm done with her games.

I place Brooke's drink down in front of her and seat myself at the table. The moment I do, I take a long chug of my beer, now wishing it was straight scotch.

"She deserves everything she gets. She's a gaslighting narcissist, and she brought this on herself." My words are laced with venom, but I can no longer hide my disdain for that woman.

"He needs to be around family," my mum says. "Not with strangers."

I agree. I'd take him in a heartbeat if I didn't have Brooke living with me, but I can't force him on her right now. Their situation is fragile.

"He can't stay here, Patricia."

"But Robert."

"No buts," my father says, putting his foot down.

There's no way my mother is going to disagree with my father in front of us. Growing up, she never did. She'd keep her opinions to herself until my sister and I were safely tucked away in bed, and then she'd let him have it. It didn't happen often, but it felt like retribution when it did. She's the only one who can get away with speaking to him like that.

My gaze moves to Brooke, and I find her staring down at her lap. I reach for her hand under the table, wrapping it in mine. I'll sort something out. I don't want her worrying about this.

Chapter 42

Brooke

My cheek is resting against Logan's bare chest, as his hand lightly skims over my hair. We've been lying here in silence for the past twenty minutes.

"You're quiet this morning."

"I'm just tired, I didn't sleep well last night."

His hand stills. "Are you okay?"

"Yeah, I just have a lot on my mind."

"Like what?"

"John."

Logan shifts, rolling onto his side to face me. "That isn't your concern, babe," he says, gently brushing the hair from my forehead with the tips of his fingers.

"I'm not sure a nursing home is the best place for him."

"We'll work something out."

"I think he should stay here."

In my heart, I know it's the right thing to do. Logan is close with his uncle and if it wasn't for me, he wouldn't hesitate to bring him here.

"You want my uncle to stay here, with us?"

I go quiet. This is where my predicament lies. I'm

pretty sure Logan won't agree to this if it means me moving out, but on the other hand, I'm not sure I could handle being under the same roof as that man.

"This arrangement was never permanent."

"What does that even mean, Brooke?" he asks, frowning. "Are you breaking up with me?"

"What? No. I love you," I say, resting the palm of my hand on his cheek.

"I love you too, but if having him here means I'll lose you, then the answer is a definite no."

"I had a feeling you'd say that, but we always knew that I'd move out eventually."

"I don't want that; I need you here. My home is nothing without you in it."

I sigh. "Well, I'll just need to find a way to deal with having him around, then."

"I don't want that either. If it's going to make you feel uncomfortable, then again, the answer is no."

"He's your uncle. He needs you."

"I know, but you are my life. You'll always come first."

His sweet words bring a lump to my throat. "He's family and has nowhere else to go."

By family, I mean *his* family, not mine. He may technically be my father, but I can't ever imagine myself looking at him that way.

"You have the kindest heart. You always put other people's wants and needs before your own."

"I had a good teacher," I say. "That's exactly how my mother was with everyone."

"I wish I could've met her."

"Me too." A sadness washes over me just thinking about it. "She would've loved you."

"I'll let my uncle come here on one condition."

"What's that?" I ask.

"If at any stage it gets too hard for you, you need to tell me. This is your home, and I don't want you feeling uncomfortable."

"Okay."

"I mean it, Brooke."

"I know."

"I'll call past the hospital on my way to work and discuss it with him." Lifting his head, he looks at the time on the clock. "Speaking of work, I don't have to get up for another half hour."

Logan effortlessly drags my body over his, and I can already feel him hardening under my weight. "I wonder how we can pass the time?"

Flipping me back down onto the mattress, he settles between my legs. His mouth moves to my jawline, as he trails kisses down my neck.

Blindly reaching for the drawer beside the bed, he retrieves a condom. "I plan on spending it inside you."

He uses his big strong arms to push himself into a kneeling position. My eyes follow his every move as he rolls the condom down his impressive length. Although we've been intimate more times than I can count, my body still vibrates with anticipation as I await his next move.

Cupping his hands behind my knees, he pushes my legs toward my chest and spreads me wide. "Here with you, is, and always will be, my favourite place to be."

For some reason, his words fill me with dread. I've never felt as close to anyone as I do with him, but I know how cruel life can be, and how fast things can change. My marriage to Jake is the perfect example.

"I hope what we share never changes."

"Never," he says with such conviction I feel tears sting my eyes.

My hands reach up to cup his face. "Promise me." I know it's unfair to even ask, but the insecure side of me needs to hear it.

"I promise I'll love you until I take my last breath. Even then, I won't stop."

"What I feel for you, it scares me at times," I admit.

"I feel the exact same way." He shifts his body until he's completely covering mine, and I anchor my legs around his waist. Grasping my wrists, he drags my arms above my head and laces our fingers together. His eyes never leave mine as he slowly sinks himself inside me. "You consume my every thought ... my every breath, and that will never change."

My eyelids flutter close as he withdraws slightly before rocking his hips forward, filling me completely.

A part of me wishes we could stay like this, lost in the moment forever. "I love you," I whisper.

"I love you too ... *so damn much*, sometimes it hurts."

Butterflies churn in my stomach as I sit in front of the television, trying to distract myself. Logan texted me half an hour ago to say he was on his way back here with his uncle. Although I was trying to do the right thing by suggesting he come and stay here until he's fully recovered, I'm now having second thoughts.

Just thinking about being in this house with him, with nowhere to escape, makes me incredibly anxious.

"I'm heading off now," Jill says, coming into my view. "Is there anything I can get you before I go?"

Take me with you. "No, but thank you."

"Dinner is ready to be dished up when Mr. Cavanagh and Mr. Sanders arrive."

"I appreciate that, Jill."

"I've made up Mr. Sanders's room. I've put him at the end of the hall to give you and Mr. Cavanagh some privacy." I nod. "I'm looking forward to having him stay. He's such a nice man."

"So I've been told."

I place the remote down beside me. Everybody seems to forget all the awful things he said, and how poorly he treated my mother. There was nothing *nice* about that.

Lowering her bag to the floor, she takes a seat beside me. "I know this isn't easy for you, dear," she says, placing her hand on my leg. "But I think spending some time together will do you both some good. A chance to get to know each other better." I shrug my shoulders because it's easier than voicing my true feelings. "Just give him a chance." I give her a half-hearted smile. What chance did he give my mother, or me, for that matter? She sits there silently for a moment before standing. "I'll see you in the morning then."

"Okay."

She leans down and places a soft kiss on the top of my head. "It'll all work out. Just have faith."

Her words do nothing to calm me. If anything, they only increase my uneasiness. I don't want this to come between me and Logan, so I'll be polite, but having a relationship with that man is the furthest thing from my mind.

Standing, I head into the kitchen and pour myself a glass of wine. I'm not much of a drinker, but I manage to consume the entire contents of my glass in two large gulps before pouring myself a second one. I need something to take the edge off.

I'm busy setting the table when they finally arrive. "Hey, babe," Logan says, crossing the room to plant a chaste kiss on my lips. He has a suitcase in his hand, which I presume is John's.

"Hey. Dinner is prepared, I'm just setting the table."

My eyes remain on Logan. I can't bring myself to look in John's direction.

"Hi, Brooke," John finally says, and my gaze briefly darts to him.

He looks much better than the last time I saw him. In his hands, he's holding a wooden box about the size of a shoebox. The sweet smile on his face has my stomach in knots. I'm in two minds; for Logan's sake I'm glad he's here, but I feel like I'm doing an injustice to my mother.

My eyes move back to the table before I answer. "Hi, John."

"I appreciate you letting me stay here until I can make other arrangements."

I force a smile and nod. I don't trust myself to speak.

"Jill made up the room at the top of the stairs," I say as my attention moves back to Logan. "I'll get dinner dished up, while you take John's things to his room."

I don't even wait for a reply before turning and heading towards the kitchen.

I busy myself placing the prepared food onto plates. I'm so lost in thought that I don't hear Logan enter. He startles me when his arms slide around my waist from behind.

"Are you okay?"
"I'm fine," I lie, glancing at him over my shoulder.
"Remember our deal?"
"Yes. Honestly, stop worrying. I'm good."
"Okay." I can hear the uncertainty in his voice, but

I'm grateful he doesn't push further. Instead, he places a soft kiss on my cheek. "Let me help you with these."

"That one is John's," I say, pointing to one of the plates. The less I have to interact with him, the better. "And this one is yours."

He picks them both up and heads towards the dining room. I take in a few deep breaths, preparing myself to sit down for a meal with a man I have absolutely no respect for. I usually love this time of night when Logan and I get to unwind as we share stories of our day. The way I'm feeling right now, I'll be lucky if I can keep my food down.

"How was your day, babe?" Logan asks the minute I'm seated.

"Good. Busy." I shrug.

I'm usually more detailed, but tonight I feel awkward talking about myself in front of John. I don't want him to know anything about my life.

My eyes move to Logan, and I find him watching me intently. I'm not good at stuff like this. I thought I'd be able to fake it through the next week or so, but now I'm not so sure.

"How are the plans for the concert coming along?"

"Good," I say. "It's chaotic, but an organised chaos, if that makes sense." I force out a smile. "How was your day?"

My eyes quickly dart to John as I await a reply from Logan, and I find him staring at me. I wish he'd stop.

"My day was pretty uneventful."

"Your sister called me this morning; she wants to do lunch one day this week."

"That's nice," Logan says, his face lighting up. "I'm glad you two are getting along."

"She's a good egg, that one," John adds, trying to insert

himself into our conversation. I begin eating, hoping that they both follow suit. "This is delicious, by the way. Did you cook this, Brooke?"

"No, Jill did," I reply with my eyes still focusing on my food.

It's funny; when I was a little girl, before I knew the depths of betrayal this man bestowed upon my mother, I would've given anything to sit and have a meal with him. *Anything.*

"Brooke's a great cook, though," Logan says. "You might get to taste some of her cooking while you're here."

I clear my throat before shoving a fork full of food into my mouth.

"I'd like that. Your mum was a great cook too. It must run in the family."

My head snaps in his direction, and I'm thankful that I'm still chewing because my response to that statement wouldn't be a pleasant one. I'm pretty sure the look on my face says it all. How dare he bring her up like that. He has no right to reminisce about my mother.

Logan's hand moves below the table, coming to rest on my leg. He gives me a sympathetic look before focusing his attention on John.

"After dinner, we can head into my home office and discuss what we're going to do about Kathleen."

"Sure," he replies as a look of sadness washes over him.

When I see it, I instantly feel bad. My emotions are giving me whiplash. I'm all over the place. The last thing he deserves is my compassion, but my traitorous psyche doesn't seem to comprehend that notion.

Thankfully, the rest of the meal is eaten in silence.

"I'll clean up here," I say once everyone is done.

"Let me help," Logan replies, standing.

"No, I'm fine. You two go and do whatever it is you need to do."

"Are you sure?"

"Yes."

He leans over the table and places a kiss on my forehead. "We won't be long."

"Take your time." I'm hoping by then I'll be in the safety of my bedroom.

As I collect the plates, Logan moves around to where John is sitting and helps him stand. Again, I'm filled with empathy. It's like an internal battle raging inside me; I want to hate this man, but a part of me won't allow it.

"Morning, beautiful," Logan says, nuzzling his face into my neck. My back is plastered to his front, and I'm wrapped tightly in his arms. It's a place where I feel safe.

"Morning, Hot Stuff."

He grilled me last night when he finally came to bed, but I remained strong and tried my best to reassure him that I'm okay with John being here. It's not like it's permanent, and I'll be working extra hours over the coming weeks, so that's going to make things easier.

"Don't make any plans for tonight," he says, running his tongue along my skin.

"Why?"

"I'm taking you out?"

"Really? Where?"

"It's a surprise," he says, sucking my earlobe into his mouth. "And you'll finally be able to wear one of those dresses I bought you."

"So, we're going somewhere fancy?"

Excitement bubbles inside me. It's been a long time since I've been able to dress up, and I've been dying to wear one of my new dresses. However, my enthusiasm dies the moment John enters my mind. Chances are, he'll probably be going with us, and that definitely puts a damper on things.

"Yes, just the two of us. I've organised for Jill to work late so my uncle won't be alone."

A huge smile breaks out over my face, and my eagerness returns. "Are you at least going to give me a hint?"

"Nope," he says, throwing back the covers and rising. "Like I said, it's a surprise."

"But I don't like surprises," I retort, pouting.

"You'll like this one."

I sit up the moment he disappears into the en suite and leap from the bed, dashing towards the walk-in robe. I wish I had more of an idea of where we were going. It would make my decision regarding which dress to wear a little easier.

Pulling the baby blue dress out first, I hold it in front of me in the mirror. "Wear the black one," Logan says, startling me.

Swinging around I find him in all his naked glory, leaning up against the architrave. My eyes drink him in. This man is flawless.

"And you need to wear something that shows off this," I reply, closing the distance between us to run my fingertip down his sternum and over his abs.

"Is that so?"

"Ah huh," I say, looking up at him through my eyelashes.

"Keep looking at me like that," he replies, pulling my body into his, "and I'm going to be late for work again."

"You're the boss, so it's not like you have anyone to answer to."

He chuckles. "Actually, today I have to be in court, so I'll have the presiding judge to answer to."

"Ugh."

Bringing his face forward, he captures my bottom lip between his teeth. "I promise to make it up to you tonight."

"I'll hold you to that."

"I don't doubt it," he says, slapping my arse.

"What time do I need to be ready?"

"I'm hoping to be home around five, so I can have a quick shower and change. I'd like to leave here by six at the latest."

I wish I knew where he was taking me, but I trust him when he says I'll like my surprise. He hasn't disappointed me yet, and always goes above and beyond.

Chapter 43

Brooke

Butterflies churn in my stomach as I descend the stairs that lead into the great room. I'm secretly praying that John is still in bed. I noticed his bedroom door was closed when I passed.

"Shit," I mumble under my breath when I reach the bottom and see him seated at the dining room table. His head is bowed as he flips through today's paper.

Lifting his coffee to his mouth, he raises his head and his gaze moves straight to me. The smile that bursts across his face hits me right in the chest.

"Morning, sweetheart," he says.

"Good morning." I'm not sure how I feel about him calling me sweetheart. "I hope you slept well."

"I did. It was great to be back in a real bed, and no longer hooked up to those machines."

I force out a smile as a wave of guilt flows through me. Despite everything I feel towards him, this man took a bullet for us.

"I bet," I say, moving past him into the kitchen.

"Morning, dear," Jill greets as I enter.

"Good morning, Jill."

"How are you this morning?" she asks, running her hand affectionately down my arm. "You were on my mind all night."

"To be honest, I'm struggling."

"Poor thing," she says. "You're not running this morning?"

"No, I have a big day at work. Our end of year concert is coming up, so I have routines to finalise."

"Can I get you a coffee?"

"Please."

"Do you want muesli and yogurt for breakfast?"

"Thanks."

I stand there stalling for a moment until Jill eventually shoos me out of the kitchen. "Go sit, I'll bring it out to you."

As much as it pains me, I have no choice but to join John at the table. He closes the paper and puts it to the side the second I sit down and gives me his full attention.

"Do you have any plans today?" he asks, and I hate the hopeful look I see in his eyes.

"Just work."

"Oh, I was hoping we'd have a chance to spend some time together."

"I'll be gone most of the day," I say, trying my best to remain polite.

I'm surprised when John reaches out to place his hand on top of mine.

"Sweetheart." My gaze darts back to him and I have the urge to pull my hand out from underneath his, but I don't. "I know this isn't easy for you, but if you could find it in your heart, I'd like the chance to explain."

"Explain what, exactly?" *That you're a cheater, a liar, a baby killer?*

"My marriage to Kathleen was purely one of convenience, you could say. We had a mutual admiration between us, but never love."

"I don't know why you're telling me this."

"In the hope that you'll understand things a little better."

Nothing he can say will make this okay. Even if their relationship was just one of convenience, they were still married. He didn't just deceive my mum; he betrayed his wife as well. That is inexcusable.

He lets out a long breath before continuing. "This is going to sound completely shallow, but our marriage was more of a business arrangement. I was young and very career driven when I met her. She pursued me, God only knows why, but she was relentless. Even back then she was a master manipulator and she stopped at nothing to get what she wanted."

"You still married her though."

"Only because I loved my job. Her brother was my boss, and she made me feel like I didn't have a choice." He pauses for a moment. "My life was quite miserable until I met your mother. Please believe me when I say, I never planned on deceiving her. I fought my attraction to her for as long as I could." A smile spreads across his face before he shakes his head. "Maree had the power to leave me breathless. She was an absolute stunner, but it was her inner beauty that captivated me the most. She was like a breath of fresh air ... I'd never met anyone like her."

I see Jill enter the room out of the corner of my eye. After placing the cup of coffee in front of me, she makes a hasty retreat.

"Right from the very beginning, I was utterly mesmerised. That's why I never mentioned my relationship with Kathleen—I was afraid she wouldn't understand. It was wrong of me, and completely selfish, but I didn't want to lose her. The deeper I fell, the harder it became." He pauses again before bowing his head. "I never knew a love so deep was possible, but I loved your mother with every fibre of my being."

I raise an eyebrow. "Really?" Sarcasm lines my voice because the way he treated her, in the end at least, wasn't with love.

"Can I show you something?"

I shrug. I can't think of a single thing that would make any of this okay.

Reaching under the table to the chair beside him, he produces the wooden box I saw him holding last night when he arrived.

"I've held onto this box for twenty-seven years," he says. "It was all I had left of her." I sit up straighter in my chair as an uneasy feeling settles over me. I hold my breath as he removes the lid. The first thing he pulls out is a strip of photos, the kind from a photo booth. "These, apart from the one in my wallet, are the only images I have of her."

He's grinning as he looks down at them, but I can't miss the sadness in his eyes. It reminds me of how my mum looked whenever she spoke of him.

He passes the photos to me, and immediately I'm overwhelmed with emotion. My mum looks so happy. There's a sparkle in her eyes, one I don't remember ever seeing.

"I miss her so much," I whisper.

"I do too." Something about his response warms my heart. Is it a sense of camaraderie I'm feeling? I thought I was the only one who felt her loss. "This is the watch she gave me for my birthday," he says, reaching back into the box to retrieve it. "As you can see, I wore it to death." He places the watch on the table, sliding it over to me. The band is broken, and the face has a crack across its centre. "I dropped it a few years ago, and it hasn't worked since. I was going to get it fixed, I just haven't gotten around to it. Read the inscription on the back."

Turning it over, I see the engraving—*I'll love you till the end of time.* Tears fill my eyes as I read her words to him.

"I think she did," I admit.

"Did what?" he asks.

"Loved you until the very end."

"Not a day has passed that I haven't regretted all the things I said to her." He reaches into the box again and pulls out a pile of letters. "After she left, I was lost. I couldn't function for weeks. I wrote to her often, begging for her forgiveness and pleading for her to come back to me. Even years later, I still continued to write to her." I hear his voice crack as he speaks. "I never gave up hope that one day I'd get to see her again and make amends for all that I'd done. I guess that's why I held on to the letters." He lifts one shoulder. "But know I'm thinking maybe I kept them for you ... so you can see that everything I'm saying is genuine." He places the letters back into the box and pushes it towards me. "I want you to have these. I hope you can find it in your heart to read the letters one day. There's a few at the bottom that your mother wrote to me when we were together. If nothing else, it will allow you to see that what we had was real. We loved each other very much." I see tears brimming in his eyes as he uses the table to help him stand. "I've missed out on almost twenty-six years of your life," he says, and his bottom lip quivers as he struggles to hold himself together. "I'd hate to lose another second of my time with you."

With that, he turns and heads towards the stairs. I just

sit there dumbfounded as a myriad of emotions run through me.

I'm putting the finishing touches on my makeup when Logan appears in the doorway of the bathroom. I'm almost ready—all I need to do is slip into my dress. My hair is slicked back into a low bun since I didn't have time to get it done professionally.

I watch him eye me from head to toe in the mirror. I'm dressed in skimpy black lace underwear.

"Fuck, baby," he says, closing the distance between us and rubbing himself against me from behind. "Are you trying to kill me?"

"Never." I turn to face him, placing my flattened palms on his chest.

His fingers dance over my hips before his big strong hands move down to cup my arse. "Do you have any idea what you do to me?"

"If it's anything like what you do to me, then yes." I fist his tie in my hand as I speak.

"I have a good mind to cancel our plans for tonight and have my way with you now."

"I don't think so, Mr. Cavanagh. You promised me a night out, and that's exactly what you're going to give me. Besides, good things come to those who wait," I say, placing a chaste kiss on his lips before slipping out of his embrace and stepping around him. "If you want to leave by six, you best jump in the shower." His eyes are glued to my backside as I exit the bathroom. "And you better make it a cold one." I'm grinning to myself when I hear him mumble something under his breath.

I lay Logan's tuxedo out on the bed before re-entering the walk-in robe to slip into my black dress—the one he requested I wear. I'm smiling as I admire it in the mirror. The dress has an off-the-shoulder neckline with an intricate lace bodice and a full-length flowing satin skirt. It's even more beautiful than I remember.

I've been in a strange mood all day: somewhat happy —lighter even—but still deeply confused. I haven't been able to bring myself to read the letters John gave me this morning, but my opinion of him has definitely softened since our conversation. Too much has happened for us to ever share the close father/daughter bond I once yearned for, but hopefully one day we can have some kind of a relationship.

Walking towards the dresser, I reach for my favourite perfume and spray a small amount behind each ear and on my wrists.

I spin around when I hear Logan exit the bathroom, the towel is draped low on his hips and my eyes drink him in.

"Wow!" he says as a huge smile explodes onto his face. "Look at you."

I spin, giving him a twirl. "You like?"

"I don't just like, I love," he replies, approaching me. "You look ... breath-taking, but there's something missing."

"Huh?" I'm confused. He reaches around me to open the top drawer where he keeps his ties. He slides his hand towards the back before pulling out a large, square velvet box. "What's this?" I ask.

"A gift, for you. Open it."

My hands slightly tremble as I do what he asked. "Hot Stuff," I gasp.

Inside is the most exquisite jewelled necklace I've

ever seen. It reminds me of something that would adorn the neck of royalty.

"It's a choker. The dark stones are black diamonds. I took a photo of the dress with my phone and gave it to my jeweller."

"It's beautiful," I say, "but it's too much. Way too much."

"Turn around." He removes the necklace from the box, unclasps it and slips it around my neck. "You deserve all the beautiful things," he whispers into my ear. "I'd give you the world if only you'd let me."

"I have no words," I say as tears well in my eyes. Facing him, my fingers delicately run over the stones. "You don't have to buy me beautiful things."

He places his finger over my mouth. "I know. But I want to."

"Do you know how much I love you?" I ask as my hand comes to rest on his cheek.

"I love you more."

"I don't think that's possible," I say with a smile.

"It is. I love you the most—the end, I win."

"You don't play fair," I say, laughing.

"When it comes to you, my love, never." He slides his hands around my waist, drawing me closer. When he runs his nose over the skin on my neck, he inhales deeply. "You smell just as delicious as you look."

"It's Opium."

"Mm," he hums, peppering kisses across my bare shoulder. "Like the drug? No wonder you're so addictive. I'm going to be walking around with a hard-on all night, especially now that I know what you're wearing under that dress."

Chapter 44

Logan

"We're heading out," I say to John as we walk towards the lift.

He uses the side of the sofa to help himself stand as we approach. It pains me to see how much he has changed since that night. I'm hoping he continues to improve.

His face lights up as soon as his eyes move to Brooke. I know it's hard for her with him here, but I really feel it's best for them both. I want them to get to know each other. She needs a man like him in her life. I had the pleasure of growing up with him, and he was always such a positive influence on me.

"You look beautiful, sweetheart."

"Thank you," she says, and if I'm not mistaken, the smile she reciprocates is genuine.

Last night at dinner, all of her interactions with him seemed forced. Something has changed between them since then.

"I hope you two have a great night."

Brooke hooks her arm through mine, and I can clearly

see the love in her eyes as she looks up at me when she speaks.

"I still don't know where he's taking me, but I'm sure we will."

"How comfortable are your shoes?" I ask as we step into the lift.

"They're fine, why?"

"We are going to start off our evening at the Bennelong restaurant in the Opera House, I've booked us a table for dinner. I can drive, or we can walk, whatever you prefer."

"Oh, we're starting at the Opera House, so there's more than one component to our evening?"

"Nice try," I say, chuckling.

"You're no fun."

"I'm plenty of fun. Just wait until I get you back home and strip you out of that dress. Then you'll see how fun I can be."

Sometimes the depth of my feelings for her are so overwhelming they frighten me, but I refuse to let my mind go there tonight.

"Can we walk? It's such a beautiful night."

"Of course," I say, placing a kiss on the top of her head.

All eyes are on my date as we walk hand-in-hand along the harbour-front. Surprisingly, the desire I see in the other guy's faces as we pass doesn't upset me in the slightest. I've changed since she came into my life. My ex robbed me of trust when she betrayed me as she did, but things are different now. I am proud to have Brooke on my arm, and I know with all certainty that she loves me just as much as I love her. I trust her implicitly.

Brooke's eyes are everywhere when we enter the restaurant. "It's so beautiful in here."

The high cathedral ceilings that create the shape of the opera house sail, and the curved wooden beams that run parallel down each side of the interior, make it a spectacular sight. The large triangular windows adorning three sides, giving us a panoramic view of Sydney's beautiful harbour, only enhance the space.

"I have a reservation for two, under Cavanagh," I say to the maître d.'

"This way, sir."

"You're so lucky you get to see this kind of view every day," Brooke says to me once we're seated.

"You have the same view as me at the Penthouse."

"I know, but you live there. Technically, I'm only staying with you."

"We could always rectify that," I say as the waitress lays the crisp white napkin across her lap. "You could officially move in."

"Don't you think it's a little early in our relationship to be making such a huge commitment?"

I try to hide my disappointment, since that wasn't the response I was hoping for.

"Normally, I'd say yes, but things are different with you." I lift one of my shoulders. "When your heart knows, it just knows."

Reaching across the table, she places her hand on top of mine, but says nothing. I decide to leave it at that. I don't want to do or say anything that's going to ruin this night for her.

"I still can't believe you got tickets to the ballet," Brooke says, bouncing on her feet, as we enter the Joan Sutherland Theatre.

"Best seats in the house too."

I must remember to send some flowers to Claire as a thank you. We're in private box seats, next to the stage, and the view from here is better than I anticipated.

"I've wanted to see a real-life ballet performance since I was a little girl. You have no idea what this means to me, Hot Stuff."

Her arms slide around my waist, and although she's smiling, there are tears brimming in her eyes. Seeing this reaction means everything.

I take my seat, but Brooke remains standing as she grasps the rail and looks around the theatre.

"It's so beautiful in here."

Her eyes are wide as she takes it all in, and the delight on her face reminds me of a small child in a candy store. It's so endearing.

"You're talented enough to perform here. Have you ever considered dancing professionally?"

"I entertained the idea for a while, but honestly, my passion is teaching. Dancing was my life when I was little, my escape from ..." She bows her head but doesn't finish her sentence. From what she's told me about her upbringing, I'd say it was her escape from the loneliness she felt due to her somewhat absent mother or possibly the poverty. "If I could just give one little girl what I got out of dancing ... I can't even begin to tell you what that would mean to me."

I reach forward and drag her onto my lap, placing a

kiss on the side of her forehead, right beneath the scar on her hairline. It's more visible tonight with her hair pulled back.

I blow out a long breath as images of that night flash through my mind.

"Are you okay?"

"I'm perfect," I lie.

Brooke's hands are trembling with excitement when the curtains finally open. I fucking love her purity, and how the smallest things mean so much to her. I barely watch any of the performance; I'm captivated watching her take it all in. She sits forward in her seat the entire time, and the smile on her face warms my heart. I even witnessed her wipe a tear from her eye on a few occasions.

It's not until the intermission comes that she finally leans back in her chair.

"I take it you're enjoying the show."

"That's the understatement of the year," she says, making me chuckle. "It's a dream come true." I bring her hand to my mouth before placing a soft kiss on her knuckles. "When I was young, my dance troupe was invited to tour The Australian Ballet—like an excursion," she says. "I was so excited when I took the note home to my mum, I thought I was going to burst."

"That's sweet. Was it everything you hoped?"

"I didn't end up going," she says, averting her gaze to her lap.

"Why not?"

"It was a tough time for my mother. Her car registration was due, and she needed new tyres. I understood because it was necessary for her livelihood; she couldn't get to work without a vehicle."

"I'm sorry."

She shrugs her shoulders. "I knew my mum was disappointed we didn't have the money, so I lied and told her I didn't really want to go anyway. That night I cried myself to sleep. The truth was, I was utterly heartbroken."

"Fuck, babe."

My heart hurts for that little girl. Her life would've been so different if John had been present. The hardship she faced growing up helps me understand some of her resentment, and why letting him in is so hard for her.

As soon as the second half of the performance begins, Brooke slides to the edge of her seat, resting her chin on her forearms against the banister. Once again, I can't take my eyes off her. She's far more entertaining than anything that's happening down on the stage.

When the ballet finally draws to an end, she jumps to her feet and applauds loudly. I'm so glad I could give her tonight. I knew she'd enjoy it, but I had no idea how much.

She's quiet as we leave—I think she's still trying to digest it all. That is, until we step out into the night air where she stretches her arms wide and turns in a circle. "I have no words for how incredible that was." I chuckle at her theatrics.

I'm pretty sure I got more out of tonight than she did. "So, I did good?" I ask, pulling her into my arms.

"You did better than good. It was the best night ever." Her flattened palms rest on my chest as she speaks. "Thank you for taking me to the ballet, and for dinner, my dress, my necklace ... *for everything*. I don't know what I've done to deserve you, but not a day passes where I'm not thankful for having you in my life."

I'm not sure why her words choke me up, but they do. She's like a breath of fresh air, and grateful doesn't begin to cover how she makes me feel.

Removing my jacket, I drape it over her shoulders. "Come, let's get you home. The night isn't over yet."

Thankfully, my uncle has turned in for the night by the time we arrive back at the apartment. Grabbing Brooke's hand, I lead her straight to our room. This was the part I was most looking forward to, but I doubt if anything can top the pure enjoyment I experienced watching Brooke at the ballet.

"I've been waiting to undress you all night," I say, closing the bedroom door and flipping the lock.

Her arms encircle my neck, as she pulls my face down towards hers. When our lips connect, all my plans for slowly unwrapping my prize fly out the window. I crave this woman ... tonight more than ever.

I reach for the zipper at the back of her dress and tug it down in one swift motion. When she lowers her arms, it glides down her body and pools at her feet. "I'm desperate to be inside you," I state, scooping her into my arms and crossing the room.

Our lips are still connected as she fumbles with my bow tie. I reach around behind her to unclasp her bra. As soon as I place her back on her feet beside the bed, she moves to the buttons of my shirt. My hands grasp the sides of her lace underwear and I effortlessly tear them from her body.

Her wide eyes meet mine as she pulls out of the kiss. "Did you just rip them?"

"I'll buy you a new pair," I answer, crashing my mouth back to hers.

We've had rough sex before, but tonight we're travelling at a frenzied pace. Desperation accompanies every movement. It's like we can't get enough of each other. Personally, I want to fuck this woman into next week.

As soon as Brooke undoes the last button, I frantically remove my cufflinks and toss them aside before shrugging out of my shirt.

Placing my hands under her arms, I lift her off the ground and gently lay her on the bed. "My shoes," she says, looking down at her feet.

"Leave them on." I smile wickedly as I raise her legs in the air and place one on each of my shoulders. She looks like a goddess lying there in nothing but a quarter-of-a-million-dollar necklace. I'm pretty sure she'd be mortified if she knew how much it cost me.

"Hot Stuff," she cries out, as I fall to my knees and bury my head between her thighs.

Briefly looking up, I flick my head towards the door. "You might want to keep it down tonight."

Her eyes widen as colour rises on her cheeks when she remembers John is down the hall. I laugh when she quickly removes her hands from my hair and covers her mouth.

Bringing my face forward, I spread her wide and lick a path along her slit. "Oh god," she whimpers, throwing her head back and fisting her hands in the sheets. I love how responsive she is to my touch. This woman drives me wild.

My tongue circles her clit as I plunge two fingers deep inside her, causing her to moan and buck her hips forward. My cock is so hard, I'm surprised it doesn't burst through the zipper of my trousers. Just her taste has me almost blowing my load.

"I love your pussy. *Fucking love it.*" As soon as her inner thighs start to squeeze my head like a vice, I know she's close. "Come for me, babe."

"I ... I am."

I don't stop until I've drained every ounce of pleasure from her body. Drawing back, I wipe my mouth with the back of my hand before digging into my pocket for a condom. I came prepared. It's all I've thought about since I found her in the bathroom in that skimpy black lace.

"Stand up," she says, moving to sit on the side of the mattress. "Let me help you."

"You need to be quick; I'm dying here."

"I seriously doubt that you're close to death."

Unbuckling my belt, she makes fast work of the button and zipper. I rip the condom wrapper open with my teeth as she reaches inside my boxer briefs to free my rock-hard cock. I'm ready to roll the rubber over my length, but she appears to have other ideas as she leans forward and wraps her lips around the head, swirling her tongue as she does.

"Babe," I pant. "I'm already on the edge." She places her palm flat on my abdomen, pushing me back slightly to give herself enough room to slide off the bed and onto her knees. Her teeth lightly graze over my length as she takes as much of me into her mouth as she can manage. My legs threaten to give out when I feel the tip hit the back of her throat. I don't even want to know where she learnt to suck cock like this. "Fuck." My hands grip her head as I rock my hips forward, and when she gags, my balls tighten. "Babe, I'm ... coming."

I try to withdraw, but she holds fast and I have no

choice but to unload into her sweet mouth. Tilting my head back, I groan. I probably should be embarrassed by how fast she made me come undone, but in my defence, I've been walking around with a semi all night.

"How was that?" she asks, looking up at me innocently through her eyelashes. There was nothing innocent about what she just did.

"Mind-blowing," I reply, dragging her to her feet. I'm still clutching the condom between my fingers as I lie her back down on the bed. I may have just come, but I'm not done with her yet ... *I'm only getting started.*

Chapter 45

Brooke

"Morning," I say to John when I descend the stairs and find him once again engrossed in the day's paper.

There's a touch of apprehension still present, but no butterflies this morning. It definitely seems like I'm more open to getting to know him better. Or maybe I'm still riding my high from last night.

"Good morning, sweetheart." Closing the paper, he gives me his full attention. "How did last night go?"

I grip the back of the chair on the opposite side of the table. I'm pretty sure nothing or nobody could dampen the glorious mood I'm in.

"Amazing." I'm still floating. "Logan took me to the ballet."

"He mentioned he bought tickets."

Resting one of my hands over my heart, I sigh. "It was the most tragic, yet beautiful, performance. It moved me to tears a number of times."

The smile on John's face grows as he listens to me speak. "I'm happy to hear that you enjoyed it so much."

"I did." I look down at the empty mug in front of him. "I'm going to grab a coffee. Would you like a refill?"

"I'd love one, thank you." Holding his mug out for me, I take it from him.

"Morning, Jill," I say, entering the kitchen.

She studies me for a moment before answering. "Morning, dear. I'm guessing by the smile on your face that last night went well."

"It was wonderful." Placing John's mug down on the counter, I open the upper cupboard grabbing one for myself. "The best night of my life."

"I'm so glad you had a nice time." Jill reaches for the mug in my hand. "Coffee?"

"Please. Oh, and John would like a refill too."

"You seem more relaxed this morning." She gestures her head in the direction of the dining room table as she says it.

I shrug. "We had a nice talk yesterday. I think it helped me understand him a little better."

"I'm pleased to hear that. You'll find he really is a lovely man if you give him half a chance."

"So everyone keeps telling me."

"Because it's true."

"I still feel like I'm betraying my mum by associating with him."

"That's understandable. I'm not your mother, so I can't profess to know how she'd feel. But if my daughter was left all alone in this world, it would give me comfort knowing her father was looking out for her."

"Maybe." I've never thought of it like that. "When she was dying, leaving me alone was one of her greatest fears."

"I can only imagine." Jill reaches out and tenderly rubs my back. "That would've been hard for her—for you both."

I nod my head, emotion clogging my throat. I try not to think about those times. It hurts too much.

Once our coffees are ready, I carry them to the table and place John's in front of him before taking the seat opposite.

"Can I ask you something?"

"Sure."

"That perfume you were wearing last night, was that Opium?" he asks.

"Yes. How did you know that?"

"It's the same fragrance your mother used to wear."

"It was. That's why I love it."

"It reminds me so much of her. I even bought a bottle of it after she left. It may sound silly, but smelling it gave me comfort."

"It gives me comfort too," I admit.

He nods his head and smiles. It's funny how we both have that in common.

"There were times I even sprayed it on my pillowcase ... it helped me sleep." His eyes move down to the coffee in his hand as he clears his throat. "You probably think that's weird." *I think it's kind of sweet.* "I used to close my eyes and imagine she was lying beside me."

"Your wife never queried the smell of women's perfume on your pillow?"

"We slept in separate rooms. As I told you yesterday, our marriage wasn't a conventional one. We have never shared a bed."

A feeling of pity washes over me. He gave up a life with a woman he obviously cared about, for an illusion.

"I always wear my mum's perfume when I'm missing her. It makes me feel like she's with me."

He reaches across the table for my hand, wrapping it in his. "We're a sad and sorry pair, aren't we?" He releases a small laugh. "I guess when you love someone as much as we loved your mother, it's only natural we'd want to feel her near."

We have a lot more in common than I ever felt possible. It's nice that I have someone to share these small things with. Jake was never able to grasp the level of grief I felt when I lost her.

"I wish you had gotten the chance to make amends. It would've meant the world to her."

"Thank you, that means a lot. It will always be one of my biggest regrets."

"She talked about you sometimes."

"She did?"

"I don't think she ever got over you."

He bows his head. "I never got over her either."

"I can take you to visit her gravesite one day if you like. It's not the same as ..."

"I'd like that." He sits back in his chair, and that's when I see the tears glistening his eyes. "I still can't believe she's gone."

After greeting Chris, I slide into the back of the limousine. It's been a long, tiring day.

Relaxing back into my seat, I fumble in my bag for one of the letters John gave me. The once white envelope has slightly yellowed with age. I planned to read it during my lunch break, but that never came to fruition. I barely had time to eat.

My stomach churns as I slide my finger under the edge of the envelope and break the seal. I feel like John and I made some headway this morning, so I'm anxious that what I'm about to read might set us back.

Taking a deep breath, I unfold the piece of paper enclosed.

> *To my dearest Maree,*
> *I don't even know where to start because there's so much I need to say to you. I must start by expressing my most heartfelt apology. I'm sorry I never told you I was married. I know it's no excuse, but I was scared I'd lose you and the deeper I fell, the harder it became. Please believe me when I say it's not a marriage based on love—it never has been. Nevertheless, I should have been honest with you from the start.*
> *Hurting you was the last thing I ever wanted to do. I hate myself for the things I said earlier, especially about the baby. Our baby. The product of our love. Just thinking there's a chance you'd consider listening to my deplorable demands, fill me with an enormous sense of dread. You must think I'm a monster, but please, please, I beg you not to go through with the termination. I don't know what I was thinking. I'll give up everything I have if you'll just promise to give our child a chance at life. I was scared, and I panicked, but the moment you walked out of my office, I knew I'd just made the biggest mistake of my life. I hate myself for the things I said. I've lost the best thing that has ever happened to me—you.*
> *I love you, Maree. I love you more than I have*

loved anyone or anything. You may be doubting that right now, but it's the truth. I can't even comprehend life without you in it. I never knew the true meaning of happiness until I met you.

It's currently 2 am and tears are streaming down my face as I sit here and write this. I spent the better part of the night driving around looking for you. I stopped by your apartment earlier, but your roommate told me you'd packed up your things and fled. I've been going out of my mind with worry ever since.

I can't eat. I can't sleep. I won't be able to rest until I find you. Even if you don't want me in your life anymore, I need to know you're safe, and that you and our child are okay.

I can see the water stains on the page where his tears have smudged the ink. Refolding the letter, I place it on my lap as I wipe away the moisture from my eyes. I thought I was ready to read these, but I'm not. This letter alone is almost five pages long, but those first few paragraphs are enough. They tell me all I need to know: *Everything he told me is true.* He did love my mum as much as he claims. He's sorry for the dreadful things he said. And most importantly, he did want me.

I can't even begin to process what this means. Maybe that's why I've been fighting this so much. Was I trying to reject him like he'd done with me all those years ago?

Bowing my head, I blow out a puff of air.

"Are you okay, Miss Ryan?" Chris asks, eyeing me with concern through the rear-view mirror.

"I'm fine, Chris," I reply as my gaze moves to the window.

To be honest, I'm unsure how I feel. In a way, I gained a sense of peace from reading the letter, but on the other hand, I feel an incredible loss. Not just for me, but for my mother, and for John. Our lives could've been so different, but I, of all people, know you can't turn back time. Those years are gone, and we can never get them back.

When I enter the apartment, I find Jill sitting at the table with John. I'm tired and have a splitting headache. All I want to do is lock myself away and soak in a hot bath.

"Here's my girl," John says when I enter the room. *My girl.* "We were just talking about you."

"Nothing bad I hope."

"Never," Jill replies. "Come sit. I'll get you something to drink."

She goes to stand, so I hold out my hand to stop her. "I'm beat. It's been a long day. If you don't mind, I'm going to head up to my room."

"Okay, dear."

The disappointment on John's face is unmissable. We parted on good terms this morning, but now I'm feeling so overwhelmed by it all.

Dropping my gaze to the floor, I make a beeline for the stairs.

After closing the bedroom door behind me, I flop onto the bed. I stay there for a moment, collecting my thoughts until my phone rings.

Sliding my bag onto my lap, I open it. The first thing

that greets me is the letter. I pull it out and place it on the bed beside me before retrieving my phone. I smile when I see *Hot Stuff* on the screen.

"Hey," I say, answering the call.

"Hey, babe. Is everything okay?"

"Of course, why?"

"Chris called me to let me know you got home safely. He said you seemed upset."

"I'm fine. I just have a lot on my mind."

"Like what?"

"Just stuff."

I don't want to burden him with any of this. Besides, he made it clear the moment things get too hard for me, he'll find somewhere else for John to stay. I'm not sure I want him to leave just yet.

"What kind of stuff?" I can hear the concern in his voice. "Work? John? Me?"

"I'm just tired, that's all. Don't worry about me, I'm fine."

"Brooke, do I need to come home?"

"No." I blow out a puff of air because I know he's not going to let this go. "Things are full-on at work with all the concert preparations, and—"

"You're struggling with John being there," he says, finishing off my sentence.

"Not struggling, *per se*."

"Then what? Do you want me to see if Michelle can take him?"

"No, she's in the middle of renovations on her house, so things are crazy for her right now. I don't mind him being here, honestly. It's just ... can we talk about it later? I have a splitting headache."

"I was going to work late tonight. I've been out of the

office for most of the day, but I think I'll come home now. I can try to catch up on everything tomorrow."

"No don't," I say. "I'm okay."

"I'm worried about you."

"You're sweet, but don't be." My gaze moves down to the envelope sitting beside me on the bed. "John gave me some letters ... letters he wrote to my mother after she left."

"I see."

"I read one today—well, part of one—in the back of the limousine on my way home from work."

"And the letter upset you?"

"Yes and no." My voice cracks as I speak. "It's just ..." Tears fill my eyes, so I take a deep breath and try to compose myself. "It made me sad. I hate the last things he said to her. It's so tragic. It upsets me that they both suffered so much because of it."

"Oh, babe."

I swipe my finger under my eye, wiping away the stray tear. "I'm going to have a long soak in a hot bath."

"You know that only makes me want to come home more."

His comment makes me laugh. "Stay at work, you sex fiend. I promise I'm okay. We can talk tonight when you get home."

"Are you sure?"

"Yes."

"I'm not going to be home for dinner, so eat without me. I'll get Claire to pick me up something here." He sighs through the line. I can tell he'd rather be coming home to eat with us. "All right?"

"Okay."

"I love you."

"I love you too, Hot Stuff. Thank you for calling."

Placing my phone down, I scoop up the envelope and head towards the walk-in robe. Reaching up to the top shelf, I pull down the box John gave me and place the letter back inside. One day I'll be ready to read them in their entirety, but not today.

A smile tugs at my lips as I stare down at the photos of my parents together. They're a good-looking couple. My fingertip skims over their faces, and the sorrow I was feeling earlier returns. *So many lost opportunities.*

Picking up the photo, I clutch it to my chest before closing the box up and sliding it back onto the shelf. Reaching for my photo album that sit alongside the box, I open it to reveal an image of my mother smiling down at the tiny baby clutched in her arms. It's the first photo of the two of us, taken the day I was born. Carefully, I peel back the clear film and place the photo booth image of my parents beside it. Would Mum be pleased that John and I have found each other? I guess I'll never know the answer to that question, but I can only hope that she would be.

Chapter 46

Brooke

When the song comes to an end, I turn and face my students. "That's a wrap for today, girls," I say, clapping my hands together. "For homework, I want you to work on your turns. We only have a few more weeks to get this perfect." This is one of my advanced classes, so the routine is complex.

Over the past few weeks, things have settled down—at home, anyway. The studio is still crazy busy as we get the finishing touches in place for the concert. It's hard work, but it's what the students have strived for the entire year: a chance to perform for their family and friends. The end result will be worth it.

My days have been long, and even more so for Logan. Our time together limited as a result. I still get to see him in the evenings and briefly before work, but he's been even busier than I am. He's working on something big that's taking up all his time, but he assures me things will slow down soon. I hope so because I've missed our quality time together.

With Jill fussing over John like a mother hen, John has regained most of what he lost that night. Although he hasn't said anything, I think he loves all the attention he gets. It's the kind of attention I doubt he got from his wife.

I'm pleased he's doing well, but he's already talking about leaving and is shopping around for an apartment. I'm not sure how that makes me feel. Each day we've gotten to know each other a little bit more. It's been nice. Some of my walls are still up, but I'm working on that part.

This week John started driving again, and today, over breakfast, he offered to pick me up from work. He's ready to go to the cemetery. I've only visited my mother's grave once since I returned to Sydney, and I'm wracked with guilt regarding it. Even after all these years, going there hasn't gotten any easier. I always leave feeling a thousand times worse than I did when I arrived. But today, I'm doing this for him. I'm guessing it will be an emotional time for us both.

After my classes are over, I grab my phone from the dock and scoop up my dance bag, before heading towards the change rooms. Since Chris usually escorts me to and from work, I travel in my dance gear, but today I brought regular clothes to change into.

When I reach the reception area, I find John already waiting for me. His face lights up when he sees me. I've grown fond of that look.

"Hi, sweetheart," he says as he stands. "Are you ready to leave?"

"Yes." I turn my attention to Laura. "I'll see you tomorrow."

"Okay." She yawns before focusing back on the computer screen. She looks just as tired and ragged as I feel.

"I got to watch the last part of your dance routine,"

John says, holding the door open for me. "Logan was right, you have a gift."

"Thank you. I love what I do."

"It shows."

We cross the road to where his car is parked and, like Logan, he's a gentleman, and opens the door for me.

"Would you mind if we stopped off at a florist? I'd like to get some flowers for my mum."

He points to the back seat, where I see a large bunch of yellow roses. "I hope you don't mind, but I took the liberty of getting some on the way here."

"Yellow roses—"

"Her favourite," he says, finishing my sentence.

"How did you know that?"

"I use to buy her a bunch every Friday. She loved them."

I smile to myself. I'm starting to realise that a lot of things my mum liked are somehow connected to him. Her perfume, the flowers, and the other night, Jill made a lemon meringue pie, which turned out to be John's favourite dessert of all time. It was also my mother's.

Once John's seated behind the steering wheel, he drapes the seatbelt across his body and clicks it into place. His car reeks of wealth and is a far cry from the bomb my mum used to get around in. Many times, it wouldn't even start. On more than one occasion, it happened outside my school and I'd have to push her down the hill so she could clutch start it. All the kids would point and laugh, which was humiliating. It wasn't my fault we were so poor. We were rich with love, but not so much with material things.

My eyes scan over John's expensive gold watch. It's a lot more lavish than the one my mother once gave him. It makes me second-guess the surprise I have for him in my bag. When my gaze moves to his Ralph Lauren polo shirt, designer pants, and tanned Italian leather moccasins that match his belt perfectly, I can't help but feel a touch of resentment towards him as I compare the different lives we've led. It leaves a bitter taste in my mouth.

Growing up, most of my clothes came from the op-shop, and it was only on the rare occasions my mum could afford to buy me something new. She always did without to make sure I was taken care of first.

"I spoke with Logan earlier," John says, briefly looking over at me before pulling away from the kerb. "He's working back again tonight."

"I know. I was texting with him between classes."

"He said he won't be home until around eight." I just nod because he told me the same thing. I trust him implicitly, but there's a small, insecure part of me that worries about the long hours he's putting in. Jake used to say he was working back too, but he wasn't. I push those thoughts out of my mind. "I made a dinner reservation for us at this little Italian restaurant on the other side of the city. It's a place I used to take your mother." His eyes dart back to me. "I'd love it if you'd join me. Only if you want to, of course. No pressure."

"I'd like that," I say, giving him a small smile.

"Great."

While the rest of the trip is silent, I can't help feeling more anxious the closer we get to the cemetery. It's one thing to fall apart when I'm on my own, but something completely different when it happens in front of someone I barely know. I'm hoping I can keep it together today, but only time will tell. Coming here has always been hard for me, which is why I haven't been in so long.

"You take a right down here," I say. "Her grave is towards the back. You should be able to park further down." When he doesn't reply, I glance at him. His face is stoic, and he's clutching the steering wheel so hard, his knuckles have turned white. "Are you okay?"

"No, not really. I use to daydream about seeing your mother again, and what that would be like. Never did I imagine our reunion would be here ... at her gravesite."

"I hate coming here," I admit. "I prefer to focus on the good times before she got sick. This place brings back all the terrible memories."

He reaches across the centre console, placing his hand just above my knee. "I'm thankful I have you with me, sweetheart. I only wish I'd been there for you back then."

"The day I buried her is a bit of a blur. The doctor gave me some sedatives to take that morning. It was the only way I could've gotten through it."

I bow my head as shame seeps through me, and his grip on my leg tightens. The night before the burial, there was a viewing. The person who lay in that coffin looked nothing like the woman I'd grown up with. The funeral home had made her up, but she wasn't one to ever wear makeup. And the awful wig they'd placed on her head was nothing like her real hair. She looked more like an oversized doll than a person. I thought seeing her one last time would help, but instead those images haunt me. Every time I come here, that's all I see.

"I can't even begin to imagine how hard that must've been for you."

He pulls the car over to the side of the road, and I remove my seatbelt. I gaze out the window as I reach for the door handle. She's only a few rows back. Unlike some of the fancier large headstones around her, I could only afford to get her a small plaque. She deserved better.

I stand beside the car while John retrieves the flowers from the backseat. When he rounds the vehicle, he reaches for my hand and clutches it in his.

"You're shaking," he says.

Part of me is having second thoughts about agreeing to this. I hope she's okay with me bringing him here.

We cross the lawn in silence, and when my mother's grave comes into view, my guilt magnifies tenfold. Her once shiny plaque is now covered with dirt and leaves, with weeds growing around the edges.

I immediately fall to my knees and hastily brush the debris away with my hands.

"I'm sorry, Mum," I whisper as tears fill my eyes. "I'm so sorry."

"Let me do that." I turn my head to look at him, and when he sees the tears pooling in my eyes, he drapes his arm over my shoulder and pulls my body to his. "Don't cry, sweetheart."

"I should've come sooner."

"You had your reasons for not coming," he says, placing a kiss on the top of my head. "Your mother was the most forgiving person. She would understand." His words give some comfort. Releasing me, he starts tearing out the weeds surrounding her plaque. "I have some wet wipes in the glove compartment. Do you want to grab them?"

"Okay." I scramble to my feet and jog back to the car.

When I return a minute later, I find John hunched over with his hands covering his face. There's no sound coming from him, but I can tell he's crying by the rise and fall of his shoulders.

Kneeling, I place the wipes beside me and rub my flattened palm over his back. No words are spoken as I let him grieve for his lost love.

He eventually removes his hands and turns his face towards me, the sadness in his eye's breaks my heart.

"Even after all these years, losing her still hurts. I can't believe I'll never see her again."

"I can't either," I say, wiping a stray tear from my cheek. "She was only forty-three years old when she passed."

"Way too young."

I pick up the wipes and pull a few out. Big fat tears roll down my cheeks as I clean the inscription. *'You were loved beyond words, and you'll be missed beyond measure.'*

When I'm done, John's fingers lightly caress her name before he places the flowers down beside it.

"It's a beautiful inscription," he says. "Very fitting."

"It's simple, but something from the heart."

"It's perfect."

I can see he's struggling to hold himself together, and strangely enough, I feel closer to him because of it. It's nice to know I'm not the only one who feels her loss so deeply.

"I have something for you," I say. "It's in my bag in the car. Let me go and get it."

I'd planned on giving it to him later, but this seems like the perfect moment.

Reaching out, he helps me to my feet, and I scoop up the wipes as I go.

He's still on his knees when I return. His head is bowed, and his hands are clasped together in front of him. I think he's praying. Is he a religious man? There's so much I don't know about him.

Standing back, I wait until he's finished before I take a seat beside him and unzip my dance bag. My eyes move down to his watch again. "I'm not sure how you'll feel about this," I say, pulling out the small box. "But I had this repaired for you."

His bottom lip starts to quiver the moment he opens the lid. "My watch."

"It's working as good as new. I had the glass face and band replaced."

"Thank you," he says, his voice cracking. I'm about to tell him he doesn't have to wear it if he doesn't want to, but before I get the chance, he removes it from the box and then takes off the expensive gold one he's wearing. "You have no idea how much this means to me."

He is overcome with emotion as he straps the watch on. "I think I do," I reply.

"It means even more to me now than it did the day your mother gave it to me."

"I'm glad," I say, smiling. "I have something else." I pull out the album.

"What's this?" he asks when I pass it to him.

"Mum made me an album before she passed. It's full of photos of both of us. A lot of me when I was little and growing up. There are some beautiful ones of her in there too. I had copies of the images made for you."

"Oh, sweetheart." Bringing his legs out from underneath him, he sits beside me. I smile as his hand gently runs over the cover. The moment he opens the first page and finds the image of my mother holding me just moments after my birth, his hand flies up to cover his mouth as a strangled sob comes from the back of his throat. My own eyes well up as I watch him. "I have no words," he says, shaking his head. "No words."

"It's a cute place," I say as John pulls out my chair at the restaurant. We ended up staying at the gravesite for over an hour, going through the album, as I told him stories to accompany the pictures. We had a few laughs and a few more tears. He told me I gave him a glimpse into my past, something he thought he'd never get. It was nice to be able to give him that.

"It's changed hands a few times over the years, and while the new owners have put their own stamp on the place, the food's still delicious."

"Good, I'm starved," I say, reaching for the menu. "You must like it if you still come here."

"I'm a creature of habit. A small part of me always hoped I'd run in to your mother here again. She loved this place too."

My eyes move around the room, taking it all in. It's hard to comprehend that over twenty-seven years have passed, and here I am with him, just like my mother once was.

"So, tell me, how did you get into dancing? From the pictures in the album, you've been doing it for a long time."

I place the menu on the table to give him my full attention. "Music was always my first love. Miss Jones, the lady who looked after me when my mum was at work, taught me to play the piano."

"You play?"

"Yes."

"Will you play for me one day?"

"Of course."

"I'd love that, now tell me about the dancing."

"A studio opened up down the road from where we lived, and it was the music that first drew me there. I used to hear it playing as I passed by on my way home from school. One day I went inside. That's when I saw the dancers ... I was mesmerised. I went every day for weeks and just sat and watched them. I would go home and practice all the steps I'd memorised. One day the teacher approached me and asked if I'd be interested in taking lessons." John is smiling as he listens intently. "She gave me a price list and a timetable to give to Mum, but I knew she couldn't afford it." I bow my head. "I wanted to dance so badly, but money was always tight."

"So, what happened?"

"I stuffed it into my school bag, and I stopped going there."

"I'm sorry," he says, reaching across the table and placing his hand on mine. "I hate that you both had it so tough."

We may have been poor, but we were happy enough.

"A few days later, when I came home from school, I found a pair of ballet shoes sitting at the end of my bed. They were second-hand, but that didn't bother me. I'd never mentioned anything about the classes to Mum, so I was confused. Turns out, she'd found the price list in my bag, and went down to the studio to make inquiries. When the teacher told her I'd been going in there every day after school to watch, she signed me up for a class. The rest is history."

"What a beautiful story."

"She didn't have much, but she always went out of her way to give me everything she could. She was a great mum."

"I wish I'd been around to make life easier for you both."

"If there's one thing I learnt growing up, it's that money doesn't buy happiness. I went without a lot of things, but I had a good life. If I could change one thing, it would be that Mum didn't have to work as hard as she did. It was my dream to open up my own studio one day so I could look after her, just like she had done for me for all those years." I blow out a puff of air, and my voice cracks when I speak again. "I hate that I never got to do that for her."

"You have a beautiful heart," he says, "just like your mother."

Chapter 47

Logan

When my mobile rings, I turn away from the window in my office and approach the desk. An uneasy feeling settles in the pit of my stomach when I see Brooke's name on the screen. I have things I need to discuss with her, but not now, not over the phone. I take a deep breath before answering it.

"Babe."

"Hey, Hot Stuff."

"I was just thinking about you.".

"I was thinking about you too, hence why I'm calling. I know you're super busy right now, but I don't have to be at the studio until two, so I thought maybe we could do lunch ... I miss you."

I run my hand nervously through my hair. I'd like nothing more than to have lunch with her, but I can't today. Jesus Christ, how am I going to get out of this one without lying? I feel like I've been deceiving her a lot lately, but with good reason. This, however, is on a totally different level.

I sigh. "I wish I could, but I just can't swing it today. I'm sorry." I feel like such a cad.

"That's okay," she says. I can hear the disappointment in her voice, and it makes me feel even shittier. "It was worth a try."

"How about we organise lunch for tomorrow? I'll move mountains to make it happen."

"I'll settle for tomorrow."

As I go to speak again, Rose buzzes me. "Hold on a minute, babe."

"Yes, Rose."

"Mr. Cavanagh, Amanda Campbell just called. She said she's running about twenty minutes late for your lunch date." Tilting my head back, I pinch the bridge of my nose. *Shit.*

"Thanks, Rose."

"Are you there, Brooke?" I say, placing the phone back to my ear as I silently pray she didn't hear that, but knowing she did.

"You're having lunch with Amanda? Please tell me it's not Amanda your ex ... the waitress from the restaurant."

I blow out a long breath. "Brooke, it's not like that. Let me explain."

"Oh my god, it is her. I ... I can't believe you."

Before I get a chance to speak again, the line goes dead. "Fuck!"

I burst out of the lift as soon as the doors open and run through the apartment. "Brooke!" I call out at the top of my voice. *Please still be here.* "Brooke."

I'm pretty sure I forced Chris to break every road rule on the drive over here.

"Mr. Cavanagh," Jill says, exiting my office. She has a dusting cloth clutched in her hand.

"Where's Brooke?"

I've been calling her nonstop since she hung up on me, but her phone continues to go to voicemail.

"I think she's upstairs. Is everything okay?"

I don't bother replying as I rush towards the stairs, taking them two at a time. I'm relieved she's still here; I was worried she may have left already.

Flinging open the door, my heart drops the moment I see her packing her suitcase.

"Brooke." I waste no time closing the distance between us, but when I reach for her, she shuns away.

"Don't touch me," she says with her back still to me.

My hands drop down by my sides, but when I observe her wiping her eyes, I know she's crying. Stepping forward, I wrap my arms around her tightly from behind.

"Babe." She struggles to free herself, but there's no way I'm releasing her until she hears me out. "It's not what you think."

"I was right all along. You lawyers are all the same. I feel like such an idiot."

Her comment stings, but I let it go. *I'm nothing like them!*

"Amanda called my office this morning. It's the first time I've heard from her since the restaurant, I swear to you. She asked if I'd represent her; she's chasing Brent for child support, amongst other things. I told her no, that I couldn't help. I don't want anything to do with either of them. Please believe me." I'm rambling, but I need her to understand.

When she stops resisting, I release my grip a little and turn her in my arms so she's facing me. The moment I see her red swollen eyes, my heart breaks.

"But you thought you'd have lunch with her for old times' sake?" she says, choking on her words as she speaks.

I'm responsible for her distress, and I hate myself for hurting her.

"No. I didn't want to do that either." I let out a long breath. "When I told her I couldn't help, she started to cry. She said she's struggling to get by on her own, that her kids are doing without because of it. I felt bad for her. I told her I could give her some advice as a friend and recommend a good family law lawyer, but that was it."

"Over lunch?" she challenges, arching an eyebrow.

"Lunch was her idea. I should never have agreed to it."

"Then why did you?"

"To be honest, I felt sorry for her. I also didn't want her in my building. I was going to tell you everything tonight. I just didn't want to do it over the phone." She buries her face in my chest and starts to cry again, so I tighten my hold on her. "She means nothing to me. It's the truth. Even if I didn't have you, I still wouldn't touch her. That part of my life is over. I love you. You're all I want ... *all I'll ever want.*" Cupping her face in my hands, I tilt her head back slightly so I can see her. The pads of my thumbs brush lightly across her cheeks to wipe away her tears. "I'm sorry I didn't tell you straight away. I just thought it would be better face-to-face. Please forgive me, I don't want this to change things between us. I can't lose you."

"I thought I could trust you, but now I'm doubting everything we have."

"Fuck." I glance up at the ceiling. How am I going to fix this? "You *can* trust me," I state, moving my gaze back to her. "I would never disrespect, or hurt you like that."

"Is she the reason you've been putting in such long hours lately?"

"What? No! I told you, today was the first time I've heard from her. I've just had some big things going on that are monopolising all my time, and before you ask, there's *nobody* else either. Please tell me you believe me?"

Tears shine in her eyes, but she remains silent, so I know she's still harbouring doubts. I have to do something.

Taking a step backwards, I pull my phone out of my pocket and dial Rose. I'm not sure if this will help, or make the situation worse, but I need to try.

"Rose," I say when she answers the call. "Can you text Amanda Campbell's number to me please?"

"Of course, Mr. Cavanagh," Rose replies. "I'll do it right away."

My request has Brooke shaking her head in disgust, and when she goes to turn away from me, I reach out and grasp her elbow. "Don't."

"Fuck you," she snaps, thrashing her arm, trying to free it from my embrace. "Let me go."

"Brooke ... baby," I plead, sliding my arm around her waist, and resting my forehead on her shoulder. "Give me five minutes. I'm going to call Amanda and put her on speaker. If you still don't believe me after that, I promise I won't stop you from leaving."

It will kill me to let her walk away, but I'm a man of my word.

When my phone chimes with the text from Rose, I let go of Brooke and open it. I click on Amanda's number and press call, the entire time praying that this doesn't backfire in my face.

"Amanda," I say, the moment she answers.

"Logan, hi." She sounds breathless. "I'm almost at the

restaurant. The traffic in the city is horrendous, so I got the taxi driver to let me out, and I'm walking the rest of the way."

Brooke's back is still to me, but she hasn't moved, so that's a plus.

"Actually, that's why I'm calling. I'm cancelling lunch."

"Why?"

"Because I'm an idiot. I never should've agreed to meet you in the first place."

"Then why did you?"

"If I'm being honest, I don't know. When you started to cry, the compassionate side of me felt bad for you ... *for your kids*. But what I failed to realise, is that I don't owe you anything."

"But we have a past."

"We *had* a past. One I'd rather forget."

"You don't mean that," she dares to say which pisses me off.

"Yes, I do. You betrayed me in the worst possible way, Amanda. Not only were you sleeping with my best friend behind my back, but you also ended things between us via text. *On my fucking birthday!* Before blocking my number like a coward so I couldn't even respond."

Brooke turns to face me. I never told her that part of the story. It's one of the things I struggled with most. At first, I thought it was a joke, but when I tried to call Brent only to find he'd blocked my number as well, I knew it was true. That kind of betrayal, from two people you care so much about? It's a hard pill to swallow. I was never granted any kind of closure. To this day it still burns.

"I'm sorry," Amanda whispers into the phone.

"What you two did, it changed me. You killed my trust. It took me a long time to work through it, but I realise now you did me a huge favour." My eyes lock with Brooke's as I speak. "My fractured heart sat in a state of limbo for ten long years, just waiting for the right person to come along and put those pieces back together. So, for that I thank you."

"Why would you thank me?"

My free hand reaches up to caress the side of Brooke's face.

"If it wasn't for your deception, I never would've found what I have now ... a beautiful, healthy relationship with the kindest, sweetest and most loyal person I know. The woman I love more than anything in this world. The one I plan on growing old with."

With that, I end the call and drop my phone to the floor.

"I love you with every fibre of my being ... please never doubt that."

"I love you too, Hot Stuff," she says, her voice catching.

Thank Christ for that.

Pushing up onto her toes, she places her lips against mine.

I walk us back towards the bed. I refuse to leave this room until I know with all certainty that we're going to be okay. The meetings I have this afternoon will have to wait. None of that is as important to me as she is.

Chapter 18

Brooke

Lifting my arms above my head and straightening my legs, I stretch my body before rolling over. I'm wearing a huge smile, but the moment I see Logan's side of the bed is empty, it instantly drops from my face. I'd been looking forward to this all week: our first weekend off with just the two of us.

John moved into his own place during the week. He's renting a small apartment until his property settlement with his wife goes through. It's not far from here, so I'll still get to see him often.

Throwing back the covers, I rise from the bed and go in search of my man. He's been run off his feet with work, and it shows. He looks worn out. I was hoping we could spend a lazy day in bed. We both need it.

"Good morning," Jill says when I enter the kitchen.

"Morning. Do you know where Logan is?"

"He had to go into the office."

"But it's Saturday!" I say, feeling hurt that he didn't mention this to me last night, or at the very least wake me before he left.

Is he really at the office?

I never would have doubted him before, but things have changed. It might just be my insecurities, but that seed has been planted, and I can't seem to shake it. While he has constantly been reassuring me since the Amanda incident, I can't help wondering if he would have even told me about his lunch date with her if I hadn't caught him out? What would have happened between them if he *had* met her that day? I want to believe what we have is different, but at the end of the day can anyone ever really be sure?

"He left you a note. It's on the counter."

"Thanks," I say, picking it up.

"Are you okay? You look upset."

"I'm fine." I'm probably overreacting. Or it might just be the birthday blues.

"If you say so, dear. Coffee?"

"Please."

Although I'm upset, I waste no time tearing open the envelope.

> *I've organised for Michelle to pick you up at ten. She's taking you for a day of pampering at the spa. My treat. Tonight, we're going out on a date, just the two of us. Be ready by six. Wear the blue dress.*
> *Love,*
> *Logan. xx*

Refolding the note, I swallow down the bitter taste of disappointment. I don't know why I'm so upset that he never mentioned my birthday. Does he even realise it's today? I haven't mentioned it. Or am I more concerned about where he is? I never suspected Jake was cheating on me every time he told me he was working back; I just believed him. Look how that turned out for me.

"Here you go, dear," Jill says, placing the hot coffee down in front of me.

"Thank you." Standing, I pick up the mug. "I'm going to take this upstairs and drink it on the balcony." As much as I care for Jill, I'm not up for talking right now.

"Okay. Would you like me to bring your breakfast up to you?"

"No, thanks. I'm not very hungry this morning."

I hear her sigh as I walk away.

My mood has turned around somewhat by the time I arrive back home in the afternoon. It is just after four, and I've had the most amazing day with Logan's sister. We spent two hours at the day spa being pampered, followed by a long lunch, and then she took me to her hairdresser.

Michelle didn't realise it was my birthday either, and I didn't tell her. It was just nice to do something special today. My mum always made a huge fuss about birthdays when she was alive, but Jake often forgot.

I didn't hear from Logan all day, which concerns me. I almost brought it up with Michelle so I could hear her take on Amanda, but I decided against it. I have to let this go or it's going to destroy us.

Arriving back home, I can't help the smile when I see Logan waiting for me in the foyer.

"There's my girl," he says, his smile matching my

own. When he opens his arms, I practically leap into them. "I missed you so much today."

"I missed you too, Hot Stuff." Drawing back, my eyes meet his. "You look tired."

"I am. It's been a long day."

"Why don't we give tonight a miss and stay home. We can go on a date another time."

"No can do, I'm afraid. Besides, I can sleep in tomorrow." Releasing me, he reaches for my hand. "Come, I have something for you."

"You do? What?"

"It's in our bedroom."

"Oh," I say, laughing. I should've known ... this man has a one-track mind.

When we enter the room, he leads me towards the bed where a small gift bag sits on top of the covers. Picking it up, he hands it to me.

"Happy birthday, babe."

"You remembered?"

"How could I not? I'm sorry it's taken me," he pauses to look down at his watch, "until four twenty-three to say it. But it was five o'clock when I left this morning, and you looked too peaceful sleeping. It didn't feel right to mention it in the note or say over the phone. I wanted to do it in person."

"So, tonight isn't really a date night?"

"No, it's *I'm taking the love of my life out on the town for her birthday*, which was previously disguised as a date night."

"You're the sweetest."

"If you're lucky, there may even be some dancing involved." He cocks an eyebrow as his arms slide around my waist, drawing me closer.

"You hate dancing."

"Not with you, I don't. You've changed me for the better. Now anything that involves you is my favourite thing to do. Plus, it means I get to hold you close, and that's always a good thing."

"Well, I look forward to that part of the evening then."

"Open your gift."

Removing the tissue paper on top, I pull the small box out of the bag and open the lid. "Hot Stuff," I gasp.

"It's not as extravagant as the necklace I gave you when we went to the ballet, but I had this one custom-made. A ballerina, for my ballerina."

"It's the most beautiful thing I've ever seen." I pull out the fine gold chain on which the ballerina pendant hangs. The tutu she's wearing is diamond encrusted. "I love it."

"I'm glad," he says, brushing my lips with his.

"I'm going to wear it tonight with my blue dress."

"I was hoping you would. Your hair looks nice," he says, wrapping one of the soft curls around his finger.

"After lunch, Michelle took me to her hairdresser's. I had my nails done too." I hold my hands out to show off my French polish. "Thank you for the day of pampering. It was nice. I also enjoyed spending time with your sister. I really like her."

"I'm glad, babe. She really likes you too. Hopefully, you'll become good friends."

"I'd like that."

I've had plenty of friends over the years, but never anyone I've been exceptionally close to like a sister. Maybe it's because I'm an only child, but I've always longed for a relationship like that.

"You look nervous," I say as we ride in the back of the limousine to our unknown destination.

"I'm okay," he replies, placing his hand on my leg. "I just hope tonight is special for you."

"I'm with you, so it already is."

He smiles. "Have I told you how beautiful you look tonight?"

"Yes, but I don't mind hearing it again." My fingertips skim over the ballerina necklace adorning my neck. It looks beautiful paired with the baby blue one-shouldered dress I'm wearing. The sheer chiffon outer layer accentuates the femininity of the gown. "You don't look so bad yourself, Mr. Cavanagh," I say, arching a brow as I lean over to brush my lips against his.

He looks down at his watch for the umpteenth time before gazing out the window. "We're almost there."

Is he nervous about tonight, or is something else playing on his mind?

"Almost where?" I ask, hoping for a hint.

"Almost at our destination," he replies, chuckling.

Reaching into the pocket of his jacket, he pulls out one of his ties.

"Oh, I thought you were opting for a more casual look tonight by not wearing one. I think it looks sexy with the top buttons of your dress shirt undone. And on the plus side, it's less for me to undo when we get home later."

"The tie isn't for me—it's for you. I needed a blindfold, and it's the best I could come up with on short notice."

"A blindfold? Chris is in the front seat," I whisper.

"It's not for that," he says, laughing. "But we can definitely recreate this moment when we get home. Turn around."

"I thought you were getting kinky."

"You'd like that, wouldn't you?"

"Not with Chris so close," I admit.

"And if we were alone?"

I lift one shoulder. "I wouldn't mind."

"Of course, you wouldn't you little minx."

"If we're only going to dinner, can I ask why the blindfold?"

"All will be revealed shortly," he answers, covering my eyes with the silk of his tie.

"Should I be worried?"

"No." The limousine comes to a stop moments later, and I hear the car door open. "Give me your hand," Logan says before helping me out.

"Can I take this off now?"

"In a minute."

He guides me a few steps away from the vehicle, then places his hands on my shoulders and turns me around to face him. He reaches behind me to untie the blindfold. When I open my eyes, I find him smiling down at me.

"Hi," I breathe.

"Hi." He takes a deep breath before reaching into his pocket and pulling out a small rectangular box. "I have another gift for you."

"You spoil me. This necklace is more than enough." He tenses as he places the box in my hand. "Are you okay?" I ask, resting my palm on the side of his face. He's starting to worry me.

"I'm just a little anxious," he says.

"Why would you be anxious?"

"Open the box," he commands. "And please know, this has come from the best possible place."

"What do you mean, 'the best possible place'?"

"I just want to make all your dreams come true."

"That's sweet, but I still don't see where you're coming from with this."

"Open the box," he says again, so I do.

Inside, I find a single key. "A key? Is this about moving in with you?"

"No," he says, shaking his head. "Although I'm still waiting for your answer to that."

"What is the key for then?"

"Please don't be mad at me," he begs, prompting me to turn back around.

My eyes take in the vast, bright yellow building before me. "Why would I be mad at ..." The question vanishes the moment I see the enormous, illuminated sign positioned above the glass doors.

Brooke's School of Dance.

The ballerina on the accompanying logo looks just like the one on my necklace. My hand immediately covers my mouth as I take everything in.

Spinning around, I stare up at Logan.

I can feel his hands trembling as he cups my face. "Before you say it's too much, or you don't want me to spend money on you, or give you expensive gifts, just hear me out." His eyes scan my face as he speaks. "I know opening your own studio has been a lifelong dream of yours. But the reality is, by the time you save enough money to actually do it, you'll probably be too old to ever see it through. So, in that box, is the key to your dreams. It's yours, babe, all of it."

I stand there speechless. When what he's done finally sinks in, my legs almost give out from underneath me.

"Steady there," he says, grasping my waist. Tears rise to my eyes and before I get a chance to speak, I break down crying and bury my face in his chest. I can't believe this is really happening.

"You don't like it?"

"Are you kidding me?" Drawing back, I lift my tear-stained face so I can meet his eyes. "You have no idea what this means to me."

"I think I do." A smile tugs at his lips. "So, I'm not in trouble?"

I grasp the lapels of his suit jacket, tugging him closer. "You're most definitely getting laid tonight, mister."

He chuckles at my response. "Well, maybe now is a good time to tell you that I've been lying to you for the past month."

"You've been lying to me? About what?"

"All of those extra hours I've been putting in at the office, it was all a ruse. I've actually been here, coordinating this. And before you say anything, I only did it because I didn't want to ruin the surprise. I know you've been worried since Amanda, and I even contemplated telling you everything, but it wouldn't have been the same if I had. I hope you can forgive me."

"Only if you forgive me for all the times I doubted you?"

"It's water under the bridge, babe. I've been burnt too, remember? I know firsthand how it feels. So long as you know in here," he says, tapping the tip of his finger over my heart, "that I would never knowingly do wrong by you. What we have is special, don't ever lose sight of that."

This man.

"What did I ever do to deserve you?"

"It's not anything you did, but rather everything you are. I could never repay you for what you've given me."

I slide my arms around his waist and hold him tight. "I love you so much."

"I know, and not a day passes that I'm not thankful for your love." He leans forward, brushing his lips against mine. "Do you want to go inside and check the place out?"

I bounce on my feet because I'm absolutely dying to go inside. "Yes!" Releasing me, he reaches for my hand. "I still can't believe you did this."

"You deserve it all and so much more."

Chapter 49

Logan

All the pressure I've put myself under for the past few weeks vanishes the instant Brooke unlocks the door to her future with a huge smile on her face.

"Wait here," I say as I rush in and turn on the lights.

I only hope this proves to her just how much she means to me.

She is my future. My everything.

The foyer lights up, and Brooke lets out a small gasp before whispering her pet name for me, *"Hot Stuff."*

She moves to join me inside, but I hold out my hand to stop her. "Hold on."

Returning to her side, I scoop her up into my arms bridal style. "What are you doing?" she laughs.

"I'm carrying you over the threshold."

"Isn't that something you're supposed to do when you get married?"

"I'm just practising for when I actually get to marry you, Miss Ryan ... and what a sweet day the will be."

She doesn't say anything, but when her hand caresses the side of my face, I can see her emotions shining bright in her eyes. I can't wait until the day she becomes my wife.

I take a few steps into the room before placing her back down on her feet. "What do you think?"

Her eyes dart around the space before returning to me. "You did all of this on your own?"

"No, I hired contractors. Plus, I had some outside help from our family and friends."

"They were all in on this?"

"Yes. My parents, John, Michelle, Craig, Chris, Jill, even Ellen."

"My boss, Ellen ... she knew about this?"

"She helped me tremendously, especially with the layout."

"Wow," I say. "I can't believe you did all this for me."

I drape my arm over her shoulders. "They all love you and wanted to help make this possible for you."

"You're going to make me cry again," she says, swiping her finger under her eyes. "I bet my makeup is ruined."

I place my forefinger under her chin, turning her face towards mine. "No, you're still breathtaking."

She places her hand on my abdomen as her head rests on my shoulder. "I can't even find the words to do this place justice. This would've cost you a fortune."

"I can afford it," I say, placing a kiss on the side of her head. "I'll never be able to spend what money I have in my lifetime. Our children, even our children's children, will be set for life."

"Our children?"

My lips curve upwards when I see her eyes widen. "Yes, our children." *One day we will have a family together.* "As you can see, you're all set to go. You have a front desk, and over here is a place for you to display all your merchandise."

"It's perfect."

"There's a sofa for parents to sit on while they wait. There's a coffee bar set up in the corner. I couldn't install a glass viewing window like Ellen has because this is a load-bearing wall, but all these monitors along here," I say, gesturing towards them, "are wired to a series of cameras inside the studio."

"You've thought of everything."

"Only the best for you, my love."

"That must be why I have you then. You're the best boyfriend a girl could ever ask for."

I puff out my chest. "You better believe I am." I smile as she bursts out laughing. "There's more."

"I'm not sure if I can take any more."

"Come." I lead her towards the back of the reception area. "The toilets and change rooms are off here."

"What's up there?" she asks, pointing to the staircase.

"I'll show you." At the top of the stairs there is a small hallway leading to two doors. "You go first," I say.

She opens the first door, and her eyes widen. "A piano."

"Just like the one at home. I thought you might like to have music lessons here as well. You already have your first client."

"I do?"

"Lara. She was here today helping us while you were out with Michelle. She wants to start dance classes as well."

"I'd love that," she says, placing her hand on her chest. "She's so sweet." Brooke walks towards the piano and skims her fingers over the surface. "I'm blown away by everything." Her eyes move to me. "Thank you doesn't seem enough."

"Seeing you smile is all the thanks I need."

I'm just relieved she loves it. There was a part of me that worried she was going to be upset.

"What's behind the other door?"

"Go see."

Cautiously she opens the door. "Oh my god, all my stuff from the terrace house is in here," she says, as her head snaps in my direction. "You said you were going to put it in storage."

"I did, for a month or so, then I brought it here."

When we packed up her old place she wanted to keep her furniture for when she moved out. As I have no intention of letting her go, I found a way to repurpose it here at the studio.

"Wow. I could almost live here."

"Not possible. You're not allowed to live here."

"Why?"

"Because you have a home with me. You can come here to relax in between classes."

"That is so thoughtful—and perhaps, a little cunning," she says narrowing her eyes playfully.

"I have no idea what you're talking about," I retort, giving her the most innocent look, I can muster.

"I bet you don't," she laughs. She encircles my waist with her arms. "I love it. I love all of it."

"The best is still to come."

"The studio?"

"Yes."

"I can't believe you did all this in such a short span of time."

"You underestimate me, Miss Ryan."

As we walk down the small corridor and descend the stairs, she notices the pictures hanging on the walls.

"What are these?"

"This place used to be an old warehouse. It was built in 1905. I had Claire do some research for me and she found these old images at the library. These ones," I say, pointing to a few further down, "were taken during construction. I thought it was a nice touch to have them framed."

"They're amazing." She moves in for a closer look. "There's just so much to see, it's hard to take it all in."

"You'll have plenty of time over the coming weeks, months, and years to do that."

"I can hardly wait to get started."

"You're going to be a huge success."

Reaching for her hand, I entwine our fingers and lead her towards the studio. When she approaches the double doors, I stand back, giving her the space to take this in.

"I'm nervous," she says, grasping the handle. Brooke has no idea what awaits her behind those doors.

"Surprise!" everyone calls out startling Brooke so much she stumbles back into me.

On cue, the DJ plays happy birthday. She once told me she'd never had a party, so I had to give her one.

"What's all this?" she says, swinging around to face me.

"It's your surprise birthday party."

"Here I go again," she says, fanning her eyes. "I can't believe you're throwing me a party on top of all this." She flings her arms around me. "It's too much. It's all too much."

"And you deserve every bit of it," I reply, placing a chaste kiss on her sweet mouth before turning her around. "Go. Your guests await."

Shoving my hands into the pockets of my trousers, I hang back to observe Brooke as she moves around the room greeting everyone. Her unwavering smile warms my heart. The extremely long hours, and every damn obstacle I faced during this mammoth project was so worth it.

There is easily twenty people her, including Jill and Chris—who had to sneak inside while I showed Brooke around the mezzanine level—and my family. The rest of the attendees are friends from her dance studio. I left those invites up to her boss.

Ellen has been fantastic throughout all of this. Although she's sad to be losing Brooke as her head teacher and choreographer, she's been very supportive.

When Brooke finally makes her way back to me, I drape my arm over her shoulder and take her on a tour of the studio. The bonus of this place being so large, meant I was able to install a stage at the far end of the room where she can hold her concerts.

"Look at all the mirrors and the ballet barre," she says, running her hands over everything.

"There's a smaller barre on the opposite side of the room for the little kids."

"Perfect. I'm blown away by the sheer size of this room." She spins around in a circle with her arms held out wide. "What's that down there?" she asks, pointing to a curtained-off area.

I move her to the centre of the room. "Stand here," I instruct as I head in the direction of the stage.

The floor-to-ceiling, theatre-style red velvet drapes almost weren't ready in time, having only arrived this morning.

After grabbing the remote, I go back and stand beside her. Pressing the button, I watch her face intently.

"Get out of town," she squeals, smacking my arm. "A stage?"

"Not just any stage, a concert-worthy one."

She holds her arm out towards me. "Pinch me. Am I dreaming? Actually," she says, dropping her hand back down by her side, "don't pinch me. If this is a dream, I want to savour it a little longer."

"You're not dreaming," I reply with a chuckle. "Come on, let's go join the others. You'll have plenty of time to look around tomorrow."

She slides her hand through my arm and hooks it around my elbow, as we walk back towards the long table where our guests are seated.

"Look at all the beautiful helium balloons on the ceiling, there must be at least one hundred."

"Three hundred, actually," I say.

"And the exquisite table setting. It reminds me of how grandly decorated the tables were the night I first met you."

"One of the best nights of my life," I admit. "Except for the part where I almost lost you, of course."

"You saved my life that night, and I'll be eternally indebted to you for that."

"Do you ever wonder if it was fate that brought us together?" *I've often wondered this.*

"Whatever it was, I'm grateful."

The party is in full swing, and everyone seems to be having a great time, especially Brooke. I hired caterers for the event, as well as wait staff. Michelle and Mum offered to make the food, but I wanted everyone to be able to relax and enjoy the celebrations with my girl.

Even my father seems to be enjoying himself. I've caught him smiling on a few occasions. I half expected him to bail early or not show up at all. I was shocked when he turned up here this morning with my mother to help set up.

After the second course is served, most of the women head out on to the dance floor, so I move down the table to sit with John and my father.

"Thank you for everything you've done tonight," John says, as his gaze moves to where the women are dancing up a storm. "Brooke looks so happy."

"She does," I reply, and my smile grows as I drink her in.

"It was a really nice thing for you to do," my father adds, catching me off guard.

"Thanks, Dad. She's had a tough life, so I was glad to be able to do this for her."

The song the DJ is playing comes to an end, and the girls stop moving, but as soon as the next tune starts to play, they all cheer. Brooke turns to look in our direction, and my heart sinks.

"Oh shit," I mumble under my breath, as she makes her way towards us. I promised to dance with her tonight, but I was aiming for a slow song so I could hold her in my arms. The 'YMCA' was not what I had in mind.

As she nears the table, I have an overwhelming compulsion to flee, but to my relief—or pure joy—she grabs my father's hand and coaxes him to stand.

"I think I'll sit this one out," he says with a look of panic on his face. It amuses me more than it should.

"Please," Brooke begs. "It's my birthday. Look, your wife is out there. Come join us."

I'm holding my breath as I wait for him to lose his cool, but to my surprise, he doesn't. "Okay, just one song," he grumbles. I literally can't believe my eyes.

"Well, I'll be damned," John says from beside me. "How much has your father had to drink?"

"Nothing, he's driving."

My eyes seek out my sister. "What the hell?" she mouths, and I can tell she's just as perplexed as I am.

This is a side of the old man we've never seen. I watch Brooke show him the moves to the chorus, and I half expect him to either walk away or just stand there for the entire song. When he actually starts to copy her, I scramble to get my phone out of my pocket in time. I need to capture this on video.

As soon as the song is over, he thanks Brooke before making a beeline for us. His hasty retreat makes me laugh. I'm so glad he's being a good sport, and that I have footage I can look back on when I need a laugh.

Deciding to head back to my original seat, I stand. Michelle grabs me as I walk away. "Please tell me you got pictures of that."

"Even better, I got the whole thing on video." She high-fives me.

"I need a copy."

"Definitely. I might even upload it to YouTube."

She throws back her head and laughs. "Brooke's having the best night."

"She is," I say, smiling as we both turn and face the dance floor.

"You did good, big brother. I'm so happy for you both."

"Thanks, sis." I drape my arm around her shoulder. "I've never felt like this about anyone."

"Brooke is perfect for you, and I couldn't ask for a better sister-in-law."

"Slow down, there," I say, laughing. "You sound like Mum."

She nudges my side with her elbow. "You're going to marry this one. You know it as much as I do."

Chapter 50

Brooke

I slide my arms around Logan's waist. "Are you enjoying your birthday?" he asks.

"Are you kidding me?" My cheeks are hurting from smiling so much. "This is the best night of my life. And don't forget, you promised me a dance."

He chuckles at my comment, and I narrow my eyes.

"Come get me when a slow song comes on."

"I almost grabbed you for the 'YMCA,' but I saw the panic on your face as I approached and took your dad instead."

"I'm eternally grateful for that."

"I still can't believe this is all mine," I say, glancing around the room.

"You deserve it all and so much more."

"One day I'll pay you back for all that you have done for me, Mr. Cavanagh, and that's a promise."

"Shh," he says, placing his finger on my lips. "Did I forget to mention the 'no payback clause'?"

"What clause?" I say, fighting a smile.

"It was in the fine print."

"Right," I say, laughing.

"Besides, you can't pay someone back for a gift. It's against the law, and I'm a lawyer, so I should know."

"You don't play fair," I say, poking him in the side.

"When it comes to you, Miss Ryan, never."

Leaning closer, I whisper into his ear, "What if I said I wanted to pay you back in blowjobs?"

Throwing back his head, he groans. "Then we'd have a problem."

"How ironclad is this contract?"

"A few minutes ago, I would've said unbreakable, but now that you've thrown blowjobs into the equation, I'm going to have to find a loophole."

"I figured as much," I say, and we both laugh.

"Just the thought of your sweet lips ..." He presses himself against me, and I feel him hardening.

"I love you so much, Hot Stuff. Even without all of this. If we were dirt poor and lived in a trailer park, the depth of my feelings for you wouldn't change."

"I know." When he covers my mouth with his, my body instinctively melts into him. "Mm," he hums when our lips finally part. "I can't wait to get you alone."

Reaching up, I slide my fingers into his hair. "I can't wait for that either. It will be the perfect end to a perfect day."

Our little moment is broken when John appears at our side. "I hate to break this up, but I was wondering if I could borrow the birthday girl for a few minutes."

Logan's eyes move to me, and I give him a tiny nod of reassurance. Even though things have improved dramatically between John and I, I appreciate that Logan still checks in to see if I'm comfortable.

When Logan turns to leave us, I give his firm, round arse a sneaky pinch as he walks away.

"I'm all yours," I say, giving John my undivided attention.

"Do you mind if we step outside for a moment?"

"Sure."

"You look to be enjoying your night," he says holding the studio door open for me.

"It's been amazing."

My eyes take in the foyer once more as we pass through. John reaches for the exterior glass door, and I thank him as I step out into the night air.

He shoves his hands into the pockets of his trousers before stopping beside me. "You're probably wondering why I brought you out here."

"Yes."

"Come," he says. "I have something for you."

"You do?"

"Your birthday gift."

"Oh my god," I say when we round the corner of the building and I see a bright yellow car sitting there wrapped in a big red bow.

"Happy birthday, sweetheart." He pulls a set of keys from his pocket and places them in my hand.

"John, I can't accept this. It's too much."

He chuckles to himself. "Logan warned me you'd say that."

"I don't mean to sound ungrateful."

"Come take a look at it," he says, placing his hand on my elbow and guiding me in that direction. "I had the studio logo put on the back and the sides. It will be great advertising when you're driving around the city."

"That was really sweet of you, but—"

"But nothing. I've missed out on all your birthdays and Christmases. Besides, plenty of fathers buy cars for their daughters."

"John."

"Please let me do this for you." Facing me, he places his hands on my shoulders. "It would mean so much to me if you'd accept this gift. You have no idea how bad I feel for not being there for you when you were growing up."

I bow my head because I can't stand to see the pleading look in his eyes. "It's just ..."

"Just what?" he asks, placing his finger under my chin and raising my face to meet his. "To be honest, I'm overwhelmed and a little embarrassed by everyone's generosity. Just having you all here tonight is more than enough for me. I've never owned a car as nice as this."

"It's only a Mini convertible, not a Lamborghini."

"It's still nicer than anything I've ever had."

Releasing me, he steps towards the car and opens the driver's door.

"Come take a look." Joining him, I bend down to look inside. "She's a beauty, isn't she?" I can smell the new leather from where I stand. The interior is so fancy. It's black with splashes of bright yellow here and there that match the exterior colour perfectly.

"It's beautiful," I say.

"So, you'll accept it?"

Tears pool in my eyes as I meet his gaze. "If it means that much to you."

"It means the world to me ... as do you," he says, wrapping me in his arms.

"Thank you."

"You're welcome, sweetheart."

"For the record, this present not only makes up for all my missed birthday and Christmas presents, but it will also cover me for the rest of my life," I say with a small laugh, but I'm deadly serious. I don't want or need to be showered with expensive gifts from him as well.

"Let me be the judge of that."

Picking up one of the flower arrangements from the table, I inhale the sweet, perfumed scent of the yellow roses. A small smile lingers as I think of my mother. She would've loved tonight.

A sense of peace settles over me. Although I didn't fulfil my promise to her the way I'd planned, I know she would be proud of me, proud of the direction my life has taken. For the first time in a long time, my future looks promising.

"Are you okay, babe?" Logan asks, coming up behind me and sliding his arms around my waist.

"I'm more than okay," I reply, leaning my head back into his chest.

"John asked if he could order the flowers for tonight," he says, nodding at the arrangement in my hand. "It's uncanny that he chose yellow roses when I didn't request any specific type of flower."

The smile on my face widens because I know exactly why he chose them. "They were my mother's favourite flowers," I reply, placing them back down on the table and turning in his arms.

"I didn't know that."

"John brought them for her when they were together."

"Really? And now I buy them for you. How weird."

"I wouldn't say weird." Giving Logan a kiss, I revel in

the extraordinary circumstances that have led me to where I am in this moment, to a life I could've only once dreamt about. "Do you know how happy you make me, Hot Stuff?"

"Even if it's only a fraction of the joy you've given, then yes." He cups my face in his hands before continuing. "I've lived thirty-two years without you, and it's only taken me a few short months to realise the rest of my life would be nothing without you in it."

"I feel exactly the same way." I've survived many heartaches over the years, but I'm certain if I ever lost him, it would break me. "Can we stay here tonight?" I ask.

"Sure, if you want to."

Releasing him from my embrace, I grab his hand and lead him out of the studio and into the reception area. We are the only ones here; all the guests have left. When we reach the bottom of the landing, Logan throws me over his shoulder and slaps my arse as he takes the stairs two at a time.

The moment we reach the private sanctuary he set up, he places me back on my feet. "This tie has been burning a hole in my pocket all evening," he says, retrieving it from his jacket.

"Why?" I ask, giving him an inquisitive look. When he raises an eyebrow and gives me a sexy smirk, the conversation in the limousine earlier springs to mind. "Oh!"

"Turn around," he orders. My body trembles with anticipation as I let him secure the blindfold over my eyes. The room is mostly silent, except for the sound of my own erratic breathing.

The clunking of his shoes against the wooden floor alerts me that he is on the move.

"Hot Stuff," I whisper as my longing for his touch intensifies.

"Shh," he utters, leaning in towards my ear. His warm breath against my skin makes it pebble with goosebumps.

"You're teasing me."

"And you love it." He continues walking in circles around me. "Lift your arms in the air," he commands. I feel like his prey awaiting the attack.

Moments pass before I feel his featherlike touch against my side, as he slowly and meticulously draws down the zipper of my dress. He lowers my arms before his fingers skim across my shoulder, gently pushing the fabric down my arm. I hear him take in a sharp breath the moment the garment pools around my feet, exposing my sheer, baby blue strapless lace bra and matching g-string. I bought them especially for him.

"Beautiful," he murmurs, leaning into me once more. He brushes his lips softly against mine, but when I reach for him, he steps back. "Hands by your side."

Unable to see, my hearing is amplified. When a sharp clicking sound fills the room, I listen intently trying to identify what it is before it dawns on me what is happening.

"Are you taking photos of me?"

"Yes. You have no idea how good you look standing here like this." He's near because I can feel his breath tickling my ear. "You're a walking fucking wet dream," he grates out, making me shiver. I tilt my head back and whimper when he runs his finger from the base of my bra to the waistband of my underwear. "Every single inch of you." I take in a sharp breath when his fingertips disappear underneath the fabric, and I ache for him to go lower.

I feel his tongue circling my belly button. The sensation is almost too much. My other senses seemed heightened by my loss of sight.

"Please touch me," I beg.

"Quiet."

"But you're slowly killing me."

His strong hands grip my hips as he turns me around, and I yelp when he bites my arse cheek. It sends a combination of pain and pleasure surging through my body.

"Are you aching for my touch?"

"Desperately."

"Where?" I whimper when he runs his tongue along the length of my spine. "I need your words, Miss Ryan."

"Everywhere." Logan's hands softly glide over my ribcage, until both his palms are covering my breasts. Tilting my head back, I moan into the silence when he tweaks my nipples through the lace. "Oh god, I need your touch everywhere."

A growl permeates from the back of his throat, and his movements suddenly become desperate. He yanks my g-string down and turns me to face him. Grasping one of my ankles he raises my foot slightly off the floor before removing my high heel and then my underwear. A whimper escapes my lips when he continues to lift that same leg higher, before resting it on his shoulder.

'Thank god,' I silently chant. I wasn't sure if I could stand much more of his taunting.

He places his palm on my inner thigh to spread me wide as he blows warm air against my sensitive flesh. "I love how flexible you are," he mumbles before his mouth finally bears down on me.

He's like a starved man at an all-you-can-eat buffet, but I'm not complaining.

"Hot Stuff," I breathe as my hands fist his hair to hold him in place.

"You taste so good."

"I need more," I say, pushing my pelvis towards his face.

I'm perplexed and disappointed when Logan suddenly pushes my leg off his shoulder and stands. He tugs off my blindfold, before sliding his hands under my arms, lifting me off the ground and moving across the room until my body slams into the wall.

"Wrap your legs around me," he demands. "I need to be inside you."

Dragging down his zipper, he pulls out his cock and after lining himself up, he wastes no time plunging himself deep inside me.

Barely audible vulgarity spills from his mouth as he withdraws almost to the tip before plummeting back in. This isn't lovemaking; it's raw, unadulterated fucking. He's like a savage animal as he impales me over and over again. I'm loving every second of it and I can already feel my orgasm building.

"Fuck me harder," I beg. He draws his face back and grins.

There's pure lust smouldering in his emerald eyes. I've never spoken to him like that before, but like him, I can't seem to get enough.

Clutching my hips, his fingers dig roughly into my flesh as he somehow manages to pick up the pace. "Fuck," he grates out, throwing back his head. Seconds later, he withdraws from me and ejaculates all over my stomach. His breathing is rapid, as he rests his forehead against mine, trying to get air into his lungs. "I'm sorry. I couldn't hold back."

"I'm not complaining."

"I didn't hurt you, did I?"

"Not at all."

"I don't know what came over me."

"I don't know either, but I liked it."

"I liked it too," he chuckles as he carries me towards the bed, gently laying me down. I smile when I see he's still fully dressed, apart from the zipper on his trousers being down. "Are you sure I didn't hurt you?"

"I'm fine, honestly." I bite my bottom lip. "Can we do it again?"

"I owe you a couple of orgasms first," he says, wasting no time stripping out of his clothes and joining me.

Reaching over the side of the bed, he picks up the dress shirt he was wearing and wipes his cum from my stomach.

"This mattress feels different, almost softer," I say squirming on the bed. "Or am I just used to your bed now?"

"Our bed," he scolds, "and I bought a new one."

"You did? Why? The other mattress was less than a year old."

"Because I didn't want you sleeping in a bed you may have shared with another man."

Pushing him onto his back, I straddle his lap. "Nobody else shared my bed. I haven't been with anyone since I moved back to Sydney ... except you."

"You bring out a side of me that I never knew existed."

"What do you mean?"

"I guess you could call it ..." He pauses for a moment.

"Call it what?"

"My jealous side. I know you have a past, babe—we both do—but just thinking about another man having his hands on you makes me all kinds of crazy."

"That's sweet," I say. "In a caveman kind of way."

"I've never loved anyone as much as I love you. I don't know any other way to explain it."

"I understand. That day we ran into Amanda, I wanted to scratch her eyes out."

He chuckles at my comment. "As I've told you many times, she's no threat to you. You're all I want."

"You're all I want too. And *yes,* by the way."

"Yes?" He gives me a puzzled look.

"To the question you asked me the night of the ballet."

When his features relax and a smile bursts onto his face, I know he's figured it out. "You're staying at the penthouse indefinitely?"

"Yes."

He flips me onto my back and covers my body with his. "Was it that hard fuck against the wall that sealed the deal?"

"No," I laugh, slapping his chest. "Although it definitely helped tip things in your favour."

"My dirty girl," he teases, nipping at my neck. When he draws his face back, he grinning. "Just so you know, you can't take it back. It's a done deal."

"I don't want to take it back," I say, cupping his face with my hand. "I'm at my happiest when I'm with you. So, my home is, and always will be wherever you are."

Chapter 51

Logan

"Good morning, beautiful," I say as I place a soft kiss on Brooke's shoulder.

She arches her back, stretching out her body. "Morning." I love the raspy sound of her voice when she first wakes.

"How'd you sleep?" I ask when she turns to face me.

"Good. It seems weird waking up here though. I'm so used to our bed back in Sydney." I grin when she says that.

Although it's been nearly two months since her birthday, the night she officially agreed to move in with me, I still love that she called it our bed.

It's mid-December, and we arrived in Melbourne yesterday. We're staying for a week. Brooke's been busy getting her dance studio ready for its grand opening in January, and Michelle's been helping her, which has been great. But it means she's also been away from home a lot, so I'm looking forward to having her all to myself for the next few days.

Tonight is my Melbourne office's Christmas party. I moved it from its usual Friday night to Saturday. I wanted it to coincide with our anniversary: exactly one year to the day since I first met the love of my life.

Rolling onto my back, I reach into the top drawer beside the bed. "I have something for you," I say, grabbing the box I stashed there last night while she was in the shower. "Happy Anniversary."

"Anniversary?"

"Yes. I know we haven't been together the entire time, but exactly one year ago today, you walked into my life and changed it forever."

"A year. I'd forgotten about that. So much has happened since then."

"Some good, some not so good," I state sliding my arm around her waist. "But I'd go through it all again if it brought me to this exact spot with you."

"That's sweet." She runs her hand softly over my hair. "I'm glad we ended up here."

"Me too. From the moment I laid eyes on you that night, I knew you were special."

"You did?"

"Never in my life have I been so deeply affected by another. I was instantly drawn to you ... like a moth to a flame."

"I didn't know that."

"You took my breath away the moment I saw you appear in the doorway. You still do that to me now."

"Who knew back then that we'd end up here ... together?" She pauses, averting her eyes. "And that Jake would be ..."

When her gaze moves back to mine, she forces out a smile, but the sadness in her eyes is unmissable.

"I'm glad we're still together, despite all the obstacles we've faced." I'm still haunted by that night as well. I'm not sure that will ever change. "What happened to Jake was a shame, but he chose that path."

"I know, but it's still hard to believe." I place the box on top of the covers so I can use my hand to drag her body closer to mine. "I received a letter from his mother about a week ago, along with a Christmas card."

"Oh."

"I was going to tell you." She shrugs. "I don't know why I didn't."

"It's okay," I say, tucking her hair behind her ear. "I'm sure you had your reasons."

"I feel for them. They're really struggling to come to terms with his death. He was their only son."

"I can't even fathom what it would feel like to lose a child in that way."

"They were estranged from him, which hasn't helped their grieving process. His mother said he moved back home when he arrived in Sydney, but after he stole a large amount of money, and some jewellery from them —probably to support his habit—they ended up asking him to leave. They never heard from him again after that."

"How awful for them."

"I know." She blows out a puff of air before continuing. "They feel partly responsible for his death, just like I do."

"What?" I raise my upper body, hovering over her. I'm shocked that she feels in any way responsible for what happened. She's the victim here. "You're not the bad guy, Brooke. You had no control over what he did. You're—"

She cuts me off by placing her finger over my mouth. "Can we change the subject?"

"I don't want you to feel responsible. None of that was your fault."

"I know, but he was my husband, I can't help feeling I could've done more."

I bite the inside of my cheek, so I don't end up saying something I'll regret. The last thing I want is to get into a fight with her over this.

Scooping up the box, I hold it out to her again. "Open it."

"You spoil me, Mr. Cavanagh."

"And that will never change."

"I feel bad that I have nothing for you."

"Your love is more than enough. It's all I need."

"You say the sweetest things, but I still wish I had something to give you in return."

I use my fingertip to trace her lips. "You have a perfectly good mouth."

I cock an eyebrow and fight a smile when she rolls her eyes at my suggestion.

"I'm still paying off my dance studio with this mouth. I'm going to end up with lockjaw if you keep adding to my debt."

Burying my face in the crook of her neck, my body shakes with laughter. I love her wit.

"I don't expect anything in return, babe," I say when I pull myself together. "Some terrible things happened to you the first night we met, and I'm in no way trying to dismiss any of that. This gift is something small to celebrate the positive things that came from it."

"Not everything about it was bad. I met you, didn't I?"

I release a long breath. "Fuck, do you have any idea how much my heart broke for you that night?"

"You were so kind to me," she says, bringing her face forward until our lips meet. She's smiling when she draws back. "My knight in shining armour. I was so grateful to have you there at the hospital."

It was that very day when I was sitting beside her hospital bed, that I realised there was nothing I wouldn't do to see her smile. A year later, I still feel that way.

"Are you ever going to open your gift?"

Her eyes widen the moment she removes the lid and sees what's inside. "Hot Stuff," she breathes. The earrings were made especially for her, along with a few other pieces that I plan to give her during our stay here in Melbourne. "They're exquisite."

"Not nearly as exquisite as you, my love."

Her fingertip lightly glides over the earrings. "I love that the diamonds are heart-shaped."

"Every time you wear them, you'll be reminded of how much I love you."

"Not a moment passes that I'm not thankful for your love."

I place a soft kiss on her nose before throwing back the covers. As I climb out of bed, I reach for her hand. "Come."

"Where are we going?"

"To shower. I'm taking you out for the day."

"Look at you," I say, pausing in the doorway of our bedroom to admire my girl.

She still manages to steal the air from my lungs. I purposely kept myself busy while she got ready. I didn't want to see what she was wearing under her dress; I can't be walking around with a semi in front of my employees all night. Besides, it will add to the excitement of unwrapping her later when we get home.

"You like?" she asks, doing a small twirl.

"I love." Stepping into the room, I close the distance between us. "The green suits you."

"It matches your eyes," she says sliding her arms around my waist.

"You look beautiful."

"Thank you, and you look handsome in your tux. I like this too," she says, running her fingers over the stubble on my face. "Very rugged, it suits you."

"I can't believe tonight you'll be walking into that party on my arm."

"It will be my honour," she says. I've never taken a date with me to any of my company's functions, but Brooke's my future and I want to show her off to the world. "I'm wearing the earrings you gave me. See."

"That reminds me." Releasing her, I pull a thin, white, rectangle shaped box from my jacket pocket. "This is for you."

"Logan," she says, frowning. "You can't keep doing this."

"Yes, I can," I reply with a grin. "Open it."

It's a tennis bracelet to match the earrings I gave her this morning. The heart-shaped diamonds form a continuous line and are set in an almost invisible setting. She gasps the moment she opens the lid.

"Oh my god, it's beautiful."

"It doesn't hold a candle to you." Taking the bracelet from the box, I drape it around her slender wrist and fasten it. "Perfect."

"You're perfect," she replies.

"Hardly," I say, brushing my lips over her knuckles before letting her hand go. "Are you almost ready to leave? Claire likes to go over all the arrangements with me before the guests arrive."

"Just let me throw some things in my clutch and I'll be ready to go."

"Did you even hear a word I said?" Claire asks, frowning.

"Of course," I reply glancing over my shoulder once more. "Why would you ask that?"

"You seem off tonight, or should I say *preoccupied*."

"I'm fine," I lie, as I impatiently await Brooke's return from the bathroom.

"Are you sure?"

"I'm sure," I say forcing out a smile as I fidget with my bowtie.

"If you say so, boss."

My breath hitches the moment I see my girl appear in the doorway. It's like déjà vu. My eyes dart to Claire, and she's studying me intently.

"Did you two have a fight?"

"Of course not."

"I've been working with you long enough to know when something's up."

I look down at my watch and see that the guests will be arriving soon. If I'm going to do this, it's now or never.

"Hold that thought," I say, leaving her side to head in Brooke's direction.

Butterflies swarm in my stomach as I approach her. I wasn't this nervous when I crossed the room to meet her a year ago, but I guess my entire future wasn't on the line then.

"Hey," she says when I reach her.

Despite the nerves, I still can't help but smile as I gaze into her beautiful brown eyes.

"Hey." Leaning forward, I place my mouth on hers and slide my hands around her waist.

Her flattened palms glide over the satin lapels of my tuxedo jacket. "Are you okay? You're shaking."

"I will be in a few minutes," I reply. *Well, I hope I will be.* Glancing over my shoulder, I give the DJ a small nod. "Dance with me."

"Really?" she asks, beaming. "Right now?"

"Yes."

"Okay."

As soon as the introduction to 'Can't Help Falling In Love With You' begins, I tug Brooke closer, until our bodies are flush.

The first time she played this song for me on the piano, she said it reminded her of us. Like the besotted fool that I am, I googled the lyrics first thing the next morning when I got to work. When I found a video of Andrea Bocelli and Katharine McPhee's more recent version on YouTube, I was instantly overcome with emotion as I listened to it. In my mind, it officially became our song.

My emotions are running high as I glide her around the dancefloor. I hope this woman knows just how much she means to me.

"Such a beautiful song," she says smiling.

"I thought you'd like it."

"It was the first song I learnt to play on the piano—the Elvis Presley version—it was my mum's favourite."

My grip on her tightens as she rests her cheek on my chest. I can hear her humming the tune as our bodies gently sway in unison.

I try not to think about what I'm about to do and focus

on this moment instead. Slowly my body starts to relax. Once the music stops, however, my nerves come back with a vengeance.

"That was nice," she says when I release her and take a step backwards. "I love dancing with you, and the song choice was perfect."

I smile as I inwardly encourage myself to make my move. I know we've gained the attention of the others in the room, but I try to block that from my mind. There have been so many times over the past few weeks when I wanted to do this, but I chickened out every time.

Man the fuck up Cavanagh.

I retreat another step as I slide my hand into my pocket. "I've been carrying this around for weeks." I pause as I pull out the small white box. "I've been waiting for the right time, but since meeting you, I've realised there's never a wrong time when it's with the right person."

Brooke's eyes widen as I proceed down to one knee. I swallow hard when her hand flies up to cover her mouth.

"One year ago to the day, you walked through that very door," I say, flicking my head in that direction. "The moment I laid eyes on you, you awoke something inside me. But timing was not on our side, or maybe it has been all along." I release a nervous chuckle. "One thing I am sure of, meeting you was the start of something beautiful. A moment that would change both of our lives. Eight months later, fate brought us together again, and although it's only been a-hundred-and-twenty-eight days since you officially became mine, I already know," I say as I gesture my hand between us, "this is something I want for the rest of my life."

"Oh, Hot Stuff," she whispers, tears filling her eyes. I'm not sure if that's a good or bad sign.

"Will you marry me, Brooke, and be my *forever*?" I open the box to reveal the five-carat, heart-shaped diamond ring that matches the earrings and bracelet I gave her earlier today.

I'm left holding my breath as she remains silent and unmoving. It's not the reaction I was hoping for. When I see a tear cascade down her pretty face, my heart drops. Have I fucked up? Although I've known for a while this is what I want, is it too soon for her? With every second that passes, my desperation grows.

"Are you going to put me out of my misery?" I eventually ask, standing and bracing myself for her answer.

"Yes."

I arch an eyebrow. "Yes, you're going to put me out of my misery, or yes, you'll marry me?"

"Yes, I'll marry you, silly," she says, as a huge smile bursts onto her face.

I intake a sharp breath and pull her into my arms. "Thank fuck," I murmur into her hair. For a moment I thought this was going to blow up in my face. "I love you so much."

"I love you more," she says, before throwing her arms around my neck.

"I think we've already been over this," I retort, drawing back so I can see her face. "I love you the most— the end. I win!"

"You suck," she says, lightly pinching me. It makes me laugh.

"Not half as good as you, babe." Her mouth gapes open as I wink at her.

Cupping her face in my hands, my lips meet hers. And for the first time in days, I can finally breathe easier —I have what I've always wanted: *her*.

Finding Forever

Keep reading for a sneak peek of Finding Forever (Book 2) ...

Logan

I lean back into my chair and release a long, frustrated breath when I see my aunt's number on the screen. I've been waiting for this call, but this is not how I wanted my Friday afternoon to end. She must have just been served with the court papers and is seeking retribution.

"What do you want, Kathleen?" I snap the moment I answer the phone. I know my greeting is harsh, but this isn't a cordial call. She's not stupid. She knows I'm the reason behind my uncle's change of heart. Like him, I'm over this woman and her constant mind games. This bullshit needs to stop.

"How rude," she quips, and I roll my eyes. "I shouldn't have expected anything more." She's been anything but affable with me throughout my life. She epitomises rudeness and indifference.

"That's rich coming from the likes of you."

She pauses briefly before releasing her attack. "I'm disgusted by your behaviour. How could you treat your own flesh and blood this way? I ... I demand you stop representing that man and filling his head with garbage.

So help me god, if you don't put a stop to this ridiculousness, you'll feel my full wrath."

I pull the phone away from my ear. She is yelling so loud Rose can probably hear her in reception.

"I can't do that, I'm afraid."

"Ugh!" The pure frustration in her voice makes me smile.

After everything she's put my poor uncle through over the past few months, it gives me a sense of satisfaction. I cannot be manipulated like John and my father and that gets under her skin.

"John has been more than compliant with your demands up until now, but no more. You've gone too far this time."

She is quiet for a moment before deciding to take a different approach. "You have no idea how hard this is on me, Logan," she says, changing her tone to sweet and adding in a sniffle for extra effect. "I'm all alone now. I'm devastated that I don't have your support. We're family, after all."

"Save the crocodile tears for someone else, Kathleen. They won't work on me."

"You're a heartless bastard."

"And you're a cold-hearted, manipulative bitch. You don't fool me for a second."

"Nobody messes with me; do you hear me? Nobody!" And just like that, her true colours return.

"And nobody messes with the people I love and care about, which unfortunately is a category you no longer fall under."

"Don't push me," she threatens.

"Look, I don't have time for you or your idle threats. I have two companies to run and a wedding to plan."

"Your father told me you are marrying that gold-digging whore. You're a bigger fool than I thought."

She's baiting me, and as hard as it is, I try my best to keep my cool. I also need to remind my old man not to tell her anything about my life. What I do is none of her fucking business.

"I have nothing further to say to you. I'll see you in court, Kathleen. Goodbye."

"I'll make you sorry you were ever born!" she screams down the line as I'm ending the call.

Her threats don't scare me. John only wants what's rightfully his so he can move on with his life, but she's fighting him every step of the way. It's wearing him down to the point that both Brooke and I are extremely concerned about him.

Dropping the phone onto my desk, I pinch the bridge of my nose. John didn't want to take this route, but unfortunately, it was the best solution. It took me weeks to convince him this was the only way to go. He was hoping they could settle this amicably, like two adults, but deep down we all knew my aunt wasn't going to make this easy for him. She's greedy, materialistic, and completely self-centred. The only person Kathleen cares about is Kathleen.

"Your four o'clock is here, Mr. Cavanagh," Rose says, buzzing my office.

"Okay, just give me a few minutes, then send them in." My eyes scan the desk. When I don't find what I'm looking for, I press the intercom. "Rose, is there a file?"

"It's a new client, but I'll get one made up for you now." I hear her giggle before she releases the button and my jaw ticks. I'm in no mood for this.

Sitting back in my chair, I run my fingers through my

hair. I don't want to be here today. I want to be at home where I can lose myself in my girl and not deal with this crap.

A few minutes pass before Rose knocks on my door and enters. I turn to look at her, but instead of my receptionist, I find my beautiful fiancée standing just inside the doorway.

"Brooke."

"Hey, Hot Stuff."

Standing, I round the desk as she approaches. She's a sight for sore eyes. Her presence is just what I need. Pulling her into my arms, I bury my face in her hair and inhale her familiar scent. It instantly calms me.

"I wasn't expecting to see you until tonight. Shouldn't you be at the studio?"

"Michelle is holding down the fort," she says, encircling my waist with her arms. "I'm your four o'clock."

"What? You don't need to make an appointment to see me. You know I'll always make time for you, no matter how busy I am." Tucking her hair behind her ear, I bring my lips to hers. "I'm so glad you're here."

"I'm glad I am too. Our time together has been limited lately, and as much as I miss you, I'm actually here on official legal business."

"Really?" Releasing her, I guide her towards the chair opposite mine and gesture for her to take a seat. As Brooke sits down in front of me, I lean against the corner of my desk, before crossing my legs at the ankles and giving her my undivided attention. "I'm intrigued, Miss Ryan."

She inhales a sharp breath before speaking. "Hot Stuff," she says, scooting forward and placing her hand on my leg. "I may as well just come out and say it. I want you to draw up a prenuptial agreement."

I stand quickly as my temper goes from zero to a hundred in a millisecond. That was the last thing I expected her to say.

"You're kidding me, right?"

"No, I'm deadly serious," she says, her face dropping.

Pushing away from the desk, I walk towards the floor-to-ceiling windows and gaze out over the city skyline. This day is going from bad to worse.

"That's not happening, Brooke. I can't believe you'd even suggest such a thing."

"Hear me out," she says, coming to stand beside me.

"Nothing you can say will make me change my mind."

"Please, Logan."

She rarely calls me by my birth name, a point that only manages to make my irritation grow. Turning my head, my eyes meet hers. "Don't do this," I plead.

"Don't do what?"

"Sabotage our marriage before it's even begun."

"How am I sabotaging our marriage?" she asks as her pretty face screws up. "That doesn't make any sense."

"You're setting us up for failure."

"That's ridiculous."

"Really? You wouldn't even be suggesting a prenup if you didn't have reservations about it working out."

"That's not it at all," she says, reaching for me. "There are valid reasons why we should do this that have nothing to do with us, or our marriage."

"Give me just one."

"Okay ... I'm a realist. I've been through enough in my life to know that things can change in a blink of an eye. Look what happened between me and Jake. When I married him, I thought it was forever too."

I scrub my hand over my face. I hate that she was

once married to that dickhead. "What we have doesn't even compare to what you had with Jake. You said so yourself."

"It still doesn't change the fact that I never saw it coming."

"It's irrelevant." I flick my hand, dismissing it completely. "Our circumstances are nothing like yours were with him."

"But don't you see? Things happen sometimes that are completely out of our control. We can't even pretend to know what the future holds for us."

"A beautiful life," I snap as I rub the heel of my palm over my pectoral muscles in an attempt to relieve the sharp pain in my chest. "That's what our future together holds, Brooke." I refuse to consider anything less. "Let's just drop this nonsense."

"It's not nonsense. I'm doing this for you. To protect everything *you've* worked hard for." She pokes me in the chest to emphasise her words, and I have to hide my amusement. She's sexy as hell when she's mad. "I love you, not your bank balance. I don't want you, or anyone else, for that matter, thinking I'm doing this for the money."

"I know you're not marrying me for my money. Christ, you won't let me buy you anything without questioning it."

"But you still do."

"What?"

"Buy me things, even when I tell you not to."

"Because I love you. I want to give you nice things. Is that so bad?"

"No," she replies, bowing her head. "But as beautiful as all those things are, none of it is as important as you are to me. It's you that makes me happy, not your gifts."

"I know." I place my finger under her chin, drawing her eyes back to mine. "It's just one of the many things I love about you. As for worrying about what everyone else may think, I don't give a flying fuck about that. When this marriage happens, *and it will happen*, it's going to last. End of story!"

"I want that too, but how can you be so sure?"

"Because my life without you is unimaginable. Don't you see that? This," I say, gesturing between us, "is *forever*. I'll fight until my fucking death to make sure that happens."

Her hands fist my dress shirt as she moves her body closer to mine. "I want forever too."

"Well, then that's settled."

"I still think a prenup is a good idea."

"I swear on my life if you don't stop this madness, I will sign over every cent and every property I own ... including this company, into your name, which, in turn, will negate any prenup."

Her eyes narrow. "You wouldn't dare."

"Try me."

"You'd be a fool to do that."

"A fool who is in love with his fiancée and refuses to do life without her." When she blows out a puff of air I know I've won. Gathering her in my arms, I crush her body to mine. "So, we're in agreeance?"

"Ugh, fine, you win. No prenup."

"That's my girl," I say, resting my chin on top of her head. "You're stuck with me for life."

"I can live with that. There's nothing we can't get through as long as we face it together."

"Exactly."

Her words should be calming, but instead I'm left with a sense of foreboding. The truth is, she's right—who knows what the future holds for us? I can only hope the unwavering love we share in this moment will last ... *forever*.

Made in the USA
Monee, IL
28 April 2026